Th̶ Way

Tormod Cockburn

A "Mysterious Scotland" novel.

Set on the Firth of Forth

Mys.Scot

First published by Mys.Scot Media in 2023

Copyright © Tormod Cockburn, 2023

The moral right of the author has been asserted

Print ISBN: 978-1-915612-07-6

E-Book ISBN: 978-1-915612-06-9

Cover photo credit: Alba Imagery, licensed by Canva

This is a work of fiction. Names, characters, places, and incidents are the products of the author's imagination or are used fictitiously. Any resemblance to actual events, locales, or persons, living or dead, is entirely coincidental.

For updates and free books, we invite you to join our Readers Syndicate. Either click the logo above in a digital copy or see details at the back of this book.

Mys.Scot

Dedication

Dedicated to the memory of Alexander William Lillico

Born 1891 in Hawick, Roxburghshire. Died 1917 Cambrai, France

Let us imagine the life you didn't get to live

Also by Tormod Cockburn

The Bone Trap
The Ness Deception
The Stone Cypher
This Jagged Way
The Ice Covenant

Chapter 1

National Museum of Scotland, Edinburgh – Present day

Adina Mofaz glances out of the window into Chambers Street. It's still pouring. No thunder, no lightning, but a storm nevertheless. As much as she loves living in Scotland, this driven Edinburgh rain is something she'll never get used to. The three years spent gaining a professional doctorate in Tehran had its risks, but at least the sun always shone. She looks at her watch. Almost 8 pm on a Sunday evening. Douglas will have the kids fed, bathed, and ready for bed. And here she is. Still working.

She crosses the floor of the Grand Gallery with only the sound of her own footsteps for company. The bright lights that normally illuminate the vast four-storey hall are dimmed for night-time, allowing streetlights to throw areas of the room into comparative shade. Not someone naturally afraid of the dark, Adina's pulse quickens as she falls into the shadow of the most dangerous creatures ever to set foot on Scottish soil. Feeling an unnatural sense of threat, she pauses to look up at the waterhorse skeletons, eternally locked in combat at the centre of the gallery. The bones have been in place for a full year now, and although they're deeply familiar, she never quite feels she should turn her back on them. Especially when she's working alone.

'Hello, boys', Adina murmurs as she picks up her pace again.

'How are you tonight?' She glances at the crossed tusks, feeling as perplexed as ever to live in a world where unicorns once existed. 'Not for talking tonight? No? Okay, then. Behave yourselves. I'll catch you later.'

She walks on, leaving them behind as she enters the special exhibitions space and moves to the last presentation in the sequence. The exhibition opens tomorrow and as head of the Department for International Culture, this is her last chance to spot anything out of place. Not that she expects a problem. This exposition of Persian Technological Advance represents nine month's work, and she is delighted with every detail. Starting at the visitor exit, she walks backwards through the exhibit, forcing her brain to see past the already familiar displays. Slowly, meticulously, she scans every inch of the room examining every aspect. She's almost finished when she feels her phone vibrate in her jacket pocket. She ignores it until her survey is complete and she can lock the door with the certainty she's done her very best work on this.

She doesn't look at the message until the door is secured, expecting it to be Douglas, checking if she's on her way home. Instead, the WhatsApp message is from an unknown number.

'QX73Y. Standby', it says.

Adina grips the phone tighter in case she drops it. She's not seen a message like this in a very long time. Not since London in 2008. And with rising dread, she enters the nearest lift and moves swiftly to her desk.

She is opening her laptop when her phone vibrates again. The message repeats her agent number and then a separate message contains an authentication code. The next message says. 'Respond.'

She is already opening her code file. A page on the dark web, password protected and containing authentication codes listed by date. She checks the one she's been sent, validating it, and responds with her own unique code, using the algorithm she holds in her memory to adjust it for the date and time.

'Confirmed', comes the next reply. 'Mission orders. Artefact YH77Q is now in play. Acquire and transport'.

Twelve years ago, when she'd been a fresh graduate, her heart would have leapt with this opportunity. She would have embraced her orders with zeal. But that was a long time ago. Today, this message might mean the end of her career. And the end of her marriage. Depending on what comes next, perhaps her very life.

Another text arrives. This one has an image of a QR code with a locker location somewhere in Waverley Station.

'Use of force is authorised', says the next text. 'Threat level KP41R. Acknowledge.'

With shaking hands, she types, 'Acknowledged.'

The final text says simply, 'Message ends.'

She tries to commit the codes to memory but can't get her brain to work. Instead, she opens an Excel spreadsheet and types them in.

Then she deletes the texts.

'Threat level KP41R', she murmurs, tabbing to her dark web files. 'Damnit', she says out loud, before glancing around self-consciously. The highest level of force applicable to her rank. To achieve her orders, she is permitted to commit violence against her adopted home. The QR code for the locker will provide her with a package. Inside the package will be a Glock 22 semi-automatic pistol.

'But, why? Why here?' is her whispered protest to the empty room.

She tabs to the artefact file and scrolls to find item number YH77Q. As she reads the article's description, and the small amount of data that will allow her to authenticate it, her hand flies to her mouth. It only takes a few seconds to comprehend the earth-shattering importance of this object. And how hard she must push to obtain it.

She swallows as she realises the storm that will soon break around her.

And the life she's known – the life she loves, slips quietly from her hand.

Stirling Castle – 3 weeks ago

In the early light of a Thursday morning in March, he edges along Castlehill Road and parks opposite the cemetery. He hasn't driven in a while. Even for this short distance, early in the morning, he has to proceed with extreme care. He gets out and slams the door, seeing himself reflected in the glass. A tall man, with swept back, overly long, salt and pepper coloured hair. He doesn't consider himself old, but seeing his reflection, realises he now looks older than his years. Stepping slowly along the perimeter of the graveyard, he's looking for the spot where he knows there's a gap in the fence. As he studies what's ahead of him, his hand slides up into his thicket of a beard, tugging at what was once a handlebar moustache, but which now hangs from his face like an overgrown vine. In his fitter days, even just a year ago, he would have seen this as a light walk. In his condition today, with the illness attacking him in new and ingenious ways, this will be a drawn-out, energy-sapping expedition. He stops for a second and considers what it will cost him.

The information he needs concerns a room in the castle. He has seen it in his mind and needs to know if it's real. Confirming it will have ... *implications*. Or maybe, it's just another ghost in his fractured, decaying memory. Either way, he agrees with himself that this expedition is a test. Of his physical and mental fitness, and the veracity of his dreams. His vivid night-time trances. Do they represent something real or are they imagined? Is this experience simply about him, or does it have implications for others? It's a small thing really, but it's the only question that burns in his brain as his life shuffles towards an untidy end. So, he begins to move, slowly, conserving his strength for what lies ahead. Shambling over the grass, he joins a thin path skirting the battlements that eventually takes him to the west wall of Stirling Castle.

Arriving at a heavy cast iron gate set into the lower stone rampart, he stops to rest. Reaching into his pocket for the keys, heavy-duty and hanging from a worn steel ring, he prays the locks haven't changed since last he passed this way. In his capacity as a building contractor and stone mason, he'd spent long periods working on these walls. Repointing the mortar, replacing crumbling stones, and occasionally carving a replacement for one of the sculpted pieces, earning a good living maintaining the boundary he's now determined to breach. He shouldn't still have the keys. But so frequent were the days he'd had to borrow one from the estate manager to access some part of the castle or another, eventually they'd just given him a set.

The old steel lock opens with a satisfying click. Now he's faced with a stairway and knows this will be a challenge. Moving forward - taking one step at a time - sucking three hard breaths - he gradually ascends - until he is inside a part of the castle identified on documents as the Nether Bailey, more colloquially known to insiders as "the arse end". Moving ahead, and uphill, he stays close to the wall until it intersects with another fortification protecting the main body of the castle.

Another gate. Another long flight of stairs, until he emerges beside the old powder store. It was in this robust, low stone building, the castle's defenders used to keep their gunpowder. Set apart from the main building, he is nevertheless getting closer to his goal. It's too early for visitors on the site, so he keeps himself hidden while his body recovers again.

A quick glance at his watch. He needs to get a move on if he is to finish and be back at the house before Alasdair realises he is missing. And now for the riskiest part of the venture. Another gate gives him access to a maintenance corridor running below the castle building. This part of the castle was a billet for soldiers until quite recent times. These days the old regiment abides in less salubrious quarters and the space is given over to exhibitions. And long before the regiment, these had been the kings' rooms. Physically distinct from the palace where they'd governed, these chambers are where they'd ate and slept. Where they'd lived and died and, with any good fortune, managed to sire successors that would live long enough to follow them on the throne. A royal residence, and away from Edinburgh, the most favoured palace of all the Scottish kings, the castle had been the centre of the Scottish court until the union of the crowns in 1603.

At the branch in the corridor, he turns right and comes to a final locked gate. This one leads out onto the ramparts of the highest part of the castle. Protected by a thin railing, this route, little more than a ledge, leans out over the sheer south wall. Looking out and down, he can see the treetops forty metres below. Beyond that, new build residential developments are spreading across the valley floor as the City of Stirling devours the land around it.

Nearby on the left is a window. It is set into the sheer south wall and is the objective of his trek. He's been here before, of course. Years before. With safety ropes and tools, and a young crew to do the work under his supervision. He remembers the outside of the window – its shape and style. But he never recalls ever having looked inside. And never had cause to be inside this room, nor even considered how he'd find it if he had free rein of the internal corridors. He clicks his tongue impatiently. The ledge here for his footing is particularly narrow. He'd forgotten about that and now will need to take extra care. Without safety gear, he only has experience and a consequential head for heights to see him to his goal and back. Taking a deep breath, he summons an energy that has eluded him these past weeks and strides out onto the ledge.

Brushing the stone wall with his left shoulder, the sheer drop to his right seems to suck him down with an unnatural force. So his body is shaking when he finally grasps the handholds provided by the window opening. He clutches the angular stone and feels his heart beating wildly in his chest.

Whether it is purely the exertion, or his rising excitement, he isn't sure.

Establishing hand holds, he heaves himself onto the window ledge which is deep enough for him to rest safely. For several minutes he recovers. Until curiosity builds. Then, with the impudence of a child, presses his face against the glass.

The room inside is large. At one time it might have been ornate, though today its furnishings lie covered by dust sheets. He rubs at the glass with sweaty fingers, twisting left and right to examine everything he can see. A little gasp erupts from him. It's true! He's now certain this is the room at the centre of his dreams, albeit a faded shell of the place. Its shabby colours strike a pallid contrast to his night-visions full of colour, pageantry and assuring company. Closing his eyes, he can see the space before him all decorated and lived in, populated by characters as vigorous as they are beautiful. When he opens his eyes again, the room seems so dead.

He eases back from the window and thinks. Everything about these past months with his dreams and sensations has been speculative; easily dismissed as a symptom of the disease that's slowly killing him. But this room is proof. Proof that he is seeing something beyond the physical and into the realms of the mysterious and strange. He resolves to call the journalist again. He'll explain what he's seen and to hell with the misgivings of his oldest son. Yes! Let's see what the journalist makes of this discovery. And without much extra effort, can already see the magazine headline in his mind's eye – *Window on a different Scotland*. Perfect! That's what he'll do.

Satisfied, he begins the arduous journey home. Crawling backwards, he dangles his right foot down the outside of the wall and feels for the access ledge. But these old limbs are stiff and his joints protest as he stretches them far beyond their normal agility. Grunting with effort, he realises both legs will need to slide down the wall, manoeuvring his hips so his feet can find the narrow strip. Growling in discomfort as his belly rolls against the stone, he clenches the window surround, digging his fingertips into any cranny so he can control his descent. But as soon as the fingers of his right-hand spring free, he realises he's in trouble. As his body swings out of control, his left hand loses grip, and his torso slides painfully down the wall and onto the battlements. But his feet find the ledge, and for a moment he feels elation, believing himself to be out of danger, even as his arms swing wildly to recapture balance. But his centre of gravity is already too far from the wall and danger looms to swallow him.

The low guard rail is his final undoing, catching the shift in his body weight and tipping him sideways. As he flails for some final redemption, the tops of the trees rush up to meet him.

Chapter 2

St Andrews, Scotland – 6 weeks ago

Gill McArdle shook the final stiffness from his limbs and accelerated as he reached the midpoint of his run. Salina's sofa wasn't quite long enough for his six-foot frame, and he'd woken before 7 am with grumbling pains in his legs and back. Now, an hour later, the pain was gone. Coasting to the far end of West Sands Beach, he reached the point where he could see the old paper mill nestling at the bottom of Eden estuary. As he turned, his eyes roved over the old town of St Andrews, with its rows of stone mansions perched on a low cliff above the sea. Looking south he could see a cluster of historic towers, comprising the university, St Rule's, and components of the Cathedral ruins. These latter fragments were all that remained of what was once the biggest church in Scotland, and in his mind's eye, Gill tried to paint the absent building back onto the cliff top. Despite its age, St Andrews was still a small town, and viewed from West Sands, it was merely a smudge on the shoreline. To Gill, it was a familiar townscape and though he now lived in Dundee, it had been his home for the better part of a decade.

He'd stayed at Salina's the previous night despite his earlier protestations that he should get back to his own flat in Broughty Ferry. They'd eaten together, then sat talking until around midnight when he'd realised she'd drifted off to sleep in his arms. He'd sat like that awhile, with his nose buried in her hair, listening to her breathing, and thanking the creator of every good thing on the earth that this woman existed and was fastening her life to his. Their relationship remained, in the rather outmoded language of his father, unconsummated. And that wasn't a problem to him just now. Such was his fascination for her that every tiny new intimacy was like unwrapping a new facet of an even bigger treasure. A few evenings before, Salina had worn a simple black dress to a dinner date with friends. She'd looked amazing and when they were alone again in her flat, she'd pulled his head against her chest with a ferocity he'd not encountered before. In variations of this position, he'd spent the rest of the evening brushing his face against her upper arms, enjoying the warmth of her skin and the smell of her hair as it drifted across his face. He could relish these moments for a long time yet, but the truth was, he burned for her.

A watery winter sun sent shimmers of light along the beach as Gill ran. There was no wind and the gentle conditions had allowed the outgoing tide to form countless trillions of salt crystals in rippling trails. He loved these rare conditions and picking up the pace, he followed these silvery paths all the way back to town.

The last part of his circuit followed East Sands Beach almost to the door of Salina's apartment. He stopped to buy her a coffee down near the harbour and wandered the last few hundred metres, crisscrossing the beach, stepping on the empty shells of razor clams; enjoying the crunch of them under his feet while he thought about his day. This afternoon held a team meeting with the magazine crew. But he'd another appointment before that. And if he was honest with himself, the occasion prickled with challenge.

Gill stood at the front of the lecture hall and tried not to look intimidated by the gathering of young people. A few boys, but mainly girls, were scattered around a venue that was too big for the event. The host was already on her feet and would introduce him shortly. He took a deep breath and nervously waited his turn. Like him, the principal of Tayside College was a runner. A wiry, wild-haired woman in her early forties, he met her from time to time along the Broughty Ferry esplanade. One morning, while they cooled down after a jog, they'd walked together and chatted about a new initiative she was planning. By "chatted", he now realised he'd listened while she'd spoken passionately about the challenges of equipping a generation of young people with the necessary skills to flourish in the world of work.

'Too many children never read at home these days', she had complained. 'The schools do their best but many fall behind. And for the struggling readers, college is often their last chance to catch up.'

He'd nodded along; concerned of course, but wondering what any of this had to do with him.

'I'm starting a new scheme', she explained. 'Bringing volunteers from industry and education into college to give our disadvantaged youth the one-to-one attention they need to get back on track.' She'd smiled sheepishly, 'And what I need, to get them motivated, and help recruit volunteers, is a local celebrity to front the launch.'

He'd nodded along sympathetically until he'd realised she meant him. 'I'm not sure celebrity is the word I'd choose', he mused. 'Notorious?'

'Controversial', she'd suggested, before adding, 'But everybody in Dundee loves you.'

He wasn't sure that was true but nevertheless had offered to help.

And now, on the morning when he needed to make good on that promise, he felt hopelessly out of his depth. In his mid-thirties, Gill's school days seemed a long time ago, and honestly, his memories were mixed. He'd never struggled academically, quietly absorbing any knowledge on offer. Socially though, it had been tougher. Never enjoying the competitiveness of his male peers, he'd found it easier to spend a Saturday morning engrossed in a new book rather than outside playing sports. And girls! He'd never found it challenging to talk to grown women. But around his high school classmates, he'd generally felt lost at sea. He was attractive to them – he knew that - and attracted by them, but never really grasped what was going on. So much complexity - too many competing impulses. Each girl utterly different from her friends. The minds of teenage girls had been a mystery to him back then, and looking around this room full of eclectic fashions, he suspected nothing had changed.

When his moment came to take the floor, he filled his lungs and thanked the principal for her kind words. He spoke to the room for a few minutes about how excited he was to be a journalist, and how he'd never have found this career if he hadn't learned to read first. Then he asked for questions.

'Did he believe in ghosts?'

'Was it true he'd cheated at Uni?'

'Did he have a girlfriend?'

He engaged with every ounce of energy he could muster and twenty minutes later, was thoroughly enjoying himself.

During the second half of the session, volunteers paired off with the young people and were asked to spend a short while guiding their reading. Uncomfortably, Gill sat down with a sixteen-year-old lass called Frankie. She was bursting with energy and enthusiasm as she recounted a weekend at the football, watching Dundee United with her dad. But when Gill finally coaxed Frankie to open her textbook, all that confidence fell away and he saw a different side to her. Trying desperately to impress Gill, the girl struggled to sound out unfamiliar words. Gill thought the reading material looked rather simplistic for someone Frankie's age, but even when she finally conquered a difficult word, she would turn the page to find exactly the same arrangement of letters and the whole struggle would begin again. As Frankie tired of the exercise, she retreated into sullen embarrassment. Showering her with encouragement, Gill began to appreciate the mountain this young woman had yet to climb to find a well-paying job in a little over two years' time.

'Everybody could read when I was at school', said Gill later as the principal walked him to the door. 'What's changed?'

'There have always been a few stragglers; you probably weren't aware of them. But a multitude of things makes it difficult for this generation. They still suffer from the disruption of covid. Then we have the proliferation of digital devices; changing parenting styles. Don't get me wrong; most of our students thrive. But the twenty per cent at the bottom

...' she shook her head. 'Unless we do something quickly, they'll find the workplace a very tough environment.'

'What you're doing here is great', said Gill. 'I'm sure it'll make a difference.'

'Oh, we've run trials', she said, pausing at the college reception area. 'The student you read with, Frankie. She's just received a late diagnosis of dyslexia. Now we know that, and assuming she'll work with us, we'll be able to give her all the help she needs. My volunteer readers will spend two hours a week with Frankie, using the skills we'll teach them. Lots of one-to-one. A year from now, she could be back on track.'

'If there's anything else I can do?' asked Gill.

She smiled sadly. 'We'll do our best. In an ideal world we'd take this remedial work into our high schools and our primaries. But the expense would be enormous, Gill.'

They shook hands, and soberly, he realised his encounter with these disadvantaged young people would haunt him until a time came when he could do something about it. Acknowledging this new burden on his conscience, he stuffed his hands in his pockets and walked back into town towards the rest of his day.

An hour after he'd finished at the college, Gill enjoyed a short walk by the river while he processed his thoughts. He took his own education for granted so he'd never realised how much of a battle it was for some others. A text came in from Cassy, reminding him about the team meeting. He tucked his musings about young Frankie and her peers in a mental back pocket and strode into work.

'What happened to you this morning?' said Cassy, dispensing with any weekend pleasantries.

'Meeting someone in town', he responded.

'Oh? Business or pleasure?'

'Volunteering at the local college. Remember?'

'Great', she said, clasping a pile of files. 'It's just it wasn't in the diary.' She addressed the rest of the team, still working at their desks. 'Gill has graced us with his presence. Shall we crack on?'

Cassy bolted for the conference room, followed by Larry, Craig and Mhairi, and finally, Gill, feeling chastised but without really knowing why. As office manager, it fell to Cassy to leap in and start the meeting by highlighting the remaining tasks between now and closing the current issue of *Mysterious Scotland*. As the editor, Gill was ultimately responsible for the product they produced, but Cassy's organisational skills outshone his, and he had long since delegated this side of the business to her. He tapped a flurry of actions into his laptop and waited for Cassy to finish.

'Any other business?' asked Cassy, already closing her computer.

'I had an interesting text on Saturday evening', Gill said. 'It might impact our line-up for issue 22.'

'We're ten days from closing issue 21', said Cassy. 'You thinking of buggering up my editorial plan?'

Gill considered his response. Petite and pretty, with dark eyes and dark hair, Cassy's fiery persona kept them all in line. 'A plan is just a plan. If I get a new lead, we might need to create a bit of space, that's all.'

'Tell us then', said Mhairi, straightening her glasses.

'Ed Johnson is consulting on the dig at Airth. He says they've found something that would benefit from my expertise.'

'Hang on', Cassy interrupted. 'Airth? That's already a total bun fight. There are more archaeologists digging down there than gulls on a rubbish tip. What possible help could the good professor need from us?'

'We have unique skills', Gill declared.

'I believe it's a positive thing he wants our help', said Mhairi. 'It could help restore our credibility.'

Craig nodded, smirking at Mhairi's clear spoken English accent. 'Aye. After Orkney, it wouldnae do us any harm.'

'Orkney was good science', Gill protested. 'And if someone hadn't been trying to kill me, our discoveries would have made headlines around the world.'

'Aye, but you fluffed it', Craig replied. 'I mean, I'm not judging. In the circumstances, I might have messed it up too.'

'And we did make the news headlines', said Cassy brightly, grinning through a plastic smile. 'Unfortunately, just the wee endy-bit where they talk about something sad and strangely funny.'

Gill lifted his palms up to his team. 'We're a crypto mag, guys. Our legitimacy is meant to be tenuous.'

'Ed Johnson', barked Cassy. 'What does he want?'

Gill swallowed and tried to reignite his enthusiasm. 'Part of their site includes a ruined church. And this church has a stone tablet with an inscription.'

Cassy's eyes blinked at him. 'Don't all old churches have stone plaques with inscriptions?'

'That's what I said, but Johnson says this one is strange.'

'In what way?'

'He wouldn't tell me. Once I've got issue 21 safely into your capable hands, I'm going down to take a look.'

'Okay. You're the boss.' Cassy cast her eyes around the room. 'Anybody else got a wild goose chase Gill can embark on, rather than hanging tight in the office and doing some proper work?'

'Well, actually, I've got one', Mhairi said with a bright tone.

'Really?' said Cassy, not sounding like she meant it. 'Oh good.'

'Do you remember the articles we wrote about the ancestral lines of Scotland's royal families?'

'Aye, grand work', said Craig. 'Who'd be king today, if Scotland were still a kingdom.'

'Gill received a call back from an elderly gentleman in Stirling. His surname is Canmore', Mhairi explained.

Gill didn't even look up. 'I spoke to him in early January. He doesn't want to talk to me.'

'Well, he does now', Mhairi huffed. 'As soon as possible, please.'

'What's changed?' asked Gill, remembering the old man's frosty reception.

'He explained that he's been having peculiar dreams. He remembers you and thinks you might be able to help.'

'No. Please don't', said Cassy, pointing her biro at Mhairi.

'I might be with Cassy on this one', muttered Gill.

'He claims to be seeing a different Scotland in his dreams. An independent country with a king and a commonwealth. He's keen to discuss it with you.'

'We're doin' dream interpretations now', said Larry, perplexed. 'On top o' the day job?'

'Sounds like a political séance', muttered Craig. 'Calling up the ghosts of long dead governments.'

'There was something about him', Mhairi said defensively, her voice rising. 'He's a bit distressed by what he sees in his dreams. But he's coherent. Not your typical Scottish eccentric.'

Larry sat bolt upright, his long grey hair flicking out behind him. 'Careful there, darlin'. You're playin' wie fire.'

'What's the issue, Larry? Am I not Scottish enough to work here? Am I not entitled to have an opinion?' Mhairi retorted.

'Have as many opinions as you like, lass. But ken you sound like a BBC newsreader.'

'And DON'T call me "darling".'

'Come on, guys', said Gill, crumpling his empty coffee cup and launching it, accurately, at a waste bin in the corner. 'Canmore didn't mention anything like this when I met him. The only thing he said to me with any clarity is how far I should sling my hook.'

'The man I spoke to seemed gentle, even apologetic', Mhairi added. 'It wouldn't be right not to at least return his call.'

'In the service of our readers', Gill drawled. 'But he's not going to be top of my job list.'

'Glad to her that', Cassy muttered. 'Cause your job list is as long as the A9 to Inverness.'

Chapter 3

Bothered by the tensions in the team, Gill spent his afternoon spreading encouragement and following up on action points from the meeting. He was just starting to think about heading home when a text came in. It caught his breath as he already had the sender's number in his phone from an incident five months ago. Back then he'd been uncertain if he was communicating with an individual or an organization, so he'd simply recorded it as *Rex Gladio*.

Today's message said simply, 'V&A 6 pm.'

He thought about this for a second. It had been five months since he'd last had contact from this number. That had led to an enigmatic encounter with the young man Gill knew as "Barcode Charlie". In this intervening time, he'd heard nothing, nor seen Charlie around. Nor had he seen the unnatural, sword-bearing individual called Raphael, aka Bikerman. Their invisibility was a problem for Gill because he was accumulating questions and had nowhere to take them. Something had ignited in him around the time of his last encounter with Charlie. Returning from Orkney, Gill discovered he had a voice, audible in his head, intermittent and calming. And Raphael's sword, which Gill has understood to be a token or symbol, sometimes seemed so real he could feel it in his hands. He'd dived into research, looking for a rational explanation for these encounters. And he found many, though none fitted his experience exactly. So, against all his preconceptions and prejudices, he'd accepted a supernatural dimension to his life. Reluctantly, though he didn't broadcast it, he'd come to believe that the God of *The Book* was real.

In the intervening months, he'd nursed a bundle of questions. Now this potential meeting with *Rex Gladio* was an opportunity to seek some answers. Not that Gill had any clue whom he was meeting. It might be Charlie. But then, Charlie had said all those months ago that it was someone called Solomon he needed to talk to. Was this Charlie's mentor figure? Gill didn't know. Resolving to lean into these questions rather than walk away, he responded to the text with a *thumbs-up* and got back to work.

Leaving his Dundee office, Gill glared up at the sky. He'd grown to like Dundee, but its weather mirrored the temperament of Salina's sole nephew. Sunny one minute; squally the next. The cool February evening seemed to be sulking towards a storm of rain and he wasn't going to make it to the meet point without getting wet. He pulled his Gortex over his waistcoat and headed in the direction of the V&A museum.

Forty-five minutes later, he shook the rain off his jacket and stepped back under the archway for cover. There was still no sign of Charlie. The arranged meeting time had been half an hour ago. Under the shelter of the new museum on Dundee's waterfront, he'd lingered by the river; he'd fiddled with his phone. Eventually, he'd taken a stroll around the perimeter just in case there was some confusion about location. He even attempted to make conversation with a lady in her mid-sixties who also seemed to be waiting around for the rain to blow over. But the man he was waiting for still hadn't shown up. At least, he'd assumed Solomon was a man. When he tried to imagine Charlie's mentor figure, he could only picture a tall man with powerful arms, plastered with saintly tattoos.

Exasperated and disappointed, he gave up and started to walk towards the bus station. It was only when he entered the underpass taking him back into the city centre, he noticed the lady had started walking too, falling into step with him some forty metres behind. In the poor light, he felt his pulse tick up as a lean figure sprang nimbly out to obstruct the exit ahead of him. The man stood, his athletic body held taut and his arms poised by his side. Gill slid to a halt, his path blocked. With daylight behind him, Gill couldn't see the man's face. Mercifully, he didn't appear to be holding a weapon.

'You can tell a lot about people by the way they manage delay', said the woman calmly, catching up with Gill.

Gill jerked around. 'I'm sorry?'

'I mean, you didn't sit passively, but neither did you get agitated and grumpy. I admire that in a person.'

'Ah', said Gill, understanding. 'Is this some kind of initiation test? Perhaps I should have seen that coming.'

'Not a test. Simply an observation.' She stopped and examined Gill for a moment. Her pale blue eyes scanning him from under close-cropped grey-blonde hair. Abruptly, she offered him her hand. 'My name is Solomon.'

Gill stared back into her intelligent, slightly troubled eyes, then accepted the single stiff handshake on offer. 'Is that some kind of code name?'

She stepped up close to Gill and cast her gaze about him for several long seconds. 'Not really', she said in a low voice. 'My name is Rosemary Solomon. Or Rosie, but generally, I'm just called Solomon. It's what my pupils always called me and somehow it fits this adventure we're all on.'

His attention flicked back to the lean man as he stepped out of the shadows and strode towards them. A sodden jacket clung to his body over a skin-tight dirty T-shirt and the closely cropped head of a man Gill had already met.

'Hey, Charlie.'

'A'richt, Gill.'

'You folk like your secrecy', said Gill, the thumping in his chest starting to subside. 'What's with all the cloak and dagger?'

Solomon stepped back from Gill. 'The answer to that question is for another day. At this point, we're just trying to determine if you're one of us.'

'One of who?'

'It sounds a little pretentious', said Solomon with a flicker of a smile. 'But we need to know if you've been … chosen.'

Gill looked back and forward between them, uncertain of the question. 'Chosen? That's a tricky one. I hope you folks realise I'm not in any way religious.'

'Naebody is these days', said Charlie, dryly.

Solomon glanced at Charlie. 'I think we can all agree that none of us are energised by hard pews and organ music.'

'How's it gaun wi' th' swuird?' asked Charlie.

Gill thought for a moment, thinking about the perplexing mornings and evenings he'd spent studying *The Book*, and its inexplicable link to the symbolism of the sword in a way he hadn't quite fathomed. Eventually, he sighed and replied, 'When I start to get my head around one mystery, I find three more ready and waiting for me.'

Charlie cast a look around, alert to threats. 'Yon's natural. We micht be able tae help.'

Solomon moved around and positioned herself at Charlie's side. 'Before we get to that, please tell us who gave you the sword?'

Gill considered the woman's intense expression and wondered if he could trust her. 'Is that another initiation test?'

Solomon chuckled dryly. 'Let's just say I'm looking to find mutual ground.'

'Okay then. A big, olive-skinned guy. Said his name was Raphael. But you know all this. I've told Charlie already.'

Gill watched Solomon's eyes flit from him to Charlie and back again. 'Charlie. You've met Raphael, haven't you?'

'Aye. Wance oor twice.'

'I don't think he's entirely natural. Would you agree, Charlie?' said Gill.

Charlie ignored his question. 'A'm aff tae leave youse tae blether. A'm aboot if ye need me.'

'Thank you, Charlie', said Solomon.

Gill studied her face, busy with the lines and creases weathered by life's heartbreaks and joys. 'What happens now?'

Solomon silently watched Charlie's retreating figure and Gill sensed she'd have felt safer if her protégé had stuck around. 'We talk', was all she said.

'Mutual ground?' parroted Gill.

Her nod was curt. 'Let's find somewhere to get out of this rain.'

'You were telling me how unreligious you are', said Solomon, sipping her coffee. They'd found a large café bar on the perimeter of Slessor Gardens. The place was busy with folk on their way home from work and the background noise suggested they were unlikely to be overheard.

Gill nodded. 'Other than letting my mum drag me to kirk a few times a year when I was a kid, I've been utterly agnostic. Until recently, it never occurred to me that any of this might be real.'

'And if you're not religious, what are you?'

Gill paused to muster the right words. 'I've come to believe in the supernatural realm. Reluctantly, however. It wasn't exactly in my life plan.'

'Define supernatural realm. Fairies? Witches? Werewolves?'

Gill cooled in the face of her gentle sarcasm. 'Not yet. I'm still stuck at "A" for angels.'

A flicker of a smile crossed Solomon's face. 'A believer, then. And since you've opened the door to the supernatural, how's it working for you?'

'I'm still in research mode.'

'And where are you doing your research?'

'I'm reading *The Book*, obviously. Trying to get a grip of it.'

'And how's that going?'

'I thought it was a bit dated at first. Iron-age tribes and ancient rituals. But as I kept reading, I started to see a meaningful order to things.'

'What kind of things?'

He flexed and unflexed the fingers in his right hand. He was tiring of her questions. 'Lot's of stuff, but I've taken a particular interest in angels. Their creation, their purpose. The fact that a bunch of them rebelled against God.'

'Why?'

He suppressed a tremor of irritation. 'Because I believe Raphael is an angel.'

'Good angel or bad angel?'

Gill noted her face didn't even flinch at his suggestion. 'He's fierce, but he's gentle. He's only ever tried to protect me.'

'And on the occasions you've met him, what was his business with you?'

'On two instances when we've talked, he offered me a sword. Last time we met I decided that taking the sword seemed the right thing to do.'

'And do you know what the sword represents?'

Gill sucked his teeth and sat back in his chair. He felt about as comfortable in this moment as he'd felt facing waterhorses back on Harris. 'I know that symbolically, the sword relates to *The Book*. That somehow, it's the word of God. Or the words that God has uttered? I dunno. It all sounds so insane. But sometimes, the presence of the sword is so real, I can feel the physical weight of it in my hand.'

'Interesting', said Solomon. 'Like a material object?'

Gill shrugged, feeling like he was the only person in this conversation with all his cards on the table. 'There are moments when it seems to manifest into something physical. I feel the weight of it for a few seconds; catch a glint of light reflecting off the blade. Quite honestly, I find that a little freaky.'

Solomon looked away somewhere to Gill's right. 'I understand. But stay aware of that feeling. Practise it if you can.'

'Why? Is it significant?'

'Charlie has experienced something similar.'

'With a sword?'

Her head shake was just a tremor. 'Your angel friend, Raphael. He gave Charlie something else.'

Gill tilted his head towards her. 'What's the deal with you and Charlie? Are you related or is he just your hired muscle?'

Solomon smiled with embarrassment. 'No. I met him a couple of years back. At an addiction recovery centre where I do some volunteering. Physically, he was doing okay, but his head was a mess.' She looked over her glasses at Gill and studied his reactions. 'Poor Charlie was struggling with psychosis.'

Gill shivered. This wasn't an attractive trait in a new friend. 'What was up?'

'He kept telling his therapist about meeting a strange individual that no one else ever saw. Like an adult's version of an invisible friend. And he claimed this man was an angel in a biker jacket, with *Rex Gladio* written on his back.'

'Yep', said Gill, aligning himself to Charlie's experience.

'After the medical people did what they could for him, Charlie was referred to me and I counselled him for a while', she continued. 'And I simply proceeded on the basis that his experiences were real.'

'You just accepted his angel stories?'

'Professionally, that was the right thing to do.'

'And then?' said Gill.

Solomon sighed. 'Every time the angel appeared to Charlie, he offered a gift. I asked Charlie how he felt about that, and he explained that he wanted to accept, but didn't see why an angel would offer something so special to someone, who in their own eyes, was the lowest of the low.'

'And how did you resolve that?'

'I asked Charlie if the angel had made a mistake. He thought that was unlikely, so then I asked who the gift was really for.'

'And Charlie realised it was genuinely for him?'

'Yes. On the next encounter, he accepted it. And his health improved almost overnight. He strengthened physically. Started a new job. We stopped our formal counselling sessions and instead, we started to meet to help him explore his new gift.'

'And are you planning to help me?'

Solomon smiled into her lap. 'That depends.'

'I get it', said Gill, trying and failing to keep frustration out of his voice. 'You'd rather not say.'

Her eyes closed for a moment. 'I don't mean to be rude. If you give us time, you will come to understand.'

He forced a more conciliatory tone into his voice. 'Has your work with Charlie helped him?'

'Yes. We started a year ago. It was good for a time. Lately, it's become complicated.'

Gill looked at her over his coffee cup, urging her to go on.

After a pause, Solomon seemed to calculate this was information she could share. 'Based on something the angel told him, Charlie became convinced there were others like him. More people carrying a gift.'

Gill realised he'd been holding in a breath, and slowly, he released it. 'Hence the advert in *Mysterious Scotland*?'

'And in a few other places.' She looked up at him and for the first time, he saw a mash of emotions behind her eyes.

'You need to understand', she continued. 'When Charlie first came up with the idea of finding what he'd call, "the others", I didn't believe him.' She stopped to stare out the window as Dundee's rainy tantrum came to an end and streaks of sunlight sprang out across the Tay. 'I worried his psychosis was returning. And on a personal level, I fretted I'd wasted a lot of time on him …'

'And then Charlie found me', said Gill, completing her line of thought.

Solomon released a long, juddering sigh. 'The day you showed up at the *Desperate Dan* statue was the worst day of my life', she said plainly.

Gill flinched back from her. 'Why? Charlie's instinct was vindicated. Surely that meant you were on the cusp of some kind of breakthrough?'

She shrugged. 'Maybe I'm more like you than you dare imagine. I didn't get up one morning and go looking for angels under my bed. I believed in God; that's true. And I'm sorry to disappoint you, but if you knew my lifestyle, you might judge me to be conventionally religious. But I didn't come looking for this, whatever *this* is. I had God in a box, and all was well with my world.'

'I see', said Gill.

Solomon tapped the table nervously. 'Since Charlie found you, God is most definitely *not* in his box.'

Gill felt puzzled. 'And that's a bad thing?'

'I just don't know how it plays out', said Solomon. 'And in time, if Charlie is right, we'll find others.'

'To what end?'

For the first time since the start of their encounter, vulnerability flashed across her face. 'That's the million dollar question.'

'And *Rex Gladio*?'

'It's become our call sign if you like. If there are others like you and Charlie, somehow they'll find us.'

'There must be a reason.'

Solomon took a last sip from her cup and gently pushed it away. 'I agree. But at the moment, I just don't know what it is.'

Gill could see her closing signals. 'You, me and Charlie. What happens next? Will I see you again?'

'Probably. But let's not make any immediate plans', she said, getting to her feet.

'Solomon, I have so many questions.' Gill realised his voice sounded pleading.

'Maybe, Gill. Down the road a little when I can see more clearly.'

Gill felt a tremor down his left shoulder, as if someone had leaned on him and then moved away. He pulled his hands to his temples to exorcise the feeling.

Solomon seemed to see his discomfort. 'Perhaps we can make a pact' she continued. 'We have each other's numbers. If we see anything unusual, let's get in touch.'

Gill dropped his elbows on the table and spread out his hands. 'I work for a crypto mag, Solomon. My day job is a creative mix of pseudo-science and rumour. Please define unusual?'

Solomon nodded as she took Gill's point. 'Something unusually, unusual.' Then to Gill's frustration, she brushed his shoulder with her hand and quickly walked away.

Chapter 4

Gill crossed the Kincardine Bridge out of Fife and into Stirlingshire, then immediately turned off the main road to follow a country lane along the south bank of the River Forth. It was Tuesday and he was on his way to view Ed Johnson's stone slab. Once Gill's friend and mentor, their relationship had soured many years before when another student discovered Gill had cheated on a PhD project. From this low ebb, their friendship had rekindled again since Gill had left university life to work for *Mysterious Scotland*.

Reaching the outskirts of Airth village, temporary traffic signs guided him down a narrow lane towards the archaeological dig and the car park that serviced it. Gill drove into a field and along a plastic trackway until he found a parking space between a gleaming new 4by4 and a university minibus. Leaving his car, he wandered through the encampment, looking for the man in charge. He allowed himself a smile. 'The Forth Gateway Project' was a fully serviced dig, running eighteen months and funded to the tune of three million pounds. Quite possibly, it was the largest dig ever undertaken in Scotland.

The dig HQ comprised four modern portacabins sitting on an area of hardened ground. A girl in a hard hat pointed Gill in the direction of the man he was looking for. He found

Professor Ed Johnson leading a briefing. Tall with glasses, and an appearance that was rather bookish no matter how much dirt he got on his clothes; his mouth working faster than his hands as he passed out duty rosters to a circle of bright young faces. Gill waited patiently for the informal meeting to end, then stepped forward to shake his old friend's outstretched hand.

'Almost as fancy as a *Mys.Scot* dig', he said, nodding at the multi-stage plan-of-works mapped out on the walls around him.

'We've got the scale to do some wonderful work', said Ed. 'Have you got time to walk the site with me?'

Gill shrugged. 'If you think we can manage it all in a single morning. You got something to show me?'

Ed smiled. 'Bits and pieces. Firstly, I have something I want you to see in person before you hear about it on the grapevine.'

'You look embarrassed, Professor.'

'No. Just pleased.'

'I hope you've not found anything mysterious. That's my turf, I hope you'll agree.'

Ed laughed. 'Not mysterious, per se. Just special. Come and see.'

The dig HQ sat on flat ground half a mile from the river. Around them, good farmland covered the gentle gradient to the water's edge under the watchful gaze of two giant pylons. They stood with their arms resting solidly on their hips, carrying the weight of massive powerlines high above the River Forth. Here and there, excavations pocked the landscapes like battlefield scars. Gill stopped at the portacabin door to take in the scale of operations. 'Pity they couldn't get a brownfield site', he said. 'Hard to believe this will all be housing in a few years' time.'

'Proximity to Edinburgh. Access to rail and motorway networks. You know the drill.'

'But still. I drove through the village. It's quite bonny.'

'Not our problem, Gill. Recording the archaeology is our goal.'

'How did you decide where to dig?'

'Mixture of old maps and interesting locations identified by ground surveys. We're not under any pressure here, so we can take our time.'

Gill shook his head. 'If this was a *Mys.Scot* dig, we'd have three or four undergrads working out of a borrowed tent to grab what they could in a two-week window.'

Setting off, Ed nodded and threw Gill a sideways wink. 'Sometimes, it pays to do it right.'

A few minutes later they stopped at a large area of cleared ground, some two hundred metres from the river. Ed waved his left arm at the landscape in front of him. 'We've been excavating the sixteenth-century dockyard. Scotland's kings used to build warships here and some of the most famous boats ever to fly the saltire first sailed from this spot.'

Gill studied the stone jetties, running through excavated farmland towards the river. He could see the digging extended for several hundred metres along a stream called the Pow Burn. 'Was this all part of the boatyard?'

Ed shook his head. 'Only from here to the river. Landward of here lies an area of carse and reclaimed land. We're currently excavating a silted-up tributary of the burn.'

'Why?'

'You'll see', said Ed walking on.

'Bloody hell', said Gill a few minutes later as he stared into the manmade basin. Below him, a thicket of bones tumbled towards the unmistakable skull of a whale.

'Ninety-eight feet', said Ed, proudly. 'We've sent a DNA sample to the lab, but we're almost certain it was a blue whale.'

'Seriously?' said Gill. 'Here?' He watched two field assistants stepping through some of the skull bones as they continued to prise the beast from it's peaty grave.

'Back in the eighteenth century, there was a seventy-five-foot long animal found even further up river near the site of Stirling University. When we've dated our new find, we might deduce they came up river together.'

'Amazing', said Gill. 'Can I take a few photos for my mag?'

Ed shook his head. 'We'll be sending out press packs in a couple of days. You'll have to make do with those I'm afraid.'

'Well, I'm impressed. And I thought you were going to show me an old gravestone.'

'Coming to that', said Ed. 'Just wanted to get your juices flowing first.' He led Gill back up the slope, pausing to point out some of the other dig sites and speculating what might be discovered. Walking up the track past the portacabins, they paused to cross a main road.

'Who are those guys?' asked Gill, nodding at a clutch of middle-aged men in camouflage jackets and matching binoculars.

'Bird watchers', muttered Ed. 'Been here off and on for a couple of days. Apparently, there's a rare wader down in the carse.'

'Something special?'

'Lesser Yellowlegs, or something like that.'

'Each to their own', said Gill, checking the traffic before he crossed over.

'We let them use our loos. Keeps them out of the bushes.'

Once over the road, they joined another temporary track and a few minutes later, they climbed a gentle gradient and arrived at a fence surrounding a ruined church. Ed explained the building had, in recent times, been smothered with trees. Now these had been cut back to allow an archaeological assessment. Denuded of their cover, the ragged masonry of the old church pointed at the sky like a row of shattered teeth.

Ed pointed at a pretty stone castle just a short distance away. 'The hotel is listed, so its grounds won't be incorporated into the new housing scheme. And the old church is a scheduled monument, though it's in very poor condition. If the developers get their way, they will stabilise the building by reducing its height and incorporating the remaining ruin into the castle gardens.'

Gill followed Ed along a walkway and accepted the offer of a hard hat plucked from a nearby portacabin. 'Much of what you can see here was built in the seventeenth century, but all of that was raised on the original structure which is estimated to be one thousand years old.'

'Ancient, even for Scotland', said Gill as they strode into the roofless shell of the church under the looming gaze of a weathered square tower. It was a damp place and the air hung heavy with the smell of mouldy leaves.

'And this is what we've found.' Ed knelt by a rectangular slab set into the floor of the original church. Made from an iron red sandstone, it carried a two word inscription. "Fatis Lapis".

'How's your Latin?' asked Ed.

'Rusty', said Gill. 'But good enough to translate that. "*Fated Stone*".'

'Exactly', said Ed. 'What do you think it means?'

Gill knelt and peered at the slab. Ed's team had done great work just to find the thing, judging by the multiple layers of stone and sand separating the working floor of the old church and the slab that was now their focal point. After a minute of prodding and rubbing he stood up and enacted an exaggerated shrug.

'Thanks, Gill. As ever, your professional insight is breathtaking.'

'How was it found?' Gill asked.

'There was a newer floor laid on top of an older surface. That layer comprised of mainly seventeenth-century grave memorials. Very worn, but worth preserving, so we lifted them. Below these layers we found a bed of sand, protecting this.'

Gill knelt again, close to the inscribed stone and ran his fingertips across the letters. 'It's very well-defined. I doubt this slab has been exposed to the elements since it was laid.'

'Which is why it intrigues me.'

'And there's nothing else at the same level?'

'We've looked. Can't see anything else.'

'And beneath it?'

'The radar survey suggests the slab is lying on the base clay. No hint of historical ground disturbance below it.'

'Are you going to lift it?'

'Of course. But I wanted you to see it in-situ first.'

'Somebody back in time has left you a puzzle', said Gill, remembering his experience with the Chi Rho stone back on Orkney.

Ed looked from Gill to the slab. 'Agreed. I've got Historic Scotland coming in on Tuesday to talk about relocating or modifying the church. I'll get documented permission', he added.

Gill wondered if Ed's words carried implicit criticism. And his reproach was justified. Six months earlier, Gill had compromised a potentially momentous discovery with a single impetuous decision. Ed Johnson was an old hand. He wasn't about to make the same mistake.

'Any chance I could tag along? To see what's underneath?' Gill asked.

Ed half turned to walk away. 'After what happened in Orkney? Sorry, Gill. But when we lift this slab, I don't want you within a mile of this place.'

'Why'd you call me then?' Gill called to Johnson's back.

'I wanted to get your instant reaction to this.' Ed half turned and smiled. 'But mainly to brag about my whale.'

Gill laughed.

'Don't worry', called Ed. 'I'll let you know if we find anything.'

Gill watched him walk away, then stooped to rub the inscription again, the letters as sharp as the day they'd been cut. Why create something so carefully and then hide it under a floor? A feeling rose up in him, and his senses suddenly heightened. The sweet, unmistakable smell of mystery. There was something here, and he needed to see it.

'Are you sure you want to go so soon?' asked Salina as they sat on the windowsill in Gordon's room. It was Thursday evening and Gill had taken the opportunity presented by a quiet week to bring Salina up to Montrose and visit his father. Gordon himself sat in an armchair; present but not aware of them - staring intently out the window, but seeing nothing. His dementia was advancing quickly, and Gill had been warned his father didn't have long.

Gill sighed. 'I've told him my news. And that I love him.' He flicked his forehead at Gordon. 'I think he's about all out of chat.'

Salina squeezed Gill's hand and said nothing. Her parents were far younger and fitter. Visiting this strange-smelling care home with Gill was perhaps a glimpse into a future she wasn't yet ready to contemplate.

Gill stood up and kissed his father's head. Then he turned to Salina and offered her his hand. 'Thank you for coming. Let me buy you some supper.'

She smiled sadly and whispered goodbye to Gordon, a man whom she'd known so briefly before the darkness had closed over his life. Then they headed for the car.

'Have you thought about what you're going to do with your dad's house?' said Salina as they walked out into the fresh air.

'Some clinging part of me wants to keep it as a connection to him. But my practical head says sell it, so you and I can have a bigger place. What do you think?'

'I do love Stonehaven. And it would be so good to have a bolt hole. Have you considered running it as a holiday let?'

Gill sucked his teeth. 'That'd make me popular with the neighbours.'

'But you know what I mean. There must be some way you could hold on to it and still cover the expenses?'

Gill didn't respond, holding an unrealistic fear that Gordon might get to hear of their conversation.

'Never mind. It's just that you'll have to think about it one of these days.'

'I know, Sal.' He threw her a pained smile. 'There's always so much to think about.'

'You got a busy week?' she asked, clearly changing the conversation.

'Routine. We're midway between issues, so not too bad.'

'It's just that you've been distracted this evening.'

'Sorry. I'm still chewing over my encounter with Rosemary Solomon.'

'What's the problem?'

'Just that she seemed so wary. I mean, I'm not offended, but I imagined that once I started talking about angel encounters and strange self-materialising swords, she'd be curious.'

'And she wasn't? Bear in mind I still haven't seen this little party trick of yours.'

'Nothing I said surprised her. It implies she's already seen even crazier stuff.'

'You sensed she's at the edge of her comfort zone?'

'Yeah.' Gill remembered the wariness in Rosemary Solomon's eyes. 'I think she's doing whatever it is she's doing, for Charlie. A big part of her is terrified of what might be around the corner.'

'Well, you might never hear from her again.'

He stopped at the car door. 'But if I do, I'd like you to meet her. See what you make of my enigmatic friend.'

'She might not see me as part of this secret cabal she's running.'

'She's not running anything at the moment', sighed Gill. 'And if she decides she wants me to be involved, she can either have us together or not at all.'

Salina smiled as they both got in. 'Ooh! Fighting talk.'

He reached his hand across the narrow gap and brushed hers. 'We'll see if it develops. Long term, unless we're in it together, I'm not in it.'

'Well then. If love knows no boundaries …', said Salina leaning over to kiss him, her face cracking into a wicked smile. 'I quite fancy another dive in Loch Ness. Coming?'

Gill snatched the kiss, then blew out the breath it seemed he'd been holding since they'd sat down in Gordon's room. 'Rephrasing my offer, we're in it together unless you're diving. Or piloting a DSV. Or flying in a small aircraft over Arctic wastelands. Or going clubbing on Glasgow's southside.' He conjured up a mock frown. 'Thinking about it, there's quite a bit I'm not up for. Maybe we should draw up a contract?'

She tugged his arm. 'Gillan McArdle! What happened to your sense of adventure?'

He pondered this question for a second. 'Last time I saw it, I was lying under a sandstone slab in Orkney. I suspect I left it behind in all the excitement.'

Chapter 5

Three days later, Gill was pulling together an action plan for issue 22 when Ed Johnson's email dropped onto his screen. The message was terse. 'Lifted the *Airth Slab* at 3 pm today. What do you make of this?' Gill opened the attachment which was a high-definition photo of the stone from the church. He called Mhairi over and she pulled up a chair.

'From Airth', he explained. 'It's the flip side of Ed Johnson's slab.'

'Latin', Mhairi remarked while studying the image. 'Must be quite old.'

'How old would that make it?'

'Its never been commonly spoken in Scotland', Mhairi explained. 'But it was the main language for recording important documents in the Middle Ages. Assuming the *Airth Slab* is a thousand years old, the Scottish gentry would likely be speaking a form of Norman French around this time but writing in Latin.'

'The original floor of the church was at least one thousand years old.'

'Alright, then it's most likely a burial stone or memorial. It's remarkably well-preserved for its era.'

'It looks to me like the slab was laid to protect the engraving.'

'I noticed that too', said Mhairi. 'There's almost no lichen or weather stains.'

'Can you translate it?'

'Sure, give me a moment.'

Gill went to grab them both a coffee. This was yet another moment when he was so glad to have Mhairi on his team. Still working as temporary staff for the magazine, she had a classics degree and was Gill's go-to person whenever he needed forensic desk research. Despite having what she described as a "useless" degree, Gill found her remarkably valuable. And she had abundant ancillary skills, like a working knowledge of Latin, so that when he returned with the coffees, Mhairi already had a sheet of paper with scribblings, and crossing outs, deciphering the *Airth Slab*.

'It's a lament', Mhairi said. 'I'll double-check with some university contacts to make sure I haven't missed any nuances, but it seems straightforward.'

'Okay.'

Mhairi scratched in one last correction and then read aloud. "The survivors of the storm raise this church to the glory of God and to the memory of Scotland's precious and most revered object. The *Fated Stone*, lost in the year 980 being progressed from the *Pilgrim Isle*. May he avert his anger and grant his people wisdom."

'Fascinating', said Gill. 'The reference to the *Fated Stone* on the top surface is repeated. I wonder what they mean by *Fated Stone*?'

'It could be anything, though it does remind me of the 'Lia Fáil' in Ireland.'

'Ireland's very own *Stone of Destiny*', said Gill.

'Yes. Or simply another piece of revered masonry. A thousand years ago, carved stone thrones were common amongst British tribes. Well, English tribes. In other regions, they were just rocks, really.'

'Some kind of precious artefact?' mused Gill, ignoring the jibe.

'And now lost forever', Mhairi said in a sing-song voice one might use when speaking to animals or small children.

'I wonder.' Said Gill. 'If these survivors founded their church at Airth, would it make sense to assume they lost this *Fated Stone*, nearby? Close to this so-called *Pilgrim Isle*?'

'The stone doesn't explicitly say that, but you can infer it from the text.'

'Makes me want to speculate on the island's identity.'

'The Firth of Forth is dotted with little islands, Gill.'

'Could you dig around and see which ones are contenders?'

'I'll pull together a list for you', Mhairi said after a moment's thought.

'Great. And for context, can you find everything you can on the *Stone of Destiny* by Tuesday afternoon?'

'It might earn me the wrath of our office manager', whispered Mhairi with a glance over her shoulder. 'But I'll get it done.'

'Thank you.'

The meeting ended and Gill took a few moments to gather his thoughts. On impulse, he picked up the phone to Ed Johnson. 'Afternoon, Professor. I take it you've got it translated by now?'

'Aye, Gill. I've one or two scholars I can call on. What do you make of it?'

'Intriguing reference to the loss of a revered stone. I mean, why mourn a missing stone, rather than men drowned and a ship destroyed? Must have been a very special stone.'

'Well, you know the Scots. We do like our cherished lumps of rock.'

'Well, that's just it. Do you think your carving could be referring to the *Stone of Destiny*?'

Ed sighed. 'I didn't realise it was missing.'

'But you see my point. Historically *Fated Stone* and *Stone of Destiny* are pretty much the same thing.'

'Do we, Gill? Do we really know that?'

'And you know the stone they're setting up in Perth is a fake. I mean, we tolerate it, but it's red sandstone, with a distinct pattern of micro-fossils. It's a matter of scientific record it came from a quarry near Scone.'

'Yes, but it's the *Stone of Destiny* with all its contingent history. It's long role in British coronation ritual. Where it comes from isn't important.'

'You don't believe the myth about Scotland's *Stone of Destiny* being the same stone as *Jacob's Pillow*?' asked Gill.

'I suspect that's just middle-ages guff. That was the era of bone relics and wood fragments imbued with the blood of Christ. They invented a pseudo-Christian backstory for everything back then. Just retrofitting Christian orthodoxy on the pagan rituals of earlier times.'

'Okay, that's possible. What about the inscription you found? Why was it there?'

'If it was so important, Gill, why was it laid face down?'

'To hide it, perhaps. Or delay its discovery.'

'Or maybe it was never very important in the first place and the slab just got recycled into the floor of a church.'

'You mean, hidden, below the floor of a church?'

'Was it hidden, Gill? Or are you conjuring a mystery where none exists?'

'You thought it was strange enough to draw it to my attention!'

'Aye, but now all I'm seeing is a very old, remarkably preserved memorial stone. As far as I can see, that's the beginning and end of it.'

'And the survivors it mentions – why go to the expense of creating this, before hiding it? Generally, when folk sponsored the construction of a new church, they engraved their names over the door, or in the body of the kirk. They most definitely didn't hide the record of their good deed where it was unlikely to be found.'

'Perhaps their thinking was they would be seen by God and that's all that mattered to them.'

'Well, I might have a poke around. Are you okay with that?'

'Gill, I'd rather you stayed away from the site. It's been useful to hear your musings but the more we talk, the more I'm certain the inscription is just a memorial stone laid the wrong way up.'

'Can I get a look at it?'

'No, Gill. You can't.'

'Can I have a sample at least? Trace where it came from?'

Ed exhaled. 'I'll be doing that analysis over the next couple of days. I'll send you the results.'

When Gill and Cassy walked into the conference room on Tuesday afternoon, Mhairi was already waiting for them, the table in front of her piled with printouts and books.

'This looks like it's going to be a heavy one', said Cassy with forced brightness.

'Gill wanted everything I could find', said Mhairi.

'And you do like to excel.'

'I follow your lead', sniffed Mhairi.

'We can always take a break for coffee', said Gill. 'Go ahead, Mhairi. Scotland's *Stone of Destiny*. The complete history. What have you got for us?'

Mhairi drew a deep breath. 'So, we're already familiar with it, as it was used for Charles the Third's coronation. But its history goes back a long way. According to a mix of reliable and dubious historical records, it's been used in king-making ceremonies as far back as the Scots' sojourn in Galicia, even before the creation of Scotland.'

'I didn't realise it was that old', said Cassy.

Mhairi leaned forwards. 'Legend has it that on its way to Scotland, the stone passed through Ireland and was known as 'Lia Fáil', which translates to 'Destiny Stone' or '*Fated Stone*'.

'*Fated Stone*', repeated Cassy. 'Like on the *Airth Slab*.'

Mhairi nodded and continued. 'The Irish still claim to have the original stone, set up at a place called Tara, in County Meath.'

'Aye', said Gill. 'But it's brutally big. Let's stick with the Scottish variant just now.'

'St Columba is reputed to have brought that stone with him to Iona from Ireland', Mhairi continued. 'An historian called Walter Bower wrote a history of Scotland in the late fourteenth century. He records a stone, carried by the Scots from their Middle Eastern beginnings, until it was brought to Iona by Saint Columba. He notes that as Columba lay dying, he rested his head on the stone and had a vision of angels going up and down to Earth.'

'Same experience reported by Jacob', said Gill.

'Jacob?' asked Cassy.

Mhairi blinked through her glasses. 'We'll come to him.'

'This chap, Bower', said Gill. 'What are his credentials?'

'He was the Abbot of the Augustine priory on Inchcolm island, which was founded by Columba.'

'In the Firth of Forth', observed Gill. 'And not far from Airth. Any suggestion the stone was ever transported to Inchcolm?'

Mhairi shook her head. 'The first reliable sighting of the *Stone of Destiny* in Scotland is during the coronation of Kenneth MacAlpin in the year 843. MacAlpin is known for uniting the Picts and the Celts and relocating the centre of his kingdom from Argyll to Scone in Perthshire.'

Gill nodded.

'This is where we get our first nugget of useful data', said Mhairi happily. 'And it concerns the stone's appearance. In the time of these early Scottish kings, they all had seals carved so they could authenticate documents. You know; the kind of thing they used to stamp wax on the backs of envelopes.'

'Tenth-century security tags', said Gill.

Cassy rubbed her chin. 'Got any pictures?' She nodded her thanks as Mhairi passed them around.

'The *Stone of Destiny* is depicted in the royal seals of nine different kings, each time with the monarch sitting on it. You can see the stone is longer and flatter than today's accepted stone. You can't exactly tell from the etchings, but it may even have been an oval shape.'

'Okay' said Gill, looking up from his notetaking. 'And I'm forced to observe that the object we acknowledge today as the official stone, the one sitting in Perth Museum, is a rectangular block.'

Mhairi raised an eyebrow. 'And there's one other bit of intrigue. From its dimensions, it appears that the official stone was originally cut to be a door lintel. The English added two iron rings around 1320, making it easier to move, and there's speculation they trimmed the stone to fit the chair Edward had commissioned.'

'Hang on', said Cassy. 'The official stone is the wrong shape?'

'It gets worse', said Mhairi. 'When you realise where the stone actually comes from.'

'Go on', said Gill with a mischievous smirk. 'Tell her.'

'Geologically speaking, the stone is Lower Old Red Sandstone. And in keeping with myths about the stone, it is possible to find this material in the Middle East. However, a study in 1998 under the auspices of Historic Scotland and conducted by trusted academics, demonstrated that the stone came from a place called Quarryhill near Perth.'

'How could they know that?' Cassy protested.

'Micro fossils', said Gill. 'And the detailed chemical composition of the stone. These days, every rock has a chemical fingerprint. Give me a stone from anywhere in the world, and with the right lab work, I could take you to where it was quarried. Ed Johnson is running that analysis for the *Airth Slab* as we speak.'

Cassy sat with her mouth open, staring at Gill. 'Quarryhill? But isn't there meant to be some crazy backstory associated with the stone?'

'Yes', said Mhairi, nodding at Cassy. 'And now I get to tell all about Jacob and the *Jacob's Pillow* myth. To get your mind around this juicy Biblical legend, you have to cast back almost four thousand years. While fleeing his brother, the Jewish patriarch, Jacob experienced a personal encounter with God while sleeping with his head resting on a stone.'

'Hence the word, *Pillow?*' said Cassy.

'Yes. And tradition claims that Jacob was so taken by this experience, he collected the stone and carried it with him wherever he lived. Some years later, due to a famine, Jacob and his family ended up in Egypt, and the story has it, they took the stone with them. Jump forward four hundred years and the Biblical Jewish exodus from Egypt is underway. The stone is carried along to the Jewish "Promised Land", where eventually, it gets incorporated into the temple in Jerusalem. There it rests until the year 586 BCE when Babylon attacks, scattering some of the twelve tribes of Israel. Rescuing *Jacob's Pillow*, one tribe flees to North Africa, and from there they migrate to Galicia in modern-day Spain. Under constant military pressure, they move on again to a newly discovered island in the north which we now know as Ireland. From there, this fugitive tribe morphs into the Kingdom of Dalriada until eventually, it spills across the Irish Sea into Argyll. All the time, carrying *Jacob's Pillow* in its care.'

'Wait, wait, wait', spluttered Cassy. 'According to this myth, the Scots are Jewish?'

'Not just the Scots', said Mhairi. 'If you believe the story then all Celts, and by extension, all Britons.'

'If I can weigh in', said Gill. 'Even if the story was true, any Jewish DNA and cultural references would have been diluted by the time Scotland achieved nationhood.'

'Which bits of this history *are* we certain of?' asked Cassy.

'We can only be confident as far back as the Galician connection' said Mhairi. That's because DNA from the Galician celts is present in the contemporary Scottish and Irish gene pools. Before that, it's conjecture, really.'

'It's a grand yarn. And maybe I'm missing something', said Cassy. 'How does a rock from Perth, travel to Israel, acquire mystical status, then find its way back home again?'

'Because', said Mhairi, triumphally. 'It's not the same rock.'

'How can you know that?'

'It's shape depicted on the seals for one. And also because Walter Bower, our fourteenth century historian, records the stone as being black marble.'

Cassy sat back and pursed her lips. 'Which means the established *Stone of Destiny* is a fake?'

Mhairi nodded. 'Substitute, might be a better word. But yeah, basically.'

'Why are we tolerating it then? Nothing you've said is secret information.'

Mhairi's gaze fluttered across to Gill. 'Because of Scottish politics.'

'Well, don't tell Tony', Cassy muttered. 'He's terrified of being caught up in the independence debate.'

'Far older politics than that. Thirteenth century to be exact.'

'Coffee break', declared Gill, standing up. 'Thanks, Mhairi. This is great work.'

Chapter 6

'Politics', said Mhairi. 'Are you ready? We're leaving those ancient kings of Scotland behind and jumping ahead to the year 1296. That's the year when Edward the First of England invades Scotland and captures the *Stone of Destiny*.'

'Why does he do that?' asked Cassy.

'Not because he covets it', Mhairi replied. 'But because he wants to deny its king-making power to the Scots. By removing it, he hopes to deny future Scottish kings their traditional legitimacy.'

'Didn't the English want it for themselves?' asked Cassy. 'I mean, they're still using it for coronations.'

'Records show, Edward left the stone in an Edinburgh fortress for almost a decade. And although he commissioned an English throne containing the stone, it wasn't used in any coronation until Henry the Fourth, more than a hundred years after its theft. In those early days, it just wasn't a big deal to the English kings.'

'Did the Scots try to get it back?'

'Not by force. They used the only diplomatic channel available to them and petitioned Rome.'

'Why Rome?'

'Back then, the Catholic church was fighting to be the universal church. Basically, they were trying to stamp out competitors. This forced the Celtic church founded by St Columba onto the back foot. By the Eleventh century, there was a real risk that Scotland could be targeted by a crusade to wipe out religious practices deemed inconsistent with Rome.'

'Hang on a second. Weren't the Celtic church, and Roman church both Christian?'

'They were', said Mhairi. 'But Rome abhorred the pagan practices the Celtic church had absorbed on its way to replacing indigenous religious belief.'

'Rituals like crowning kings while they sat on sacred stones', Gill added.

'Well, that's religion for you', sniffed Cassy. 'Always at war with itself.'

'On one hand, the Scots might have been relieved when Edward removed the stone, effectively eliminating this old pagan tradition', Mhairi continued. 'While at the same time, they set about elevating the stone's legitimacy by creating the Judaeo-Christian backstory, which we know today as the *Jacob's Pillow* myth.'

Gill added to his notes. 'Either way, the people running Scotland are diplomatically tilting towards Rome and away from early Celtic traditions.'

'Absolutely', said Mhairi. 'And as well as the little matter of not facing a crusade they also are cosying up to the pope as he's the arbiter of disputes between nations. Think along the lines of an early version of the European Court of Justice.'

'Nice analogy', said Gill. 'Basically England takes Scotland to court.'

'In the early fourteenth century, Edward tries to argue the English are a superior race and are therefore qualified under God to rule the entire British Isles. In response to this litigation, the Scottish nobility make what's called the *Declaration of Arbroath*.'

'Give me a wee refresher on that please, Mhairi', said Cassy.

'The *Declaration* was a letter to the pope, signed by every significant Scottish nobleman. It recounted the tale of Scotland's old origin story with the aim of convincing the pope that the Scots were an ancient people with Middle Eastern roots. The goal was to get Rome to acknowledge the Scots as a distinct people group, separate from the English.'

'Does Rome buy it?'

'Not at first. A short while later the Scots double-down by adopting St Andrew as their patron saint. That's another gesture towards Rome, which side-lined domestic Celtic Christianity in the process.'

'Okay', said Gill, trying to sum up. 'You're saying the signatories to the *Declaration of Arbroath* in the year 1320 might have conjured up a biblical provenance for the *Stone of Destiny*, casting it as *Jacob's Pillow*? And all this smoke and mirrors is probably just a ruse to give the Scots distinct religious significance in the eyes of the pope?'

Mhairi nodded. 'It's possible.'

'Can we prove that?'

Mhairi referred to her notes. 'The first reliable document suggesting the stone was *Jacob's Pillow* doesn't appear until two decades after its theft by Edward the First. Which is a hint the Christian origin story was appended to the stone.'

'Still, we're left with only two possibilities', said Cassy. 'Either Scotland's *Stone of Destiny* was an authentic Biblical artefact, which has since been lost, or swapped for a block of local sandstone …', she paused to let Mhairi nod her assent. 'Or maybe the stone portrayed as *Jacob's Pillow* was a fabricated story right from the start, retrofitted onto a rock most likely used in pagan coronation services.'

'Yep', said Mhairi. 'That about nails it.'

Cassy turned to Gill. 'So we have a substitute stone sitting in Perth. And potentially, the real one, lying somewhere at the bottom of the Firth of Forth. Am I getting that right?'

'You are', said Gill. 'But we've got to be careful. Even if the contemporary stone is a replacement, it's been part of the British constitution for seven hundred years. Faked or not, it's an immensely historical artefact in its own right.'

Cassy clicked her pen a few times. 'And no one is going to thank us if we draw attention to the facts suggesting it's just a random rock.'

Gill nodded. 'Both the Westminster government who has hoarded it for seven hundred years and the Holyrood government who demanded its return would both be embarrassed by that kind of revelation.'

'Makes me wonder if the history of the stone is even relevant', said Cassy. 'The English monarch stole it to undermine the legitimacy of Scottish kings. Nowadays, the Scots use it to accuse the English of imperialism.'

Mhairi straightened her back and ostentatiously cleared her throat.

'Sorry', said Cassy, looking like she'd forgotten her friend harked from Kent. 'Not all English are imperialists. Well, not these days.'

'The stone is still a political tool', said Mhairi. 'When it was returned to Scotland in 1996 by John Major's unpopular Conservative Government, he was trying to curry favour with the Scottish electorate.'

Cassy shook her head. 'All this fuss over a rock.' She turned to face Gill. 'You're the one responsible for making a magazine out of this bag of weasels. What do you want to do?'

Gill tapped the table a few times with his knuckles. 'Apart from the newly discovered *Airth Slab*, are there any other clues as to what happened to the original?'

'It might still be buried at Scone', said Mhairi. 'There are legends about Edward being duped with a substitute stone. And they're strengthened by the fact Edward came back to Scone two years later and sacked the Abbey. Partly to keep the Scots under his heel, but perhaps to have another look for the original stone.'

'And there's the seed of a story', said Cassy, leaning back with her hands splayed on the table. 'Because the old royal seals depict a stone, we know an important artefact existed. Just not the one Edward took to London.'

'Which means the original stone is probably still out there', said Gill. 'Waiting to be found.'

'Agreed', said Mhairi.

Gill drummed his hands on the table. 'And that my friends is a story I'd like to print.'

Chapter 7

Gill was gathering himself to spend the rest of the day out of the office. He updated his "to-do list" with Cassy before placing a couple of reworks on Craig's desk.

Craig looked up. 'Are you really planning to see Conall Canmore?'

'I going to try', Gill replied. 'I'll call in on my way to Airth. See if I can meet him.'

'I thought you were at the dig site last week?'

Gill nodded. 'I want to see it again.'

Craig glanced at his watch. 'Seen the time? You'd better hope Johnson's excavations glow in the dark.'

'I've got my reasons. But the point is, if I leave now, I could spend an hour in Stirling on the way.'

'This Canmore fella.' Craig paused. 'You do realise who he is, right?'

Gill blinked twice. 'A one-time wannabe king of Scotland?'

'And an ardent nationalist in his day', Craig said quietly. 'I googled him. He even contested a parliamentary seat for the Nats in the '90s.'

'Okay', said Gill, considering if this information impacted his plans. 'Thanks for the heads up.'

Cassy breezed over, catching the whiff of contentious conversation. 'Yeah. I was going to say the same. My advice to Gill, if you're hanging around the Canmore's, make sure you're wearing tartan.'

Gill laughed.

'I'm not messing, Gill', Craig continued. 'Old Conall Canmore never achieved an election win, but his eldest lad has been a member of the Scottish parliament for the best part of a decade. Quite a high-heidyin.'

'No kidding! I assume you mean, Roddy Canmore? The Justice Secretary?'

'Aye, and aspiring First Minister if he wasn't such a hardliner.'

Cassy swept humour off her face. 'Not too late to change your mind.'

Gill waved a hand a her. 'I'm popping in to have a wee chat with his dad. What could go wrong?'

'Just saying! You know how Tony feels about politics. If Roddy Canmore is about when you're making your house call, please tread carefully.' She dropped a furtive glance in the direction of the team working on the cat mag. 'And please make sure nobody dies.'

'Thanks.' Gill winked. 'I'll carry a first aid kit and wear a sprig of heather in my waistcoat. Stay on the right side of them all.'

Gill found on-street parking a short distance from Stirling city centre and checked his watch. He still had half an hour before his appointment, so he climbed up to a narrow cobbled street known as The Esplanade and walked around the perimeter of the castle and the centuries-old buildings that stood in its shadow. At one time, this had been the very centre of Scottish government and the prestige and history of the place seeped out of the stones like last night's rain. The view out over the rest of the city was spectacular and, in the moments when he had an easterly view, he could see the wide coils of the River Forth as it meandered its way towards the sea.

Timing his arrival to the minute, he stood in front of a detached stone villa on the old castle approach road, called Broad Street. Like many buildings of its era, the house looked like it needed fifty thousand spent on it, just to keep it standing. No one answered his first two rings and he was just about to try one final time when the door swung open and a fit-looking man in his early forties gave an apologetic smile. 'Sorry. I was in the middle of something. Can I help you?'

'Gill McArdle. My office phoned ahead to make an appointment.'

'Yes. They spoke to me.' He reached out and shook Gill's hand. 'I'm Alasdair Canmore. You've come about my father?'

'Aye. If that's okay?'

'Fine. Come in.'

Gill stepped into a dimly lit hall and through into an old-fashioned family lounge, laden with books. The house wasn't unclean, but Gill surmised no women lived here. The décor, like the exterior of the house, looked faded and old.

'Sorry about the state of the place. It's my dad's. He's not given it much attention since my mother passed a few years back.'

'No problem. You should see mine', Gill lied, thinking about the modern flat he rented in Broughty Ferry.

'Have you come far?' asked Alasdair.

Gill shook his head. 'I've got another appointment in the area. I found I had a gap in my schedule and decided it would be a pleasure to meet your father.'

Alasdair pointed to a couple of mismatched wooden chairs and stifled an embarrassed smile as Gill sat down. 'Until you called, I hadn't realised my father had contacted your magazine. To be honest, I'm surprised you've come to see him.'

'Don't be. When I spoke to your father a few months ago, I was researching the contemporary bloodlines of old Scottish kings. He wasn't keen to chat. I'm rather hoping he's changed his mind.'

Alasdair looked at Gill. 'You might find it's him asking the questions.'

'How so?'

'My father isn't well. He has a progressive disease affecting his memory.' Alasdair waved a hand in the air. 'He has strange dreams. Upsetting visions.'

'I see', said Gill, remembering Mhairi had alerted him to this possibility.

Alasdair dipped his gaze and nodded at the floor. 'I wonder how lucid you'll find him. I've no idea what undercurrents are driving his imagination.'

'I'll take the conversation as it comes. I won't judge him.'

'Thank you. He has lymphoma, you see. And it's spawned a rare form of brain tumour.'

'Ah', said Gill. 'I'm sorry to hear that. My dad is suffering rapid onset dementia so I know how you feel. It's hard to lose them piece by piece this way.'

'It was quite sudden with Dad. He just woke up one day and decided he was having dreams about living the wrong life. That somehow his wires were crossed. We'd have panicked if he hadn't been so damn reasonable about it.'

'Still, it must be very difficult for you all.'

Alasdair swept his hand at books scattered around the room. 'And now he doubts all his accumulated knowledge of the world. Hence all this reading material. British history, world history, and the history of scientific advance. He reads it all, trying to make sense of his dreams.'

'And Scottish history?' said Gill, lifting the nearest volume.

'Initially, yes. He doesn't talk about it now. He says he finds it too upsetting.'

'For the sake of our conversation, can I ask what your father did for a living?'

'He was a stone mason. We all were in this family. From a long way back.' Alasdair pulled another embarrassed face. 'Not that you'd know it looking at this place.'

'And he retired, when?'

'He was still working when all of this kicked off. Not heavy stuff. He loved having a nice piece of detailed work to tinker with. Architectural dressings. Finials and the like. He was really quite good.'

'And this stopped at the onset of his disease?'

'Yes. He woke up one morning imagining himself in some crisis or other. He hasn't worked since.'

Gill nodded, remembering his father and how quickly his mind had ebbed away.

'Instead, he's acquired all these airs and graces. My father has always been what he'd call, "a snappy dresser". Fastidious about his hair. But he was a working man, if you know what I mean. Comfortable with the hard language around a building site. But now his demeanour is quite formal, and he gets distressed about his appearance. They're just a couple of things about him that are weirdly changed.'

'I'm sorry', said Gill, again. 'You must find this harrowing.'

'Anyway', Alasdair continued. 'I'll take you in to see him. All I ask is that if he seems tired or becomes upset, you don't stay long.'

'Of course. Will you be staying in the room?'

'I would like to, but Dad will probably chase me off. I'll give you twenty minutes or so, then interrupt.'

Gill smiled his confirmation. 'Agreed.'

Alasdair stood and led Gill out of the room and across the entrance hall. Outside what might have been a dining room in the old villa, he paused and looked at Gill. 'I know you came to research our family. I hope my father doesn't say anything that leads you to mock him in your magazine.'

'Let me give you my word', said Gill. 'This is a courtesy call out of respect to your father. I won't be gathering quotes.'

Alasdair nodded, though he didn't look particularly encouraged by Gill's honesty. He knocked on the dining room door, before continuing into the room. Gill followed and found a tall, almost regal-looking man with a mass of well-tended facial hair, sitting reading near a window.

'Dad. I've got Gillan McArdle from *Mysterious Scotland* magazine here to see you.'

The old man looked up. 'Ah, yes. Thank you, Alasdair. Mr McArdle. Please excuse my reduced circumstances. Come in and have a seat.'

'Would you like tea?' said Alasdair.

Canmore deferred to Gill, who shook his head. 'Thank you, Alasdair. That will be all.'

Alasdair flicked his eyebrows at Gill in an exasperated gesture and left the room.

The old man flipped his book over and laid it across his thighs. He studied Gill with dark chestnut-coloured eyes that managed to be warm and penetrating at the same time. He lifted his left hand, and perhaps subconsciously, started to rub the ends of his moustache with his fingertips.

'Thank you for seeing me, sir', said Gill.

'Please, call me Conall. I have my fill of formality while I'm asleep.'

'And I'm, Gill. People only call me McArdle when they're cross about something.'

Conall laughed hoarsely. 'The girl from your office said we'd spoken before?'

'Yes. We stood on your doorstep a couple of months ago and briefly discussed the short life of the *Maid of Norway*, plus the state of modern Scotland. Then, if I'm honest, you slammed the door in my face.'

Conall gritted his teeth in embarrassment. 'I am sorry about that. I've … I've not been myself.'

Gill forced his face into an expression of reconciliation but said nothing.

'*Maid of Norway*', Conall repeated.

'Ancestor of yours', said Gill. 'Her premature death in the year 1290 ended the Canmore royal line.'

'Yes', he said. 'I seem to recall a queen of that name, though in my memory, her reign was far from short.'

'It was a tough moment for Scotland. Historians argue the power vacuum left by her premature death gave Edward the First an excuse to invade.'

'Fascinating', said Connall.

'What are you reading?' asked Gill, pointing at the upturned hardback on Conall's knees.

'British history. A sorry tale of how the English built a kingdom, then lost an empire. And how they won a war but squandered the peace.' He rubbed his unshaven chin. 'Somehow, I remember it differently.'

Gill nodded but said nothing.

'I'm surprised you came', said Conall. 'Please tell me why you did?'

Gill cleared his throat. 'We've been writing a series of articles on the old royal Scottish houses. And of course, the Canmores were on our list.'

He smiled. 'Well, I'm glad you're here, Gill.'

'Alasdair told me you're having strange dreams. He seems to think I might be able to help you.'

Conall gave one abrupt nod. 'I am. I dream I am the king of Scotland.'

Gill gave him an encouraging smile as if this was the most normal claim in the world. 'Do you mean, a king back in the days of the old Canmores?'

'No', Conall shot back. 'In this period. A contemporary twenty-first-century king.'

'I see', said Gill, feeling like a woefully underprepared psychologist. 'When did these dreams start?'

'About eight weeks ago. Not long after you and I first met, I suspect. And your next logical question is when was I diagnosed? That was three months before. Any reasonable person can deduce my mental capacities are impaired.'

Gill nodded. 'Excuse me, but I don't know a lot about dreams.'

'But you do know I'm ill? I'm dying and when this thing in my head decides to pop, that will be the end of me.'

'And you have my sympathy.'

Conall looked away and for a few moments looked frail and sad.

'Is there something specific I can do to help?' Gill asked.

Conall glanced upwards and thought, then clutched his right hand into a fist. 'I keep seeing snatches of a kingdom. Of a different Scotland where I'm king. One that's been prosperous and progressive for one thousand years.' He dropped his fist and wrung his hands for a few moments. 'This other Scotland does have its problems; these are the things the dreams focus on. The threat of war. The sudden decline of the kingdom. A succession crisis as I become progressively frailer. But do you know, despite its problems, it's still a very attractive place. I'm wondering, did a Scotland like that ever exist? Was it ever real? Or is it the figment of a diseased imagination? Can you help me with that, Gillan McArdle?'

Gill studied his own hands as they rested in front of him. 'You'll need to tell me more about it. The mind is an incredible tool. Perhaps you've read a history book, or a novel and your mind has interpreted it in your dreams. In just the same way people present Shakespeare's plays in contemporary situations.'

'Yes, that might be it.' The old man turned to face Gill with sad, watery eyes. 'But it all seems so real.'

Gill leaned a little closer. 'Tell me more about it.'

Conall smiled. 'My dreams always start in a bedroom. It's large and has an anteroom, which is like a porch that sits between a bathroom and a dressing room. On the wall facing you as you walk in, hangs a sword.'

'A sword?' said Gill, coming to attention. 'What kind of sword?'

'A gleaming weapon. Somehow, I know it as *The Royal Claymore*. In the abstract knowledge of my dreams, I'm aware of its name and that it's cast from a single piece of the purest steel.' He rocked in his chair and laughed. 'But what kind of man would keep a sword in his bathroom?'

'You see yourself as the king in the dreams. Where do you rule from?'

'Stirling Castle, of course. I can see the city from the bedroom window. From there, I progress to the rest of the castle, attending meetings and functions.' He flashed Gill a shy smile from the midst of his facial hair. 'I must say, in my dreams, I'm awfully busy. And desperately important.'

'Stirling', said Gill, thinking. 'A favourite royal residence of many of the old kings, but never the permanent seat of government the way Scone or Edinburgh have been.'

Conall nodded. 'It's the same city. Though it's much larger in the dreams than the town I've known all my life. And the castle is greatly expanded. Royal palace and parliament of the commonwealth, all in one place.'

'Commonwealth? Are we still talking about Scotland?'

'I've seen documents.' Conall screwed up his eyes and thought. 'The *Global Alliance of Celtic Nations*. Yes, that's it.' He looked away. 'But of course, we don't have that here.'

'But you perceive it is based in Stirling?'

Conall smiled knowingly. 'Yes.'

Gill sat back and puzzled at this. Although he could see no logical way a commonwealth of nations could end up based out of Scotland, the idea tickled him. And he realised he was quietly enjoying Conall's gentle imaginings.

'This king you see', said Gill.' 'I mean the role your dreams cast you into; does he rule as monarch, or hold a ceremonial and constitutional role?'

'Half and half. Parliament seems to do most of the detailed work, as it does here. But I have the impression that politics has to work hand in hand with the monarch. Win his or her support for government policies and be prepared to explain themselves if they act without royal ascent.'

'Sounds like a recipe for conflict.'

'The dreams hint at tension, though I haven't seen conflict. But yes. I imagine there'd be lots of horse trading in that kind of system.'

'Is the technology in the dreams the same as here?'

'More or less. To be honest, the dreams are sucking me into a rising sense of crisis. I'm not very good at noticing things like digital devices.'

'Do you recognise anybody, portrayed in the dream?'

'Yes. Alasdair and Roddy. Though they're ... different.'

'In what way?'

The old man looked away. 'I'd rather not say.'

'And when you sleep, do the dreams pick up from where they left off?'

'Like episodes in a TV drama', said Conall, wearily. 'Each chapter ramps up the pressure on the king, played skilfully by my dreaming self. The same man, who in real life, is barely able to go to the bathroom unassisted.'

'Incredible', said Gill. 'Let's talk about this commonwealth you mentioned. How could something like that come to exist?'

Conall coughed and looked away. 'That's a big question and I doubt I have the resources to answer it.'

Gill remembered his promise to Alasdair. 'Perhaps we should leave that to another day?'

'Of course.' Conall rubbed his palms on his trousers, perhaps driving feeling back into weary limbs. 'Tell me, Gill. To the best of your knowledge, did a Scotland like this *ever* exist in the past?'

Gill considered his response carefully. 'I'm an archaeologist rather than a historian. Some parts of your dreams sound very plausible. Other pieces ... have no historical precedent as far as I'm aware.'

'I thought as much.' Conall lifted a weary hand. 'A different place or a different time. A part of me wishes it could all be true.'

'Sounds like a wonderful vision of Scotland', said Gill.

Conall nodded weakly and looked away.

'I should leave you.'

'Thank you, Gill. Call for Alasdair. He'll see you out.'

Gill stood to leave, uncertain how he should wrap up this strange encounter.

In the end, Conall had the last word. 'Might you be passing this way again?'

Gill nodded. 'I'm working around Stirlingshire for a few days. There's a dig at Airth.'

'Well, please call in. If I'm spared, we might talk again.'

Gill said farewell to Alasdair, then left the house. Rather than go straight to his car, he walked the short distance to Stirling Castle, its doors now closed to visitors for another day. As editor of *Mysterious Scotland* for the best part of two years, he'd had many surreal conversations. The magazine's readers and contributors brought him all manner of thoughts, sightings and theories, and he'd become quite practised at greeting each one as if it was the most reasonable thing he'd ever heard. Conall Canmore had stretched even that worthy record to breaking point, and yet, there was something coherent and attractive about his dreamt flashes of an alternative Scotland.

Gill shook his head at the madness of it all and turned his mind to what he was going to do over the next few hours. It was a sly undertaking that would have no place in Canmore's idealistic Scotland. Under a darkening sky that was a fair representation of his mood, he drove the few miles to the Clackmannanshire bridge, battling his misgivings for what he was about to do.

Chapter 8

Ed Johnson didn't want Gill anywhere near his dig site. He'd been one hundred per cent clear about that. Consequently, Gill nursed a certain amount of guilt as he stopped at the protective fencing, separating the hotel from the churchyard.

He'd arrived at the Airth Castle Hotel an hour before on the pretence of looking for a wedding venue – another small lie that weighed on his conscience. Having had a tour of the recently refurbished facilities, he'd enquired about the state of the ruin next door. In response, his host had shown him an artist's impression of how the hotel gardens would look a year from now. The illustration suggested the crumbling towers of the church would be gone and a new interpretation of the old building crafted from the remaining stones. It would stand at no more than head height, surrounded by neatly mown grass. Thanking his host, he'd stepped outside.

Under the shadow cast by the hotel, he slipped through a gap in the fence and into the churchyard where the old building had not yet surrendered to the developer's plan. He was acting on an urge rather than a strategy. He wanted to see the context in which the *Airth Slab* had rested for a thousand years. If there was anything to learn beyond the words on the underside of the artefact, he was confident he would see it. And if nothing was visible, he'd feel it, employing that inexplicable part of his senses more useful to him than underground radar in moments like this.

Stepping through broken walls into the centre of the derelict kirk, he searched for the spot where the slab had lain. Lighting a small torch with a very confined beam, Gill studied the excavated floor. Millimetre by millimetre, he looked for any continuation of the stone or evidence of anything further beneath. The bed of sand that had supported the underside of the stone had been swept away, presumably for further analysis. All that was left was a roughly cut hole in the base clay. Ed Johnson's ground survey had reported there was nothing else beneath the floor, and after seeing the void for himself, Gill was inclined to agree with him.

Slowly, he studied the immediate vicinity. Was there anything else here hinting at another element to the puzzle? Finding nothing, he stood up and stepped through the rest of the building, looking for anything that seemed out of place. Or anything to suggest the whole set-up was faked. In its dilapidated state, it was hard to see anything significant, other than the scars left by the church's modifications over the years.

Summing up, all he had was a message on a slab, purposely hidden from sight, until when? Until a day like this when the building would be torn down? If this was a message in a bottle, it was a long shot indeed. All the more perplexing then that Airth church should yield the slab a few weeks before the *Stone of Destiny* went on permanent display in Perth. A coincidence? Gill had stopped believing in coincidence. There were forces at work here that seemed to stretch beyond the natural. Dropping his hands to his hips, he realised this was why the *Airth Slab* now lodged in his curiosity. It had captured his attention and metaphorically, he'd carry the slab on his back until he'd figured out why.

Frustrated, Gill walked through the broken walls and out to the perimeter of the demolished woodland that had engulfed the building in the century since its retirement. The night was still, and a fresh salty smell drifted up from the Forth, rising as far as the church, but no further. In the darkness, he imagined the green landscape running downhill towards the river and tried to picture the church in its original context. In this area one thousand years ago, the estuary had been wider, before land reclamation and the natural processes allowing silts to gather had added the broad fields below this one-time coastal community. Try as he might, he couldn't see the significance of Airth. Despite its age, it had never grown very big, although that was something about to change with the developments underway. And then he realised, perhaps that was the point. For rescued sailors making landfall, this might simply have been a cherished place. And if you needed to post a letter to the future in the form of the *Airth Slab*, maybe this place was as good as any. As for who and why? Those were questions he might never answer.

Below him ran the main road into the village and beyond that, a kilometre distant towards the river, there was sufficient ambient light to make out the excavations around the old dockyard and the last resting place of Ed Johnson's whale. He imagined the survivors of a shipwreck, deposited in the dockyard and giving thanks to God before progressing on their way. Except that it wouldn't have been the James the Fourth dockyard, but rather, a far smaller facility some five hundred years earlier. The land would have looked very different too, with the ground below the village still a water-logged carse, with the Pow Burn winding through it. Was there anything else of significance here? The slab was in a laboratory for analysis. This letter from the past had been received. Now all that remained was the churchyard itself, representing an empty bottle.

Distracted by movement on the main road, he picked out the profile of an old 4by4 sitting in a layby. Several men stood by the car with their backs to Gill and their focus towards the river below. They were too far away to hear their voices, but as they turned to talk to each other, Gill could see they held binoculars. For a moment Gill was suspicious the men were studying Johnson's dig site, but when they became momentarily excited by a skein of geese flying overhead, Gill remembered what they were doing. Birdwatchers, he told himself, remembering the mudflats around the bridges contained a thriving nature reserve.

Somewhere behind him in the hotel car park, he heard a car door slam and women's voices, laughing. He decided he'd done enough. Leaving the birders to their hobby, he stepped gingerly back through the trees and into the body of the church. He stopped to listen to his senses one last time before going home. But … as he stood at the base of the ruined tower, he heard something move. Suddenly alert to danger, he stood quite still and listened intently. And heard nothing. Trying a new tactic, he turned slowly through the full three hundred and sixty degrees and tried to detect movement. He was struck by how dark it had become. Where, a few minutes before, he'd been able to step through the ruined church without stumbling, now everything seemed smothered in a suffocating blackness. There were the lights and sounds of the hotel car park, barely forty metres away, but in this immediate spot, even the night-time wildlife was silent.

A grown man, he wasn't afraid of the dark, however, his encounters with Raphael had taught him to listen to his instinct. He'd seen a pattern over the last two years. In the moments before Raphael had appeared, Gill had already heard some small internal alarm bell - some inner sense that his life was in danger. And even without Raphael's presence, he felt that now.

Above him, there came the sound of rock rubbing against rock. He didn't look up; electing instead to leap into the clear void at the centre of the church. That choice he realised later saved his life. Even as he plunged to safety, he heard the crash of a large chunk of masonry hitting the hard floor behind him, sending shards of stone against his legs. He spun onto his back to see a tall figure slither out of the tower stairwell and approach him with some kind of metal bar with a blade fashioned at each end. His attacker adjusted his grip on the bar as he stepped forward.

As Gill turned and struggled to crawl to safety, he heard footsteps among the leaves as his attacker strode towards him. He spun onto his back again and saw the black figure had raised his weapon, shoulders tensed, ready to put his full force behind his blade. As the blow started to fall, Gill flung his hands out in a futile effort to protect himself and immediately felt the weight of a heavy object in his hands.

With a clash of sparks, his attacker's blow landed inches from Gill's face, hitting whatever it was Gill held in his hands. The ringing of metal on metal seemed as unexpected to the attacker as it was to Gill, and he paused momentarily before lifting his weapon to strike again. Gill slithered back a few more inches and gripped his defence. He could feel it now; the hilt of a sword in his right hand and a sticky soreness in his left where the blow had forced Raphael's blade into his flesh.

Another car arrived at the hotel and swung into a parking bay only twenty metres from where Gill was defending himself. Strong blue LED beams cut into the darkness and illuminated his attacker's face. An ugly face, covered in scars, and gone in a flash as the man turned his head away and raised a hand to shield himself from the light. The beam was only going to delay his attacker's advance, but it created a pause just long enough for Gill to scramble to his feet and sprint to the gap in the fencing he'd entered twenty minutes before. He kept running and didn't stop until he burst into the hotel reception. The host who'd shown him around earlier looked up in alarm.

Gill stood, smeared with soil, and with his sword tucked behind him, while his left hand dripped blood on the carpet. 'Sorry', he said politely. 'I need to hide in here for a second while I call the police.'

An hour later, Gill sat sheepishly on the hotel steps being chaperoned by a young police officer. His sword had evaporated as mysteriously as it had appeared, and his damaged hand hung in a temporary bandage. Once he'd answered a few questions, he would need to make a hospital visit to have the wound cleaned and stitched.

'Just so you know', said DI George Wiley, lighting a cigarette and tossing away the burnt match as he stomped up the steps towards Gill. 'Other Detective Inspectors are available.'

'You're the only one I have on speed dial', replied Gill, tugging on the tails of his waistcoat.

'Lucky for you I've finally been promoted to Bathgate. There's some talk about me setting up a special unit. Help Police Scotland deal with all the mumbo-jumbo crap you keep throwing at us.'

'No mumbo-jumbo, this time, Inspector. Just some nutcase trying to kill me with blocks of sandstone.'

Wiley flicked his head at Gill's bandaged hand. 'They didn't do that with sticks or stones.'

'He'd some kind of weapon'. Gill used his good hand to wipe his face. 'Didn't get a close look.'

Wiley took a long drag and exhaled a stream of smoke. 'In a minute you can take me in there and walk me through what happened. First, tell me what you were doing in a ruined kirk in the middle of the night?'

Gill shrugged. 'Checking out some archaeological work, obviously.'

'In the dark?'

'Yes.'

'Hunting for luminous unicorns?'

'No. The site has restricted access. This was … an out-of-hours call.'

'You were trespassing?'

Gill paused. 'Yes.'

'Ah. The great Gill McArdle reduced to playing Wee Willie Winkie.'

'If I did commit a crime, I think a far greater one was committed against me.'

Wiley huffed. 'We'll see.' He swung his fag in the general direction of the church. 'Whose dig is this?'

Gill told him.

'I'll chat to this Professor Johnson and see if he'd like to press charges. For trespassing, that is. In the meantime, any idea who wants you dead?'

Gill shook his head.

'Brilliant', spat Wiley before taking a last long pull on his fag and tossing it away. 'Let's go and join the uniform guys under the spotlights and see if we can salvage any indisputable facts from your little midnight jaunt.'

Chapter 9

Wednesday morning saw Gill back in the office feeling worse for wear. His adventures in Airth the previous evening had been followed by several hours in the A&E department of Kirkcaldy's Victoria Hospital. As he reached his desk Cassy glanced at his bandaged hand, then met his gaze, but said nothing. When her back was turned, Craig slid his chair over beside Gill and flinched when he saw Gill's injury.

'Roddy do that to you?'

'I didn't get to meet our illustrious Justice Secretary. This was a separate incident.'

How'd it go with Canmore, senior?'

'Lovely old gent. But probably losing his marbles. Some kind of degenerative brain disease.'

'Nothing we can get a story out of, then?'

Gill pulled a face. 'Nothing. Besides, I promised I wouldn't write about him.'

'And are you going to tell me what happened to your hand?'

Gill had already resolved to keep this one vague. 'I cut myself on a site visit.'

Cassy appeared a few moments later with a laptop and a bundle of files clutched to her chest. 'You guys ready to go?'

Five minutes later, the whole team gathered in the conference room to firm up the plans for the next issue. As usual, Cassy led the meeting while Gill focused on fine-tuning the content and tone of the articles. The meeting format was well established and the key agenda items already agreed, so with practised efficiency, the conversations happened quickly. With all actions, alterations and additions squared away, Cassy moved to close the meeting.

'Before we go', said Gill, staring at the centre of the table. 'I visited the Kincardine dig again last night. And I got into a spot of bother.'

'Oh, aye?' said Larry, while Cassy folded her arms and slumped further back in her chair.

Gill cleared his throat. 'I visited the ruined church in Airth.'

'The one Ed Johnson told you to stay away from', observed Cassy.

'Aye. And I would have got away with it if someone hadn't tried to kill me.'

'Kill you, as in "Stop, thief, I've got a gun"?'

'No. Kill me, as in try to drop three hundred kilos of crumbling church on my head.'

Only Mhairi's face seemed sympathetic. 'Goodness! Who would do that?'

'I've no idea. And I didn't hang around to chat. I called DI Wiley as I kinda hoped he'd be too lazy to do the paperwork on it. But apparently, he's got a new minion. A Detective Constable Lillico. By all accounts, he's a straight by-the-book kind of guy, and in light of my trespassing in a secured area, he'll be inviting Ed Johnson to press charges.'

Craig shook his head. 'You're a head case, Gill McArdle.'

'The bad boy of contemporary archaeology', muttered Cassy. 'A red-haired Indiana Jones without the hat.'

'So, my apologies in advance if this goes public and I end up bringing the magazine into disrepute.'

'Again', added Craig.

'Leave the laddie alane', barked Larry, who as the oldest member of the team was the only one who could legitimately make that statement. 'Ye don't git to be a hard-hitting in-vest-tig-gative journo wie oot turnin' a few heids.'

'Thanks, Larry', said Gill, trying to look grateful and repentant at the same time. 'But look, here's my instinct. And probably the thing that put me in harm's way. The inscription on the *Airth Slab* has really tickled my curiosity. Aside from its local origin, it's further proof the *Stone of Destiny* going on display in Perth is not the original.'

'It's only nine days until the official stone gets its shiny new museum', said Craig. 'You sure someone's not having you on?'

'Looking at the site last night, I'm certain the *Airth Slab* is authentic.'

Craig acknowledged Gill's comment. 'Aye, but if you go saying the Perth stone isn't the real deal, that won't be popular.'

'Maybe', said Gill. 'Or maybe there's no better time to cast the harsh light of day on a thousand-year-old forgery.'

'Gill, listen', protested Cassy. 'If we debunk the *Stone of Destiny,* we'll be depriving the Scots of their national icon. We might as well blow up the Tennant's Brewery for all the joy that's gonna bring.'

'Not if we could find the real stone', said Gill. 'Take away the fake stone and give them back the authentic mascot they didn't know they'd lost.'

Cassy clutched her fists. 'And how are you going to do that? All you've got is an ancient inscription on a slab, not a treasure map.'

'Aye, but if we could work out the *Pilgrim Isle's* location, then we could check the records for any marine or land-based archaeology and see if anyone has turned up anything interesting.'

The rest of the team glanced at each other, and then in silent unison, they all stared at Gill. 'Yeah, I get it', he said after a while. 'Long shot.'

'Doesn't even start to describe it', Cassy mumbled.

'Is it even worth it?' said Mhairi. 'I mean the history is fascinating, but it's not exactly a treasure hoard.'

Craig mumbled to himself, then eased the open palm of his right hand towards Mhairi. 'Ah, now let's be clear about one thing. The *Stone of Destiny* is the ultimate symbol of our nationhood. It talks to our mythical past as the earliest Scots journeyed towards their ultimate homeland. Then it speaks to our connection to our land – our kings and queens sitting on the stone during their coronation.'

Mhairi shook her head. 'Yeah, I know the history. But at the end of the day, it's just a rock.'

'Think what the Liberty Bell means to the US. Or the crown jewels to the English', Gill added. 'Nationhood expressed and condensed into an item easy enough to be carried by a horse and cart.'

'But if the English chose jewels', said Mhairi, with a jubilant smile. 'Why did the Scots settle for a stone?'

'It's got a cracking back story', said Craig energetically. 'Movie material.'

Mhairi smirked. 'Just an old myth.'

Craig's eyes fluttered like he was struggling to keep a straight face. 'Back in time, the Scots felt more prosperous and protected just having it around.'

'Oh, right. So you're saying it was essentially a national good luck charm', said Mhairi, folding her arms.

'Something like that', Craig muttered, running out of steam.

'And then', said Cassy, picking up the thread, 'Edward the First nicked it. And in the centuries that followed, the stone became iconic in Scotland's continuing battle to be independent of English persecution.'

Mhairi's face flared. 'Persecution! You don't honestly believe that?'

Cassy shrugged. 'Not personally, but if you ask the average guy in any Dundee pub.'

Larry nodded vigorously. 'Specially on a match day, ken.'

'As the only English person at the table, I'm actually starting to find this line of conversation a tiny bit offensive', sniffed Mhairi.

'Sorry', said Cassy. 'And for the record, I lived in London until I was two. What you got to realise is that to most Scots, the anti-English thing is a bit of an in-joke. Like Londoners talking about the weather. Or house prices.'

Gill slumped in his chair and raised his hands. 'Folks, can we get back on track?'

'Yes please', said Mhairi, thinly masking her indignation.

'I'm gonna park my idea of finding the *Pilgrim Isle* and the *Fated Stone* while I do some more thinking', said Gill. 'Before we wrap up, is there anything else happening in the logs?'

'Pretty quiet', said Cassy, winking a smile at Mhairi. 'Loch monsters, ghosts and unidentified predators are having a quiet month.'

'It's yon miserable weather', said Larry. 'Keeps 'em indoors.'

'Nothing at all to distract me from the *Airth Slab*?' Gill asked, making no attempt to hide his disappointment. Using reports from readers, the magazine kept a weekly journal of strange sightings from around Scotland. In the past this log had offered him story leads during quiet weeks for news.

'I have something', said Mhairi, opening a tab on her laptop. 'We've had three reports of strange blue lights in the sky. That's a new one.'

'Whereabouts?' said Gill, sitting up.

'The Firth of Forth.'

Gill felt his pulse ticking up. 'Near Ed Johnsons dig site by any chance?'

'No, Gill. At the mouth of the Forth. Fifty miles away.'

'Okay. Probably nothing then.'

Cassy nodded. 'Almost certainly nothing.'

'It'll be the English getting ready to invade', said Craig, leaning across to poke Mhairi's shoulder.

'Watchin' us frae drones', agreed Larry.

'Stop it!' she laughed, her tension suddenly released.

Gill listened to the continuing banter and resisted fanning the flames. What he needed now was a distraction from the tugging in his brain that wanted to rush back to Airth. 'Well, thanks, everyone. Great work on issue 21. And we're looking good for 22.'

Returning from lunch and a brief walk around central Dundee's green spaces, Gill was carrying a coffee back to his desk when Cassy waved her phone at him. 'Ed Johnson left a message for you. He wants you to call him immediately.'

Gill's heart sank and all the benefit from his refreshing lunchtime air evaporated in an instant. He elected to step out into the small glass mezzanine at the top of the stairwell before he dialled Ed's number. He wasn't expecting an easy call.

When the line connected, Gill leapt in first. 'Ed. I'm so sorry. I thought I could just take a sly look around. I didn't mean to cause you any bother.'

'Aye, well. That's three strikes now, Gill. You'll understand if you're not the first person I call the next time I find something interesting.'

'Again, I'm so, so sorry.'

'What I don't get about you is why you're always in such a tearing hurry? I could have put your PhD cock-up down to youthful enthusiasm, but Orkney and Airth, Gill? Those are career-ending mistakes. You know you'll never work in academic archaeology ever again?'

'I figured', said Gill, trying to sound humbly repentant. In reality, the thought of ever going back to the dry world of academia brought him out in a cold sweat.

'Anyway. Aside from all that, I'm calling to keep a promise. You wanted to know where the stone for the *Airth Slab* originated.'

'Yes. It was a red sandstone I recall, so the fossil fingerprints should give us a clue.'

'More than a clue, Gill. It's a hundred per cent match to Quarryhill, which you might recall is a long abandoned sandstone pit near Perth.'

Gill thought for a moment. 'The same quarry as the *Stone of Destiny*?'

'Exactly the same.'

Gill let out a long breath. 'You do know that can't be a coincidence.'

'I know. And my team will research all possible theories and record them in our final report.'

'When will that be issued?'

There was a pause while Ed consulted his diary. 'Approximately thirteen months time.'

Gill tried to resist sounding rude. 'I'll wait with bated breath. And again, I'm so sorry for the intrusion.'

He hung up the call and thought. The *Airth Slab* and the Destiny Stone, hewn from the same rock? It could only increase the likelihood the original stone was lost and the current one; the one now adorning Perth Museum, was a substitute. Thirteen months! He could smell this story brewing and it was way closer than that.

Taking Cassy with him, Gill put his head around the publisher's door. When he saw Tony wasn't on the phone, they slid in, and Gill closed the door behind them.

'*Stone of Destiny*', Gill began.

Tony thrust a hand at him. 'What about it, Gill? No politics, remember?'

97

'There's been a development', said Cassy. 'Something important. And a massive story opportunity.'

Tony's head cocked to one side, and over several minutes, Gill brought him up to speed. Eventually, Tony got up, stepped to the window, and stood with his back to them. 'Barely a year ago we killed the Loch Ness Monster. And now you're about to debunk the *Stone of Destiny*?'

'If that's how the story plays out.'

Tony leaned his face against the glass. 'I've never been chased by angry men with pitchforks. The way you two are talking, it won't be long.'

'The *Airth Slab* pulls the rug from under the old stone', said Gill. 'And it also declares the original stone was lost in the Firth of Forth. And there's a hint of where it might be. What if we mount a search for the lost stone?'

'Hang on', said Tony, looking stressed. 'Old stone – lost stone; you're confusing me. For goodness sake, agree on your terminology.'

'What do you suggest?' said Gill, feeling stung.

'Let's stick with *Stone of Destiny*, for the one sitting in Perth, because that's its name. And *Fated Stone* seems a suitable label for the one you seem to think is lying in the Forth somewhere.'

'Agreed', said Cassy diplomatically.

'This *Fated Stone*. Where is it then?'

Gill flinched. 'Being honest, Tony. It's not like we've got coordinates. I'll need to do more research. At this stage we don't even know which of a dozen islands might be the *Pilgrim Isle.*'

Tony's nod was brief and didn't brim with enthusiasm. 'I'm not an expert, but even if you did know the right island, the stone was lost a thousand years ago. It could be lying under several metres of sediment.'

'Didn't say it would be easy', Gill muttered.

'Easy? I've done a bit of sailing. The Firth of Forth must be about sixty square kilometres. Even if this *Fated Stone* exists, it's a needle in a marine haystack.'

'Maybe we don't need to find it', said Cassy. 'Our existing information undermines the *Stone of Destiny* while the *Airth Slab* introduces the concept of an older, authentic *Fated Stone*. When you boil it down, that's the story.'

Tony laid his hands on his desk and took a deep breath. 'If we're going to run with this, I'd really like us to have a more positive angle.'

'What are you saying, boss?'

'That you can't kill Scotland's *Stone of Destiny*, without having a new contender to put in its place.'

'That's almost impossible, Tony', Cassy huffed.

Gill nodded slowly. 'I'll go over the data again. Narrow down the search for the island.'

Tony waved a hand at him. 'Your girlfriend has a submarine. Maybe she could help?'

Gill sat back and suppressed a smirk. 'My fiancé works for a university that occasionally hires submersibles to conduct scientific studies. It's not like she has her own personal sub parked on a trailer in her backyard.'

'And she lives in a flat', Cassy added, impishly. 'Imagine the hassle from her neighbours.'

'But you know what I mean. We have access to certain skills.'

'I can have a very, very general conversation with her', said Gill cautiously. 'But until we have a search area, it's all a bit moot.'

'But as you say, Tony', said Cassy, serious again. 'Pre-emptive speculation about the *Stone of Destiny* could get intensely political. We shouldn't advertise what we're doing.'

'Which means we'll have the opportunity to kill the story if we don't like the way it's panning out', said Tony, turning his body to fully face Gill. 'Tread carefully. Can you do that?'

Gill nodded, and then he and Cassy left Tony's office. Under his breath, he said, 'I think that was the publisher's permission to start digging. Would you agree?'

Cassy checked she'd closed the door behind her. 'Yep. I heard full steam ahead.'

'Still think I'm wasting my time on this story?'

'I'm enjoying the hunt', she said, stepping towards her desk. 'But there's no way you're ever gonna find anything.'

'Ya reckon?' he called as she walked ahead of him. 'Challenge accepted.'

Chapter 10

Monday saw the team musing over the first printed copies of issue 21. They all agreed it was solid work, but nothing that was going to break any records. They'd need a big news story in issues 22 or 23 to keep the magazine's numbers on track. Eventually, they all drifted back to their desks to work independently as preparations for issue 22 gathered pace. Gill remained standing, hanging by his desk and wondering if he could afford a couple of days pursuing speculative stories.

'Cass', he said. 'Can you print off the reader sightings Mhairi mentioned on Friday.'

'Lights-in-the-sky thing?'

'Aye.'

'Sure. After the meeting?'

Gill flashed her a pleading smile.

'You know it's a shared document? You could print it yourself.'

'I'd need to set the filters and that takes me ages. You'll do it in moments.'

'Okay, tech boy. Gimme a second.' She flashed a few keystrokes on her PC before walking to the printer and returning with a sheet of paper, her trademark, baggy shirt, swaying as she walked. Rather than pass the sheet to Gill, she stood and stared at it.

'Problem?' asked Gill.

'We've had two more entries since the weekend.' She thrust the paper in front of Gill. 'And do you see the first name on the list?'

'Corrie McCann', Gill read. 'Is he a frequent flyer?'

Cassy let her jaw drop open and her head hang at an angle. 'You're kidding me? Corrie McCann, as in guitarist for *Black Scabbard*.'

Gill thought for a second, then shook his head. 'Celtic rock's never been my thing.'

'Gill! This guy is huge. He's like my biggest all-time hero of Scottish folk rock.'

'Was huge', muttered Craig from the fringes. 'Last time I saw *Black Scabbard* was their end-of-the-road tour in 2010.'

'Yon was braw', said Larry. 'An they did anither in 2014. An' again in 2016. They wurnae as gud.'

'There are probably dozens of Corrie McCanns', reasoned Gill, taking the sheet from Cassy.

Cassy snatched it back. 'He left a mobile number. I'm going to call him.'

'Cass. Our meeting …?'

Cassy was already dialling. The others watched while she waited to see if the call connected.

'Hello. Is that Corrie McCann?' Cassy bit her lip and glanced around their faces. 'Great, but are you *the* Corrie McCann?'

She listened for a few moments then made a fist-pumping motion and lifted her gaze to the ceiling. 'Thanks for picking up. It's Cassy Tullen here, from *Mysterious Scotland* magazine. You were good enough to leave a report on our message board last week.'

Another pause. 'That's right. Lights in the sky. The thing is, we've had several similar reports and our editor would love to come out and interview you if that's okay.'

Gill held out his palms in silent protest and Cassy responded by pulling a forefinger to her lips. 'Great. Thank you so much. When works for you?'

She nodded a few times and scribbled a few notes on her pad. 'So, just to repeat that; you're working a gig near Crail this week ...' pause for Cassy to do a little happy jiggle ... 'and you'll nominate a precise meeting spot if we text you one hour before the meet.'

She listened to the response at the other end of the line. '... and absolutely no cameras. I hear that loud and clear. Thank you. We'll see you then.'

Cassy ended the call while Gill folded his arms and slumped back against his desk. '*We'll* see you then?'

'This afternoon', announced Cassy. 'And you'll need an escort.' Her dark eyes flashed at him. 'That's me by the way.'

'To think, you hassle *me* about time wasting', Gill protested.

But she'd already lifted her hands to her hips. 'All the favours you owe me? It's your chance to pay me one back.'

'You'll like Crail, boss', said Craig. 'It's nice.'

'In July, mebbie', muttered Larry.

Cassy lifted her laptop and a clutch of files to her chest. 'Now that's settled, I'm in my happy place. Let's go and beat some sense into issue 22.'

Gill liked a wild goose chase as much as the next person, but even to him, the McCann appointment felt like a wasted trip. He'd planned to spend the day driving around Mhairi's list of candidate islands for the *Pilgrim Isle*. Cassy's ambush had arm-twisted him into a long detour.

'You been a fan of McCann for long?' he said, making conversation as they wound along the coastline road running east through agricultural land from St Andrews.

'Since high school. An old neighbour taught me to play the fiddle when I was still a kid on Raasay. But it took the bright lights of Portree to open my eyes to the contemporary Celtic rock scene.'

'I've never heard you play. Are you any good?'

'Of course! I'm awesome at everything I do.' She left a slight pause. 'Well, almost everything.' She turned to slap his arm. 'When are you going to come to see us perform?'

Gill winced. The fact he'd not seen *Calum's Road* live on stage was a serious oversight. 'Sorry, Cass. I will soon.'

'You'd better. Catch us soon before we're famous.'

He smiled at her, and after a moment, she smiled back. In fact, she beamed at him.

'You're really excited to meet this guy?' Gill said.

She nodded. 'He's a songwriter as well as a guitarist. The way he's reworked some of the old Scottish melodies is sublime.'

Gill cleared his throat. 'I hope you're not disappointed.'

'What do you mean?'

'I've researched Mr McCann. When the band went megastar in the nineties, he kinda went off the rails.'

'He's had his struggles. Haven't we all?'

'But this guy? Serious alcohol issues. Lots of rehab, and almost torpedoed the band.'

'And the reason for this wee health warning, is what?'

'Just, don't be devastated if he's not the man you hope he is. I mean, seeing lights in the sky is all very well, but this guy's grip on reality might be tenuous.'

'Says the editor who believes in time travel.'

Gill sighed. 'My job is to find the unexplained. Run a wary eye over it – kick the tyres. Not everything makes sense. I tell the facts as I see them and then leave people to make up their own minds.'

'Let's give Corrie the chance to explain his facts as he sees them, shall we? Then we can make up our minds about him.'

Gill nodded. Cassy made a fair point. 'You gonna ask him for his autograph?'

'You mean, go all fan-dom, and *I'm soooo in awe of you*, thing?'

'Aye.'

'Yes. Definitely.'

Arriving in Crail from the north, they drove down a shortbread-tin-pretty high street of independent shops and crow-stepped gables. Gill parked on the main road and got out to stand by a wall, looking down on a pocket-sized stone harbour while Cassy texted Corrie's number. His response came through a few minutes later, asking them to join the coastal path heading west out of town and walk for half an hour until they reached some caves. Groaning she hadn't worn more sensible shoes, Cassy accepted a battered waxed jacket from Gill and together they struck away from the road and onto the path. They stopped only once, to look back on the village where narrow streets of stone houses clung to the steep hillside. All roads seemed to lead down to the harbour where a pair of solid little creel boats sat with their engines idling, making ready for the sea.

Back on the path, they followed a narrow track that rose and fell amongst the various geological barriers nature had placed in their way. Passing a pair of derelict stone cottages, they caught up with a slow-moving man carrying two black sacks of rubbish in each hand. Wearing a faded brown body warmer over a stained tee shirt, the man's arms bulged with muscles and his strong sinewed neck stuck out through a thicket of grey facial hair. Completing this feral look, long grey locks spewed out the back of his baseball cap.

'Excuse me. Are we on the right track to reach Caiplie caves?' asked Cassy, moving her feet from place to place to keep them dry.

'Aye', said the man. 'Just ower the next rise.' He set down the bags. 'Are you folks lookin' for Corrie?'

Gill glanced at Cassy. 'We might be.'

The man looked at the bags and rubbed his forehead. 'Catch a haud of those then', he said, nodding at the sacks. 'And I'll tak these.' He squatted to pluck two ruined lobster creels from a stack of derelict fishing gear and gesticulated with his chin to start moving.

Gill lifted two of the sacks and Cassy managed one, and together they trailed behind their burly guide, up an incline and down into a verdant hollow trapped between the sea on one side and the mouths of half a dozen caves on the other. The man added his creels to a great stack of garbage in front of the caves, nodding at Gill and Cassy to do likewise.

'Are you folks frae the magazine?' asked the man.

'Yes', said Gill. 'And I take it you're Corrie?'

The man, Corrie, swung his right arm theatrically. 'Welcome tae my humble abode.'

'Sorry', spluttered Cassy. 'I didn't recognize you.'

Corrie tugged his beard. 'I'm in disguise.'

Cassy threw him an embarrassed smile then took a few steps into the mouth of the nearest cave and surveyed camping gear with a black ring of stones forming a well-used hearth. 'When you said you had a gig near Crail ...', she began.

Corrie's mouth twisted into a suppressed smile. 'I'm beach cleaning', he said, waving a hand at the pile of garbage. 'Spent the last eight days clearing frae Crail to Anstruther. And now I'm humpin' all they bags to a shore-side farm where Fife Council assure me, they'll place a couple of skips.'

'And you're living here?' said Cassy, pointing at the cave.

It was in reality a series of caves and Gill had seen similar examples in other places around Scotland, cut by the sea some thousands of years before, then left high and dry by a drop in sea level. The sandstone ran from yellows to reds to browns and back again, due to weathering, or the presence of natural minerals, Gill didn't know.

Corrie had chosen the largest for his habitation. It was deep and clearly offered protection from the elements. But the walls had suffered graffiti and even Corrie's efforts hadn't fully addressed the litter problem.

'Stayed in a hotel for a couple of days, but that wasnae workin' for me.'

'Better than this', muttered Cassy, perhaps without thinking.

'Braw wee hotel. But the other guests got on my goat. I suppose, when you spend half a lifetime singing angry songs you attract a lot of crabbit folk.' Corrie waved a hand dismissively. 'Anyway, the further I cleaned, the longer the step each morning. Thought I'd plant my flag here for a couple of days.'

'Excuse me for asking', said Gill. 'But how does a rock star end up living in a cave and cleaning beaches?'

'Penance for bein' a lifetime shit-head, pal. Had a holiday hoose aroon here for a couple of years. Didnae behave myself very well. My agent saw the beach clean as a way to recondition my persona as errant high priest of Scottish rock.' He shrugged. 'But I kinda got into it. While the weather's fair, I'll keep going.'

'And no one bothers you?'

Corrie vigorously rubbed his beard. 'Out here, naebody recognizes me.' He stopped and pointed at Cassy. 'But I ken your face. Saw your band play a talent gig at the Caird Hall. *Calum's Road*. Am I right?'

For the first time in his life, Gill watched Cassy blush. 'You've seen me play?'

Corrie closed his eyes and rocked on his heels. 'Oh my goodness, the fiddle playin'. Pure magic. These days, I have you on Spotify.'

Cassy had to pull her hands from her face before she could speak. 'Thank you. I'm genuinely flattered.'

'Don't be flattered, lass. Just be the best you can be. Who's your manager?'

'We're indie', Cassy fired back. 'No label, no agent, no manager.'

'She's their manager', said Gill. 'It's why they're so damn driven.'

Corrie nodded an acknowledgement. 'Well, after today, you hae my number. When you're ready to move on to the next level, drop me a text. I might be able tae make some introductions.' Corrie glanced at Gill and rubbed his hands on his trousers. 'I was just about to take a break. Would you folks like a cuppa?'

Gill glanced at his watch.

'We'd love some', said Cassy, watching as Corrie decanted water from a plastic drum. 'Look, this is cheeky, but can I get a selfie with you? Just so I can have a wee brag to the rest of the band.'

'Aye', said Corrie, leaning in close to Cassy so she could grab a couple of shots. When Cassy finished, he knelt on the ground by his stove. 'You've come tae ask me about what I saw?'

'Aye', said Gill. 'You reported a sighting last week, I believe.'

Corrie lit the gas burner and stood upright. 'Wednesday night, or early Thursday morning. There's nae light pollution out here, so I was watchin' the stars. There'd been a storm earlier but when it finished, I could see the Isle of May silhouetted against the night sky. About midnight, I started seein' pure-weird lightning.'

'Weird, how?'

'It would start like regular lightnin', except it was a kinda lilac, pale blue colour. And it wasnae here-and-gone like regular lightnin'. Each flash hung aroon for ten or fifteen seconds.'

'Did you see where it originated?'

'Well, that was the other thing. Regular lightnin' is high up, ken. This stuff was down low, I'd guess about two hundred feet. Maybe lower? It started out over the wind farm and worked it's way west until it reached the northern tip of the isle. Then it disappeared.'

'Could it have been boat flares?' mused Gill.

'Or drones?' said Cassy.

Corrie was dropping teabags into three stained mugs. 'No. Yon things just materialised in the dark. No idea where they come frae. If you want to corroborate my story, you might need tae talk to NASA.'

Gill shook his head. 'I'm not doubting what you saw, Corrie. And we've had a few other reports along this coast. We're just trying to puzzle out the source.'

'Definitely a UFO', said Cassy. 'Another first for *Mysterious Scotland*. Give it a week 'til Gill finds aliens living on an island.'

Corrie and Gill both looked at each other simultaneously and smiled. 'I doubt it', said Corrie. 'There'll probably be a perfectly rational explanation.'

'Would you say you had a clear head', said Gill. 'Whenever you saw whatever you saw?'

'Do you mean, was I drinkin'?'

'Sorry. I don't mean to offend.'

'I've offended lots of people, Gill. These days, you'll find I'm pretty forgiving.' He reached down into a rucksack and pulled out a small silver tin. 'I'd had two of those. They're low alc shite, so I ken what I saw.'

'Thank you. And again, sorry.'

Corrie shrugged. 'Don't apologise. I'm a one-time piss-head. Your scepticism is justified.'

'Have you seen the lightning since that night?' asked Cassy.

Corrie ran hot water over the teabags. 'I'm out cold most nights afore midnight. Not seen anything since.'

'What did you make of him? Cassy asked as they walked back to the car.

'I was expecting a vain, hollowed-out husk of a man. Turns out he's the opposite of all those things. What about you?'

'I need to inform you that your status as the third favourite man in my life has been relegated to fourth.'

'Okay. Besides Corrie and your dad, who's the other guy?'

Cassy's eyes flashed to his and then away. 'I can't believe Corrie is so grounded. He has this wonderful peaceful atmosphere. Just being around him hugs you like being in a cosy blanket.'

Gill tried to imagine that for a few seconds. He didn't think the blanket would smell all that fresh. 'Looks like he's been off the hard stuff for years.'

'What did you think about his lightning story?'

'Intriguing. The man is credible, so you have to conclude he's reporting what he believes he saw. Do me a favour when we get back to the office. Phone the other folk who reported seeing something. See how closely their stories tally with Corrie's.'

'And I might try the coastguard. Lights at sea are often a sign of distress.'

'You're not pouring water on this lights-in-the-sky thing anymore?' said Gill.

Cassy flashed him a happy smile. 'If Corrie says they're legit, then I'm on board.'

Chapter 11

The long walk to Caiplie Caves on Monday meant Gill's tour of Mhairi's candidates for the *Pilgrim Isle* was pushed back into Tuesday. He drove west along the Fife coast all the way to Kincardine Bridge, then east along the Lothian coast until it faded into the North Sea. Periodically, he would park up and study the nearest islands with binoculars. He didn't have time to visit them – a distant survey was all he could afford.

At the far reaches of his trip, he left North Berwick and drove down to Tantallon Castle. He'd visited once as a child and took a few minutes to climb the battlements and stare out over the Forth. The castle itself was a work of deception. From the perspective of a fourteenth-century sea captain, the immense wall of mud-brown sandstone suggested a mighty fortress, no doubt impregnable and bristling with canons. In reality, the long narrow structure was an imposter, baring its belly to any passing guns in the hope that its sheer size would ward off attack.

As a vantage point over the Forth however, the castle was unsurpassed. Standing on the high walls, perched on a cliff, Gill felt on a level with the Bass Rock, a prominent island just a short distance away. From here, the mass of the volcanic plug drew the eye with its one hundred metres of vertical black rock towering out of the sea. Clouds of gannets circled the island, hunting for nest sites and restoring old bonds. Against the blues of the sky and the sea, the big white birds were easy to spot as they plunged off the cliff and down onto prey in the clear waters below.

Gill stayed for a few minutes just enjoying the air. There was something about mid-March around here that brought a change in the sea. Perhaps it was the fresh plankton growth adding scent to the atmosphere, their oily bodies throwing off chemicals that allowed a rough sea to foam. Or maybe it was just the lengthening days, with all manner of land and sea-borne vegetation surging into new growth, filling the sky with oxygen and fresh smells. In any event, the experience was the high point in an otherwise dubious road trip. He'd planned it as a shout-out to his inner sense that might detect if a mystery was in the offing. But as he clambered down off the walls of Tantallon, he admitted to himself the trip was entirely hypothetical and probably a waste of time.

On the return journey to Dundee, he stuck to motorways and major roads. With all that time alone, his mind drifted back to Mhairi's research, specifically the royal seals depicting the *Stone of Destiny* as a slab rather than a block. Finding he still had a little time left in the day, he decided to make a speculative visit in Stirling.

Standing outside the rundown stone villa, Alasdair Canmore tentatively opened the door to him. 'Mr McArdle. How are you?'

'Good thanks. Busy. I was in the area and wondered if I might have a moment with your father?'

Alasdair glanced at his feet. 'He's quite frail today. Good days and bad days. You know what it's like.'

'I do. And I promise only to stay a few minutes.'

'Sure. Come in. Wait in the hall while I see if he's awake.'

Gill stood by a vestibule table, loaded with bills and semi-digested correspondence; the flotsam of a family stumbling towards a death. When Alasdair reappeared, he spoke quietly and said he would stay in the room. Gill could have two minutes.

Walking in, Gill could see immediately that Conall had lost something of his presence. His facial hair was lank, and his demeanour carried a similarly frayed look.

'Good afternoon', said Gill, working hard to stop his face from reflecting Conall's decline straight back at him.

The old man raised a thin hand to Gill by way of a greeting. 'You find my circumstances further reduced', he said.

'I think you look well.'

Conall grunted. 'You're a liar, sir! But it's good to see you again.'

'Are you still having your dreams?'

Conall gave an uncomfortable snort. 'It's like you said last time. I'm a powerless observer in an unfolding Shakespearean tragedy.'

'I'm sorry about that.'

'If the alternative is not sleeping, or simply dying, I can bear it.' He turned his head. 'Have you had any ideas for me?'

'Honestly, Conall, a psychologist might rationalise your experience. I find your situation fascinating but cannot explain it.'

'Never mind. Maybe the story will have a happy ending.' He grunted. 'Just pray I get to see the final episode before I go.'

'Can I ask you something? A question about the Scotland you see in your dreams?'

Conall paused to discharge a string of hoarse coughs. 'What do you want to know?' he said, his voice straining.

'Does the Scotland you see in your dreams possess a revered stone? Something linked to its kings and nationhood?'

'Like the *Stone of Destiny*?'

'Yes.'

Conall thought for a second. 'I haven't seen it. Perhaps I could take a look for it next time I dream.'

'You can do that?'

'I seem to be able to wander at will, so I'm happy to try.'

Just then, there was a disturbance as the front door opened wide on rusty hinges and slammed shut again. They heard footsteps cross the hall and the door to Conall's improvised bedroom swung open.

'Evening, Pops. How're doin' today?' The man stopped; his attention shifting between the three faces already in the room before he pointed at Gill. 'Who's this?'

Alasdair took a few steps towards him. 'Roddy, this is Gill McArdle. He's a journalist visiting with Dad.'

Roddy looked at Alasdair, then at Gill, then back to Alasdair. 'Are you naturally stupid or are you having to work at it?'

'Roddy, Dad invited him.'

'And that makes it okay? I'm four days away from the biggest event of my political life, and you're letting a journo worm his way in here under false pretences?'

'He's not wormed his way into anything, Roddy. Dad invited him. And although you consider yourself to be the most important thing in the universe, he hasn't asked a single question about you.'

Roddy made a show of looking away, drawing his hands to his hips and looking exasperated. 'That's the way they do it, you moron. Wander on in, chat about the weather, while all the while they're sniffing for clues so they can concoct some ridiculous story.'

'I didn't mean to cause any trouble', said Gill. 'If you want, I can leave.' He moved towards the door but found Roddy Canmore blocking his way.

'Who are you? BBC? I bet you're BBC.'

'No. A local magazine.'

'What've you been asking, then?'

'We're writing a series about old Scottish royal families. Your father had read some of our pieces and asked to see me.'

'Maybe it's because I'm a politician, or maybe it's because I'm a suspicious bastard, but I don't think you answered my question.'

Gill sighed. 'Your father was telling me his dreams about another Scotland.'

'Aye, pal. We all get those dreams. Me more than most. A Scotland where we tell Westminster tae bugger off so we can run this country without a single unionist politician in sight. Is that the kind of dream you were chattin' about?'

Gill glanced back at Conall. 'No. And I expect you're aware, but your father's dreams are more elaborate than that.'

'And you indulged him? We're doing our best as a family, to hold things together in the face of his mental illness, and you bust in stoking it up?'

'I'm still here', muttered Conall. 'Roddy, if you want to fight about this, can you do it somewhere else?'

'Aye', spat Roddy. 'Good idea, Dad. Me and the journo should step outside.'

Gill cleared his throat. 'Again. Your father invited me.'

Roddy thrust the forefinger of his right hand towards the door. 'Aye, and you've done enough damage. Now I'll ask you tae get tae … outta here.'

Gill raised his hands and moved to work his way around the bulky, red-faced man.

'Roddy!' called Conall. 'I'll say farewell to my guest.' He beckoned Gill to come over and did his best to shake his hand. 'Thank you for coming', he said, glaring at his son.

As they shook, Gill felt Conall's whisper more than he heard it. 'The stone', he said. 'I'll try to find it in my dreams.'

But the looming presence of Roddy chased Gill away from Conall's side before they could talk anymore. Roddy followed close enough for Gill to feel the man's breath on the back of his neck until he was over the threshold and the front door slammed behind him.

Chapter 12

The following morning, Gill McArdle stepped off the Broughty Ferry bus and began the short and very familiar walk to his office. The last few days had been unproductive, and he yearned for the weekend to come so he could sweep Salina off to Stonehaven and close the door. He realised he'd been deeply unsettled by yesterday's encounter with Roddy Canmore. Waking early, he'd made a coffee and sat at a screen researching Roddy and his father. What he'd read about both characters wasn't particularly attractive. In his recent speeches, the younger Canmore said he wanted to shake Scotland out of its moribund union with England. Gill didn't begrudge the man's right to state his case, but found himself unsettled by the vitriol of Roddy's language and his thin grasp of basic economic realities. And reading the older Canmore's flowery words, mingled with thorns, Gill recognised he'd heard that kind of rhetoric many times before. To his rational mind, it sounded like Conall Canmore's vision of a modern, prosperous Scotland would be built on shortbread, and the oil industry. Or just shortbread, depending what era of the speech you read.

Exasperated, he'd turned away from the Canmores and turned instead to *The Book*.

Ruefully, he found himself in the Psalms and found echoes of Scotland's current power struggle already presented for him on its pages. And as had happened so many times in the months since he left Orkney, he found his prejudice against this book being overturned by the words he ultimately read. Since childhood, he'd believed that good and evil existed in the world. And like his peers, he understood that the two forces were locked in an eternal battle for supremacy; two mighty powers, powerfully armed but equally matched. Today he realised it wasn't like that at all. Today, if he'd understood it correctly, the Creator stood ready to crush evil under his heel. And the fact that it still persisted was because the Creator permitted it. Evil endured in the world to grant human beings the right to choose between the two forces. Gill had made his choice. He had no idea what it was going to cost him, but his instinct said it was going to be worth it.

He reflected on this later, during his morning run, along the esplanade built on top of Dundee's new sea defences. He ran it five minutes faster than usual because he always worked harder when he was angry. He was angry with Roddy because the man was so coarse. But more than that; he was angry with the folk who ran Britain and Scotland because they spent so much energy chasing fashionable politics rather than pursuing the self-evident problems that were the real malaise. And maybe, it was ever thus. Men were persistently ambitious, cruel and exploitative, though there were still wise words in *The Book* that could speak to any of these situations. And he wondered about Conall Canmore. Was this dying mind, still deeply in love with his homeland, trying to imagine how things could have turned out better? Perhaps he was weighing the outcome if he'd made fewer left turns and a few more rights? If he'd made better choices throughout this journey; this jagged way of life and nationhood.

He was still mulling this as he left the bus station and strode into town, his shoulders high as he rode out his anger.

The city centre was busy with shop and office workers like himself, pushing past each other to be nowhere especially important in a hurry. People didn't normally greet each other in Dundee, but on this particular morning he was starting to feel strange. Most folk ignored him, as they usually would, but now and again, someone would glance at him, smile sheepishly, or glare at him and walk on past. He swung around a bend to come face to face with a sallow-faced lady who saw him, yelped and stepped backwards. He held up his hands in surprise, but the lady just scowled at him, then with a glance over his left shoulder, she swore under her breath and rushed away. Perplexed, he picked up his pace to cover the last few hundred metres to the office, swerving around a buggy with a child who squealed and used both her arms to point at Gill. He slid past, turning a few steps later to find the child's mother staring at him open-mouthed.

Deeply unsettled, Gill paused. What was it about his appearance, causing these reactions? He stepped up to a shop window and studied his reflection. He could feel the weight of it before he could see it – around two kilos of what looked like translucent glass. The hilt, high and visible over his left shoulder; perfectly positioned to be grasped by his right hand. He'd felt the weight before, reasoning this was the weapon that had manifested in Airth, materialising in his hand and blocking a mortal blow. Yes, he'd glimpsed it before, but not like this. He slowly drew the weapon from its sheath and brought it to a side stance, a natural defensive position without implying threat. Well over a metre from hilt to tip, he touched the weapon on the pavement near his right foot and caught the "ting" as it made contact. He studied it in this position and watched shimmers of light running up and down its length.

Two young women came around the corner and he glanced at their faces to observe how they would react. But they walked past him, clearly not seeing what he held in his hands.

'This is crazy', he whispered to himself. 'What? What am I meant to do with this?'

He sheathed the blade and continued to his office. As he walked in, he scanned the room for anyone startled by his appearance. In the end, only the layout artist on the cat magazine looked up and stared. But then, Gill reasoned, she often did that. He sat down at his desk and pondered what to do. He couldn't wander around Dundee with a sword strapped to his back. And how would he explain it when someone, understandably asked about it? Mercifully, no one in the team seemed to notice. On impulse, he decided to text Solomon. 'There's been a development. Could she meet him?' He wasn't sure if she'd respond. But after a while she did, suggesting they meet at the end of his working day. He accepted, and gradually, the physical sense of the sword ebbed away.

As Gill and Solomon walked along the river, he sheepishly told her about his experience that morning. It was late afternoon and the dusk was already well advanced.

'Can you feel it now?' she asked, referring to his sword.

He shook his head. 'Not for hours.'

'And no one in your office noticed?'

'Maybe one person. But she didn't say anything.'

In a voice, cut from the coal face of decades spent teaching small children, Solomon said, 'I'm not sure I've grasped your concern.'

'I don't know how to control this thing. I think it happened because I was angry this morning. With a guy I met yesterday. And then I was angry after reading *The Book*.'

'Must have been the right kind of anger', Solomon mused. 'Given its provenance, I doubt the sword would manifest if you were nursing unforgiveness or revenge.'

'I was thinking very clearly at the time. Then I noticed some people were staring at me.'

'You're modest, Gill. You don't like to stand out in a crowd. If it's any relief, I can't see anything now.'

'But what if it happens again?'

Solomon took a few steps without saying anything. 'The same thing happens to Charlie from time to time.'

'Oh, yeah?'

'Raphael's gift to Charlie manifests, physically, in moments of stress.'

'And how does Charlie deal with that?'

Solomon pursed her lips, perhaps choosing her words carefully. 'I don't think he's as sensitive about it as you are.'

'You're saying I should just man up and deal with it?'

'In a sense. At least until we understand it better. You said Raphael carries his sword with dignity.' She emitted a deft little shrug. 'Maybe you should learn to do the same.'

'I guess', said Gill, staring down at his feet. 'Let's hope I'm not arrested in the meantime.'

'What happened to your hand?' Solomon asked suddenly.

'I cut myself visiting an archaeological site in Airth.'

'Looks painful.'

'It was at first. Now it's just a nuisance. To stop me from flexing my palm, the hospital staff bound me up like a boxer.'

She half turned to face him, and he sensed what he'd felt around Ailsa's friend Mrs P, that somehow, Solomon was reading his mail.

'Must have been quite a shock', she said. 'Cutting yourself like that. Do let me know if you ever want to talk about it.'

'Thank you. I will.'

'If that's such a private thing, did you have anything else on your mind, or are we done here?'

Gill did have a question and he asked it now. 'What do you know about dreams? In *The Book*, I mean.'

Solomon stared out over the water as she walked. 'Can you rephrase your question?

'I have an acquaintance who's struggling with his dreams, so I was researching them. Are dreams simply our brains doing their daily maintenance, or is it possible in a dream, we can touch a form of alternative reality?'

'Hmm', said Solomon. 'Did you find any dreams like that in *The Book*?'

He flicked his gaze towards her before continuing. 'For reasons to do with my work I've been reading about a character called Jacob. In the story, he's fleeing to his uncle's home to escape his brother. Justifiably, as it happens as he's treated his brother like a rat. But on his journey, he lies down to sleep one night, using a rock as a pillow. During the night he dreams some weird stuff and then he's wrestling with God. And in the morning, he seems transformed by the experience. The sounds to me like Jacob was touching an alternative reality.'

'Well, let's look at it in context', said Solomon. 'Jacob's grandfather Abraham was credited with being a friend of God and therefore the first man of true faith. His son, Isaac followed Abraham in matters of belief and in due course, became Jacob's father.'

'But the people before Abraham, they believed in God, didn't they?'

'It was the iron age, Gill. Culture was primitive. Maybe in those early days, everyone believed. There were a plethora of gods to choose between, so Abraham had a choice. He made a few wrong turns here and there, but ultimately, he came to be regarded by Jews and Christians as the father of all believers.'

'And Jacob?'

'When Jacob flees his father's household, he reaches a moment where he has to decide whether he believes or not. He's no longer covered by his father's faith and can either turn sharp left into unbelief, or sharp right and develop his own faith.' She looked up at him. 'What do you think happened, Gill?'

Gill had already thought about this. 'In his dream, he'd wrestled with God. At that moment, God became real to him.'

'And isn't that a landmark moment? Judaism and Christianity exist today, despite the wrong turns made by some of the key characters in our shared story. And both faiths continue to weave through history, getting some things wonderfully right, like poverty action and campaigning for freedoms, and at the same time, getting many other things horribly wrong, such as the abuse scandals and exploited privilege.'

Gill nodded. He'd observed *The Book* recorded that all the so-called heroes of the faith were flawed in some way. 'If Jacob hadn't grown into his personal faith, then Judaism and Christianity might not have happened. Or at least, not as we experienced it.'

'I suspect for Jacob the dream was the culmination of his faith journey', Solomon continued. 'For him, it must have been a *blue pill-red pill* moment. Should he restrict his life to the physical realm he can see and feel? Or should he push forward with God and see how deep the rabbit hole goes?'

Gill stopped and looked around him. The city, the river, and the hills beyond, were all so present, immediate and demanding. And yet, with each passing day, he could see this was just a painting on a veil. In a sense, he understood how Jacob must have felt.

'What's going on, Gill?' Solomon demanded.

'What do you mean?'

She gave something halfway between a shrug and a shake. 'There are lots of dream stories in *The Book*. Why are we talking about Jacob's dream?'

Gill sighed. The same sixth sense that acted in him to detect mysteries, seemed to operate in Solomon to detect invisible wheels in motion. 'I'm working on something that might relate to Jacob', was all he said. 'If it comes to anything, we'll talk. I promise.'

Chapter 13

By Friday morning, Gill was already anticipating a quiet weekend with Salina in Stonehaven. His mood brightened when Salina phoned, hopefully, to fine-tune their plans, then it crashed again when it transpired her mother had arranged a surprise sixtieth birthday party for an aunt. Because Salina wasn't out of the country, or away on a job, she felt a crushing pressure to attend. Of course, the invitation extended to Gill, but he needed to spend time with Gordon. Nursing his disappointment, he decided to go to Stonehaven on his own.

'Gill. A word.' Tony Farquharson was standing in his office doorway and calling loud enough for most of the floor to notice what was going on.

'Yes, boss', said Gill, trotting over to Tony's office, pushing the door closed and moving a pile of magazines so he could sit down.

'Had a bit of a complaint', said Tony.

'Just a bit? I need to try harder', said Gill.

'Something about the abuse of press privileges, invasion of property, exploitation of a vulnerable adult. Ringing any bells?'

Gill's shoulders sank. 'Let me guess. Roddy Canmore?'

'The one and only. He called earlier and is demanding a meeting. Anything you need to tell me?'

'My visit on Tuesday afternoon was legitimate because Roddy's father invited me.'

'I'm sure. But Roddy is a prominent political figure. *Mys.Scot* can never be political. Never. Do you hear me? You cannot be seen to pick a side in the independence debate. It could kill us in a heartbeat. Why did you have a confrontation with this man? Did you not do your research?'

Gill patted away Tony's torrent of questions. 'Until I met him, I'd no idea he would find me so objectionable. The other brother, Alasdair; he was quite reasonable and wanted to honour his dad's request to see me.'

Tony grunted while peering over his glasses at an email he was midway through writing. 'If this ever goes to court, let's hope Alasdair remembers it the same way.'

Gill sat back, stung by Tony's suggestion. 'Why would it ever go to court?'

'That will depend on what, if anything, we print. Until then, I'm hoping we haven't done or said anything he can hold us accountable for.'

'Let's talk to him', said Gill. 'See if we can sort this out.'

'I'm glad you said that', muttered Tony. 'Because he's on his way to see us right now. I think his game plan is to see you sacked, followed by a grovelling apology from the new editor.'

When the receptionist rang to say Roddy Canmore had arrived, Tony indicated with a curt nod that Gill should wait in the conference room. Resenting this interruption to his work and nervous about what was coming next, he prowled around the glass box and was still on his feet when Tony led Roddy into the room. Gill offered the visitor his hand, which Roddy ignored, sitting down before he was invited and waiting for Gill and Tony to join him.

'I'll be brief', said Roddy. 'You met my father, at his instigation, I understand – I don't have a problem with that. But I'm concerned about what happens next.'

Gill did his best to look puzzled. 'What might happen next, Mr Canmore?'

Roddy leaned back and sighed. 'My father wasn't well when you met him. He said things … things that were completely off guard, and to be frank, I'm concerned that a magazine with your kind of reputation might spin his comments into something false. Defaming him and embarrassing me. And thereby impugning the worthy cause to which we've devoted our adult lives.'

Gill arched his eyebrows. '*Our kind* of reputation?'

'Last year you ran some cock and bull story about time-travelling neoliths. And not long before that, you were tramping all over the highlands trying to prove the existence of the Loch Ness Monster.' Roddy stared at Gill with cold, clear eyes. 'Not exactly the stuff of serious journalism.'

Gill pointed at a display of the company's award-winning magazines. 'You've either not read my articles, or you're wilfully misrepresenting them. Let me assure you that our writing is thoroughly researched.'

Roddy looked away and shrugged. '*Mysterious Scotland* isn't my kind of rag. Which is a pity as I'd like to celebrate anything with the word "Scotland" in the title.'

'I'm sure we could debate the various merits of our writing all morning', Tony interjected. 'Roddy, why don't you save us some time and tell us exactly what you want?'

'Simply, that nothing my father said to you, will either be reported, or implied, in your media.'

Tony turned to face Gill. 'You're the editor. How do you feel about that?'

Gill shifted his weight in his chair. 'I didn't hear enough about Conall's dreamt experiences to form any kind of view. I offered him a kindness by honouring his request to meet. I don't have a story here, or at least, anything I'd want to print.'

'Last time you called, you spoke with my father about Scotland's *Stone of Destiny*?'

'I did.'

'Why?'

Gill paused. His question about the stone had been his motive for visiting Conall.

'Come on. What was your angle?' Roddy snapped.

Gill considered his words. 'Some folk think the stone about to go on display in Perth isn't the original and authentic stone. And I've seen some data backing up that suggestion. I was curious if your father concurred.'

Roddy snorted a laugh. 'The stone lay in Westminster for over seven hundred years. There's no doubt about its authenticity.'

'For seven centuries, yes. I agree. My data suggests a substitution before then.'

'Based on what?'

Gill decided not to expose the Airth inscriptions to Roddy's scrutiny. 'Two things. The seals of several Scottish kings before its removal by Edward the First include depictions of the stone. In all of them, it is a flat slab, rather than the block we have today.'

'Seriously? You're treating government insignia from a thousand years ago as a reliable source?'

'And then', said Gill, ignoring him. 'The microfossils in the sandstone suggest the current stone was quarried from near Scone rather than the Middle East.'

'Why's that important?'

Gill wasn't sure if Roddy was being obstructive or just didn't know his history. 'Well, if you take the *Declaration of Arbroath* seriously and buy into the whole origin story for the Scottish people, then you'd expect the stone to have been sourced in the Middle East.'

Roddy's round face pulled into a puzzled snarl. 'Why?'

'Because of the legend about it being *Jacob's Pillow*', said Gill patiently.

'Now you're talking myths and legends. More your bag than mine.'

'But for the stone to have the legitimacy that originally made it famous …' said Gill before Roddy interrupted.

'Our First Minister has invited me to take a key role in the opening ceremony for the new Perth Museum. The star attraction, as I'm sure you're aware, will be Scotland's *Stone of Destiny*, back in its rightful home. Do you, or do you not agree, that this is the same stone made notorious during its theft by Edward the First in the year 1296?'

Gill thought for a moment. 'Yeah. Based on that description, I'm sure it's the same stone.'

'And that's what we'll celebrate. The physical object we have in our possession, returned to us from England, set in the context of its long history, displayed for every Scottish citizen to scrutinize and enjoy.'

Gill tapped his chin and tried to look engaged in Roddy's logic. 'I don't see how you can just wander up to a local quarry and hack out any old stone, then set it up like some kind of idol.'

'Not an idol, Mr McArdle. A rallying point for every Scot who opposes English hegemony.'

Gill held up his hands in defeat. 'Mr Canmore, I've got a magazine to produce. And quite legitimately, I might research the *Stone of Destiny*. However, if I give you my assurance that I will not print anything that mentions you or your father by name, or alludes to his dreams, will you be happy?'

Roddy smiled and spread his thick hands on the table. 'Can I have that in writing?'

Gill and Tony glanced at each other before Tony spoke. 'You can.'

'Then, gentlemen, you have my thanks. And to show my appreciation, I'd like to offer you both a personal invitation to tomorrow's opening ceremony for the new Perth Museum. I'm sure once you have a chance to stand up close and personal with the one and only *Stone of Destiny*, any reservations you have will evaporate.'

Gill and Tony walked Roddy back to the second-floor mezzanine and then Tony joined the politician in the lift back down to reception.

Gill tried to settle back to work but jumped up as soon as Tony returned from seeing Roddy off the premises. 'You gonna take up his offer for tomorrow?' Gill asked.

Tony shook his head. 'I've got a bunch of things in the diary. You?'

'I was meant to be busy with Salina, but that's not happening now. Means I'm available. Tell you what though. I'd rather have another hour with Conall Canmore.'

'Ah', said Tony. 'That won't be possible.'

'Oh, I believe you. Not with Roddy standing in the way.'

'It's more than that', said Tony. 'Conall Canmore died yesterday morning. Which is probably why we have a grieving Roddy picking this moment to take a pop at us.'

Gill couldn't quite mask his shock. 'When did you hear that news?'

'Just now in the lift. Once he'd got our vow of silence, he went back into politician mode and wanted to be pals again.'

Gill drew his hands up into his armpits and said, 'Sorry, Tony. I stepped on an emotional landmine there.'

Tony strode towards his office without looking up. 'If you do go to Perth, Gill. Please stay out of Roddy Canmore's way.'

Gill murmured his ascent and wandered back to his desk. He'd not known Conall Canmore long enough to form a relationship with him. But his two encounters with the man had been gentle and his passing was sad news. Being honest with himself, Gill admitted his curiosity had stirred. There had been something, something, *something* about Canmore's dreams. But he was gone now, taking his dreams with him. And Gill would never know what that *something* was.

Corrie was chopping bits of driftwood from his stash at the back of his cave. The sun had fallen and now he needed a little heat. To be honest, he loved this part of the day. As the day cooled, the number of passers-by on this remote section of path dwindled, so that his chance of being recognized fell away and he could properly relax. He was a long way from the road and the only light pollution came from the distant shoreline villages of Crail and Cellardyke. Once he had the fire lit, it was just him and nature.

On this particular evening, one last lone walker came wandering by. A large man, bordering on fat, studiously ignored Corrie, while his binoculars rose up and down as he scanned the sea for signs of life. Below the caves was a rocky promontory, forming a defensive barrier, and probably the only reason the soft sandstone structures still stood. The man was strolling out on the rocks, picking his way carefully in the failing light. Only after giving up his hunt did Corrie recognize him.

'Well, Billy', he said as the figure approached.

'Och, Corrie. What a surprise.'

'Surprise, my arse', said Corrie. 'What are you doin' here?'

Billy let his binoculars hang from his neck and tossed his hands out from his sides. 'Bird watching. What about you?'

'Got a gig in five minutes. Can ye no hear them chantin' my name?'

Billy looked around at the bags of rubbish. 'I remember seeing *Black Scabbard* at the O2 arena in Glasgow. How the mighty have fallen.'

'I get by', said Corrie, breaking a stick over his knee and laying the pieces on the fire. 'Whatja want, Billy?'

Billy glanced down the shore in the direction of Edinburgh. 'The boss is getting impatient. Wants to know if you'll be in Perth tomorrow?'

'I told you when I saw you afore in Crail. I'm no' interested.'

'Nice wee hotel that', said Billy, nodding. 'Better than this shithole.'

Corrie continued to busy himself with the fire and didn't look up.

Billy thrust out a hand. 'It's going to be a laugh. Why won't you come? You don't need to sing if that's the problem.'

Corrie waved his left hand at a pile of derelict lobster creels. 'I'm otherwise engaged.'

'Seriously? Time was when you were never far from a nationalist get together. Tomorrow's going to be the biggest in years.'

'Yeah? I heard all you're doing is unveilin' a stone.' He glanced up and around the cave mouth. 'I've got plenty enough stone around here.'

'We'll be doing far more than unveiling a stone', said Billy slyly. 'But I'm guessing you know that already.'

'A few years ago, you'd'a had me. All *Braveheart* and swingin' a saltire. Nowadays, I'm a wee bit too old for all that.'

'Nah! Never too old.' Billy fiddled with his binoculars and stared along the shore. 'The boss said to remind you that you owe him.'

Corrie couldn't quite restrain a throttled laugh. 'I owe him nothing.'

'Really? What's your reputation worth? Think about that for a second.' Billy moved a step closer. 'Try and monetise the impact of the "great" Corrie McCann unveiled as a regular wee crook?'

Corrie jerked his thumb over his shoulder. 'I'm an old man clearin' garbage off a beach. I don't have a reputation worth saving.'

'But your dear, dear Denise. Would she want to hear these tales? Facing the disapproving stares of her peers each time she walks out in that pretty little town of yours?'

Corrie hung his head. 'Denise kens everything about me. I'm known and I'm forgiven. So, really, you've got nothin' on me. And when *you* stop tae think about it, the smear of all those wee favours could rub the other way. Your heid-yin might want to think about that.'

Billy took off his binoculars and gripped them in his left hand. 'Ach, Corrie. The boss said you'd be like this. And I disagreed! Like an eejit, I stuck my neck out for you. "Corrie's a patriot", I said. And now you're letting me down. What's happened to you?'

Corrie picked up another log and started to tear off some loose fragments. 'It was a different day, Billy. Different leaders. Hey, I'm not sure if I moved away frae the cause or the cause moved away frae me.'

With a conciliatory smile, Billy took a step closer, so Corrie was caught completely off guard when Billy's binoculars came slamming against his head, knocking him to the ground, dangerously close to his fire.

'Hell, man', Corrie shouted. 'What'd you do that fer?'

Billy had already moved into position to strike Corrie again, should he try to defend himself. 'Partly as a warning about what will happen to you if you're not in Perth tomorrow. And partly because I just don't like you, you leather-wearing, catwalk-strutting asshole.'

Corrie rubbed his head. 'Message received. Now piss off ya big shite!'

Billy remained standing over him, his body poised.

'Was there somethin' else?' yelled Corrie from where he lay.

'Just seeing if you'll do anything. I'm standing here remembering the happy days when *Black Scabbard* were fighters.'

'Too old tae fight', said Corrie, working his jaw to check for damage. 'These days it's about all I can do tae turn the other cheek wi out hurtin' myself.'

Billy sneered and took a step back. Collecting what was in his mouth, he spat at Corrie. 'See you tomorrow you pathetic turd', he said as he walked away.

Chapter 14

Gill wandered around Perth Museum, waiting for the show to start. It was Saturday afternoon and for once, the tens of millions of taxpayer's money seemed well spent, with the colonnaded building receiving a breath of fresh energy as the new home for Scotland's *Stone of Destiny*. The museum itself was about far more than the stone, cleverly using this central exhibit to draw together the history of the town and its surrounding region. As he finished walking the well-constructed galleries under a dizzyingly high ceiling his gaze found a banner proclaiming, "The Stone comes home". Technically this wasn't true as the nearby hamlet of Scone had been its real home base until the late thirteenth century when Edward the First of England had snaffled it and moved it to Westminster. But Perth City was a fair approximation for Scone and on a practical note, it was cheaper to repurpose an existing grand building, prematurely retired from public life, rather than build a new one in the countryside.

He joined an informal queue that wound its way towards the stone, displayed on a bed of sumptuous blue velvet. In the ten minutes it took to reach the relic he pondered if the Scots might gradually lose the quintessential British trait of polite queuing, should their nation ever become independent. When he finally reached the weathered block of sandstone, he was underwhelmed. Sure, he'd seen it before, at its previous resting place in Edinburgh castle, and since then, it had featured in the coronation of Charles the Third. As ancient artefacts go, the stone was unremarkable. One hundred and fifty kilos of weathered rectangular sandstone with an iron ring at each end. Reputed to have been a pillow used by a biblical patriarch, Gill studied the dimensions and concluded Jacob must have had a pretty uncomfortable night's sleep. He lingered for as long as he dared before the passive hostility of the stalled queue behind him forced him to move on. Gill shook his head. Something didn't add up about that stone.

He accepted a glass of wine from a waiter and mingled amongst the crowd, looking for any familiar faces. But it was all politicians and local worthies, and he was about to give up and find a discreet place to stand when he felt a tap on his shoulder.

'Gill McArdle? Yes, I was hoping our paths would cross. I saw your name on the guest list.'

Gill turned to find the sad, shy, smiling face of Alasdair Canmore. 'Alasdair. Good to see you.'

They shook hands and Gill studied the man's expression to detect if he was friend or foe.

'Nice to see a friendly face', said Alasdair, looking around. 'This is home turf for my brother. But I don't know a soul.'

'Listen, I was sorry to hear about your father.'

Alasdair nodded. 'Thank you. It's been a hard few days. Especially for Roddy, trying to keep it out of the papers.'

'Conall was ill. And a public figure in his day. I understand Roddy's desire for privacy.'

'Especially this week of all weeks. When we learned of our father's death, Roddy seemed to decide heaven and hell were set against him.'

Gill wasn't sure if he had misheard. 'You *learned* about his death? Weren't you in the room?'

'Because of the manner of his passing …' said Alasdair, stopping when he saw surprise on Gill's face. 'Ah. You don't know.'

Gill feigned interest in some activity around the podium at the high end of the hall. 'Listen, Alasdair. Your brother thinks I'm a dodgy journo. So tell me nothing you don't want to see in a newspaper.' His eyes flashed back to Alasdair, and he tried to work some sympathy back into his tone. 'What you probably don't know is that my company has signed a gagging order. We've committed to printing nothing about your brother, your father, or you. So you can tell me anything you want because Roddy could sue my ass if I ever printed a word of it.'

Alasdair sipped his drink and processed this new information. After a moment's reflection, he said, 'Dad died, falling off the battlements of Stirling Castle.'

Setting down his drink, Gill fought and failed to keep shock off his face. 'How did that happen?'

'He'd been obsessing for days about some bedroom he kept seeing in his dreams. He wanted me to take him into the castle to look for it. At that point, he was barely fit to reach the bathroom on his own, so a stiff walk up the hill and trekking around the public bits of the castle with all those stairs was out of the question. But last Wednesday, he was insistent. I deflected him as usual saying we could try the following morning. But the next day, when I brought him his morning tea, he had gone. I guessed straight away he must have gone to the castle. I raised the alarm. By lunchtime, we found his body.'

'Alasdair, that's terrible.'

'Dad knew the castle like the back of his hand. Probably slipped in from a north entrance. Our firm did a lot of work over the years, so he still had keys.'

Gill nodded silently, absorbing this information.

'And the last part of the story is this', said Alasdair, producing a small white envelope. He passed it over.

Gill looked down to see his name scratched in spidery handwriting. 'Your father left this for me?'

'He must have sealed the envelope before his fatal trip to the castle. I've no idea what's in it. Pretty tiny so I doubt it's an heirloom.' Alasdair stopped to glance around. 'Roddy doesn't know about it, but if it's okay with you, I'm curious to see what's inside.'

Gill glanced at Alasdair, then caught a loose flap of paper on the envelope and tore it open. Carefully, he shook the contents into the palm of his left hand. Then the two men stared for several long seconds.

'I'm sorry', said Alasdair. 'Dad's behaviour was very erratic towards the end.'

Gill picked up the single white pill and examined it. 'Any idea what it is?'

'Let me think. I made up Dad's daily pill pouches.' He took the lozenge, examined it and pointed to the letters ERYC. 'It's an antibiotic called erythromycin. Dad was taking it to fight a bacterial infection.'

Gill wiped his mouth. 'Any idea why he would send it to me?'

'I was about to ask you the same question. Did it relate to something you were talking about?'

Gill cast his mind back to his last conversation with Conall Canmore. 'We were talking about his dreams when Roddy burst in that last time. We'd started to discuss the *Stone of Destiny*. I asked him if he'd ever seen it in his dreams. He said he hadn't, but that he would try.'

'Can you do that? Navigate in a dream?'

'Not my area of expertise', said Gill, gripping the small tablet between his fingertips. 'Maybe the pill is a clue about the stone. I asked your father to tell me what shape it was in the Scotland he could see in his dreams.'

Alasdair glanced from the pill to the stone on display, barely twenty metres from where they were standing. 'There's no resemblance.'

'Maybe the stone in your father's imagined world was shaped like this pill?'

Alasdair sighed and took a sip of his wine. 'You're welcome to see a mystery here, Gill. All I see is a dead man's medication.'

'Can I hold on to this?'

'Of course. It was addressed to you.'

Their conversation was interrupted by the master of ceremonies calling the room to order. He introduced a couple of local worthies who spoke for a few minutes each, compressing the story of the stone into a few paragraphs – how it had travelled from an uncertain origin with the ancient Celts arriving in Scotland from Ireland. Then its resettlement at nearby Scone at the heart of the united Scottish kingdom, before its theft by Edward the first.

The tempo of the story picked up with a little humour, recalling the moment in the 1950s when the stone briefly returned to Scotland after a madcap raid on Westminster by a group of nationalist students, only to return again to London. Concluding their presentation, they stood aside, and Roddy Canmore stepped up to the podium to bring the story of the stone up to date. He spoke about the stone's return from London under prime minister, John Major, and its sojourn in Edinburgh. Finally, how it had been used in the coronation of Charles the Third before returning to its rightful home, here in Perth. As he spoke, the First Minister of Scotland stood patiently, waiting for the invitation onto the stage. As the highest elected government official in Scotland, it would be their duty and privilege to welcome the stone to its new home, and to declare the new museum open. That's what was flagged in the programme. But in the event, as Roddy Canmore continued to speak, it wasn't what happened. Not by a long shot.

By the time Gill slipped out of Perth Museum, the First Minister still hadn't had an opportunity to speak. The choreographed presentation had descended into a verbal maul with shouting and counter-accusations echoing around the room. The last few years had exterminated Gill's interest in politics, so he left the sharp suits with their cadre of supporters behind and went in pursuit of some fresh air. A short walk took him to the centre of the old Smeaton's Bridge, linking Perth city with the road leading to Scone. From here he could see some of the best bits of Scotland in the form of old stone houses, against a backdrop of forests, rivers and a skyline of rolling hills. Looking around he realised, this was the Scotland he wanted. And the curse of it was, he could stand right on this very spot and name a dozen practical ways to celebrate and protect this beautiful land. Meanwhile, a few hundred yards away, Scotland's high-heidyins were yelling at each other about the quickest way to dismantle the union with England. And he found himself thinking again about Conall Canmore's night-time dreams of a better Scotland. Had the dying Conall allowed his mind to succumb to some idealistic image of an imagined Scotland? Or could his vision have been the nation's ultimate destiny, a beacon of possibilities, sabotaged by a few too many wrong turns?

Frustrated, and a little sad, he considered driving on to Stonehaven. But then a thought occurred to him. As he was in the area, there was a place he could visit that might shed light on his muddled thoughts about the stone. After returning to his car, Gill left Perth city centre, crossing the River Tay and driving the short distance to Quarrymill Woodland Park. Tourist signs indicated Scone Palace was less than a mile away. He wasn't particularly interested in the palace itself, a relatively modern stately home, built on the site of Scotland's first parliament. Instead, Gill wound his way into the car park of a small visitor centre. The park was an area of protected forest, carefully set aside from development so the city didn't swallow it. But Gill wasn't here for the walks or the wildlife, seeking instead to find the remains of the old quarry.

He knew the excavations had long been abandoned and in his mind, he'd pictured derelict mining equipment amid high cliff faces of exposed rock. In the event, all he found was a park built around the path of a small burn. Generations of stone masons had chiselled away at the accessible sandstone, creating bays and hollows where seams of the pale red rock had provided high-quality building materials, right on the doorstep of the growing city. Today, very little stone was visible, and any he saw was weathered and crumbling, laced through with brambles and other vegetation.

He stopped and sat on one of the many benches and tried to picture the scene as it would have looked a thousand years before. Just over the River Tay, the original town of Perth would have been a fraction of its modern self, growing to serve the nearby powerhouse at Scone. Originally selected by the first king ever to lay claim to the bulk of the land that would someday be called Scotland, successive monarchs had built their palaces and adapted any buildings raised before their reign. Eventually, the site would become an Augustine abbey and the seat of Scotland's periodic outdoor parliaments. To construct these buildings the masons would have looked for a local supply of accessible and workable building materials. With its outcrop of red sandstone, close to the surface and already partially exposed by the river, Quarrymill, as it became known, was ideal. Instead of hacking into a hillside, successions of masons had lifted the riven stone from shallow pits until the area must have resembled the dusty red surface of Mars. But all good things must come to an end and in due course, the best stone was exhausted, and nature crept in to recapture the site once more. But not before the site surrendered its most important object; a sandstone block known as the *Stone of Destiny*.

Sitting on the bench, Gill studied his feelings. The inner voice that made him alert to any mystery was quiet. And yet, he experienced a twinge of uneasiness. He thought about Roddy Canmore's announcement and his shoulders sagged at the thought of more political battles ahead, plus the uncertainty they cast around Scotland's future. He saw the possibility of positive change, but experience made him sceptical; a resignation that another period of political turmoil would be just another excuse to avoid the root and branch reforms Scotland needed if all its people were to prosper. Shaking his head, he stood up and was about to walk to his car when he experienced the uncomfortable feeling of being watched. Sensing danger, Gill scanned around him. Seeing nothing, he looked again. This time, across the river and screened by the thin leaf cover of a beech hedge, he could make out two figures, each with binoculars, watching him.

Uncertain of their intentions, Gill raised an arm in greeting. The figures shifted their position, perhaps seeking more shelter, but did not respond. Gill stood up and took a few steps towards them.

'Hey! What are you looking at?' he yelled at the faraway figures. Without answering, the pair immediately moved off. By the time Gill had found a bridge and jogged to their position, they had already reached the car park. Running after them, he was just in time to see two men climb into a car and drive away.

Gill stood with his hands on his hips watching them go. Who would be watching him and why? He'd ponder this during his drive to Montrose to visit his father, and then afterwards, as he travelled on alone to Stonehaven.

Chapter 15

Monday morning and Craig was leaning over Gill's desk. Like everyone else in the office, he'd been unsettled by Roddy Canmore's announcement.

'Seriously, man?' said Craig. 'You were there?'

Gill cracked open his laptop. 'It was hilarious. Try and picture this. Canmore is giving this oration about the *Stone of Destiny*, then there comes a moment when he stops and folds up his speech. He's trying to build the impression he's feeling so inspired he's going to deviate from his script. And then, with a touch of theatre, half a dozen semi-famous people get up on stage and form a guard of honour behind him …'

'Who?' Craig asked, breaking in.

'A retired boxer. A musician. And a couple of personalities. You know the types; the ones who get all misty-eyed about being Scottish but live in California three hundred and sixty days a year. Canmore prattled on for over an hour. It was painful.'

'You don't like his ideas?'

'Whether you agree with nationalist politics or not, Canmore was just plain rude. To hijack that event to launch a new political party and scorn his former colleagues was a bit rich.'

'Aye. It wasnae fair to do that to the First Minister', said Craig, wandering back to his desk.

'I mean, a political party called, *New Scotland*. It doesn't exactly reek of innovation.'

'I don't know. Mebbe they'll need a spin doctor.' He glanced over at Gill. 'You could apply.'

'But his industrial policies are reheated schemes that failed back in the 70s. And his social policies; don't start me!'

Craig studied his screen for a few seconds and started typing. 'He's really got you wound up.'

'I don't know if it's because the guy took a lump out of me last time I met his father, or if it's because he's so darn rude.'

'Well, he's on his own now. The Nats have expelled him, haven't they?'

'Sure, but at the latest count, a quarter of their elected members decided to go with him.'

'What's going on here?' barked Cassy as she and Mhairi walked in together.

Craig nodded at Gill. 'Our illustrious editor was present for the birth of Roddy Canmore's *New Scotland Party*, but I don't think he enjoyed himself.'

Mhairi dropped her bag on her desk and smiled mischievously. 'I think it might be nice if Scotland was independent.'

'Nice!' erupted Gill.

'Save England a fortune', she added playfully.

'Hey', said Cassy, her hackles rising. 'Magazines and mystery, please. Let's park the politics for pub chat, okay?'

'Gill', said Mhairi, switching back into work mode. 'Are we still meeting to discuss the *Pilgrim Isle*?'

'Yes, please', said Gill.

Cassy stood for a second, waiting for Mhairi to walk towards the coffee machine and drop out of earshot. 'Seriously, Gill. No politics. It's too toxic', she whispered.

'Aye, I get that. But we're adults. We should be able to talk about it. Share ideas.'

'Maybe in the old days when it was just *regular* politics, whatever the hell that was. But these days? We're talking here about dismantling a country, and office chit-chat generates too much heat. I've seen families wrecked by this stuff, so how'd you think the *Mys.Scot* team would fare?'

He nodded, frustrated that the temperature of Scotland's political debate often meant that no rational debate took place at all. 'Okay. Good point. Jump in if you ever see a risk of that happening.'

She nodded in a business-like fashion and turned to her desk. 'Now away you go and find that island.'

'I took a drive around the Forth last week', said Gill, puffing out his cheeks. 'I'd no idea there'd be so many islands.'

'Eleven big ones', said Mhairi. 'That's islands large enough to have settlements. They're all east of the Forth bridges. The tricky ones are west of the bridges, where the estuary narrows to become a tidal river.'

'I didn't see any over that way.'

'That's the point', said Mhairi, unfolding an Ordnance Survey map across her desk. 'A whole bunch have been swallowed up by land reclamation and the natural sediment coming down the river every year since the ice age.'

'Like what?'

'Preston Island, for a start. It's on the north shore near Culross. It was artificially extended in the nineteenth century to allow coal mining under the Forth, then partially buried under ash from a nearby power station in the early twentieth century.'

'Okay.'

'Then there's Rosyth Castle on the perimeter of the naval dockyard. That's been subsumed by land reclamation. And at the Stirling end, you have Tullybody Inch. That was created by the loss of farmland due to collapsed mine workings.'

'What about the religious angle?'

'Inchcolm is still your best bet, really. Because of the Augustine Abbey. But lots of the islands had some form of religious building on them at one time or another.'

'We know the *Airth Slab* was laid over one thousand years ago. Do any of the islands with religious buildings correlate with that?'

'The May Isle had buildings at least that old, but again, Inchcolm looks promising.' Mhairi took her glasses off for a second and rubbed her eyes. 'The Abbey wasn't established until the early twelfth century, but there's a religious history going right back to the sixth century through the island's namesake, St Columba.'

'Aye. The Iona of the East', said Gill. 'An ancient place and probably overdue a look from *Mys.Scot*.' He tapped Inchcolm on the map. 'The inscription mentioned the stone was being moved. I have to wonder if they were moving it to protect it from raiders. Does that help us?'

'Not really. Any substantial religious building would have been subject to Viking raids from as early as the ninth century. It doesn't help us narrow the search.'

Gill scowled at the map. 'That's true.'

'Thing is, Gill', said Mhairi. 'Even if the *Airth Slab* is reporting a real historical event, and supposing Inchcolm is where the *Fated Stone* was lost, how does that help you?'

'I guess we'd take a look for it.'

'But where?' said Mhairi with an apologetic smile. 'It's a big island with lots of coastline.'

'You've not met Gill's fiancé yet', observed Cassy, overhearing their discussion from her desk.

'No', said Mhairi, slowly.

'Flies submarines for a living. Handy for underwater stuff.'

Gill smiled. 'I could always ask.'

'I forgot to tell you earlier with all the political "chat" going on', said Cassy as Gill returned to his desk. 'I spoke to the skipper of Anstruther Lifeboat on Friday. He confirms a call out the night Corrie saw his lightning.'

'And?'

'Nothing. They did two circuits of the island and didn't find a thing.'

'What did they make of it?'

'They say it's happened before. Blamed the bird watchers. Apparently, they dazzle wading birds with strong torches so they can catch them and ring them. All those flashes can look quite weird when viewed from the mainland.'

Gill laid down his coffee and thought for a moment. 'That kind of light would appear close to the sea level. Corrie's lights appeared several hundred metres up and looked like suspended lightning.'

'Agreed. But the lifeboat guy didn't see what Corrie saw. So I phoned the coastguard. They were cagey about sharing information but did admit to requesting a lifeboat launch after reports of flares over the May Isle.'

'That's more like it.'

'Aye', said Cassy. 'Still doesn't tell us what the lights were.'

'And did you speak to the other folk reporting sightings?'

'I got hold of two households on the Fife coast. Both agreed with Corrie. Trails of lingering pale blue lightning, drifting towards the island before disappearing.'

'Anyone seen this kind of phenomenon before?'

Cassy shook her head. 'Neither before nor since. But if we keep our feet on the ground, the likely contenders are drones, or flares, or some kind of light diffusing from the island.'

'Agreed. Let's keep looking for a rational explanation.'

Half an hour later, Gill was updating a few long-running stories on the magazine's website when his phone rang.

'Gill McArdle', he said.

There was a short pause on the other end of the line. 'Did you enjoy the grand unveiling on Saturday?' said a male voice with a thick west coast accent.

'Sorry', said Gill. 'Who's speaking?'

'They say the stone came home', the voice drawled.

'Sorry, caller. I'm not catching your meaning.'

'Perth, ya numpty. The new museum and all that.'

'Who is this?' Gill asked.

'Just a pal', said the voice. 'Just a friendly neighbour. I gather you caught a wee bit of fresh air after the presentation.'

Gill twigged who might be on the line. 'Were you following me?'

'Now, why would a journo like you want to take a walk in Quarrymill Park when there's proper history being made, just around the corner?'

'Sounds like you were having a stroll that afternoon as well.'

'No, pal. I was at Perth Museum watching the birth of *New Scotland*. Which is a fine enterprise, I'm sure you'll agree.'

'I try to stay out of politics', said Gill, flatly.

'Oh, I don't believe that for a second', said the voice. 'I've heard a wee rumour that you might try to undermine the legitimacy of the stone. And if you do that, you're no friend to *New Scotland*.'

'Just doing my job.'

'Would you not think of coming on board with us? You're a well-kent face with good prospects. I'm sure if you aligned with the party, you could be moving up the ranks pretty smartish.'

'You haven't even said who you are', said Gill impatiently.

'Like I said. Just a pal.' The voice left a long gap that Gill wasn't minded to fill. 'Just a pal who doesn't want to have a nasty falling out wi you.'

Gill considered this threat for a moment or two, then without further delay, he hung up the call.

By mid-afternoon, Gill was unsettled and struggling to concentrate. Distracted by Cassy's office phone ringing, he looked around to see if she was nearby. With no sign of her, he followed office etiquette, and reluctantly answered it for her.

'I'm trying to reach Cassy Tullen', said a well-spoken male voice.

'She's not at her desk just now. Can I take a message?'

'If you could. It's rather urgent. My name is Roger Elmwood. I'm a solicitor working on behalf of Corrie McCann and the other members of *Black Scabbard*.'

'Okay.'

'I gather Miss Tullen put a picture of herself with Corrie on social media. And while the law states it was her photograph and she can do whatever she wants with it, Corrie does feel that he'd expressed a preference that his current whereabouts should not be revealed.'

Gill's grip on the phone stiffened. 'I do remember him saying something to that end.'

'Thank you. So, you'll appreciate he'd like the photo deleted as soon as possible so he doesn't suffer further consequences.'

'Consequences?' said Gill.

'Early this morning, two men tracked Corrie to his current residence in the caves. There was some kind of disagreement, then things turned quite ugly.'

'That's horrible', said Gill. 'But what's it to do with Cassy?'

'I've been set an image posted by Ms Tullen and lifted off social media by a fan of *Black Scabbard*. The image contains a geo-stamp of Corrie's present location.'

'Ah', said Gill.

'If you could get Miss Tullen to phone me back, I'd be most grateful.'

Chapter 16

Cassy was utterly silent on the journey back to Crail. She wanted to apologise to Corrie in person, and in the circumstances, Gill couldn't let her do it on her own. As they drove along the coast he switched on his lights as the southern sky darkened. No rain was falling, though the bruised sky was full of menace. They parked his car and by the time they made it to the caves, the gathering dusk rendered the south-facing coastline into a mess of overlapping shadows. They found Corrie sitting with another man around the campfire while they both sipped tins of beer.

'Corrie, I'm so desperately sorry', said Cassy, her fingers clasped even as they dug into the belly of her coat.

When Corrie looked up to study the arrivals, Gill could see puffiness around his eyes. Butterfly clips attended to a wound on his forehead, and when Corrie stood up, he walked towards them with a limp.

'You didnae have to come all the way out to see me', he said.

'I feel so terrible', said Cassy. 'I didn't think.'

Corrie pulled a hand up to the back of his head and rubbed it gently. 'For my money, I don't think it was your fault.'

'But your solicitor …', Gill began.

'Is always lookin' for someone to blame.' Corrie flicked his chin at his fireside companion. 'Nah. I've made a few enemies ower the years. My guess? It was a house-call frae some of them.'

'Did you chase them away?' Cassy asked.

Corrie shook his head. 'A group of folk came walkin' frae Crail. They saved my bacon.'

'How are you?' asked Gill.

Corrie raised his left hand and touched a tender part of his face. 'Been a couple of years since I had a good kickin' like that. A local GP patched me up. I might need an x-ray, but I'll see how it goes.'

'I'd have thought you'd go home.'

'Second beating in three days. Corrie doesn't know when to quit', said the second man. 'Of his many flaws, it's his most persistent.'

Corrie swung an arm at the man, wincing in the process. 'You folks probably don't know my friend.'

'Barley McGuire', breathed Cassy. Gill half turned towards her. 'Drummer. *Black Scabbard*. Early noughties to present day', she added.

'Also in charge of the band's security', added Barley.

'Aye, and he's been crap at it an' all. Even in the days when he could walk across the room unaided', muttered Corrie, turning to face Cassy. 'Are you folks staying for a cuppa? I'd offer you a beer, but we've drunk the last of ma stash.'

'Oh, we couldn't', said Cassy. 'I just wanted to tell you personally how utterly devasted I am. I took the picture down at once and I've deleted it from my phone.'

Corrie flinched as he sat down again. 'And that's fixed. Stay for tea. I was tellin' Barley all about you.'

Gill and Cassy glanced at each other, then moved over to an upturned fish box where they sat, side by side. 'You've had another attack this week?', said Gill, ever the detective.

Corrie waved away Gill's concern. 'Friday was the first. That was just a skirmish.'

'Who did this to you?'

Corrie studied his feet for a few moments. 'I'd love to think it was artistic differences, ken. Or hardcore fans workin' out their frustrations about our current musical direction.'

'Just neds, having a go', said Barley, setting to work on the hot drinks.

'Used to be a regular thing', said Corrie. 'Back in the early days, our musical style was … confrontational', he said after a pause.

Barley's face pulled into an embarrassed smile. 'Celtic rock meted out by Pictish warriors. We were wicked. In every sense of the word.'

Corrie shrugged. 'Record company's idea. Same clowns who dreamt up the face paint and all that posturing on stage. It was even worse when we weren't singin'. They encouraged us to pick fights and never walk away frae an insult.'

Cassy's repentant face puckered back into a shocked smile. 'You were arrested so many times.'

'Not for any stretch', said Barley, leaning back and working his shoulders to relieve some cramp. 'Not proud of it, but it's what we had to do to be different. Get noticed.'

Corrie laughed, then immediately seemed to regret it, pulling a hand to his chest. 'And look at the lot of us now.'

Barley rubbed Corrie's back for a few moments. 'One band member with dementia, two half crippled with arthritis and one ancient drunk who's faded into an old-time Jesus-freak.'

'I'm no' a drunk anymore', said Corrie, tossing his empty beer can at Barley.

'Swapped one crutch for another', muttered Barley. 'Mind you, at least he still has hair which is more than you can say for the rest of us.'

'Is the band still active?' Gill asked.

'BBC Alba occasionally wheel us out for a short set. Pump us full of drugs and stick us in front of a tame crowd.'

'Coke and marijuana?' asked Cassy.

'Ibuprofen and Tramadol', said Barley, laughing at his own joke.

Gill and Cassy drank tea, enjoying the banter between the two old friends. But rain clouds were gathering and Gill eventually pulled Cassy to her feet and got ready to leave. 'Will you guys be okay out here?'

'Yon twats won't be back', said Corrie.

'You sure?'

'He can always call in reinforcements', barked Barley, making an exaggerated praying motion with his palms pressed together.

'I could an' all', said Corrie, glancing over his shoulder at his friend.

Gill offered Corrie his hand and for a moment he held Corrie's gaze. 'I'd come. In a heartbeat. If you needed help.'

'Thank you, Gill. I'll hae you in mind.'

After Gill and Cassy had said their farewells, Cassy waited until they were out of earshot.

'Corrie knew his attackers, didn't he?' she said.

Gill gave one curt nod. 'Yep. But I got the definite sense he wasn't going to talk about it.'

Billy Whyte stared at the sky. The coastal path hadn't been as quiet as they'd hoped, but the rain was coming and they needed to get this done while there was still light. Gripping his phone he pressed the call button and studied Stevie's face. The man was impassive, oblivious to the risks of what they were about to do. When the call connected, he turned away and faced the sea.

'Boss?' he said, waiting to hear who answered.

There was a pause before the voice replied. 'Why're you calling this number, ya eejit?' Another pause, then a shout. 'DON'T use any names, alright?'

'Got that', said Billy.

'What's the problem?'

'We were just about to go back in.' Billy glanced at Stevie and away again. 'Thing is boss, that guy from the magazine was here.'

'So?'

'Just that, if he and …. the caveman, are working together, I'm wondering if that changes anything?'

'Why should it?'

'Dunno. Just thought I'd make you aware, before … you know.'

The voice at the other end of the line was angry now. 'During your wee chat earlier, did the caveman agree to come in with us or not?'

'He said "Nah. Over his dead body".'

'So, what're you waiting for? Gie him what he wants.'

'But the magazine guy, boss. What if he comes back?'

'Why should that be a problem?'

'He saw us on Saturday. If he makes another appearance, he might recognize us.'

'Why? Did you boys all sup a pint together?'

'No. He was miles away.'

'Are you going soft? I think pal, you and I had an agreement?'

'Aye, and that's not a problem …'

'Just get on with it.'

The line went dead, and Billy tucked his phone away. Stevie didn't talk, just nodded once, and bent to retrieve a rucksack from the car. Reaching inside he pulled out two black balaclavas. Billy took one and folded it into a beanie shape. Then after a deep, shuddering breath he nodded at Stevie and started to walk towards the caves.

Roddy Canmore hung up the call and growled in frustration. Billy was keen, but the man was a coward. At least Stevie was still there to add a little backbone. Sinking into an armchair that should have been tossed in a skip years ago, he sat and surveyed his father's bedroom. Bedroom! In Roddy's eyes, this was still the dining room, abused and neglected; its table and chairs pushed to one side to make way for a hospital bed with all its gadgetry. And the table itself, laden with so many pills he could barely remember what they were all for. Ach, that was Alasdair's business – he could sort it out.

At least one good thing about the room hadn't changed. Roddy stood and walked over to the drinks cabinet. He rummaged through the bottles of spirits until he found the one he was looking for. Tucked at the back was an unopened bottle of Mortlach twenty-year-old. The guys in the firm had given it to Conall for a significant birthday. And then his father spent the next five years joking he'd open it on the day Scotland gained its independence. Roddy shook his head as he tore off the seal and poured himself a decent measure.

'That bloody journalist again', he spat after the third sip.

He took the drink back to the uncomfortable chair sitting beside an unlit fire and thought. Eventually, he would have forgotten the journo, sniffing around old Conall; just a pathetic creature looking for scraps. But then the rat turned up at Perth and didn't even have the decency to stay to the end! Good call to have Stevie and Billy on the lookout for him. They didn't realise the significance of Quarryhill, even though Roddy did. And now this piece of human vermin had hooked up with Corrie McCann. What had caused that? And to what end?

Roddy took another long sip of the old Speyside and considered his options. Of all his potential opponents and naysayers, McArdle was the only one he hadn't foreseen. And with his careless disrespect for the political realities of the day, McArdle was the man who could cause him the most trouble. He needed to put him back in his box, and Roddy doubted if Billy had the balls to do it. So, what else to do?

Peering into the amber liquid, he arrived at a realisation. 'If you've got a rat problem, it's time to call in pest control.'

He dug into his jacket pocket and cracked open the burner phone he kept for emergencies. Dialling a number he kept in his memory, he waited.

'Michael', he said as the call connected. 'I have a little job for you.'

Gill dropped Cassy at her flat and told her not to worry. The photo had been an innocent mistake and Corrie didn't hold it against her. Feeling a little weary for a Monday evening, he was just walking into his flat when his mobile rang. When he picked up, all he could hear at first was heavy breathing, as if the caller had been running.

'Gill. It's Corrie McCann. You gotta second?'

'Sure. What's happening?'

'After you left, I walked Barely up to his car. When I got back to the cave, those clowns were waitin' for me.' Corrie gulped a deep breath. 'This time they brought metal batons.'

'Have you called the police?'

'No.'

'Have they trapped you?'

'No. They're away.'

Gill didn't respond. Instead, he tried to decode the reason for the call.

'Gill. This guy appeared. Big biker fella. Turkish lookin'. Said you sent him.'

'Corrie, I haven't sent …'

'He had a sword, Gill. Honest tae God. Shook it at yon neds and roared at them. They took one look at him and ran. My question to you; who is that guy?'

Gill ran a hand through his dark red hair. 'Where are you, Corrie?'

'Still at the caves.'

'Stay there. I'll be back with you in a little over an hour.'

Chapter 17

As Gill abandoned his car in Crail for the second time that day, he heard a distant rumble of thunder. The brewing storm was getting ready to break. Glad of decent rain gear, and with a torch in hand, he set off down the coastal path as more grumbles drifted in from the North Sea.

'The big Turkish fella', shouted Corrie as Gill approached the caves. 'You ken that guy?'

'I encountered him a couple of years back when I was on Harris.'

'Who is he?'

Gill didn't respond until he was standing head-to-head with Corrie. 'You wouldn't believe me if I told you.'

Corrie met Gill's gaze. His face was wet, and his long grey hair plastered across his forehead. 'Try me, pal.'

Gill glanced up at the darkening sky and sighed. 'Most likely, he's an angel.'

'Seriously?'

'I said you wouldn't like it.'

Unphased, Corrie shot back. 'Good angel? Or bad angel?'

'He's saved my life a couple of times. Helped me and my fiancé on occasions.'

'Interesting'. Corrie stared down at Gill's feet. 'I take it you're a man who believes in the supernatural?'

'Reluctantly, yes.'

'Oh! Reluctance? Why the hesitation?'

'I'm not a religious person.'

Corrie grunted. 'I didnae ask if you're religious, ken. I'm askin' if you're a man of faith?'

'There's a difference?' said Gill shielding his face from the first shards of rain.

'Ya think?', said Corrie. 'Anyway. After he chased the goons away, yon angel fella said he had a message for Gillan McArdle.'

'For me?'

Corrie threw his hands out from his sides. 'That's what I said.'

'What was the message?'

'He tol' me to tell you tae watch the sea.'

'I'm sorry, Corrie. I don't understand.'

Corrie's eyes darted to the sky and back to Gill's face. 'Come intae my parlour and we can put our heids together and figure out what he could possibly hae meant when he said, "Watch the sea".'

Gill had plans for the evening but they washed away in the face of Raphael's intervention. Corrie made tea while Gill sat down by the open fire a little back from the mouth of the cave, while just outside, the rain lashed down in rods.

'Are we safe in here?' Gill asked as yet another lightning flash threw white light into the darkest corner of the cave.

'Sure', said Corrie. 'Ken, I think so. Maybe dinnae swing any metal poles at the sky.'

Gill grunted and moved a little deeper into the cave.

'So, my hesitant, most-definitely-not-religious friend. What's come across your path tae open your eyes to the supernatural?'

'It's a long story.'

Corrie's eyes flitted around the cave. 'I hae time.'

Gill accepted a mug of tea from Corrie and thought. Taking a deep breath, he went back to the beginning of his story, recounting his experiences of these last two years. And how it left him with the certainty there was a powerful and benevolent force at work in the universe.

'And does this force hae a name?'

Gill thought. 'The ancient Hebrews called him Yahweh. I like that. "I am." It seems a fitting name for God.'

Corrie nodded, offering Gill milk from a dubious looking carton. 'Aye. Specially when most folk would prefer tae talk about him in the past tense.'

He flicked his chin at Corrie. 'How about you? What's your story?'

Corrie took a long sip, then leant back against a log. 'It was all about the music for me. The girls. The drinking.' He shook his head. 'I worked so hard when I was young. Pissed most of it away by middle age. By the time I hit my fifties, I was a roaring alco and six months frae bein' deid.'

'And yet, you're still here.'

'As a last gasp, I tried the AA. Threw myself into it, like a drownin' man clingin' tae a raft. Learned the twelve-step model and eventually came to believe every word of it. I didn't want tae die, and realised that if God is real, he didn't want me tae die either.'

Gill's eyes darted involuntarily to a crushed beer can, lying at Corrie's feet.

'And you're wondering how I'm doin'?'

'You look well.'

Corrie picked up the crushed can and slipped it into a bag marked "recycling". 'Thing is, Gill. Livin' as an alcoholic, eventually, it defines you. I wasnae Corrie McCann any more, but the Alcoholic, Corrie McCann. I became terrified of booze - stayed dry for five years. And then, in what I can only call a miracle, God gae me back a workin' relationship with alcohol. Not that havin' a drink is a good thing, in and of itself, but by making my peace wie it, it no longer defined me. These days I hae a tin or two during the week and the bonnie woman I'm husband to shares a bottle of wine with me at the weekend.'

'And now you're well, have you tucked God away where you don't need to deal with him anymore?'

Corrie laughed. 'Hey, pal. Dinnae judge by appearances. But yeah. I tried to do just that. Thing is, he disnae want to go. Having refurbished one area of my life, he's been grindin' through the rest.' He laughed again. 'Yep, by the time I'm ready to die, I'm gonna be a braw citizen. Part of me hates that.'

'Hates it?'

Corrie pointed at the expression on Gill's face. 'Sure! I'm a rocker. Never destined to be nice. I had all this anger before. About the world and all the things I wanted to change. Where'd all that go?'

Gill said nothing, still trying to figure out if Corrie was just being ironic.

'Yeah', said Corrie looking away. 'Wanted to change the world, and here I am clearin' garbage off the beach.' He kicked a stone lying near his shoe. 'But honestly, Gill? In ma whole life, I've never been happier.'

Gill considered this and stared after the stone Corrie had pushed away. 'Personally, I don't find believing in God is a comfortable place at all.'

Corrie brushed away Gill's remark with a wave of his hand. 'That's because you're aye self-conscious about it.'

'Beg your pardon?'

Corrie pointed at him. 'I bet you dinnae say a word about your faith to friends and colleagues. That lovely wee lass here today, Cassy. Does she know what you believe?'

'We've not had an appropriate moment to talk about it.'

'Yep, there you go. You're sittin' on gold dust and yet you keep it to yourself. You need to buckle up, Gill.' Corrie eased himself back into a sitting position. 'What I don't get about you, is you're still squeamish about your faith, and at the same time you've got an angel droppin' in whenever you need him. Ken, what makes you so special?'

Gill shook his head. 'I honestly don't know.'

'The angel said you sent him. I'll bet he didnae make that up!'

Gill drew his fingers to his cheeks and thought. Gradually, a realisation crept up on him. 'I prayed. As we drove away from Crail, and Cassy went quiet, I was thinking about how risky it was for you, staying out here. So I prayed. I asked God to send an angel to look after you. *The Book* says you can do that.'

After a pause, Corrie nodded. 'Aye, it does.'

'That's the bit that's clearest to me', said Gill. '*The Book*. It's incredible. It's like the most intricate piece of clockwork. The way it loops back on itself; the themes weaving in and out like crafted gears.'

Corrie poured more water into his kettle and put it back on the stove. 'I like that analogy. Hit me again. What else have you seen?'

The two men talked for an hour as the night settled in under the assault of rain. Corrie was curious about what Gill was working on, and Gill, omitting a few key details, decided to tell him.

'You're searchin' for a shipwreck', Corrie summarised. 'And the only thing you ken about is that it sits near an island that used to have a church on it?'

'That's where I'm at', said Gill.

Corrie shook his head. 'And some folk think rockstars hae all the fun.'

'I've got a high tolerance level for wild goose chases.'

'And this *Fated Stone*, ken. You reckon it's the real *Stone of Destiny*?'

'Yes.'

Corrie stared at Gill for a long moment before folding his arms. 'That's weird, man. Cause three days ago I was chattin' to a fella outside this cave who was bangin' on about the *Stone of Destiny* bein' unveiled in Perth.'

Gill shrugged. 'Whatever the Perth stone is, it didn't come from the Middle East.'

'Sorry, pal. Why's that important?'

Patiently, Gill explained the *Jacob's Pillow* myth and the how a revered stone from Israel might have journeyed to Scotland, only to be lost in the Firth of Forth one thousand years ago.

At the end of Gill's story, Corrie started to laugh. 'I'd love it, pal, if you laid your hands on the *Fated Stone*. Cause I'd phone a few ... *friends* and put them right about a couple of things.'

Still laughing, he took himself off into the dark to relieve his bladder.

When Corrie got back, Gill was shivering and tugging his layers tighter around him.

'I can loan you a spare sleepin' bag', said Corrie. 'Unless you want to walk home in the rain?'

Gill shook his head. 'Looks like the storm is almost done. I'll stay a little while longer then head back.'

'Suit yourself. I'm gonna turn in.'

'What happened to, "Watch the sea"?'

'He said you were to watch, ken. Didn't say nothin' about me. Besides, tomorrow's my last day.' Corrie nodded at the diminished piles of rubbish sacks heaped on the shore. 'I'll be pullin' a long shift.'

'Understood.'

While Gill listened to the grunts and mutterings of Corrie's bedtime routine, he sat counting the seconds between each flash of the Isle of May Lighthouse. Gradually the two pulses followed by a ten-second lag became quite soporific. Running to a less predictable rhythm, flashes of lightning illuminated the gigantic wind turbines ten miles to the southeast of their position. Even in the dark, as the rain eased, Gill could make out the slow-moving blades, held in stark silhouettes by each distant flash.

'Corrie', called Gill, urgently.

'Wha'?' said a bleary voice at the back of the cave.

'Come here a second.'

'Man, I've just got my ass intae bed.'

'The lightning, Corrie. It's back.'

There was a momentary pause, then the sound of a zipper being ripped. Grumbling, Corrie stumbled back down beside him. Together, they watched a lingering pale-blue tear in the sky, pulsating with energy, and drifting east to west towards the island. After ten seconds this first phenomenon petered out but was replaced by another that lasted longer and extended further west. As this second light started to fade, Gill lifted his phone and started to video the scene. A third and final streak of lightning erupted, over the island this time, gradually dipping out of the horizontal and tipping towards the sea. Touching the surface, the phenomena seemed to lose its energy and the remaining lightning corkscrewed down towards the water until it was gone.

'What on earth was that?' said Gill.

Corrie said nothing. Instead, they both stared at the scene for ten, twenty, thirty minutes, until a small ship appeared, presumably a lifeboat, it's LED beam casting left and right across the area where the lightning fell.

'Was that what you saw before?'

'Aye, pal', said Corrie. 'Just like that.'

Chapter 18

'I saw Corrie again last night', said Gill as he laid a coffee on Cassy's desk the following morning.

'Why?'

Gill turned away towards his desk. 'He needed help with something.'

Cassy's eyes flashed up and right. 'But it was pissing with rain.'

'Aye. We went a bit caveman and sat watching the storm from the door of his hotel.'

'Did he have a moan behind my back?'

'Honestly, I don't think he's holding anything against you. And while I was there, we saw the blue lightning again.'

'No way!'

'Yep. Let me show you.' Cassy hunched over Gill's phone, watching the thirty seconds of footage from the night before.'

'Okay. I'm impressed I think', said Cassy, while the expression on her face was, *I don't know what the hell I'm looking at.*

'I know', said Gill. 'And having seen it, I really want to figure out what's causing that lightning.'

'How're you going to do that?' asked Cassy.

Nearby, Craig cleared his throat loudly. 'He's doing it by delegating that particular jobbie to me', he said. 'And yes, the pun is intended.'

Gill jerked his head at Craig, and together, he and Cassy converged on Craig's desk. 'And I suspect you've found something.'

'So far, I've two possibilities.'

'Go for it.'

'The first explanation could be ball lightning', said Craig. 'But it's incredibly rare and nobody seems sure how it works. On the plus side, it sometimes presents as multiple balls of light, generally orange in colour and slow-moving.'

'The ones I saw were pale blue, bordering on Lilac.'

'Then maybe it's the second option. St Elmo's fire. That's definitely blue or purple, but it's even rarer. Especially in the UK. You say there'd been a thunderstorm?'

'Aye, south of the wind farm.'

'Okay. That might help explain it. St Elmo's fire is only seen after thunderstorms, and typically sticks to the tops of pointed objects like masts or spires.' Craig opened a tab on his MacBook Pro and started to run through the physics behind both phenomena until Cassy started to huff with impatience.

'The fire might be created on the turbine blades, then spun off to free float like ball lightning', Gill mused. 'Have you seen any reports like that?'

'Not so far but if I get some time later I'll check again and focus on wind farms.' Craig stopped to scratch the side of his head. 'Even if that is the source of the lightning, we don't have anything to explain its behaviour. Can you show me your video again?'

Gill opened his phone and presented the footage he'd taken in front of the caves. They ran through it four times, noticing there were several conventional lightning flashes in the background.

'Must have been a pea soup of electrical charges with ions and plasmas all boiling together. Gill, this needs more than a trawl through a wiki to figure it out. You'd need to talk to a physics professor.'

'Good point.'

'Know any?'

'Only one, and he's serving a prison sentence for manslaughter. I do know a scientific journalist I could call.'

Craig nodded. 'Is it okay then if I leave that to you? My day is crammed as it is.'

Gill sat with Mhairi, Craig and Cassy in the conference room, with maps of the Forth spread in front of them. The lingering uncertainty about the *Pilgrim Isle* had been lying around like an unwashed towel and he felt the need to move forward or dump it altogether. Larry had declined attendance at the meeting citing pressure of work. When Gill had explained what they were trying to achieve, Larry was laconic. 'It's just a rock, Gill. Personally, am nae bothered.'

'Right, Mhairi', said Gill, glancing around the other faces. 'Decision time. The *Pilgrim Isle*. Which one is it?'

Mhairi threw Gill an expression of mock astonishment. 'I'm afraid it's not that simple. Most of the larger islands have had religious buildings on them over the centuries.'

'Okay then. I'll take your most educated guess?'

'And she is *very* educated', Cassy added.

Mhairi seemed to ignore the jibe. 'I still think your best bet is Inchcolm Island, really. It has connections to St Columba, which gives it the oldest religious heritage of any of the islands.'

'By my reckoning, it's also the closest site to Airth', added Craig.

'The next hottest prospect is Inchkeith', Mhairi continued. 'Saint Adomnán of Iona founded a monastery there in the seventh century, so that's pretty old too.'

'Okay. Inchkeith or Inchcolm. We're narrowing it down.'

'Hang on, Gill. There's a bunch of saints associated with some of the other islands.'

'Bit rusty on my saints', said Gill. 'Want to remind us who you're thinking of?'

'Saint Adrian of May and Saint Monance were murdered on the Isle of May by invading Danes in 870. That island has a long ecclesiastical history, including the remains of a 13th-century Benedictine church.'

'Any more?'

'An Irish missionary called Saint Baldred lived on The Bass Rock in the 8th century. And finally, you have Fidra. It has a ruined 12th-century chapel dedicated to St Nicholas.'

Gill exhaled slowly. 'So there are at least five contenders to be the *Pilgrim Isle*.'

Mhairi tapped the map. 'Those are only the big islands. Some of the tiny ones had chapels and hermitages.'

To deflect his frustration, Gill scratched the back of his head. 'Let's narrow our search to these five. Can we make any connection to the *Fated Stone* or the ancient monarchs?'

'All of these islands were vulnerable to Viking raids', said Mhairi. 'So, the clergy and their holy relics were evacuated to the mainland from time to time. There are scraps in the records but nothing relating to a stone.'

'And the monarchs?'

'Where the clergy went, the kings weren't far behind. Inchcolm scores highest but they all had royal connections of some sort.'

'Gill, face it', said Cassy. 'There's no clear favourite. The weight of evidence nudges us towards Inchcolm. But it's a big island and we don't have a clue where to mount a marine search.'

Gill got up and started to pace the room. 'I'm just thinking about our other investigation.'

'Which one?'

'The strange blue lightning.'

'Corrie McCann's UFO?' asked Craig.

'Corrie doesn't call it that. But you see where I'm going? Two lines of enquiry on totally separate stories, potentially intersecting on the Isle of May.'

Mhairi glanced at Cassy. 'Yes. But two unrelated events separated in time by one thousand years.'

'Sorry, Gill', said Cassy. 'You're gonna have to spell this one out for us.'

Gill turned to face them and leaned on the back of a chair. 'Okay. We think the original *Fated Stone* was lost in a storm a very long time ago and we don't know where. While we're considering this, we've got strange lightning dropping into a spot northwest of the May Isle.'

Cassy and Mhairi looked at each other but said nothing.

'What if the lightning is showing us where the stone lies?'

Cassy thrust out a hand. 'By what agency? Aliens?'

Gill shook his head. 'Something in the supernatural realm.'

The women sat back in their chairs and looked at their hands. Craig meanwhile had closed his eyes and was rubbing his face.

'Hear me out. The myth around the stone suggests a supernatural origin amongst the Jewish patriarchs. Somewhere along the line, it passed into the possession of one of Scotland's predecessor tribes. Is it such a giant leap to suggest it might have supernatural significance today? That it could even display an unnatural phenomenon?'

Nobody looked convinced. 'Bit of a leap', said Mhairi.

'Massive', said Cassy. 'Especially if we already suspect the *Jacob's Pillow* story was basically a political stunt.'

Gill looked back and forward between them both. 'I've mounted archaeological digs based on less.'

'Even if it were true', said Cassy, grasping for the right words. 'How would you test the link?'

'I'd go to where the lightning hit the water.'

'It's a big island, Gill. How can you be sure where to look?'

Gill lifted his phone and wiggled it at them. 'I've got video. Remember?'

Cassy thrust a hand at him. 'I get your curiosity about Corrie's lightning, but I'm struggling to make any connection between that and our search for the *Fated Stone*.'

'They intersect on the Isle of May', he repeated.

'That's coincidence.'

He stared down at his hands. 'No such thing', he said quietly.

'How are you and Cassy doing?' Gill asked Mhairi when he met her a short while later at the coffee machine.

'How do you mean, Gill?'

'Ach, sometimes you seem a bit short with each other.'

'We're friends. We work together; play in the band together. Okay, we chew each other's ears off from time to time, but she's my bestie.'

'And you still think she's doing okay?'

'Well, she works all hours, you know.'

'Apart from the band, I never hear her mention any kind of social life.'

'She's close to her mum and dad.'

'Aye, but when was the last time she went back to Raasay to see them?'

Mhairi thought for a moment. 'Her sister is getting married at the next new year. We're booked to play at that. I guess that'll be the first time in a while.'

'Ever hear her talk about boyfriends, girlfriends, past or present?'

'Gill. I'm not going to tell tales.'

'I'm just concerned, that's all. Some days she's calm, cool and professional. Other days, she's ripping strips off us all.'

'Sounds like a walking definition of a woman', said Mhairi, glancing around to make sure they weren't being overheard. She smiled and whispered. 'And it's what I'll have to do to you if you keep asking personal questions about my friend.'

Gill raised his hands. 'No problem. Leave it. I'll ask her myself when I next get a chance.'

It took Gill several attempts to reach Arnold Broadbent at *Science Magazine*, so it was late afternoon when he finally spoke with his journalist friend.

'Och, aye, it's ma wee Scottish pal', mimicked Arnold.

'Thanks, Arnie. But I think you'll find that kind of language is considered derogatory these days.'

'Ack, away! When did the Scots get so thin-skinned? Anyway, how're doing, matey-boy?'

'I'm good. Busy as ever. I see ScoCion is up and running again.'

'But on a tight leash. No more vaporised scientists.' Arnold paused. 'Sorry, Gill. I know you guys were friends.'

'Make it up to me by talking to me about lightning.'

'You get it during thunderstorms. What's your question?'

Briefly, Gill told him about the phenomena he'd seen with Corrie, plus his debate with Craig.

'Sounds like a strange one', said Arnold. 'I mean, no one's sure what ball lightning is. Based on observations, it can drift around like a soap bubble. And St. Elmo's fire is sometimes mistaken for ball lightning, but it generally remains attached to an object. You say you took a video?'

'Hang on. I'll mail it', said Gill.

He listened as Arnold huffed and panted, rubbed his bristles and swore under his breath. 'What you got there', he said at last, 'is St Elmo's fire behaving like ball lightning.'

'Can lightning do that?'

'The only thing I know about lightning is how little we know. Regular lightning is a naturally occurring electrostatic discharge. In a storm …' Arnold paused. 'This would be so much easier with a couple of pint glasses in front of us.'

'Try for me, Arnie.'

'What lightning is, at its most fundamental level, is energy leaping from the positively charged zone to a negatively charged point. And most often, that means the upper atmosphere discharging energy to the ground or some lower part of the cloud.'

'But that's flash-bang and gone in a moment. The thing I saw lingered for twenty seconds.'

'Yeah, so something else is happening, so let's dig a bit deeper. Lightning represents the discharge of very high voltages. Under the right conditions for St Elmo's fire, this energy rips apart atoms and turns them into a glowing mixture of protons and electrons. You end up with a Scotch broth of particles in the form of a highly conductive plasma. It seems the positives and negatives hold each other in balance for longer while the energy gradually discharges as light.'

'Hang on a second', said Gill. 'I'll write this down.'

'But eventually', said Arnold without waiting. 'All that energy will tend to discharge to earth. For example, do you know what your lilac lightning was striking?'

'It just hit the sea.'

'But you said your friend saw the exact same phenomena a few weeks before. In the same place, right?'

'Yes.'

'When lightning hits water, the energy spreads horizontally. But the old adage, lightning never strikes twice … you know it?'

'Of course.'

'Well, there must be something about that location, sucking the energy towards it.'

'Hard to see from the mainland, but as far as I'm aware it's just open sea.'

'Nah', said Arnold. 'There'll be something unique about that spot. Something that pulls the lightning to discharge.'

'Interesting', said Gill.

'Gimme a day or two. If I get a quiet half hour, I'll research it for you.'

'Thanks, Arnie. I owe you.'

Gill reviewed his call with Arnold. The information he'd provided wasn't conclusive, but a deep conviction was rising in him about the location of the *Fated Stone*. He abandoned his desk to stretch his legs down by the river so he could think without the blare of the office.

Hands in his trouser pockets buried deep under the tails of his waistcoat, with his chin pressed against his breastbone, he tried to think. The Isle of May was just one contender for the *Pilgrim Isle*, but it ticked all the boxes. When it came to justifying his decision to Tony and his team, it was this fact he'd have to rely on. Plus, the archaeologist's instinct that had propelled him to "lucky" finds on previous occasions. Apart from Tony, they'd all spot the link between Corrie McCann's lightning and a highly speculative archaeological dive. But Arnold had tipped the scales. Deciding on his course of action, he turned on his heel and strode back to the office.

Chapter 19

His announcement didn't merit booking out the conference room, with all the attendant fetching of coffees and "just finishing" other tasks. Instead, he got them to circle their chairs within the *Mys.Scot* pen and grabbed their attention.

'Right, folks. Decision time', he said.

'You've got *that* look', said Cassy, with emphasis.

'What look?'

'The one where you come out and say something preposterous. Then we all make fun of you. And finally, to my constant bewilderment, sometimes, you even turn out to be right.'

Gill patted the air to deflect her.

'Mhairi's done lots of great work for us, building the background picture on the *Stone of Destiny* and the possible locations of the so-called *Pilgrim Isle*', he said. 'But I need to draw a line under it so she can get back to her day job. I've got a tiny bit of budget from Tony, and Salina is offering to help for free, so we've got the resources to mount one short dive.'

'No hard feelings, boss', said Craig. 'Chances of finding it would be thousands to one. Even with a widespread search.'

'Exactly', said Gill. 'So, the only meaningful way to run with this is to double it up with Cassy's lights-in-the-sky story. My contact at *Science Magazine* thinks there must be something in the water to attract the electrical discharge. The goal of this dive will be to investigate the source of this attraction.'

'Okay', said Cassy, seeing where his logic was going.

'Just to be clear. The purpose of the dive is to figure out Cassy's lightning story. If we happen to stumble across any *other* interesting artefacts while we're down there, so be it.'

'Your call, boss', said Craig.

'Yeah', said Mhairi a little wistfully. 'It will be good to have a least tried.'

Without any dissension in the ranks, Gill closed the meeting and everyone turned back to their work. Or at least, almost everyone.

'I hear it's *my* lightning story now', whispered Cassy, appearing at his shoulder.

'You were the one with the instinct to visit Corrie McCann. If you hadn't done that, we'd not have that lead.'

Cassy's eyes darted up to the ceiling. 'Guess so.'

'And when we come to write this up, I'd like you to do it.'

'Me?'

'It's your story, so your name needs to be on the by-line.'

Cassy's face scrunched into a puzzled smile. 'Are you sure?'

'Cass, you already write better copy than just about anybody in this room. You're destined to be an editor. Might as well take a step towards it.'

Cassy chewed on his proposal for a second, then nodded once. 'Okay then.'

When Gill phoned Corrie McCann, the call went straight to voicemail and an automatic message. 'Corrie. Gill McArdle here. Just to let you know, the magazine is sponsoring a limited project, diving on the spot where your lightning fell. We're putting the logistics together now and liaising with the Trust that manages the island. We could be in there as soon as next week. Suffice to say, if we find anything, I'll let you know.' He was about to hang up when he decided to add one last clause. 'Just to be clear, our project is investigating your lightning. Any suggestion we're searching for the *Fated Stone* is entirely coincidental.'

Later that evening, Salina and Gill sat around her kitchen table, hunched over a laptop. Gill had used his video of the May Isle lightning to estimate the target point where it hit the sea. Salina refined this by calling up a detailed marine map of the sea bed north of the island and drawing a line between a physical landmark on the island and the sighting point outside Caiplie Caves.

'You're making a connection between the lilac lightning and the *Pilgrim Isle*?' said Salina while they worked.

'I've been puzzling over it for days now', said Gill, leaning over the table. 'The Isle of May was always a contender, although Inchcolm initially looked more promising. But Raphael's intervention swung my thinking. The fact that he made an appearance led directly to Corrie and me seeing the lightning. My instinct says the Isle of May is the *Pilgrim Isle*.'

'And you think the location of the lightning entering the water is significant?'

'I do. Corrie says the second incident was in exactly the same spot as the first.'

'Okay then. We know the longitude of the lightning strike', she began. 'But because you recorded your video just above sea level, we have a margin for error on the latitude. We've got to figure out how far the lightning was from the island when it struck the water.'

'And this line you've drawn is your search area?'

'Yes. And a few metres on either side. I mean, do you think the lightning was pointing straight down, or could there be wiggle room?'

Gill dropped the tension out of his shoulders and stared at the ceiling. 'I'm a grown man chasing lights in the sky. I just can't pretend to be too precise about this.'

'I know. You're basically insane.' She gave him a little nudge. 'But let me humour you by giving you a hand.'

'Could you operate a DSV safely, this close to the island?'

Salina nodded. 'Sure. But I'm not sure that's where I'd start.'

'What do you mean?'

'I'm thinking I could free-dive from a RIB. The depths range from twenty to thirty-five metres so it's the absolute limit I would consider using regular air, but it's do-able.'

Gill shook his head. 'Won't that be dangerous?'

'There'll be a strong tidal surge', said Salina, pointing at the map. 'There will be a natural eddy created by the tides rising and falling past the island. And this ridge of rock on the seabed is the feature that worries me. It runs almost parallel to our search line and it'll stir the water up a bit. Thinking about it, I'd need a dive partner and a safety guy on the boat.'

'Sal. That couldn't be me', said Gill, remembering the last time he'd dived with Salina in Loch Ness.

She laughed. 'No. I'd find somebody else.'

'And why not use a DSV?'

'The expense, for a start. And we're looking for a thousand-year-old wreck. At this shallow depth, there'll be almost nothing left. We could be combing the seabed with our fingertips.'

'Okay. How do we push this forward?'

Salina thought for a second. 'I can't do it on Uni time. Let me research what dive boats are working out of Anstruther. If I find someone I like, then we'll visit them. I warn you, we're going to need a little cash.'

'I'll speak to Tony in the morning.'

Salina grunted. 'He'll want me to do it on the cheap.'

'When we dig holes in the ground, it's not cheap either.'

'I'll donate my time; the cost of true love and all that. But we'd need to pay my dive partner.'

Gill cast his mind to any others in Salina's team he'd already met. Immediately he thought back to their project on Loch Ness and the people they'd worked with. 'Could we pay Ellie to do an ad hoc dive?'

Salina thought. 'I could ask. She and Tom are saving to buy a house. Might be interested.'

'Excellent. Tom could be our safety guy on the surface.'

'Gill McArdle', she said. 'You don't half push your luck.'

'That's all arranged then.'

'And, Gill.'

'Yes?'

'Anstruther. The fish & chips are on you.'

Chapter 20

Seven days later, Gill found himself with Salina on a large RIB, scudding towards the Isle of May. Behind them, the Fife coastline diminished rapidly as the boat's two large engines sped the craft across five miles of open sea. The island lay to the south and sat like a hunched sentry at the mouth of the Forth. Topping it off was a building that looked like a substantial Presbyterian church, but which Gill knew to be the Stevenson Lighthouse. Salina had talked to potential dive boats in the area and found a crew she liked. They'd helped her arrange permission with the nature reserve managing the island and would ferry her crew and supplies. The plan was to have a day on the island as orientation, and then the RIB would return the following day with Ellie and Tom. Ellie would dive with Salina while Tom acted as their safety guy. Gill had no particular skills to offer so would just be tagging along for the ride, though he planned to stay on the island for a few days to do more research.

The RIB slowed as it reached the northern tip of the island. Low-lying and battered by aeons of storms, the only inhabitants to greet them were a few dozen grey seals that lazed by the water's edge or bobbed in the water, their black eyes indignant at the boat's arrival.

Moving south, towards the main body of the isle, vertical cliffs of black basalt rose to over one hundred feet high, creating an impenetrable wall of rock along most of the island. The top half was stained white with guano which blighted the air with the smell of ammonia. The lower half plunged deep into the pale green water. And everywhere there were birds; on the water, on the cliffs, crisscrossing the sky like a scene from a sci-fi movie; their cries a cacophony of competition.

'Have you ever dived here before?' shouted John, their skipper, over the noise.

'Never', yelled Salina. 'Do we have time for a quick survey?'

'Sure. I'll get you in nice and close.'

As the boat throttled back, Gill was suddenly alarmed by what the skipper meant when he said, "close". Soon they were idling along, near enough for Gill to reach out and brush the rock surface. All around them, puffins were flying with great effort on short wings, or bobbing in rafts with other small auks. He knew from his research the breeding season was just getting underway, and soon, a quarter of a million seabirds would be nesting on this thin island less than a mile long.

'You've typically got twenty metres depth up against the cliff, increasing to thirty when you're a stone's throw from the island', said John. 'But take care when diving. In places, it drops to forty metres a little way off.'

'I've read there are dozens of wrecks', said Salina. 'Do they concentrate in any particular place?'

'No. They're dotted all over. Nothing very big mind you. This isn't Scapa Flow.'

'Will the seals be a problem?' Gill asked, nodding at one particularly large bull seal shadowing the progress of the boat, matching it for speed just a short distance back.

'Nah', said Salina. 'They're just curious.'

'Very abundant at the moment', said John. 'They've had a few really good years.'

While John and Salina fell into a technical conversation about diving, Gill stared around him. The Bass Rock and Tantallon Castle lay eight miles to the southwest, while Edinburgh was visible in the clear light, forty miles due west. The nearest coastal landmarks were Crail and Fife Ness, but even they were five miles away to the north. This realisation led Gill to a sudden sense of vulnerability. Sitting out here in an open boat, you were a long way from anywhere and his picture postcard image of this island masked a brooding, far-flung place.

Eventually the noise of the birds forced the three of them into companionable silence as the boat slid past a couple of sea stacks – giant slivers of black rock, split away from the cliff surface to expose dark caves behind. As they approached the southern tip, a small shingle beach offered the only break in the cliffs before the island rose again, raising great knuckles of rock to shake in anger at the distant Lothian coastline.

'Big current in here', said John as the boat traversed noticeably rougher water around the South Ness of the isle. 'Same on the north side. The island acts like a stone in the middle of a fast-moving river. It can be calm as you like in the middle but around here, you can feel the water moving beneath you like a high-speed conveyor belt.'

The eastern side of the island seemed more hospitable. The high cliffs gave way to a rocky coastline that hemmed in several low hills of sparse grazing. If anything, the water was even deeper on this side and Salina stood scowling at the depth sounder. 'We'll never be able to free dive in water like this', she muttered. 'I'm hoping for better when we hit the target zone.'

Gill nodded and passed the skipper his phone. 'Can you take us to these coordinates?'

The boat accelerated for a few minutes until they approached the northern tip again, almost completing their circumnavigation. The skipper studied the screen while he moved his vessel into position. They were back in fast-flowing water, but this time they were fighting against the outgoing tide and the long RIB pitched and bucked as it rode out a never-ending series of outsize waves.

Immediately, Gill began to feel unwell.

'There's a ridge on the seabed right below us', called John over the sloshing of the waves. 'The tide hits the ridge and forces lots of energy to the surface. I'd say this is just about the most dangerous spot around the whole island.'

'Brilliant', Salina muttered without enthusiasm. 'And depth thirty metres. Not far off the maximum I'm prepared to do without specialist gear.'

'We won't take unnecessary risks', said Gill, lifting his face from the screen as nausea started to rear up inside him. 'If you don't like it, we'll find another way.'

'We've booked the boat time and the forecast is good', said Salina. 'But it's absolutely critical we do this at slack water. If I misjudge this dive, my mouldy remains will wash up in Denmark.'

Gill gripped the console as a large wave pushed the boat backwards and sideways. 'Any chance we could go now?' he asked, slowly losing the will to live.

John laughed and threw the boat into a one-hundred-and-eighty-degree turn. 'Back to your seats, please. Let's get you folks ashore.'

He powered back to the southern tip and then executed another turn. Gill could see a second lighthouse in the lee of the eastern hill, plus a smattering of other buildings, but no sign of a harbour. He found himself gripping his seat as the boat seemed to accelerate towards a clutch of high rocks. He was just about to call out in alarm when a narrow channel materialised; a natural fissure reaching into the body of the island.

A minute later the boat was idling in a lagoon of deep water, near a sandy beach just big enough for a single picnic rug. Somehow detached from the restless movement of the sea, this peaceful place, decorated by high strands of kelp in clear water, reaching lazily up from the seabed to greet them. And all around, every form of local wildlife; birds, fish and seals, went about their business. With his nausea rapidly subsiding, Gill watched the skipper tie up to a sturdy concrete jetty. He clapped Gill on the shoulder as he went to fix the stern line. 'Welcome to the Isle of May. You can kiss the jetty if you like, but please don't puke in my boat.'

Gill and Salina carried a waterproof holdall each, plus a bag of provisions for their stay. As Gill waved to the reversing RIB, Salina unzipped her bag and extracted two black baseball caps, pulling one over her hair, and coiling the longer strands out of sight. With this done, she passed the other cap to Gill.

'Never seen you wear one of these before', he said. 'Not sure it suits you.'

She smirked and bent her knees to pick up both holdalls. 'You've never been to a proper bird sanctuary before, have you?'

'I think they make us look like special ops.'

Salina was already walking. 'Just put it on, Gill.'

Reluctantly, Gill complied, before stooping to lift the heavy bag of provisions. Salina was a few metres ahead of him and from nowhere, small white birds were rising up from the ground. With little angular bodies and jerky flying motion, they looked like colour-reversed bats.

'Mind where you put your feet', she called back to him, as the first bird to dive-bomb him impacted his shoulder.

'Hey!' yelled Gill, as several more birds clipped his head and body. But Salina was just laughing and striding away. Freeing one hand to wave at the cloud of small angry birds, he lugged the heavy bag, eventually joining Salina where the path turned uphill. A woman in her mid-twenties stood with a battered luggage trolley and a smile on her face. Wearing khaki clothes and a brimmed hat, she had the ruddy face and brawny physique of some who spent their working life outdoors.

'You came prepared', she said, nodding at Salina's baseball cap.

'You never, ever forget your first tern colony', said Salina. 'What do you think, Gill?'

'Nasty wee buggers', muttered Gill, checking his new cap for stains and damage.

'Salina Ahmed', she said, offering the woman her hand.

'Lillian Black. We spoke on the phone.'

'And this is Gill. He's not having a great day so it might be an hour or two until he finds his legs.'

Lillian moved to help Salina with their luggage. 'You'll be staying at the Low Light, otherwise known as the Observatory, or *obs* for short. Whatever name you call it, it's the smaller of our two lighthouses and lies on the eastern slope. I've got you booked for seven nights. Is that right?'

'Aye. Though I might leave earlier when we've completed our dive', said Salina.

'No gear?' asked Lillian.

'The rest of the team is bringing it on the RIB tomorrow.'

'Excellent. We're a small crew at the moment before the season properly gets underway. But come on up and I'll introduce you to whoever is around.'

Gill let Lillian and Salina lead while he followed with the trolley. The physical effort required to drag it up the rough track helped settle his stomach and he started to think about what he wanted to achieve with the remaining daylight.

'We've a French couple staying who were very insistent they should get a room to themselves, so to avoid a diplomatic incident, I've surrendered the ranger's room to them', said Lillian as she finished a whistlestop tour of the hostel converted from the old lighthouse. 'We haven't opened the accommodation on Fluke Street yet, so that leaves two bedrooms we've split into men's and women's dorms. Gill, you've got Ryan and Carlos who are both PhD students who arrived a few days ago. Salina, you've got me I'm afraid. I'll try not to snore. Oh, and we have three birders coming in tomorrow. They're staying for a few days to help us catalogue the migrants on their way north.'

'Migrants?' repeated Gill.

'Birds', mouthed Salina to Gill. 'Not refugees.'

Gill winked his thanks at her. 'Lillian. Where can we find the priory remains?'

Lillian thought for a second. 'I think they're close to where you landed. They're hard to spot until you know where to look.'

'And you probably didn't notice them because the terns were trying to eat your head', Salina added.

'Are we free to move around the island without any restrictions?'

'You are, but the same rules apply to you as to any visitor. Be mindful of the high drops on the west cliffs, and make sure you avoid nesting birds. The puffins are reopening or digging fresh burrows at the moment, so you'll only be safe if you stick to the paths. Are you planning to go anywhere in particular?'

'North Ness' said Salina. 'We're planning a dive there tomorrow and I want to study how the sea moves.'

'I can confirm it moves actively up and down and vigorously side to side at the same time', muttered Gill.

'Okay. We normally exclude visitors from that area as the terrain is extremely rough. Again, stick to the paths, such as they are, and avoid any behaviour that might disturb the seals. They like to sunbathe around there.'

Gill glanced at the cloud-capped sky. He didn't think it looked like sunbathing weather. 'Okay. We'll head out shortly and get a feel for the place.'

'We normally cook together around 6 pm', said Lillian, glancing at a bottle of wine poking out of Salina and Gill's provisions bag. 'You'll be welcome to muck in.'

'Absolutely', said Salina. 'We'll see you then.'

Feeling fully recovered, Gill started to enjoy the lonely beauty of this place. Hand in hand, he and Salina walked the circumference of the island in a clockwise direction, taking in views of the island and laughing as they dodged the terns to wander amongst the stones of the old priory. When Gill thought of a ruined abbey, he pictured the broken ribs of a multi-storey building reaching into the sky to honour the God it once served. But the building on the Isle of May wasn't large and had never been grand. Although the island had no shortage of rock, the hard basalt was unforgiving as a building material. A single low building made from scavenged beach stones formed the heart of the old priory. Gill tried to visualise the place at its prime, in the days before the Vikings, and later, as religion changed and new expressions of Christianity made their impacts on the pilgrim community.

'Folk used to come here from the mainland in large numbers', said Gill. 'They'd row in little boats, or sail. Just to sit at the feet of the old saints.'

Salina was staring at the distant Fife coastline, appearing at this distance as just a slim ribbon of land. 'What do you think they got out of the experience?'

Gill shrugged. 'You gotta wonder. Maybe some sense of having paid their dues. Or an expression of devotion. They had so little compared to us and yet took their faith so seriously.'

'Or was it just a sense of duty that obliged them to come out here?'

'I dunno. You'd have to have a good reason to want to make that journey.'

'Ready for the high cliffs?' said Salina. 'As well as being a fearless sailor, I know you've a wonderful head for heights.'

'Do we have to?' said Gill, pulling her close to him.

'You do realise I've discovered your secret?' she said, brushing the tip of his nose with her own.

'And what's that?'

'In your heart of hearts, you're not much of an adventurer.'

'So, you've found me out', he said slowly, returning her smile. 'Maybe it's time for me to hang up my gloves at

Mys.Scot. I could chat to the guy who edits the hobby mags and see if he'd like a swap.'

Salina's eyes flicked up and right. 'In your job, he wouldn't last a fortnight. Best you stick with it a while longer.'

Gill squeezed her hand. 'So, the high cliffs it is. Come on then. I'll look after you.'

Clear of the tern colony, Salina pulled off the cap and let her long black hair wash behind her as they started walking towards the island's high points. But they hadn't taken ten steps when a puffin dashed out of a burrow close to Gill's left foot. It bit him swiftly on the ankle then shot back underground. He leapt out of the way and promptly lost his balance. Falling on wet grass, he contemplated the hard colourful beak of another little bird as it appeared from a different hole less than a metre from his head. Gill flinched into a sitting position and rubbed his ankle while staring up at Salina's laughing face. 'Everything on this damn island wants to eat me!'

'Thinking about the hobby mags', giggled Salina. 'You'd probably get run over by a model train.'

Once he was back on his feet and dusted down, they proceeded with care along the cliff top. Occasionally they crept to the edge so they could peer down into the inky-blue water the RIB had carried them through a few hours before. Gripping Salina's hand tightly, Gill deflected her taunts until the path took them away from the water's edge and down a slope towards the North Ness. Here the going became slower, picking their way through boulders as they followed an intermittent path. Their final approach to the sea was blocked by a clutch of seals. Deciding they had the numbers on their side to resist the incomers, the seals brayed until Gill and Salina retreated a few steps.

'This is the ridge we saw on the RIB's sounder', said Salina, serious again while she pointed at a digital map of the seabed on her phone. 'You can see all these fissures in the seabed where the volcanic rock is eroding.'

'Makes me wonder', said Gill. 'With a map like this, why do we need to dive at all? Can't we see the wreck on the seabed?'

Salina shook her head. 'No chance.'

Gill tapped the map with the nail of a small finger. 'That's as near as we can estimate to where the lightning went in. Right where the fissures give way to this extended ridge.'

Salina nodded and tapped the map. 'Might work in our favour. Ellie and I can enter the water here where it's relatively shallow, then follow this channel to the target point in the hope of getting some protection from the current.'

'Sal, are you sure you want to do this?'

She tossed her hair from side to side. 'I'm here, aren't I? And I have the skills and the necessary back up crew. So don't worry.'

'What's your exit strategy if the current is too strong for you?'

'Our new kit allows voice comms between the active divers. Ellie and I will stick together, and if we don't like the conditions, we'll rise to the surface together at the safest possible rate. Tom can pick us up in the RIB.'

'But the current will carry you, what, hundreds of metres?'

'Tom has a microphone in the water. He won't be able to speak to us, but we can speak to him. We'll give him our speed and direction, before inflating a safety buoy just before we surface.'

Gill shook his head.

'What?' said Salina.

'Nothing scares you.'

She patted him on his chest as she turned to leave. 'Nothing that's under my control scares me. That's the difference.'

Chapter 21

Gill woke early the following morning. In the distance, and all around him, he could hear screaming. As his waking mind decoded the sounds, he remembered Fort William. While it no longer traumatised him, his memory was easily jogged by the chaos wrought by the Great Glen disaster. It was as if his mind was preparing him to walk those troubled streets once again. But then he rubbed his eyes and saw the bunk above his head. He heard sleeping sounds from his roommates and remembered where he was. Before they'd gone to bed the night before, he'd been warned about this. The screams he realised were the cries of thousands of gulls, rising from their night-time roosts to fly off the island and forage across Scotland's central belt. While the local auks, terns and gannets still ate their age-old diet of fish, the gulls had long since switched to food discarded by humans.

It was cold in the room, and he needed the bathroom, so reluctantly, he swung his legs out of bed and sat for a moment. The craic last night had been good. The three established staff seemed happy to have new faces around their table and the first bottle of wine had become two. Gill hadn't minded. Alcohol he realised helped break the ice between new housemates and because there was now only one bottle left, it wasn't a stunt they could pull every night.

And the nearest shop was ... unreachable. Nevertheless, his throat was dry and he needed to make some tea. Then he'd sit for a while, enjoying the daily ritual he'd nursed since faith had stomped its footprints onto his early morning routine.

He used his toes to drag his walking boots towards him, his right foot slipping in easily, but the left impeded by a sock or some other debris. Except it couldn't be a sock because the obstruction was moving. Gill lifted the boot and in his sleepy state, shook the contents into the palm of his hand. Two mice tumbled out, sniffing and rubbing against each other until one fell and scuttled away. The second made a move to dart up Gill's sleeve, but he took it by the tail and let it hang for a few moments. The mouse didn't seem particularly distressed, so Gill considered dropping it into Ryan's boot as petty revenge for his roommate's snoring. It was he decided, a rather unchristian thing to do. But funny, so he did it anyway.

He moved through to the empty kitchen and set an electric fire to warming the room before rustling around to make a pot of tea. He opened *The Book* on his phone and started to read. Some new aspect in the writing caught his attention, so he stood and contemplated its implications. As he did so, the impression of a sword slung across his back came powerfully. As an experiment, he went through the motions of drawing the blade and swinging from left to right, through defence and offence. He spent the next few minutes considering the context of the ancient words; what had been meant by the original writer, and what they said to him now, twenty-one centuries later. He chewed on the passage. What did it mean to him? How would he apply it? He swung the blade and wasn't especially surprised to look down and find the gleaming weapon fully visible in his hands. And for the first time, the experience didn't feel alien. He was contemplating this when the voice spoke. That small, quiet voice that so unnerved him in Dundee six months before, on the day when it first broke into his senses. He'd researched the concept later and concluded the voice was either a benevolent form of psychosis, or the onset of a brain tumour, or quite simply, the voice of God. On the balance of probabilities, given that he was neither dead, nor judged insane, he'd decided it was the latter. And today, the voice spoke again through the words he'd just read. It reassured him. And it urged him. And in a world burdened by so much hatred, it reminded him he was loved. Fifteen minutes later, as Gill sheathed his sword, he was aware his hands were trembling.

A scream from Salina brought him out of his reverie. He was on his feet instantaneously and at the threshold of the women's dorm within seconds. He found Salina, partially dressed, on her hands and knees in the centre of the room.

'What the hell', she shouted as she shook out her boots. Two mice spilt out of one boot and three from the other. The drama should have finished there as four of the mice dashed towards hiding places in disparate parts of the room. But the fifth darted up her arm and seemed to be heading for her hair. Salina squealed and swiped at it. Compelled to intervene, Gill reached down and grabbed the creature by the tail while Salina swept her shaking hands across her face. Holding the mouse far away from her, he used his free arm to pull Salina towards him. Held in this clumsy half hug, Salina's chest rapidly rose and fell until, eventually, she calmed down.

Once she'd recovered, Gill dangled the mouse in front of her wild, hair-strewn eyes, and whispered lovingly, 'If you're gonna keep this one, did you want to give it a name?'

Three hours later, Gill was helping Salina make final checks on her diving gear while Tom did the same for Ellie. They were joking with each other, Ellie's eyes sparkling at her boyfriend through a mane of wet blond hair. Behind them, John was preparing the RIB to go back to sea.

'Can we have one last check of the comms before we dive for real?' Ellie asked.

'Salina can tell you about her wildlife encounter', suggested Gill.

'Piss off', muttered Salina, hiding an embarrassed smile as she turned to face Ellie. 'Because we have our air regulators between our teeth, we can't do much more than mumble at each other. We need to stick to clear actions words, like Stop, Proceed, Up, Down, Danger, and the like.' She made a gesture with her hands. 'We'll use spoken words to accompany the core list of hand signals.'

'Do you have a hand signal for, Mouse?' said Gill, sending his right hand scurrying up her arm.

Salina grasped his middle fingers and Gill winced as she bent them back to their limit.

'Be nice', she said. 'Or we'll tie you up and leave you to the terns.'

She released him and nodded to Ellie. 'Let's jump in and give it a try.'

Gill watched from the concrete ramp as the women got into the water and settled a metre down amongst the kelp.

Tom meanwhile climbed into the RIB and lowered a microphone into the water. His head drifted from side to side, seeming unimpressed by the sounds, as if the women each had a pencil clenched between their teeth. Soon they were up again, climbing a metal ladder into the boat.

Salina glanced at her watch. It was twenty minutes until the start of the dive window. 'Better get a move on. Gill, are you coming or staying?'

'I'm going to jog over to the North Ness and watch from there. I'd rather risk the seals than experience death-by-seasickness.'

He left them, huddling around Tom in his role as dive leader, as he reiterated the dive plan and the safety protocols. Gill leaned into the hill climb, hoping to achieve his typical ten-minute mile. In the event, the combined hazards of terns, puffin burrows and antisocial seals meant it took him twice as long to get close to the water at the north end of the island. By then the RIB had been over the target location for several minutes and Salina was getting ready to dive.

'You okay?' Salina asked Ellie.

'Good. You?'

Salina pursed her lips and forced herself to nod.

'Are you sure? You don't look brilliant. Boyfriend trouble?'

Salina stared back into Ellie's kind eyes. 'What? No! If he hadn't rescued me from the mice, I'd still be screaming like a Banshee. It's this violent piece of water. Very unsettling.'

'Better underneath. Shall we go?'

Salina nodded. Then they masked up, and after an all-clear from Tom, dropped backwards into the water. As she waited for the bubbles to scatter, Salina shook herself. Sitting on the edge of the boat, getting ready to deploy, she'd grown nervous. Not that she was losing her taste for this kind of work. Simply that the two biggest scares she'd had on dives occurred while working with Gill McArdle. And the implication? Be ready for anything.

She paused at three metres depth to let Ellie get alongside her, then using hand signals, indicated they'd begin their descent. A few minutes later, they were in ten metres of water, close to the island, and eighty metres from the target zone. Water clarity was excellent, and she could see the eroded foundations of the island stretching into the inky blackness in a northerly direction. What was strange was the noise. Most of her dives had been in still water where the only sound was splashes and bubbles. But here, with millions of tonnes of water squeezing past the rocky island, the sea sounded like the roar of a busy motorway.

A pair of seals joined them, one gliding so close that Ellie could extend her hand and let it slide along the creature's back. This was their domain, and she knew from many previous dives their relentless curiosity could be as intrusive as the little kid who attaches herself to you at a party.

A shoal of tiny fish sped over their heads, pursued by a smaller shoal of mackerel. The seals sped off to try their luck, while from above, a dozen puffins whirled down from the surface, using shards of sunlight as cover, they used their short wings to propel them towards their prey.

On her signal, they started to move horizontally. Salina indicated to Ellie that they would skim the kelp beds, staying just above the oily leaves and any hazards they might hide. She was looking for the rock fissure, a natural channel just deep enough to protect them from the current. Even though they were diving at low tide, she could feel the water pressing against her. First one way, then the other, as the old tide finished draining out of the Firth of Forth and the new one bristled at the mouth of the North Sea, anxious to begin the process of pushing millions of tonnes of water back into the channel.

They were in the fissure now and Salina could see the kelp on the higher rocks leaning against the new tide. 'Current. West', she said, for Tom's benefit rather than Ellie's. If they needed to finish the dive early, it would help him know where to look.

'Wreck. Ahead', said Ellie.

She was right, though Salina hadn't seen it herself. A vessel, of twenty metres or thereabouts was discernible as a shape amidst the kelp. A metal boat – possibly war era. It wasn't in their target zone, so they passed above it. In the days before GPS and radar, the May Isle had been a hazard for any unwary sailor who didn't know these waters.

Leaving the wreck behind, the seabed lost its rock features and steepened dramatically. Salina continued their descent. Nitrogen narcosis would become a hazard once they dropped below thirty metres, and they weren't far off that already. The kelps were gone, with insufficient light to support their growth and now a fine silt ran up amongst the visible rocks.

They switched on their lights and Salina checked how far they were from the target area. She informed Ellie it was another thirty metres and used her arm to indicate the direction. This was the most difficult moment in the dive. The strengthening current would soon have enough force to start pushing them along, hindering their chance of hitting their target location.

Ellie's sharp eyes spotted another feature on the seabed. A black cable thicker than her thigh was converging with their direction of travel. A strip of double yellow lines woven around the cable body signified its likely purpose. Salina flipped over to it and started to follow, knowing it would offer her a grip point if the current got too strong. She needed to stay close to the sea bed. The vintage of Gill's wreck meant that very little would be visible. An old wooden rib or some debris would be a valuable find, though in the deepening mud, even that was unlikely.

She stopped to let Ellie catch up. They had ten minutes left on their dive clock and were less than ten metres from their goal. But they were approaching another ledge and beyond that, the deep black water yielded nothing to their torch beams.

Five metres, and they followed the cable along the top of the ridge. It was touch and go if the target point was going to be on the plateau or below the ledge. The black cable they followed seemed to hold to the top of the ridge despite the suck of gravity pulling it into the darkness.

'Wreck', came Ellie's voice.

The darkness here was oppressive. As their beams crisscrossed an obstacle right in front of them, Salina had the sense of a huge industrial pipe discarded at sea. Almost circular, it was substantial – as high as a two-storey house.

The open pipe looked damaged as the inside revealed equipment and scattered debris within the structure. Moving closer, Salina could see the hull was laced through with old-fashioned rivets, suggesting it was early twentieth century. Adding to the mystery, the object had strange circular portholes distributed at intervals along its length. Running along it and trying not to disturb any silt, Salina could see the pipe tapered at its undamaged end, and that's when she realised she was looking at the wreck of a submarine.

Glancing at her watch, she turned to Ellie and indicated two minutes. It was a tiny amount of time to try to find something of value. While the submarine was unexpected, she doubted it was useful to Gill. Controlling her agitated breathing, she signed to Ellie they would make one traverse of the wreck, taking photos on Ellie's camera. She could see now why the black cable didn't slide off over the ledge as it was snagged around the tail of the wreckage. Beyond it, the cable swung sharply eastwards and down into the deep water. Ellie was scraping at the base of the sub and Salina suppressed her frustration at the rising clouds of silt, blowing away to the west like smoke from a fire on a windy day. And moments later the alarm in her watch was vibrating. It was time to go. She tapped Ellie on the shoulder and ordered their ascent. Ellie nodded, pointing at something clutched in her hand. Salina had no time to see for herself. She checked her depth gauge and spoke once into the mic for Tom to hear.

'Rising.'

Chapter 22

Relief surged in Gill as he saw Salina's safety buoy pop up. During their controlled ascent, the current had pushed them one hundred metres west of the target point, but John was already guiding the RIB in their direction. As Tom's distant figure stooped to help one of the women clamber back into the boat, he raised a hand to Gill to signal all was well. Gill was getting used to the presence of the seals, but even in his rush to get back to Salina, he gave them a wide berth. He was already jogging over the high point of the island when the RIB overtook him on its way back to the tiny harbour.

'Well. How does it look', he asked five minutes later as he helped secure a line.

'Complicated', said Salina.

'You found something then?'

Ellie passed him a sealed plastic bag containing a dark fragment of wood. 'We might have found your wreck', she said.

Gill felt elation spill onto his face.

'Don't get excited', warned Salina, before casting around the crew to check they had time for a cup of tea together before the RIB needed to head back.

'Fancy one?' Gill asked John.

He shook his head. 'Need to make another run. I've got a couple of birders paying good money to make it to the island tonight. I'll get your crew on the return leg in two hours' time.'

'Ooh. Terns! They're so cute', cried Ellie, already wandering up the concrete ramp. 'Can anyone lend me a hat?'

Back at the *obs*, Salina opened up a map of the seabed on her pad. 'We followed this ravine until the feature was lost to the silt. There's a small wreck quite close to the island. Something pre-war like a fishing vessel. Soon after that our path converged with a major electricity cable.'

'Nothing like that on the map', observed Tom.

'No, but it does show one three hundred metres to the east. It carries power from the new wind farm to the Lothian coastline.'

'You think the map is wrong?'

'I know the map is wrong', said Salina. 'Looks like the cable is in the wrong place. When you think about it, it's far too close to the island.'

'And that's not all', said Ellie. 'There's a submarine wreck right on the target zone. The power cable is snagged around the tail.'

'It's primitive', added Salina. 'I googled it on the trip back. There was some kind of incident involving First World War subs in this area. A couple were lost.'

'And it's sitting on our target?' said Gill.

Salina turned to face him. 'Maybe the submarine is your target. If the lightning you observed was atmospheric discharge, then maybe it interacted with the iron hull of the old sub.'

'But you have some wood?' said Gill.

'There is some kind of structure underneath the sub', said Ellie. 'Probably a wreck. I took this from the most prominent part.'

'I didn't see anything', said Salina. 'It might just be debris.'

'I've got some photos', said Ellie. 'I'll mail them to you.'

'I'll get the wood sample to the lab tomorrow', offered Tom. 'Get an age at least. Maybe the tree species if we're lucky.'

Salina nodded. 'And we need to report the cable. Its interaction with the submarine doesn't look healthy.'

'Okay', said Gill, wondering what he could conclude from their findings. 'Do you think you've done all you can do for now, or do you want to have another crack tomorrow?'

'The conditions down there aren't great', said Salina. 'The sub looks like it wouldn't take much to send it sliding off into the depths. I think we should test the wood and make a plan after that.'

'And the weather forecast has deteriorated for the next few days', said Tom. 'We could come out here and find it wasn't safe to dive.'

'Okay. Let's leave it there. Do you guys want to stay over? Talking to John, he's out here most days for one thing or another.'

'East Neuk fish and chips', said Tom without missing a beat.

'Actually, that sound good', said Salina.

A rush of disappointment hit Gill. 'You're not thinking of going back?'

'I've done what I came out here to do. As much as I'd like another campfire cook-up, Chez Lillian, I think I've earned my ticket home.' She peered at him and drew the fingers of her left hand through his hair. 'Are you very upset?'

Gill did feel a little short-changed. 'I need to take a day or two to research the priory. It's much easier to write when you're working in situ. I thought we could hang out.'

Salina leaned close to his face and kissed his cheek. 'This morning, there were mice in my boots, Gill. Mice! In my sleeves. My hair.'

'Ah, Salina Ahmed', he sighed theatrically. 'I think I've found your kryptonite.'

She nodded soberly. 'I've swum with whale sharks, had an Orca attack my sub, and had glass eels burrow into my wetsuit. All of those were a breeze compared to this morning.'

'Then go, with my thanks and blessing', he said, smiling. 'Oh. and Sal?'

'Yes?'

'Enjoy the chips.'

The RIB that arrived to collect Salina, Tom and Ellie had a different skipper. He didn't introduce himself and seemed to be in a hurry to offload three new visitors in return for Salina's crew and all their gear.

'Hope you've got your sea legs, folks', was all he said by way of greeting. 'Getting a bit lively out there.'

Gill glanced at the sky. He hadn't seen the sun for days and although the westerly wind had freshened, it didn't seem particularly bad. He waved Salina off, consoling himself that even if he had cut and run, the last thing he'd have felt like arriving on terra firma was a plate of fried food.

He made himself useful, helping the new arrivals lug their gear up to the obs. Their leader was an older man called Colin Milne; a regular on the island and a one-time trustee of the group that ran the nature reserve. With him, came two burly west coasters – fellow birders who had volunteered to sit out in all weathers and record the seasonal avian changing of the guard.

'I'm Lillian', said the warden, introducing herself to the new arrivals.

Colin shook her hand. 'Sorry, when we spoke, I thought we'd come across each other a few years back. But now we're face to face, I realise we haven't met.'

Lillian briefly looked embarrassed. 'I'm a contractor. I dot around.'

'That'll be it', said Colin. 'I'll have come across your name at a different reserve.'

'Aye', said Lillian.

A brief technical discussion broke out between the three new arrivals and the PhD students who were already one week into their deployment. Everyone was studying migration and there were opportunities to combine aspects of their work. This wasn't Gill's bag, so he returned to the priory and wandered amongst the stones until it was time to cook.

Lillian was boiling an immense cauldron of pasta when he returned. She gathered the occupants and told them to enjoy it as it was or augment it from their own supplies, giving Gill cause to say a silent thank you to Salina for including a jar of pesto. The remaining bottle of Gill's wine had already disappeared and although no one owned up, he suspected the two new birders, Mick and Monty, had enjoyed an aperitif. These new arrivals were both delivery drivers for a living, and although they exuded masculine confidence, they were utterly without opinions on any conversational topic Gill tried to throw at them. They ate their food in a business-like fashion, washed up, and then announced they were having an early night.

Colin was another hard man to draw in conversation. Gill was about to give up when he mentioned a "sparrow" he'd seen down by the priory, mooching around the stones for either food or shelter from the strengthening wind. That prompted Colin, Ryan and Carlos to ask a flurry of questions. Precisely, how big was it? Exactly what markings did it carry? Was its beak finch-like or long and fine? After Gill had described it and struggled to articulate its flight pattern, the ice was well and truly broken. The French couple quickly bored and went to bed, prompting Colin to produce a bottle of supermarket whisky for them all to share. The craic was good for a while until Colin started a long discourse on the 2022 bird flu and its continuing echoes in the wild bird population. By this stage in the evening, the old gent could talk for Scotland and eventually Gill excused himself and went to bed.

Chapter 23

The new day started with mice in his boots. If he was going to stay here much longer, he'd have to figure out a strategy to deter them. When he questioned Lillian about it later, she admitted the buildings were rife with them.

'Have you considered pest control?'

'Actually, we're a nature conservancy', she observed dryly.

Gill nodded his understanding. He reasoned the timorous wee beasties had more right to be on the island than the human visitors.

Stepping outside, he found the wind had risen overnight, swinging to the south and bringing a deluge of rain. He attempted a brief foray down to the priory, but in these conditions, it wasn't safe to be outside. Giant waves pounded the normally calm lagoon with its concrete jetty, rendering it just another inaccessible piece of coastline.

'Rather exciting', said Colin as Gill struggled back into the common room and ditched his rain jacket. 'I gather we have a storm coming.'

'Coming?' said Gill.

'Oh aye', muttered Lillian from where she sat hunched over her phone. 'You haven't seen a storm until you've seen a storm from a tiny island.'

Gill glanced out periodically as the wind rose. The rain was hard and almost horizontal. From the safety of the lighthouse, it looked like it could simply lift him and toss him into the sea. The French couple asked Lillian to call the RIB so they could leave. And Lillian just laughed apologetically.

A little later, the wind swung back to the west and howled at the island. Seeking human company, Gill joined everyone else in the common room. The compact rectangular space had white-painted roughcast walls and a motley collection of old furniture. Two small windows let a little light into the room, though only one of these faced the sea. And the only mod-con was an ancient TV that didn't seem to work.

'I need to close the Heligoland trap', said Lillian to the room. 'Anybody fancy giving me a hand?'

Gill had noticed the nets near the priory. The rangers used them to trap migrant birds so they could be recorded and released. Normally just an inconvenience to the birds, the nets could be potentially fatal in this wind.

'We'll help', said Mick, tapping the dozing Monty on his shoulder.

'I can too', Gill offered.

'Three's plenty', Lillian replied. 'But do us a favour and put the kettle on the moment we get in.'

The three were gone half an hour. They returned, soaked to the skin, despite their top-of-the-range waterproofs.

'Take a look outside', said Lillian. 'We've got company.'

They took it in turns using the tiny window to peer out over the sea. A massive vessel, the length of two football pitches and the width of one was creeping into the wind shadow cast by the island. From multiple cranes and gantries, the vessel spewed harsh industrial light.

'What the hell is that?' asked Mick.

'Construction platform for the new wind farm', said Colin. 'That ship creates the foundations that sit on the sea floor.'

'The thing's barely moving, even in this storm.'

'It'll be moving all right. I gather it's got quite an unpleasant motion in a storm. It's been up close to the island during a few spells of bad weather.'

Gill's turn came to look out upon the gigantic metal beast. Two massive cranes sat at one end of the vessel, themselves at least as high as the May Isle. Indeed, the whole effect was like a separate man-made island coming alongside. He watched as giant anchors started to deploy from two corners of the platform, chains as thick as a family car dropping slowly into the sea.

'Never seen it do that before', said Colin. 'Must be planning a long stay.'

Gill considered the impact each one of those anchors could have on the sea bed and shuddered. Here he was looking for a thousand-year-old shipwreck, while all around him, weather and mechanised humanity were conspiring to make its ancient wood an ephemeral thing. Gill moved away from the window to allow the French couple a turn and found Lillian staring at a gaping tear in her rain gear.

'Wondered why I'd got so wet', she muttered. 'Must have caught it on a nail.'

'Sorry about that', said Gill. 'I hate losing a good jacket. Does Amazon deliver out here?'

'Must be joking', said Lillian. 'But yeah, I don't think this can be patched.'

The following day saw the rain ease but if anything, the wind got stronger. Gill risked a walk up onto the top of the island and stood in the shade of the modern Stevenson Lighthouse, watching the sea. The waves were large, but it was the underlying movement that caught Gill's eyes as if the Firth of Forth was rendered down to a bowl in the lap of the gods; the water tilting from side to side in a motion that made him feel seasick on land. On top of that, huge waves were passing, and upon these, the furious wind tore ripples into the water's surface. But even in this explosion of natural energy, the seabirds continued to fish. Small groups rafted on the surface and individuals swooped through the spray as water ripped from the sea's surface was flung in the air so that the whole scene was a mist of hurtling seawater.

Returning to the *obs*, he found Lillian putting on her damaged gear. 'Nothing for it', she said when she saw his expression.

'You'll be drenched', said Gill. 'Borrow mine.'

'You sure?'

'Aye. The rain's stopped but the spray still makes it feel like a car wash. But can you do me a favour?'

'Aye. What?'

'Can I borrow the key to the tower? I need to make a bunch of calls. I can't sit outside and there's no reception in the common room.'

Lillian reached up into a wall-mounted box and took several long seconds to select a bunch of keys. 'Thanks for the jacket. You're a star.'

After Lillian left, Gill put on a fleece and gathered his laptop and phone. His workspace for the day was to be the bulb at the top of the old lighthouse. Just a few steps from the hostel, the modest tower had a metal staircase attached to its inner walls. No longer illuminated, the mechanism dismantled, the space offered Gill room to spread out his gear and make himself comfortable. His first call was to Salina.

'Morning, castaway.'

'Don't joke. It's foul out here. They reckon it will be at least another day until they can get a RIB into the channel. The French are doing their nut.'

'What about you? Still communing with nature?'

'Nothing has tried to eat me today, so far. Oh, and the mice say hi.'

Their conversation rattled back and forth for a few minutes until Salina switched to a few items of business. 'I spoke to someone at HM Government's Receiver of Wreck about the submarine. He immediately got defensive about it being a war grave and that it can't be disturbed.'

'Okay. Doesn't surprise me.'

'But then I spoke to someone managing the wind farm and explained about the cable. He was just as uppity and said the cable was at least half a kilometre east of the island. So I emailed him the photos that Ellie took. They have a GPS stamp, and to be fair, he phoned back later and apologized. Looks like the cable is in the wrong place.'

'How could that even happen?'

'He wasn't about to say. But I've heard of instances where a cable-laying ship gets stuck on station for a spell of bad weather. They end up dragging the cable like it's an inefficient anchor.'

'But at the end of the day. It's just another obstacle to stop us from seeing if there's anything left of the wreck.'

'Yeah. It's hard to see us getting any closer. Sorry, Gill.'

'No worry. The whole thing was speculative. And you were so brave. At least I won't hit Tony with a huge bill.'

'You sound quite relaxed about it.'

'I'm trapped on an island by a storm, Sal. I think I'm using most of my mental energy dealing with that.'

'Once you're back on terra firma you might figure another way to get at the wreck.'

'Aye. But I might need to put it on the back-burner for a while.'

They chatted for a few more minutes before Salina had to excuse herself to go on another call. As she hung up, Gill noticed he had a missed call from Arnold Broadbent. He reviewed what new information he had to impart, then dialled Arnold's number.

'How's it going, matey-boy? Figured out your lightning problem yet?'

'Maybe. We found an old sub, with a modern, heavy-duty electrical cable wrapped around its tail.'

'What? Like a proper submarine?'

'First World War wreck. Half of it at least. I've got photos; all rivets and iron plating.'

'Interesting.'

'Could that have attracted the lightning discharge?'

Arnold gave an unconvinced grunt. 'Sounds plausible. The electromagnetic field created by power running through the cable would be quite small. Mind you, if the power is only flowing one way, then a static charge could build up on the hull of the submarine. A bit like rubbing a balloon against your woolly jumper.'

'That sub represents a mighty big jumper', said Gill. 'Do you think the build-up of static could act as a draw for St Elmo's fire?'

Gill heard Arnold rubbing his stubble while he thought. 'A ball of free-floating plasma will either be attracted or repelled by other charged surfaces in the vicinity. So, yes. I think you've got a working theory there.'

'Great. Then I'm going to put that in my magazine. Can I quote you, Arnie?'

Arnold released a breath. 'It's not really my field. And I'm still struggling to find you a proper expert to break this down into logical cause and effect. But, yeah. Quote me. No one's ever going to prove I'm wrong.'

Arnold signed off and Gill absorbed this tentative information. It appeared Corrie's lightning might be a natural phenomenon after all. And if that was the case, had he utterly misinterpreted its appearance as some kind of divine signal? He doubted that. After all, they'd found a wreck, so this confluence of remarkable events still reeked of mystery. Yes, there were obstacles in his path but he had to conclude this story still had legs. Meanwhile, Salina's dive was over, and her crew was safely out of the water. He was grateful for that.

He glanced at the time and realised he was overdue for his next call. Taking a deep breath, he dialled his team in Dundee. He'd already reviewed their stream of emails. There was so much to do.

'Oh, you're here', said Colin as Gill stepped into the kitchen that lunchtime.

'Aye. Been working my office job while the storm does its thing. Was it you trying to reach me inside the lighthouse?'

Colin looked puzzled. 'No. I didn't realise you were up there.'

'No problem. It's just that someone gave the door a shake and I was on a call so couldn't go down and see who it was.'

'Not me.' Colin glanced around. 'It's like the Marie Celeste this morning. Ryan and Carlos are braving the weather, and the DuBlancs are hiding in their room. I haven't seen anyone else all morning.'

'Lillian went out about 9 am', said Gill. 'Off on her rounds. Not sure about the others.'

Colin looked at his watch. 'Well, I'm going to have some lunch. Would you like to join me?'

The hours passed, until Ryan and Carlos arrived back, wet and cold but enthused by the weather and whatever it was they were working on. When Mick and Monty came back a little while later, Mick did a strange thing – pausing at the door of the common room and staring at Gill for several seconds before moving on to the dorm. By 5 pm there was still no sign of Lillian. And Colin was getting concerned.

'It'll be dark soon. And it's not a big island. No way she should be out that long.'

'Should we search for her?'

'Might be best. I'll round everyone up.'

The group quickly arrived at a reluctant consensus they needed to search for Lillian. While Ryan and Carlos stayed behind to warm up, the DuBlancs were sent north, Mick and Monty took the middle part of the island, while Gill accompanied Colin, towards the South Ness. They shouted for Lillian, explored buildings, peered down into gullies and braved the gale by creeping to cliff edges. As the wind howled and the light faded to an angry darkness, they met back in the common room.

'Nothing', reported Gill. The other teams confirmed the same.

'We'll try again at first light', said Mick.

'Agreed', said Colin, now their de facto leader. 'But I think I need to alert the authorities.'

'I know it's unlikely, but is there any way she could have left the island?' asked Gill.

Colin thought. 'There's a small landing point on the northwest of the island, but it would be a death trap on a day like this. No, I think for now, we need to assume she's fallen and injured herself.'

'Shouldn't we keep looking?' said Ryan. 'We've got the torches we use for dazzling the birds.'

Colin shook his head. 'There's a serious threat to life if we start clambering around in this gale. The winds will peak over the next few hours, so it's best if we try in the morning.'

'We can't just leave her, so I'm going to try anyway', Carlos announced. 'I'll stick to the paths and listen out for her.'

He made for the door, but Monty stood up and blocked his way. 'Colin's got sense. What's wrong with you?'

Carlos stared at Monty, blinking in surprise. 'If she's injured, the next few hours will be critical.'

Monty looked away and sneered. 'Lillian strikes me as an outdoor kinda girl. I'm sure she doesn't need your help.'

'I'll go with him', said Ryan, standing beside Carlos.

'Let them go, Monty', said Mick, from where he lounged across a battered armchair, reading a bird-watching magazine. 'But if these kids want to risk getting lost in the storm, they need to know we'll not be looking for them this side of first light.'

Carlos turned to Colin. 'We'll be out for one hour, max.'

'I won't stop you', said Colin. 'Just try not to add to our problems.'

Mick and Monty settled in the common room chairs, forming a wall of indomitable silence, while the DuBlancs headed for the kitchen and started to prepare food. Gill meanwhile studied a detailed map of the island while Colin phoned the coastguard and reported Lillian was missing.

'They're reluctant to launch a lifeboat unless someone saw her go into the water', Colin reported. 'Assuming the wind dies down a bit, they'll launch in the morning.'

'What would Lillian have been doing?' asked Gill.

Colin shrugged. 'A quick glance around the infrastructure, such as it is. A few observations on how the weather is impacting the birds. She'd have gone out for a couple of hours, then come back and put it in the logbook. She should have been tucked up in the common room scrounging whisky from me by mid-afternoon.'

'She'd have stayed out in this, despite the risks?'

'As one of our approved rangers, she should know what she's doing. Anyway, she'll be survival trained, so if she's injured, she'll make the best of her situation knowing that help is on its way.'

The two men gathered around the map and looked for locations Lillian might be trapped. They were drawing up a list when Ryan stuck his head around the door. 'We've found something.'

Colin lent Gill some outdoor gear and together they stepped out into the gale. The wind had eased a little, though still strong enough to take Gill off his feet as they crossed the island. Ryan led them past the main lighthouse and across the thinnest of paths, snaking across open ground to a spot where Carlos lay on his belly, close to the cliff edge.

'There's a viewpoint across this gulley called The Mill Door', he shouted over the gale. 'Lillian mentioned it's her favourite spot on the island so it appears she's taken a tumble, or the wind caught her or something.'

They followed the direction of his torchlight until they made out an object, cloaked in the navy blue of Gill's rain jacket. Assuming it was Lillian, she was caught on a ledge, ten metres below the cliff and just a few metres above the reach of the waves crashing onto the rocks below.

'Any sign of life?' said Colin.

'She hasn't moved', said Carlos. 'Though she might be unconscious.'

'No way we can reach her without specialist equipment', said Ryan.

'Can't we use ropes?' asked Gill. 'You must have something back at the observatory.'

'I agree. We need to try', said Colin. It had started raining again and bullets of hard water roared up the rock face to hit their faces with the force of driven hail.

'Carlos and I will keep an eye on her', said Ryan. 'We'll wait to hear from you.'

'Agreed', said Colin. 'Let's aim ...' But he never completed his sentence. A huge wave boomed in the cove below them, throwing shards of cold water high into the air. They all buried their faces in their arms and waited for the torrent to pass. When they were able to see again, the blue-shrouded object had gone.

'Can't see her', yelled Carlos, as his beam crisscrossed the rock face.

'Can we get any lower?' shouted Gill.

'No', called Colin. 'Look, we're all suffering out here. Let's take it back to the *obs* and work out a plan from there.'

After a few more minutes of scanning back and forth, Gill, in his ill-fitting borrowed jacket couldn't help but agree. Reluctantly, the party edged back from the cliff line and threaded their way back to the security offered by the thick stone walls of the Low Light. Standing dripping in the kitchen, a sense of shock descended on the whole team.

'I need to call the coastguard again', said Colin. 'This will change things for them.'

'Don't', said Mick sharply, as Colin reached for his phone.

'Lillian is in trouble. She needs our immediate help.'

'If that was Lillian out there, then she's dead. You call a lifeboat out in these conditions, you risk killing everyone on board.'

'That's their decision', Colin spat. 'If they judge it isn't safe, then I'm happy to leave it to their professional judgement.'

'F's-sake', muttered Monty. 'You posh old gits don't care. Never mind the regular working men and women on that boat. You'd drag them out in this?'

But Colin was already walking away to a place where he could get a signal. Monty followed him and after howls of protest, he returned moments later with Colin's phone.

'The rest of you', shouted Monty. 'Hand over your phones. You can have them back at 10 am tomorrow.'

'Monty?' protested Gill.

'He's right', growled Mick. 'You people just don't care. Hand them over. Monty – go grab the UHF radio.'

'Guys, this isn't rationale', said Ryan.

'Actually, I think it is', said Mick. 'There's nothing we can do for Lillian tonight. Let's not have a boat or helicopter crew risk their lives for nothing.'

'More democratic to discuss it first', yelled Ryan. 'Don't expect me to hide what you're doing from the authorities.'

Mick thrust a gloved finger close to Ryan's face. 'Tomorrow's another day, my soft-skinned friend. We'll let the sun come up and then you can do whatever the hell you want. In the meantime, it there's any messing around, all this kit goes in the sea.'

Ryan took a step backwards and Mick pressed into the empty space. 'Make yourselves comfortable. It's going to be a long night.'

Chapter 24

'How well do you know these guys?' whispered Gill when Mick and Monty finally left the room.

'I don't', said Colin. 'They came recommended by a friend.'

'You didn't think to check?'

'At this time of year? I was happy to take any volunteer willing to work for bed and board. And whoever these guys are, they're definitely experienced birders.'

Gill was about to press Colin again but stopped himself. Colin was now shaking and cold, the effects of shock kicking against his body. Leaning over to one of the armchairs, he gathered up a tartan blanket and draped it over the older man's shoulders.

'I've never lost anyone', said Colin. 'On the job I mean. We work in wild places, so there's always a risk …' He shook his head and his voice trailed off.

Gill leaned across him and squeezed his shoulders. 'If there's anything we can do for Lillian, we'll do it in the morning.'

'Okay, then.'

'I have to say, I don't buy this whole "protecting lifeboat volunteers" speech', said Gill.

'It's a wild night out there so it might be true.'

'Were you aware she was wearing my coat when she disappeared?'

'That's hardly an issue! You can get a new one.'

'I mean …' said Gill, considering what exactly he was trying to say. 'Mick gave me a strange look earlier today. Like he was surprised to see me.'

Colin considered this. 'You think they meant you harm? And they might have mistaken her for you?'

'Maybe.'

Colin's voice rose. 'You're saying Lillian's death … could be murder?'

'Mistaken identity, possibly. But something doesn't feel right about this.'

'If you're correct, what's to stop them now? If that was their plan, why not just march you outside and chuck you off the cliff?'

Gill glanced around the door to check they weren't being overheard. 'Maybe it's a numbers game. We're tolerating them taking our phones, but if they threatened any one of us with serious harm it would become two against six.'

'Two very strong lads against six', Colin corrected. 'And that's only if the DuBlancs pitched in.'

'We need to keep our wits about us, Colin. If this turns ugly, it could happen very quickly.'

'Agreed. But maybe when the morning comes, and they hand us back our phones, then we can all take a step back.'

'Bit late for Lillian', said Gill.

Colin sighed. 'You saw her. There was nothing we could do.'

Gill nodded but said nothing. Colin seemed to think that mortal danger had snatched one victim from their nest but passed over the rest of the brood. But Gill's instinct didn't concur. Not in the slightest.

The following morning, the group sat scowling at each other as the common room clock wound its way towards 10 am.

'We're wasting daylight', said Carlos.

'Letting the storm die down a little', Mick snarled.

Then, when the time came, Mick tossed everyone's phones into a heap on the common room floor. 'Right. Everyone make themselves useful and get out there and see if there's any sign of Lillian. Monty, you give the coastguard a call. Let them know what's going on.'

Monty gathered the UHF radio into his arms and stood up. Then he stared at the still-seated figures and shouted, 'Shoo! Go find our girl.' He was still glaring at them as one by one, they gathered their phones and filed out of the room.

Warily, they donned waterproofs and adopted the same pairs as the previous evening. The wind had died and the waves, though still large, had lost much of their intensity.

Walking away from the observatory, Gill tried to power up his phone. 'Looks like the battery's dead', he muttered.

'Mine too', said Colin. 'Annoying. It's almost new.'

Quite suddenly, Gill felt a prickle of fear. 'Let's catch one of the other groups. Check their phones.'

They struck out due south and managed to intercept Ryan and Carlos before they disappeared into the rocky knuckles on the island's South Ness.

'You guys have any reception?' called Gill.

Ryan shook his head. 'Our phones are dead.'

'Ours too', said Colin. 'It's beginning to look like we're utterly reliant on Mick and Monty to call for assistance.'

Gill scanned the near horizon. 'Am I the only one who thinks help might not be coming after all?'

'There's more of us than them', said Carlos. 'Maybe we could take the UHF by force?'

'Hang on a second', said Gill. 'Maybe there's no need.' He pointed back at the *obs,* some three hundred metres away, where Mick and Monty had just emerged carrying small rucksacks. Signalling the others, Gill flattened himself amongst the Sea Pinks for cover. Several patient seconds later he raised his head and satisfied himself they hadn't been seen. Mick and Monty meanwhile, were heading west across the island to where they'd last seen Lillian.

'Colin. Head back to the *obs* and see if you can find the radio', said Gill. 'At the very least, charge your phone and get a message out. Ryan, Carlos. You go with him. Secure the lighthouse so you can keep those morons at bay until help arrives.'

'What about you?' said Ryan.

'I'll follow Mick and Monty. See what they get up to. I can double back to the *obs* and warn you if they come in your direction.'

'I could do that', said Colin.

'I'm an investigative journalist. Besides, I don't know how to work a radio.'

'In your trade, Gill, you should probably learn', Colin huffed, doubling up and shuffling away.

Gill waited until the others were safely inside the lighthouse and the door closed behind them. There was no sign of the DuBlancs, but they'd gone north, and he imagined they were assuring their personal safety in some other way. From his position, he could see that Mick and Monty had already passed the Stevenson Lighthouse and were almost out of sight heading for the Mill Door. Gill scanned the landscape and picked the best route to intercept them. Then he zipped up his fleece and set off.

He ran quickly at first, then slowed as he approached his quarry, moving from cover to cover as best he could on the sparse terrain. It got to a point where he hadn't seen Mick for ten minutes, though Monty could be seen with binoculars, working along the cliff top in a northerly direction. Gill dropped low and moved forward, keeping two hundred metres back. For a few minutes, his mood started to rise. Colin and the others would have control of the *obs* by now. And even if the radio wasn't available, they'd be charging their phones. Either way, help would be on its way.

'Hiya', said a cheerful voice behind him. He spun around to see Lillian leaning against a rock, a steaming mug of tea in her hands.

'My goodness', said Gill, standing up straight with relief. 'I'm so glad to see you. We were so worried.'

'Aw, thanks', Lillian drawled, throwing her head sideways in a comic smile.

'Where have you been?'

She jerked her head towards a crude but solidly constructed bird hide, positioned to see the cliff face on the south side of a gulley. 'Freezing my ass off in that.'

Gill stared at her, puzzled. 'Why?'

Lillian peered at him and sniggered. 'You really want to know?'

'Of course', said Gill.

A predatory smile crossed Lillian's face. 'Dad, you can come out now.'

Mick emerged from the bird hide, stretching his arms and back, before reaching for something. When his hand reappeared, it was holding the UHF radio. Mick took a few steps towards the nearest cliff and heaved it over the edge. 'Well done, our girl', he said, stepping back to Lillian's side.

'Thanks, Dad. Amazing what you can do with a little piece of research.'

'What is going on?' said Gill, flinging out his hands.

'Nothing personal, pal', said Mick. 'Just some family business.' He pulled off his gloves and raised a hand to discourage Gill from another outburst. Then he made a call on speed dial. 'Monty. It's Mick. We've got him.'

'Family business?' said Gill.

'Yeah', said Lillian. 'Got the idea from America. Getting quite lucrative. Though it's not easy, is it, Dad?'

'Aye, love', Mick replied. 'It's murder.'

They both laughed at the shared joke and the penny dropped for Gill.

'What do you want with me?' he asked.

Mick shook his head. 'Not interested in you. Don't care why someone wants you dead. I only need to find the means and opportunity to do it.'

Gill threw out his hands. 'But why fake Lillian's death? And all that nonsense with our phones?'

Mick advanced two steps. 'I don't owe you any explanations, pal.'

'My idea. In the heat of the moment', said Lillian, brightly. 'A little sleight of hand to get you all focusing on my little fabricated tragedy so Dad could sweep in and control the situation.'

'You didn't care a fig about the potential rescue teams?'

Lillian and Mick looked at each other and laughed. 'Not them, not you. And now, with a wee bit of help from the weather, you've made it easy for us.'

But Gill wasn't going to make it easy for them. Judging he'd seen a gap, he dashed from their reach and sped along the cliff top. He could already see Monty marching towards him, the man picking up his pace once he saw Gill hadn't been contained. Gill spotted a side path; just a track through the grass and sea pinks. It still took him too close to Monty for comfort, but as Gill had the benefit of a firm track, it was worth a punt. Sure enough, whether it was a puffin bite or a puffin burrow, Monty threw his arms out and crashed to the ground a few metres before reaching Gill.

Gill knew he had to be careful. The cliff wrapped back on itself in a semi-circle, meaning it would be a challenge to get back to the observatory without being flanked by Mick. He was pondering how he might do this when he mis-stepped, tumbled into a gulley created by a landslip and slithered to a halt at the cliff edge. His heart raced. He was face down and at least fifteen metres above the sea. He steadied himself and edged back, checking himself for damage. Aside from a few scrapes, he could still run. But three unfriendly faces appeared above him. Forming a defensive ring about the gulley. They had Gill trapped.

'Tell me', said Gill, panting. 'What happens next?'

'Put it this way, pal', said Monty. 'You've seen your last sunrise.'

'Who wants me done in?'

'Official secret', said Mick, smiling.

'King of Scotland', said Monty and the others laughed.

'I'll make you a better offer', wheezed Gill. 'I'll double whatever he's paying you.'

Mick shook his head. 'We're not going to cross this guy. If you'd had any wit, you'd have known the same.'

'The authorities will catch you. You do know that?'

Monty glared at Mick. 'Gettin' cold and bored, Bro. Can we finish here?'

'Agreed', said Mick, reaching around to his belt where it hugged the small of his back. When his hand reappeared, it was holding a gleaming blade.

'Okay', yelled Gill. 'If I'm gonna die, then I want to go by my own hands. Alright?'

'Don't care, pal. For us, it's cash on delivery.'

Gill stepped to the cliff edge and looked down. The water was inky black, still tossed about by waves. He'd travelled this way only four days before in a far happier moment. 'Alright then', he said, steadying himself. With barely a flinch of warning, he lunged four long strides towards Lillian, watching the three of them lurch to prevent his escape. And then he turned, running as fast as he could in the confined space, and roaring, he leapt off the cliff.

Chapter 25

Gill woke in pain. The simultaneous crushing compressions on his chest, which he later learned was CPR, added to his body's urgent need to expel the seawater he'd swallowed. He twisted himself sideways and spewed the contents of his airways onto the deck.

'Deep breaths', said a voice. 'Slow and steady. You're safe now.'

Gill didn't feel safe. He felt like he'd been hit by a car and robbed of his senses. Sight, hearing, touch – everything was a blur.

'You're lucky we were passing, mate', said another voice.

'Where ... where am I?' sputtered Gill.

'Lifeboat out of Anstruther. Answering a call about a body in the water.' The voice was interrupted by the mechanical exchange of information. 'We'll have you back on terra firma in fifteen minutes.'

'Wait', said Gill through lips that wouldn't quite work. 'I have friends on the island. They're in trouble.'

'What kinda trouble?' said the closest man. Gill could see him now. Big and burly in a life-preserving suit of reds and yellows. The whole outfit was capped off by what looked like a motorcycle helmet. For a few brief seconds, Gill wondered if this might be some kind of technicoloured angel.

'The people who drove me off the cliff … are still there. They might … hurt my friends.'

Gill only heard snatches of the discussion that followed. Someone was wrapping him in a survival blanket and the crinkly plastic smothered the conversation.

' … not a ruddy armed response unit.'

' … serious threat to life.'

' … who else is gonna do it?'

The next statement was louder. 'Coastguard, coastguard. Anstruther lifeboat on route to continuing situation on the island.'

Gill didn't hear the next exchange of conversation as the pains in his legs suddenly burned like his ankles had been dipped in boiling water, and for a moment, he thought he was going to pass out.

'Need to get you to hospital, mate', said the first voice. 'Looks like you've broken something.'

'Soon', spluttered Gill. 'Soon.' He twisted his head and made eye contact with the voice. 'On the island. Two men and one woman. They're dangerous. Everyone else is holed up in the observatory.'

There was a mumble of agreement from somewhere above him.

'Skipper says he hears the same. We'll proceed with caution.'

Gill was glad he was lying on his back without a view of the water as the fourteen-metre craft bucked and kicked as if the boat itself sensed the danger of approaching the landing site. The deck slid and arched as the vessel navigated the narrow channel through the remnant swell of the storm. He wasn't sure, but he thought he could hear the skipper humming. Everyone else was silent.

That was until a volley of swearing exploded from the men around him. 'Where the hell did he come from?'

'What's going on?' called Gill hoarsely from his prone position.

'Big black RIB', said the nearest crewman. 'Pushed us sideways in his rush to be away.'

'Getaway car', mumbled Gill, now deeply cold.

'We're not going after him', shouted the skipper. 'But I've got the bugger's beacon number. And I'll track him on radar. Unless he's going to Denmark, we'll know where he lands.'

Another hasty conversation. This time with someone on the slipway. 'We're safe now. Yes. We thought there was someone in the water last night, but we've just seen her on that RIB.'

'No other problems?'

'Lots of questions, but no problems.' It was Colin's voice. 'They took our UHF, but our phones are working again.'

'This one's hurt. I need to get him to a hospital.'

'He's Gill McArdle… we got separated on the island … How is he?'

'Leg damage and five minutes in the water, so he's cold.'

'Go. I'll make contact with the authorities.'

The conversation ended and the boat's engines surged again. After a fleeting sense of relief, Gill felt pain course through his legs and every colour around him rushed to black.

Chapter 26

When colour returned, it hurt Gill's eyes. The strip light above his head and the guardrails around his bed were the first things that told him he was in hospital. He pulled up his left hand to shield his eyes and noticed his bandage across his palm had gone. Before he had time to think about this, a dull ache in both his legs and lower back reminded him of his jump. Anxiously, he wiggled his toes and was relieved to see movement under the sheets.

Looking around, he saw Salina was asleep in a chair at his bedside, while beside her, a young man in a suit was tapping a message on his phone. Detecting movement, the man looked up. He leaned across to Salina and gently shook her shoulder.

'Gill?' she said sleepily.

'Hi there', he said, his mouth dry. 'How long was I out?'

'Just a few hours. They decided to sedate you while they checked your legs.'

'How bad's the damage?' he said, struggling to sit up.

'Your ankles took the brunt of your fall. One fractured and the other sprained. Oh, and two cracked ribs from the CPR.'

'That's me out of the Dundee marathon, then.' He glanced across at the young man. 'Who's this?'

'DC Lillico', said Salina.

'I'm on secondment to DI Wiley', said Lillico.

'You're the copper who reported me to Ed Johnson?'

'Yes. That was my duty under the Trespass (Scotland) Act of 1865, which states …'

Gill cut him off. 'The Inspector's not here in person?'

Lillico blinked twice. 'He sends his regards. And if I summarise his colourful reaction to your accident, he thinks you should hire a bodyguard.'

'Aw', said Salina fondly, reaching in to stroke Gill's head. 'It's not his fault people want to kill him. I'm considering it myself after this latest stunt.'

Lillico looked down at his phone. 'Can you tell me what happened?'

'How much do you know?' asked Gill.

'The coastguard despatched Anstruther lifeboat in response to an SOS from the Isle of May. As they approached, still a mile off the island, they saw someone jump from the cliffs. They found you floating face down, close to the west cliffs. Two RNLI volunteers entered the water to pull you to a place where the boat could bring you aboard. They reckon another minute and it would have been too late for you.'

Gill nodded, breathing a bullet prayer of thanks for his safe deliverance. 'It was still better than the alternative.'

'Which was?'

'Being tossed headfirst onto rocks. Instead, I got to choose a spot where the water was deep and where I'd have a fighting chance of surviving a jump.' After a sip of water, Gill told them about the events leading to his fall.

'The RNLI was able to track the RIB. We arrested the driver but your three acquaintances escaped.'

'I don't understand how they were able to embed Lillian on the island before we got there?' said Salina. 'I met her. She seemed so nice. Authentic.'

'Still unravelling the details on that one', said Lillico. 'Looks like it was achieved by deceit. They lured the real ranger off the island with news of a family emergency and promised to send a substitute relief worker in her place. When in due course she discovered there was no emergency, she was talking to the grifters rather than the Trust. By that point, they had their own woman in place and fobbed her off by lying about the rota being changed.'

'And do we have any idea who would want to hurt Gill?'

'To be honest, I'm hoping you two might be able to answer that question.'

Salina shook her head.

'I can tell you what I'm working on', said Gill. 'See if that rings any bells.'

'DI Wiley is assuming this attempt on your life is linked to another at that ruined church in Airth?'

Gill took another sip of water. 'Maybe. Though I've no idea who, or why.'

'Okay. Take a few minutes, then when you're feeling up to it, I need you to talk me through the last couple of months', said Lillico. 'Mention anyone you've interacted with.'

'Okay'.

'Then when you're out of here, you might want to lie low for a while.'

Gill leaned back on his pillows. 'If someone wants me dead and has the reach to attack me on an island, I don't think hiding myself away is going to help.'

Salina stood up. 'Okay, then. On that cheery note, I'll get us all tea.' She brushed against Gill's hand. 'Don't get too comfortable in there. Chances are they'll put splints on your legs and discharge you as soon as you're able to pull on a pair of shorts.'

The following morning, Corrie put in a call to *Mys.Scot*. Cassy answered the phone and Corrie listened aghast as she explained what happened to Gill.

'He did what?'

'Salina says he jumped off the island', said Cassy. 'Damaged his legs and knocked himself unconscious. It was a miracle someone had already called the lifeboat.'

'A miracle', Corrie repeated. 'Yeah, somehow that figures. Is he gonna be aw'right?'

'Couple of days in hospital, then all being well, he'll be back in the office having the shit ripped out of him as usual.

Sorry! Did I really say that? I meant he'll be back in the loving arms of his colleagues while we celebrate his recovery.'

Corrie cackled. 'And after all that pain, did he find anythin' on the isle?'

'Not as far as I know. Salina said she has a few ideas, but I think it involves another dive.'

'Okay. Listen, I might gie you a shout for an update in a couple of days.'

'Sure', said Cassy, sounding pleased. 'Always happy to chat.'

Corrie hung up and strolled over to the floor-to-ceiling window overlooking the river. A large house, with generous gardens and a view of the pretty stone bridge joining Dunkeld to the rest of civilisation, he loved living here, although in theory, he could afford bigger. He pressed his head against the glass and stared down at the Tay, with its millions of gallons of water tumbling past his window every day on its way to Dundee.

'Hey, Babe', said his wife, striding into the kitchen. 'Had any breakfast yet?'

He turned around and shook his head. 'Thanks, Denise. I'm good.'

'You okay, love?'

'Just gettin' an update on yon magazine guy I mentioned. Apparently, he's had a fall.'

'Babe, that's terrible. What happened?'

'Jumped off that island. The one with the strange lightnin'. Got chased off by some gang frae Glasgow.'

'Is he alright?'

'Och, aye. The wee eejit's just braw.'

'Aw, I'm glad to hear that. Listen, I going to take the dogs out. Do you want to come?'

Corrie shook his head. 'Need to do some thinkin', darlin'. I'll catch you for a piece at lunchtime.'

She gave him a cheery wave, and he watched as she rounded up the retrievers and bundled them out the back door.

Denise was the best thing in his life. Standing by him year after year when all he had to offer her emotionally was a bag of nails. "For our daughter's sake, Corrie", she always replied when he'd screamed at her, demanding to know why she hadn't left yet. And when those years passed, and his personal storm was over, she'd still been there. Older, but not bitter or broken. Guarding her heart, but willing once again to share her life with him. If love existed in the world, she was its walking, joking, swearing, living embodiment. And it broke his heart to remember all he'd put her through.

He had a sudden urge for a whisky. Nothing fancy – an Islay with plenty of peat and a dash of water. Take the edge off and give his brain room to think. But he extinguished the temptation and followed Denise out the back door before turning left and down to the summerhouse. The log burner was already set, so he tossed in a match and watched for several minutes as flames licked around the tinder-dry wood. Unsettled, he thought back to the time when he'd finally kicked the booze. Not just learned to flee it, but discovered he could live detached from it. He could consume or not consume, as it no longer controlled him. And for the duration of that battle, he'd had the sense of a voice cheering him on. A small, clear voice. "The whispers of a higher power", his mentor had explained. He'd heard the voice clearly back then and never doubted it, even when it eventually fell silent. Was it silent, or had he simply smothered it again as his life gained momentum? But this morning the voice was back. Mere shards of discourse, distant snatches of words, uttered in a loving and urgent tone.

In his struggle to hear the words clearly, Corrie sat by the fire and sang a couple of tracks off an old Delirious LP, and then a ballad slated for the next *Black Scabbard* album. He paused and meditated, basking in the heat from the burner and eventually becoming drowsy and on the brink of sleep. And in that moment as his mind cleared and his head began to droop, the voice was there, as clear as a tuning fork. Corrie sat up and blinked. Clapping his hands together he laughed. 'Nae bother, my old pal. Nae bother at all.'

Chapter 27

Salina waited for Gill in the hospital car park the following morning as he hobbled towards her car. 'You're all metal and plastic from the knee down', she said. 'Like a half-finished terminator.'

'Sorry. Not sure my top speed on crutches is going to be all that exciting for a few weeks.'

Salina huffed. 'How're going to cope back on the island then?'

Gill pulled up short of the car. 'What do you mean?'

She held the car door open for him and when he'd grunted and groaned his way onto the passenger seat, she relieved him of his crutches. 'While you've spent that last forty-eight hours coughing sea water out of your lungs, I've been busy on your behalf.'

'Oh yeah?'

'The fact the electrical cable is lying in the wrong place has raised a shit storm. That it is vulnerable to damage from a rusting submarine is adding fuel to the fire.'

'Okay.'

'So, in a burst of magnanimity, the War Graves Commission is granting the wind farm permission to lift the submarine and lay it twenty metres east, in deeper water.'

'You make it sound so easy.'

'Oh, yeah. They'll provide a gigantic crane. Fortunately, there's one sitting east of the May Isle sheltering from the weather.'

'It's still there?'

'Sure. They took the opportunity to have a weeklong shutdown and address some maintenance issues. But they're going to shift the sub tomorrow afternoon. And there's a DSV going down to observe what happens to the cable.'

Gill grimaced. 'I hope someone's stopped to think about all the archaeological implications of all this jiggery-pokery.'

Her glance in his direction was faintly incredulous. 'I put it on the right desk. Then St Andrews used its clout to red-flag the situation to the Scottish government. They put us in touch with the wind farm contractor and helped us negotiate the best possible price. If we go ahead, they'll permit us to put a rep on the boat, which is me, by the way. And then, if we have archaeological artefacts to recover, we'll have use of the DSV with full support for the following two days.'

'How', said Gill slowly, 'do you manage to be so awesome?'

'Ah. But there's just one problem.'

'Which is?'

'Even though there are service providers doing this on the cheap, and the Scottish government is paying to relocate the old sub, I'd still need a tender to collect anything we find, plus a safety boat and up to twenty hours flight time on their top-of-the-range DSV.'

'How much?' said Gill, sinking deeper into his seat.

'Not much shy of one-hundred thousand pounds.'

'Okay, thanks Sal. I'll run it by Tony. I'm sure he'd love for *Mys.Scot* to be working on this.'

'No', said Tony, standing beside Gill's desk later that morning.

'This is perhaps the most significant dig in the history of the magazine', Gill protested. 'This will sell a lorry load of mags.'

Tony shook his head. 'I calculate the maximum possible return from this dig, by way of extra magazine sales, extra advertising and sales of media rights, might be a quarter of a million pounds. But you need to factor in the likelihood of success which I'm estimating is about five per cent. Even if I'm generous and call it ten per cent, that's a forecast rate of return of twenty-five thousand. As I said. The answer is no.'

'Tony, listen …'

'Gill, it would be our single biggest expense since the inception of *Mysterious Scotland*. And we've taken some long shots in our day. But this one is like placing a five-pound bet and hoping to win the lottery.'

'But our first dive collected proof there are organic remains of a boat, and in the right age range.'

'The wreck is what, a thousand years old?' said Tony, raising his voice. 'And if that wasn't bad enough, it's had a sodding submarine lying on top of it this past hundred years. The chances of making a significant find are just too low.'

Gill shifted one of his legs uncomfortably beneath him. 'And what am I going to do with all the great material we've gathered so far?'

'Speculate', said Tony. 'Write something romantic and future-focused. Then park it and move on.'

Gill was tired and sore. At this moment, he had no more fight left for this. He caught Tony's gaze, nodded once, and then turned back to his laptop.

'Sorry it's working out like this', said Cassy, sliding onto the corner of his desk after Tony had moved away.

'Nah, it's okay. Sometimes I forget I'm working for a business and not a university.'

'It's weird. I felt we were really close on this one. And even the spooky lightning seemed to be helping us out.'

'No Worries, Cass. Onward and upward.'

'I want to give you this', she said, laying a five-pound note on his desk.

He picked it up. 'What's it for?'

'Put in on the lottery', she said, walking away.

Gill stared after her until his ringing phone distracted him.

'Any chance of a wee blether wie Scotland's champion high-diver?' Corrie shouted cheerfully down the line after Gill picked up.

'How're you doing? Still in Fife, living like a hobbit?'

'Nah. Back in my Perthshire mansion wie the wife. Wanted to ask what happened on the isle. From the little I heard it wasnae pretty?'

Briefly, Gill recounted his adventures over the last few days.

'Man, that's fantastic! You have the wreck. And the chances are, if the *Fated Stone* was on yon boat, it'll still be there.'

Gill released a long slow breath. 'We're not going to be able to fund a dig.'

'What? But this could be mega!'

'The logistics of doing it underwater for a start. Then the low probability we'll actually find anything.'

'After all yon effort? You're just gonna let it slip away?'

'Sorry, Corrie. That's the reality of the situation.'

'How much cash are we talkin' about?'

Briefly, Gill told him.

'Okay. No promises, pal, but I'm gonna make some calls.'

'Corrie. I'm not trying to tap you for funding.'

'I hear you, man. But, listen. It's the authentic *Fated Stone* we're talkin' about! Is it okay if I mention this to a few folk? See if I can find a suitable sponsor?'

'Yeah, sure. At this stage, I've nothing to lose. But I'll be honest and say the odds of finding something aren't great.'

'I hear you.'

'You think there's a chance?' said Gill, after a pause.

Corrie laughed. 'I've done some charity work. It's amazin' the kinds of cash you can raise when some folk ken your name.'

Roddy Canmore tweaked the position of his telescope and leaned into the optics. Standing at Fife Ness, he had before him a wide field of vision, stretching from deep inside the Firth of Forth, past the May Isle and into the turbine field of Neart Na Gaoithe wind farm. And finally, north, almost as far as Stonehaven. This was his favourite bird watching site. It's wild location at the furthest point on the Fife peninsula gave it a remote and rugged feel. But today, he wasn't just here for the birds. A contact at Holyrood had passed him some information and he was here to see for himself.

And in the meantime, he had the birds. So far, apart from the regular stuff, he'd sighted a flock of Manx Shearwaters and a pair of Storm Petrels, and that pleased him. Those particular birds normally roosted during the day. The recent bad weather had left them hungry, sending them foraging when they'd rather be resting. But what he really wanted to see was a Bonxie. The colloquial name for a Great Skua, these birds were no bigger than a Herring Gull, but with a distinct flight pattern and a characteristic hooked beak. Shunning the ostentation of the eagle family, the Bonxies were nevertheless carnivorous. They preyed on other gulls and were Roddy's favourite animal. But the bird flu of 2022 had hit their numbers hard, and Roddy hadn't seen one of these predators for quite some time.

The shuffling of coats and zipping of jackets reminded him that his security team lingered nearby. They'd probably be feeling the chill by now and eager to be get away for some lunch. He glanced at his watch. They could shuffle all they liked. This was a rare moment of leisure time for him, and he was going to enjoy it. Even if he did have to combine it with work.

Billy Whyte was ten minutes late when he finally arrived. Roddy nodded at his security guys who let Billy pass. Gingerly, the large man stepped onto the apron of grass surrounding the Second Word War pillbox still dominating Fife Ness. The concrete structure was ugly. But if you were birding, which meant standing on the exposed shoreline for hours at a time, it made an excellent windbreak.

'Sorry, Roddy, pal. I always forget how long it takes to walk down here.'

Roddy looked his visitor up and down. It didn't look like Billy did a lot of walking. 'No problem. Thanks for joining me.'

Billy produced a pair of lightweight Swarovski binoculars. 'Seen much so far?'

Briefly, Roddy brought him up to speed.

Billy stood in uneasy silence for a few minutes, until he eventually offered, 'Had a Hen Harrier last weekend.'

'Oh, aye. Whereabouts?'

'Kinnordy.'

Roddy grunted. An RSPB reserve with plenty of car parks. It would suit Billy well.

'We should go up there', Billy continued. 'And stay in your big camper. Catch the dawn chorus.'

'My campervan is outta bounds', Roddy growled.

'Yeah. Sorry Rodds.'

Roddy cleared his throat and shifted the conversation to more serious matters. 'Billy, pal. You did me wrong last week.'

Billy's bulk diminished a little. 'Sorry, Rodds. He's got new security.'

'Stevie told me about it', said Roddy, throwing a glance over his shoulder. 'Some fella with a sword?'

'Maybe a fan. Maybe hired muscle? Looked Eastern European.'

'Still. A sword! That's more like the *Black Scabbard* we know and love.' Roddy took his time to scan the skyline again. 'Thing is, Billy. If you'd been caught … if this fella had beaten you … say, you'd ended up in custody?'

Billy blinked at Roddy, clearly wrong-footed by the direction of conversation.

'You do know', Roddy continued, 'I'd deny all knowledge'. He stopped to shrug and scan the sea. 'You're just some bloke I met at a conference. Just another ex-councillor who'd like to be on the candidate list of *New Scotland*. When I come to think about it, Billy, I don't think there's a soul in the world who'd be prepared to testify you and I are even pals.'

'Sorry, Rodds. I wouldn't have let you down.'

'Okay, Billy. How would you like to redeem yourself on another wee job?'

Billy glanced around to judge how loudly he could speak. 'I dunno, Rodds, Stevie's your man for this kind of heavy lifting.'

Roddy shook his head. 'Ach, don't gripe. I'll outsource those more ... specialist services. Your task is perfectly legit and more in line with your skills. And it's a worthy endeavour in defence of our cause.' Roddy smiled to himself. Increasingly aware he sounded like a statesman, even if just ordering a pint of beer.

'I'm all ears.'

'Then track right your glasses westwards a wee bit. Do you see that construction platform sitting on the east side of the May Isle?'

Billy followed his directions. 'Yep. Hard to miss.'

'In a few days, it's going to facilitate an archaeological dig on the sea bed.'

'Really? How d'you know that?'

Roddy gritted his teeth for a second. 'Because I'm Roddy *sodding* Canmore, and it's my job to know things; that's how. I may not be in the Scottish government anymore, but I still have ma pals.'

Billy swallowed. 'What would you want me to do?'

'It's simple. Attach yourself to the dig crew and let me know if they find anything.'

Billy rubbed the back of his neck. 'What possible reason would I have to comment on an archaeological dig?'

'You're a geologist, aren't you?'

Billy blinked. 'Yes.'

'What I need you to do is cosy up to the person leading the dig and talk geology with them. If in due course, this guy finds what I think he's looking for, you'll be at the top of his Christmas card list.' He laughed. 'That's if he makes it to Christmas. I hear McArdle walks too close to the edge.'

'The magazine guy?'

'That's the fella', said Roddy, slow enough for Billy to understand.

'How will I find him?'

Roddy jerked his thumb over his shoulder. 'Stevie will help you link up with him.'

As Roddy leaned over his telescope once again, Billy shrugged. 'You got it, Rodds.'

'Oh, Oh! Check this out', said Roddy, clutching his optics. 'I think I've got a Bonxie.'

'Lemme see', said Billy, switching positions. He stared into the telescope for several long seconds. 'Ah sorry, pal. That's a juvenile Black Back.'

Chapter 28

After the Friday publisher's meeting, Gill joined Cassy at her desk and pondered the ways they could leverage some value from the work they'd done researching the *Fated Stone*. Cassy wanted to cut the whole sequence to a speculative article buried behind their subscriber paywall, while Gill preferred to use some of the material in the magazine. Neither was giving ground to the other and the temperature of the conversation was rising. Cassy's ringing phone provided relief from the tension. Gill could see it was the receptionist from downstairs.

'Hi', said Cassy with artificial brightness, clenching the phone to her ear as she listened. 'I can come down for them. No? Okay. Just send them up and I'll meet them here.'

'Shit, shit, shit', muttered Cassy to herself as she slammed down the phone and dashed towards the loos.

'What's happening?' called Gill to her back, though she didn't stop to reply.

Gill hobbled back to his desk, but after a minute, he was aware of a hush falling over the entire publisher's office. He looked up to see Corrie McCann, flanked by two others striding down the central aisle between the magazine sections. At least, Gill thought it was Corrie. He was wearing something akin to a black leather cowboy outfit, his long greasy hair was now free-flowing in thick black curls, struck through with grey, topped off by a huge, broad-brimmed hat. The scruffy beard, now neatly trimmed to a fashionable stubble, and high-heeled boots turned his already substantial height into a towering presence. As Gill stood up to greet him, Corrie thrust out his hand and then introduced his entourage. Dressed like Corrie, Gill recognised the older man, though he too was transformed from the rough sleeper he'd met at Caiplie Caves. The other was an athletic-looking woman in her late twenties, also clad in black leather, minus the ten-gallon hat.

'Gill. You ken, Barley. And this is my daughter, Thyssen.'

'Interesting name', said Gill, shaking her hand.

'Long story', muttered Corrie. 'Best if you dinnae ask.'

Gill detected embarrassment. Realising it was mainly his own, he offered his visitors chairs within the confines of the *Mys.Scot* pen.

'There she is', said Corrie, standing to greet Cassy, who was returning to her desk after urgent repairs to her composure. 'The object of my desire.'

'Dad!' hissed Thyssen under her breath.

'I was just talkin' about her autograph', Corrie retorted, offering Cassy an ornate spiral bound notebook.

'Seriously?' was all Cassy could say.

'Best to get 'em before they're famous', Barley observed, studying Thyssen's disapproving face. 'Be worth a fortune someday.'

'Oh. My. Goodness', exclaimed Cassy, her flash of insecurity demolished by Corrie's munificent approval.

'You're in good company in that little book', said Barley. 'Take a look at it before you give it back to him.'

Moments later, a cluster of *Mys.Scot* and other staff were gathered around Cassy, variously squeaking and cat-calling as she read out the autographs.

Corrie nudged Gill. 'While they're havin' fun, is there anywhere you and I could have a wee blether?'

Gill nodded at the conference room, and moments later they were standing in relative silence.

'I can gie you the money', said Corrie. 'To search yon seabed near the May Isle.'

'Already?' Gill spluttered. 'From where?'

'One-third from me. Big sacrifice. I'll have to flog a car or somethin'. One third from the rest of the band, because they're aw mugs and easily led. And one third frae a donor who would like to remain under the radar.'

'That's amazing. Thank you.' Gill paused. 'I do need to ask; are there any conditions attached to this money?'

'Just that if we find anythin', it gets donated to the nation.'

Gill nodded.

'And, if the nation disnae want it', Corrie continued, 'we can always flog it on eBay.'

Gill just stared at him, unsure what to say.

'Is that a deal?' said Corrie, thrusting out a hand.

'I need to run it past my publisher. And my fiancé. She's the one running the dig. But yeah, in principle, we've definitely got a deal.'

'When's the kick-off?'

'There's a crane nearby ready to redeploy. We could go in as early as tomorrow.'

Corrie gripped Gill's hand. 'I'll gie you the cash by bank transfer at the end of the day.'

Gill felt Corrie's hard skin against his own and squeezed as firmly as he dared. Like Cassy, he was realising he was slightly in awe of this man.

'Taipem Three. This is DSV. Comms check.'

'DSV. Have you on comms and sounder. Proceed to lift point.'

Salina was dizzy with tiredness. This was her second consecutive weekend spent working, and all her effort assisting Gill rung with the usual high intensity. Forcing herself to focus, she peered between the shoulders of the DSV pilots sitting in front of her. This vessel was much bigger than the one she held a license to skipper, and exponentially more powerful. Earlier that day, she'd watched as its crab-like arms had placed belts around a submarine wreck known only as "K4". And in the blaze of LED lights, she could see something she missed during her survey with Ellie. At another point, some twenty metres further down the drop-off lay the bow section of K4. The accident amongst the Allied fleet back in 1918 had sheared the boat in half with the loss of her fifty-six crew. Today's action had a certain symmetry as it would place the two halves of the boat at their closest proximity in over a century.

Seals and pollack flitted at the margins of the lights while orders and data were assessed above and below. Numbers representing depths and vectors flew back and forward between the lead pilot and the massive rectangular vessel above, until finally, the order was given to lift. Salina watched as the belts wrapped around the old submarine, and stretching up to one of the cranes on the surface, began to tighten. Gradually, and respectfully, the wreck was eased off the sea bed. As predicted by the tension on the cable, it swung away eastwards and out into the dark. The DSV also drifted east for a few metres where it watched the carcase of the submarine being laid gently back onto the sea bed. Recovering the clamps that had gripped the wreck, the DSV followed the trajectory of the electricity cable now floating free as tension and gravity dragged it eastwards until it settled again on the silted floor.

'Taipem. The cable is now at rest and clear of all hazards', reported the DSV pilot.

'Good work, DSV. Please proceed with the north-south survey.'

Salina had to endure a patient hour as the DSV followed the cable in either direction of the snag. Only when the DSV confirmed no further hazards, and that its location was now accurately mapped, were they released to begin an initial archaeological survey. By now the currents had blown away all the silt disturbed by the earlier manoeuvre. Carefully, the DSV allowed its autopilot to carry them back to their original coordinates. The pilot throttled back his engines and flooded the area with light. The edge of the drop-off loomed like a black shadow, the current flowing over the freshly exposed ledge caught silt and blew it away, like snow blowing off the edge of a drift.

'Is that what you were expecting?' asked the pilot.

Salina surveyed the wooden ribs of an ancient craft emerging from the sand. She clapped him on the shoulder. 'No', she said. 'It's far better.'

Staring at what looked like the inside of a brightly painted shipping container, Gill watched Salina organising herself in front of the camera. He was working from home as his return to the island had been ruled out on health and safety grounds.

'How are your legs?' she asked quickly.

'On the mend', he said. 'How was the dive?'

'There's definitely a boat there, Gill. I saw one line of ribs in the mud.'

'That's excellent. Why are you looking so worried then?'

'Two things. Firstly, we'll only have the support ship for forty-eight hours before it returns to wind farm duty.'

'We knew that.'

'The other is erosion. The wreck is sitting on a sandbank that is rapidly changing shape. I think by lifting the submarine, we might have accelerated that.'

'I don't understand. I thought it was sitting on the sea bed?'

'It was, but this is a silted area with perpetually strong east-west currents. It's like sand dunes moving around on a beach. And historically, it's probably worked in your favour. If your wreck was buried for a good portion of the last thousand years, the submarine will have helped preserve it. The point is, now it's exposed I think it might break up.'

'Okay. What's the plan?'

'Tom and Ellie are joining me tonight. We've got three dives planned. The DSV will be with us the whole time, providing light and the occasional heavy lift if required. We'll transport anything we find to the surface.'

Gill let out a deep breath. 'Be careful, Sal.'

'I will. If the stone's there, I'll do my best to find it.'

Chapter 29

For the past two years, Gill had worked hard not to find himself drinking alone. On this particular Saturday night, he was breaking this pledge, sitting in the Fisherman's Tavern, nursing his concern for Salina. Their brief call in the early evening had revealed her to be tired and uncomfortable. Even using a top-spec submersible, the dive was not without risk. The presence of the electrical cable on the sea bed, plus the thick dark anchor chains of the Taipem raised the hazard levels to the point where even the experienced pilots were sweating. And back on board the boat, she was a beautiful young woman working alone. She could deal with it, but the constant attention was a burden.

He liked the Fisherman's Tavern. It was dark and roomy, with booths offering an escape away from the sports TV. And the ale was good. There were several real ale pubs in Broughty Ferry. Salina preferred the colourful intimacy of The Ship Inn, but Gill liked them all.

Navigating on crutches back to the bar, he faced a problem he'd never had before. How to carry his beer to his table. On ordering his first ale, the barman had taken mercy on him and carried the pint over to the distant booth Gill had selected. This time, he poured another perfect pint but was too busy to offer Gill table service. Gill stared at the settling contents of his glass and wondered what to do.

'Do you need a hand, pal?'

Gill turned around to find a middle-aged man, of substantial girth, standing with a half-drunk ale. 'Hey, thank you. I'm just over here.'

Gill led the way and after stowing his sticks, he thanked the man profusely.

'If you don't mind me asking', said the man. 'Are you Gill McArdle?'

Gill's face flushed and the bar suddenly became less anonymous. 'I am.'

The man offered him his hand. 'I don't mean to intrude. I've read your magazine. When I saw it was you, I just wanted to say how much I enjoy your work.'

'Thank you. It means a lot to hear people say that.'

The man started to move off. 'Well, enjoy your beer. Let me know if you need a hand with another one.'

Gill's inclination to drink alone and suckle his worries crumbled in the face of the man's kindness. 'Are you on your own? Would you like to join me?'

'So, Billy. What brings you to Dundee?' asked Gill as he sipped the top off his third pint, generously bought for him by his new friend.

'Scouting for business. I've got a meeting tomorrow with a prospective client.'

'What's your field?'

'I work with engineering firms. In the energy sector, mainly. I'm a geologist.'

'You know lots about rocks, then?'

Billy smiled. 'Plenty. In the old days I assisted oil companies to interpret their seismic scans of the sea bed. Helped them figure out where the oil was. But these days it's all about the wind farms. Lots of offshore work now, using the same seismic data to find suitable places to anchor these massive turbines they're building.'

'Interesting', said Gill, doing his best to look attentive.

'And in my line of work, I do bump into archaeologists from time to time. These days I take quite an interest myself, at an amateur level.'

Gill was on firmer ground with this. 'Cool. Anything I would have heard of?'

Billy cast his eyes down at his drink and thought. 'Mostly small stuff. My biggest was Tara in the Irish Republic. Have you ever been?'

'No. But I've heard of it. I know it's a big cluster of ancient monuments and earthworks. The old Irish kings ruled from there for thousands of years.'

'Yes, so I heard', said Billy. 'And I guess, because those kings preceded the Celtic incursion into Caledonia, they must have been our ancient kings as well.'

'Hey, Billy. You're a bit of a history buff.'

Billy nodded modestly. 'When I first got into this trade, I was only interested in the rocks and the application of geological sciences. I've travelled a lot around Scotland and Ireland since then, so I know there's a lot of human history embedded in the physical landscape. It gives my enjoyment of the job a wee boost.' He sipped his beer. 'You've written about Orkney, Gill, so you'll know what I mean.'

Gill nodded enthusiastically. 'I most definitely do.'

'Tara is a lot like Orkney. There's a sense of a once great civilization being slowly absorbed back into the landscape.'

'It was ever thus.'

'And the Irish have their own special monuments', Billy continued, gathering steam. 'There's a cracking specimen at Tara; a standing stone on top of a hill. It's meant to be a protected monument. But it just sits in the open. Every now and again, some eejit goes and spray-paints an emoji on it.'

'Kids', Gill surmised.

'I took a guided tour when I was there. It was the quickest way to get the context of the place. Anyway, during the talk it became apparent the good folk of Tara aren't very keen on us Brits.'

'They have good cause', said Gill. 'Did they mention the sacking of Tara by British archaeologists in the late nineteenth century?'

'Oh, yeah!' Billy stopped to snigger. 'Posh Victorian gents posing as archaeologists. They wanted to bolster the British Empire by proving the Brits had some kind of special legitimacy derived from our Celtic heritage. That we are, in fact, one of the lost tribes of Israel.'

'Oh, aye. It's a grand yarn. Something worthy of *Mysterious Scotland*.'

'What I didn't grasp was why they were digging in Ireland? Stonehenge maybe, but County Meath? I don't get it.'

'It's a question of heritage', said Gill, fiddling with his glass to slow down his beer consumption. 'Have you heard of Princess Scota? Or Scotia. Nobody seems too sure.'

'The lassie Scotland got named after?'

'Aye. She was either an Egyptian princess. Or a daughter of the last king of Judah. I find the latter idea more compelling.'

'I got the fact that she's meant to be buried at Tara, but I've no idea why she'd have been of interest to English establishment types.'

'The story goes that migrating Jews fleeing the Assyrian onslaught in the sixth century BCE, rescued important artefacts from Jerusalem and after a journey of many years, managed to squirrel them away at Tara. And that's what the Victorians were looking for. Proof that the English could claim descent from God's chosen people.'

'Yeah! And justify continued British imperialism', huffed Billy. He threw Gill a nervous glance. 'Sorry, no offence. These days you can meet a new pal and not know where they stand on Scottish politics.'

Gill shrugged. 'Don't worry about it. I swing both ways on independence.'

'Back to those Victorian gents', said Billy. 'Why brag about a Jewish connection?'

'Well, it was 1900. Society had moved past making sacrifices to the gods' said Gill. 'But even in those enlightened times, proving you have God's backing might be a handy justification if you're trying to maintain a global empire.'

Billy nodded soberly. 'From what I remember of Tara, the dig didn't produce the goods.'

'No. It ran for two years and didn't produce any discoveries that backed up the Brits-are-the-chosen-people hypothesis. Worst of all, the scattered nature of the excavations and the poor record-keeping rendered the Tara dig as the defining example of archaeological bad practice. Essentially, it was an act of vandalism.'

'Disgusting', said Billy, finishing his glass. 'At least that wouldn't happen today.'

'Can I return the favour and buy you a beer?' asked Gill, knowing that he shouldn't, but that he still fancied another.

Billy smiled. 'Normally I'd be game on a Saturday night, but I need to have a clear head for tomorrow's meeting. I mean, what's their urgency to meet on a weekend? But hey ho, in the service of my customers.'

The two men shook hands and Billy got up to go. 'Nice to meet you, Gill. That was better craic than sitting on my own in an unfamiliar bar.'

'And you, Billy. I enjoyed your company.'

Billy raised his right hand in farewell and took a couple of steps towards the door. Seemingly as an afterthought, he walked back to Gill and offered him a business card. 'Just in case you ever need a geologist', he said.

'Thanks, Billy. If I ever have to build a motorway or a wind farm, you'll be the first guy I call.'

Both men laughed and Billy stepped out into the dark and disappeared.

Gill sat cradling his almost empty glass. As he subconsciously tucked the business card in his waistcoat pocket, he reflected on this chance conversation with a stranger. In her research, Mhairi had mentioned the older, Irish connections to the Stone of Destiny. But Gill had directed her to focus on the Scottish angle. Consequently, no one had mentioned the cult of British-Zionism, a shadowy group, prevalent in the Victorian era. It was their fanaticism that had motivated the desecration of Tara. And now a dark thought occurred to him. What if their ideology still existed in the UK? As he contemplated this, he realised the logical implication. However small in number, and far from the public eye, there might exist in Scotland a small group of extremists who would love to get their hands on the *Fated Stone*. In the light of this, he reconsidered the attacks on him, at Airth, and then later, on the island. Was it possible these zealots were already on his tail?

Gill shivered. If they existed, surely they would wait and see if he recovered the stone. And right now, that felt far from certain.

Two days later, Salina stood with hands on her hips, watching a crane on the Taipem transfer its precious cargo. She was weary to her bones, and a little lonely since Tom and Ellie jetted off that morning on the Anstruther RIB, ready to get back to their day-to-day lives. As ever, the most senior person on the team was left minding the gear. If this had been pure university work, she could have delegated the task. But the fact that there were multiple agencies involved, plus the seed money donated by Corrie McCann, made the responsibility ambiguous. And so, it fell to her. She loved Gill McArdle, but he definitely owed her for this!

The crane cables were retreating now and soon a second large container was on its way. The first had been their dive gear and personal luggage. The second was … who was to say what they had found. Salina wasn't an archaeologist – to her, it was all just junk. She'd land it in Dundee and oversee the transfer to a lab Gill had borrowed. Then she was going to bed. For a week.

Just junk, but she still breathed with relief when the second container was safely on the deck of the service vessel. Meanwhile, with its duty complete, the Taipem wasn't hanging around. All around the massive, ugly vessel, she could hear klaxons sounding and see lights flashing as the two great anchors were winched up from the sea bed. She threw a wave to anyone who was watching, though she wasn't sad to be leaving that vessel, with its round-the-clock noise, the oily smells and the brutish masculinity that seemed as essential to existence on the ship as the life-preserving gear the whole crew wore.

Her own vessel was moving now; its diesel engines were barely a purr compared to the Taipem. Reversing away from the bulk of the construction platform, her tender eased away to the east, ready to navigate the rocky hazards at Fife Ness and set a clear course for Dundee a short distance away. She strolled up to the bow and took off the black baseball cap she'd worn almost constantly these past days. Some part of her would like to have tossed the greasy, oily cap into the sea. But she was a marine biologist by trade, and you didn't do that kind of thing. Instead, she shoved it in a back pocket and inhaled the smell of the sea. She closed her eyes and let the wind take her hair, tossing it behind her in a flowing black mane, as gradually, the ship turned to the east and took her gracefully, powerfully, towards home.

Chapter 30

Tucked in a nondescript store room in the Hammond Building, on Dundee University campus, the *Mys.Scot* crew were heading towards a tea break. It was Tuesday morning and they'd gathered around Gill as he sat entering data onto his laptop. He'd positioned himself in the middle of the room so he could answer questions without having to lean onto his crutches and stand. The team had been lifting and sorting Salina's discoveries for almost two full days.

'I'm tae old for this crap', groaned Larry. 'Ma back is breaking'

Cassy slid a mug of tea in his direction. 'Stop moaning. Normally, Gill has to stand in a bog for a fortnight and scrape it out of the ground. Unpacking this lot is like doing archaeology by Amazon delivery.'

'Aye, but ye couldnae get students tae dae the donkey work? At least some other gang couldae washed the barnacles off.'

Gill glanced up. 'I can't ask St Andrews just now and it was short notice to raise a crew in Dundee. You work on an investigative magazine, Larry. Think of this as on-the-job training.'

'Yeah', said Craig lifting a heavy box. 'Team building exercise combined with a decent workout.'

'Speak for yourself', came Mhairi's shrillest voice from a distant corner. She was hunched over a table with tweezers, her glasses hanging off her nose as she tried to create order out of the morass of smaller items Salina's team had hoovered off the sea bed. Grouping items by appearance or by material, she had laid out several hundred brown and grey items for Gill to review.

'We're making great progress', said Gill, turning as he felt someone rub the base of his back. 'Here she is. The hero of the hour.'

'Don't say that', Salina said, leaning in to kiss him. 'You haven't seen my bill yet.'

Mhairi got up and came across to say "hello", as she was the only one of the *Mys.Scot* team who hadn't met Salina before. 'Can't believe you actually dug this lot off the sea floor. I think you're incredibly brave.'

'It's what I do.' Salina gave an embarrassed smile. 'Worst part was getting my bum patted every time I left my room.'

Gill felt his face flush. He'd been too focused on his task. Salvaging the wreck had cost him nothing; Salina had picked up his tab.

'And now the big question', said Salina, ignoring his discomfort. 'Was it worth it?'

Gill glanced down at his screen. 'We've about two hundred ferrous items. They're badly corroded but will likely be nails or other fittings. And in that bucket of seawater over there we have the two dozen wood samples – thank you for those. That will give us another chance to carbon date the age of the timber and the likely age of the wreck.'

'Coins', Mhairi added. 'Not many and most had a high silver content so we'll be lucky to get one with a date.'

'One or two miscellaneous chunks of iron', added Craig. 'Anchors, maybe.'

'Nae human remains sae far', said Larry.

'Come on, guys', Salina protested. 'What about the main event? Do we, or do we not, have the stone?'

Gill did get to his feet now, grunting as he shifted his weight off the worst of his legs. With the aid of a single crutch, he shuffle-hopped to the far end of the room where forty smooth black rocks were laid out in the shape of a long almond. 'This is all the ballast you recovered. We've laid it out as best we can according to the photos you took and the labelling you were able to do.'

'Sorry I couldn't get a number tag on them all', Salina muttered. 'We were under such time pressure at the end.'

'No problem. You can see the complete outline of the ship, with just a couple of gaps. It's quite remarkable.'

'Hang on', said Larry. 'What's the point of building a boat tae float, then filling it full ae o' rocks?'

'Buoyancy', said Gill. 'Those old wooden sailing ships needed additional weight placed below the waterline so they didn't tip over. Some of the oldest vessels incorporated their cargo as ballast. The old Dutch traders brought in the red roof tiles that are common in old Fife buildings. When they headed for home, the ships were packed with grain. It was a good system.'

Salina pulled her face into a mock frown. 'You're thinking I risked my life down there for a load of old ship's ballast?'

'Maybe', said Gill, brightly. 'But I think we have a contender.'

She punched his arm with more force than usual. 'Show me!'

Gill pointed at a large lozenge-shaped stone that Salina herself had already numbered as MS12. About a meter and a half long, it was seventy centimetres at its widest and barely ten centimetres thick. 'This fellow doesn't quite fit. No matter what way round we shift him, even allowing for the ribs of the boat, he looks like a spare.'

'That's fantastic', Salina exclaimed. 'But can you prove it?'

'Next step is to take samples from all the stones. Science will tell us where they came from. If MS12 is from somewhere exotic, then we might be in business.'

'Might be?'

'Aye. Ships needed to adjust their ballast as they aged. Stones might be added or discarded at any time in the boat's forty to eighty working years. Meaning the origin of the stone won't be everything.'

'But it came from a wreck in the exact place you predicted?'

'Yes, which is a massive help.' Gill swept his right hand around the room. 'But we'll need all this context data to confirm we have the right kind of boat, sinking in the right era, in order to tie it conclusively to the *Airth Slab*.'

'Okay. Sounds like you have a line of enquiry. Let me know how it goes.'

'You off already?'

'Aye. I just swung by to make sure you're behaving yourself and then I'm off to work from home. I'm hoping for an early night.'

He returned her smile and pointed at his crutch. 'I promise to stay out of trouble.'

She kissed his head. 'You'd better. See you later in the week.'

Gill waved her off and then turned to find Cassy. 'Right. Now we need to do some more research on stone MS12.'

'How're you planning to do that?'

Gill smiled and produced a crumpled business card from his waistcoat. 'I happen to know a geologist.'

As expected, Billy Whyte had finished his meetings in Dundee and had returned to his home in Aberdeen. But, after hearing about Gill's unusual request, he made himself available the following morning.

'It's all basalt', said Billy the next day, having reviewed the stones. 'That was a common choice for ship's ballast. It's incredibly dense but will take a smooth edge after a little bit of handling. Some of these stones may have been in use for hundreds of years, recycled from boat to boat as needs required.'

'Are they all from the same source?'

'I'm seeing differences in grain sizes and texture, so my educated guess is the stones may have come from different places. I'll need to take some tiny core samples to tell you more.'

'Of course. What identifying factors will you be looking for?'

'Crystal size will be important for our basalts, but also the detailed mineralogical content. I'll run some tests over the next few days. Are you looking for anything in particular?'

Gill chewed on his lower lip for a second. 'I'd rather not say if you don't mind.'

'Ah!' said Billy, smiling. 'Some secret mystery you're protecting? No problem. Well, my initial analysis might not be one hundred per cent determinate, but I can tell you what I've found out by the end of the week.'

'Okay, Billy. Let's go for it.'

'I'll go to the car and get my tools.' He turned to peer at Gill, then whispered theatrically. 'If at the end of this process, any of the stones are judged to be historically significant … I can patch the holes with a sympathetic colour of resin.'

On Thursday, the team continued to split their time between the Hammond Building and their desks, so that by Friday morning, Gill was busy in the office putting the final touches to issue 22. His left leg was feeling better, and he judged he'd soon be able to remove the splint on that foot.

Even then, he'd be protecting his right leg for several more weeks. He was considering a break for coffee when an email from Billy Whyte came through. He read it before printing Billy's attachment with a growing sense of excitement. Limping over to the printer, he signalled Cassy and Mhairi to join him in the conference room.

'As expected', said Gill, clutching the piece of paper. 'The ship's ballast is all basalt. Chemical composition and crystal size conform to igneous sources around the Firth of Forth. Most are from North Berwick, with a few from Kinghorn and two he believes are from Elie.'

Cassy rolled her eyes. 'Come on, Gill.'

'What do you mean?'

'I know when you're holding out on me.'

'Okay then. The big black lozenge – the stone labelled MS12, is from northern Israel.'

'Side on, it's a slab rather than a block', observed Cassy, refusing to be shaken. 'Makes it a contender to be the *Fated Stone*.'

Mhairi's mouth dropped open.

Cassy noticed her surprise and waved it away. 'Honestly, girl. Work around here long enough and you get used to it.'

'Hang about', said Gill. 'This in itself isn't enough. It's a big leap to find a rock on the sea bed, identify its geological fingerprint and then just assume it's the original *Fated Stone*.'

Mhairi gave herself a little shake. 'Did Billy give you any more information?'

Gill studied the printout. 'He says it's strange. The rock originates from an igneous intrusion in the Golan Heights or southern Galilee, so he doesn't think it was gathered opportunistically for ballast as it wouldn't have been found on the coast.'

'Unless it wasn't ballast', said Cassy.

'It was cargo!' Mhairi shrilled.

'We're going to need some additional expertise', Gill decided, keeping his voice low. 'Someone with insight into why this stone might be special and not just a random hunk of rock.'

Mhairi tapped her lips with her pen. 'If, for the sake of discussion, we assume MS12 is the *Fated Stone*, its origin goes back to Jacob wrestling with God. We don't have a date for that but it's around 1000 years BCE. The Assyrian empire is on the rise and the Persian empire hasn't happened yet.'

'You think it might be tricky to find an expert?'

'There'll be someone', said Mhairi. 'Are you okay if I post a very general description of the task on a few message boards? See if anyone bites?'

'Keep it fairly general. I'd rather not broadcast what we have here.'

'Okay. I can hold back if you like?'

'No, just go for it', said Gill. 'I sense we're all getting excited. But until we get more data, all we have is a rock that's a long way from home.'

Chapter 31

Adina Mofaz stares out on a street still damp from last night's rain. She normally loves her short walk to work. Douglas generally takes the kids to school, and unless she needs to be in early, she's free to linger in the house, wandering from room to room with a mug of coffee, whispering prayers for everyone she loves, and a few for those she doesn't. This is her 'alone' time of day. A moment to emotionally and spiritually ground herself. To loiter in the company of her messiah; a relationship so private, not even Douglas knows her whole story. After this special time, she'll be ready to step into the endlessly busy, always noisy, rooms of the museum.

On this particular Monday morning however, her time alone gives her no peace. The message exchange the previous evening has rocked her world and her emotions ping between anger, terror and shock. Last night, Douglas noticed, of course. Even when she'd come home late. She'd murmured excuses about problems with the new exposition and though she could see he didn't believe her, the generous heart in the man she loved meant she had some hours or days before he gently asked her about it again.

She considers calling in sick. Everything is set for the new gallery, so she doesn't really need to be in. But it would be out of character for her not to be present. It's already most unlike her, not to be clucking around the exhibits before the doors open to the public, picking at tiny details as a tactic to alleviate her nerves. And yet her training says, "never step out of character". Especially in the face of a threat, or new orders coming in.

'Oh, dear God', she murmurs, stepping reluctantly into her day.

She leaves her flat on Newbattle Terrace and turns left into Clinton Road. Trees hang low over the narrow cobbled street and for a moment, urban Edinburgh seems miles away. For a few terrible seconds, it occurs to her to flee. She has the training to melt away – to a different place, using a different name. To land on her feet, catlike, and walk calmly away, as if this brush with danger means nothing to her. But Douglas and the girls? She can't do it. She made vows. To the man she married, and by implication, to the children she bore him. And now she is living under the curse of an earlier vow – a sacred confession, rising up from her past life to consume her. What a fool she'd been! Just an idealistic girl, ready to die for a cause; utterly unthinking how she might be sacrificing her own future.

She pushes back her rising panic. The movement has trained her well, and she can leverage that to her own advantage. Escape routes do exist! She runs through an imaginary conversation in her head where she explains her past to Douglas. He'll understand, with difficulty, and then they'll grab the kids and flee together. Easy for one, retorts her inner voice. Harder with four – they'll be so much more visible. But there might still be time. If she hides herself away at the museum today, she can work out a plan. By tonight, they might lose their home and their livelihoods, but they could be on their way to safety.

Struggling with these thoughts, she walks down Church Hill to join Morningside, stepping past a white van mounted on the kerb with its winkers on. A blond-haired man in the red uniform of a delivery firm apologises as he throws open his door in front of her. She takes a step back in surprise, and treads on the feet of a man who has come up behind her.

'I'm so sorry', she splutters, aware she's not been concentrating.

'Adina!' says the man warmly. 'What a wonderful surprise.'

She properly looks at the man's acne-scarred face. He's in his mid to late-forties. A few centimetres taller than her with close-cropped hair.

'Do I know you?'

'You don't remember? I am disappointed. Let me buy you a coffee and we can be reacquainted.'

'Actually, I'm late for work.'

The older man nods at the delivery driver who has jumped back in his vehicle and is starting the engine. 'The invitation is politely made, Ms Mofaz. But it isn't optional.'

As the white van drives away, it reveals in its wake a lithe young man with a fox's face and a sharp black beard looking out from under a hoodie. Realising she has no choice, Adina indicates they should walk the short distance to Morningside. The next sixty seconds pass slowly, punctuated with glances over her shoulder as her interceptor follows into the café. The people here know her well but won't be surprised to see her with an unfamiliar man. This close to the museum, she is a regular visitor with colleagues, researchers or visitors from other facilities. It occurs to her to use the occasion to shout for help. But her captor looks so calm, he just isn't plausible as an aggravating stranger any more than they'd recognize him as an assassin. She could probably manage to get away from him, escaping out the back. But all she'd achieve would be handing him a bullet.

So, they both summon civilised smiles and order black Americanos, then, at her lead, choose a seat by the window. It gives her a chance to see the man in profile. She knows immediately she made the right decision not running because she does know him. There's no sign of the blond guy, though the fox-like young man has taken up a position, half facing the shop, half watching the traffic, hiding behind the universal anonymity of a mobile phone.

'Colonel Uri', says Adina, summoning her courage. 'What brings you to my fair city?'

The man smiles and speaks in a low voice. Above the bustle and chatter of the busy shop, she can just about hear him. 'You see! You do remember me. Although, my rank was Commander when I retired.'

'You are no longer with the organisation?'

'Not formally. These days I act as a sub-contractor.' He stirs his coffee slowly while he conjures the right words. 'Serving the greater good in missions where the normal rulebook might be need to be … set aside.'

Adina wants to snort at his weasel words. 'And does your presence suggest I cannot be trusted in the field?'

Uri shrugs. 'At the request of your superior, I'm here simply to offer you whatever support you need. If you are successful in your mission, there will be certain … logistics to be organised.'

Adina sips her coffee. 'I manage high-value shipping as part of my museum role. I doubt logistics are the big challenge here.'

Yuri leans in closer. 'You know what I mean. Organising secure transportation isn't the only thing I had in mind.' His shoulders rise and fall in the whisper of a shrug. 'I can assist you in other ways.'

She considers what he means and lifts her coffee to her mouth, hoping he can't see her hands tremble.

'How long since you last saw active service?' he asks in a quiet, companionable voice.

Her eyes rove the street over the rim of her coffee cup. 'British Museum, London. 2008.'

'Ah, of course. You were still a student, yes?'

Adina has to fight to keep exasperation from her face. What point is Yuri trying to make with this ridiculous dance? 'I was. I ran security for a more experienced agent while she searched their paper archive for a record card.'

Yuri smiles. 'The British. So traditional.'

'It's been digitised since then.'

'I know', he says, turning slowly to peer out the window at the cloudy sky. 'Makes my life so much easier.' When Adina reads his meaning and looks away, he adds. 'How long since you were home?'

'Home?'

He sighs. 'Don't make me spell it out.'

'We last visited my parents before Covid. They prefer to take vacations here. Especially in the summer.'

'And yet you've been to Iran three times since the end of the pandemic.'

She cocks her head defiantly. 'I still have cousins there. And my legend says I specialise in Persian antiquities.'

He shrugs. 'You have friends in Tel Aviv as well as London. Perhaps after this new adventure you'd like to request a transfer. There are universities far superior to this old town.'

'I'm educating my girls here. It would be unfair to move them.'

'Life isn't always fair, Adina. Or do I need to remind you we serve a higher calling?'

'The artefact', says Adina, ignoring his jibe. 'Now you're here, are you going to tell me where to find it?'

For the first time in their encounter, Yuri looks shifty. The blemishes on his face become more apparent as he glances left and right before passing her a note under the table. 'The system picked this off a message board. A Scottish archaeologist looking for help confirming the origin of a stone. You can read their request when you get to your office.'

'And why me?'

He pulls a face of surprised amusement. 'You signed a pledge to further our cause. Why shouldn't it be you?'

'Because I know these assignments aren't doled out at random. What boxes do I tick that make me the agent most suitable for this job?'

'You've worked with them before', he says. 'A consumer magazine trying to pass itself off as an investigative journal.'

'*Mysterious Scotland*?'

'Yes.'

Adina casts her mind back and recalls talking to the magazine's research assistant about six months ago. They'd been writing about parallel breakthroughs in Astronomy, in both ancient Persia and an early civilization based on Orkney. 'And what makes you so certain they'll want to talk to me?'

'With your expertise? My dear, you are perfectly qualified to help them.' His shrug is almost playful. 'Besides, your technical people have smothered their digital message board. Unless someone else saw their request before us, you'll be the only person responding to their call for assistance.'

He pushes back his chair and makes ready to leave. Adina glances down. He hasn't even touched his coffee. 'Leaving so soon?' she whispers.

'It's a long time since you were active. Do you remember how to contact me?'

She nods, then lowers her head towards him. 'I still don't think I'll need your help.'

'The unexpected creeps up on us', he says, before tapping the table and standing up. 'But no matter. I will be watching.'

Adina pecks at her coffee as he exits the shop. Yuri's message, delivered so succinctly, is now heard and understood. She digs deep in her training to keep tears and emotion from blotting her face. Then she glances at her watch. Her new exhibition opened to the public ten minutes ago. Yesterday, her work had filled her every waking hour. Today, she doesn't give a damn.

Chapter 32

Monday 4pm, and Gill drove up the A92 to Montrose as fast as he dared. The alert had come through towards the end of a gruelling one-hour meeting with Tony. Gill's publisher was fretting about what they would do if the *Fated Stone* turned out to be the real deal, leaving him trapped in the twin headlights of the story potential and the political ramifications. Their opinions were at an impasse when a call from Gordon's care home alerted Gill. His father was awake and asking for him. Consequently, he dropped everything and rushed to his father's bedside; painfully mindful that this could be "goodbye" to the last member of his family.

Arriving at the care home, he tossed his car into a visitor's bay and using both crutches, limped inside. After a rushed consultation with the care team, Gill arrived at Gordon's bedside a few minutes later.

The old man's eyes were drooping, but for the first time in four months, his gaze shifted, and he looked at Gill face on.

'Hey, Dad', said Gill softly.

Gordon raised a bony hand, and in response, Gill gripped it.

'Something happened', Gordon whispered slowly.

'What happened, Dad?'

'To you.'

Gill gently squeezed his father's hand.

Gordon gave a dry cough. 'You changed. After the waterhorses.'

Gill searched his memory. After his time on Harris, he'd had six intense months learning the magazine trade. Nothing significant happened in his life until Loch Ness and his collision with Salina Ahmed. 'Did it? I'm not sure what you're thinking of.'

Gordon studied Gill's face as if seeing it for the first time in a long while. 'You're different somehow … got purpose.'

'Did I change, Dad? I guess I'm not aware.'

Gordon looked away. 'I … I dunno. Somehow.' His eyelids flickered up and down. 'Proud of you, Gill.'

'Dad?'

But Gordon's consciousness had collapsed again. Gill gave his father a little shake. But it was no good. His chest rose and fell in a gentle rhythm. He was asleep.

Emotionally wrung out, Gill sank into a bedside chair, parsing his father's few words through his brain and wondering what he'd meant. But it wasn't clear to him, and he grew frustrated. He'd been under the impression that having a faith would make a difference in moments like this. That somehow, a great blanket of peace would land over everything, and things would be … alright. He'd hoped his father's last days would pass gently, but instead, everything seemed so … incomplete. He scratched at a ragged fingernail and wondered. Questioning if taking Raphael's sword had been worth it. Measuring if this unexpected deposit of belief had made the slightest difference to the outcome of his life. And he was stuck with it now. He couldn't unlearn the things he'd seen, or un-hear the words he'd heard. So, what the hell was the point of it all?

Aware he should stay a while in case Gordon resurfaced, he dropped his face in his hands and started a long angry prayer to a God with whom he was barely acquainted. Just as he was reaching a crescendo of self-pity, the small voice in his head reminded him how he had survived the attack at Airth, and how the lifeboat had come just in time to pluck his damaged body from the North Sea. And it reminded him that someday he would lie where Gordon lay now, his body worn out and dying, ready for the great mystery of what comes after. And all the while, his father's voice, lingered like a backing track in his head. Words he'd never, ever, heard before. 'Proud of you, Gill.'

He sat for an hour, resenting his pain, yet knowing this ache was a reminder they were both still alive. Gordon had lived his last years with a similar philosophy. Had he been able at this moment to sit up and talk, he'd be urging Gill to get on with his life. Taking a deep breath, Gill stood up, kissed his father's head, and decided to do just that.

The following afternoon, Gill unlocked the door to the nondescript laboratory and switched on the lights. He knew he was taking a risk, showing the stone to someone else. But he needed to move forwards, so shuffling on his crutches, he stood aside to let Adina step into the harshly lit room.

'You don't have security?' she asked, glancing around her.

'Until we know we have something worth securing, it seems like a pointless expense. Besides you have to get through two doors to get here, and the university has night staff on patrol.'

'Impressive', she said, not sounding like she meant it.

'We have a mixture of artefacts. Lots of small metallics, some organics.' He nodded towards the centre of the room. 'And we have the ship's ballast.'

'And all this came of a single wreck in the Firth of Forth?'

'Yes. Though I'd prefer not to say where for now.'

'The age of the wreck?

'The boat was built from locally sourced oak, harvested soon after the year 900', said Gill, choosing his words carefully. 'And we have a separate record mentioning the wreck site and suggesting the loss of a valuable cargo.'

Adina gave him a thin smile. She looked cold, nervous, or both. 'Can you tell me what you're looking for?'

'I'd rather not be specific.'

Adina sighed and rubbed her forehead with the forefinger of her left hand. 'Mr McArdle. I'm a busy woman, and so far, I'm offering you my expertise for no fee. That might change if we spend the next few hours playing a game of archaeological hide and seek.'

'Okay', said Gill. 'I see your point.'

He led the way to a low platform built from a stack of wooden pallets with a protective cloth covering stone MS12.

He nodded at it. 'This is the object we're interested in. I'll give you a moment to take a look.'

Adina pulled back the cloth and sat on it, protecting her trousers while she leaned over the stone. 'What analysis have you done so far?'

'I've had a geologist look at it.'

'And what did they say?'

Briefly, Gill told her about Billy Whyte and the most likely source he judged for the stone.

'So, you met a guy in a bar. Is he any good?'

'He has a business. I gather he's quite successful.'

Adina didn't look convinced. 'Can I have his contact details? In case I need to check a technical point with him.'

'Sure'. Gill burrowed in his waistcoat pocket, presenting her with Billy's rather frayed-looking card.

Adina dropped the card in her bag and extracted a strong LED torch and magnifying glass. Then she worked in silence for ten minutes, studying the surface of the stone.

'Golan Heights, said your geologist?'

'Yes. Or southern Galilee.'

'Hmm. He's not far off. This is Yarda basalt. From further south.'

'Oh', said Gill, acutely aware this placed the source of the stone just north of Bethel and the location of the *Jacob's Pillow* myth. 'You can tell that just by looking at it?'

'My expertise is Persia. Remember?'

Gill nodded.

'Israel was part of Greater Persia for a time. And Yarda basalt is very fine. It carves well. In fact, we have several pieces in the National Museum.'

'It's a long way from home. I wonder how it came to rest in the Firth of Forth?'

Adina reverently stroked the stone. 'It will have come from the Yarmouk River which is south of the Golan Heights and feeds into the Jordan Basin. Over the aeons, the river has eroded softer rocks and now rests on a bed of ancient basalt.'

Gill stepped closer and ran his hand over the stone. 'Which would explain why it's so smooth.'

'After the raw stone was dislodged by a storm, it probably rested in the river for centuries.' She looked up at him. 'Of course, all of this is conjecture. I'd need to get it back to the museum laboratory to be completely sure.'

Gill nodded but said nothing. He watched as Adina produced a collapsible set-square from her bag and set it around the outside of the stone. She noted a few numbers and periodically moved the measuring stick through ninety degrees, before taking another reading. Watching her work, Gill detected a tiny tremor in her breath. 'It's exceptionally regular', she said, completing her measurements. 'I'm struggling to imagine that was achieved by natural erosion.'

'Sometimes miracles can happen in nature', observed Gill.

'Indeed they can', she replied quietly.

She turned to face him. 'Well, there you are. I doubt I can offer your further assistance without understanding your interest is in this particular stone.'

'We took core samples from all the ballast from the wreck. This one stuck out because it isn't local', said Gill, truthfully.

'I see. But you were specifically looking for this object?'

Gill looked away while he judged how much to say. 'As an archaeologist, I'm just following clues.'

She packed away her tools and moved around to the far side of the stone. 'I recall I helped one of your researchers on an earlier story. Mhairi Dodd. Is she still working with you?'

'Yes.'

'She wanted my point of view on the roots of Persian astronomy.'

'She did. Thanks for your help on that.'

'And I recall you caused yourself some considerable embarrassment about how you applied that information.'

Gill shook his head. 'I stand by the story. Not everybody believes it, but I can live with that.'

'And yet you are the undisputed discoverer of Equus pictus.' She formed a thin smile. 'I see your waterhorses every day of my working life. We've mounted your picture on the display board. I walk past it and shudder.'

'Actually, some folk think I'm quite good-looking', he said, running his left hand through his dark red hair.

'Your reputation, Gill. Some people think you're inspired. An equal number think you're a fool.'

Gill dropped his face towards the floor and chewed on a smile. 'It was ever thus. The difference today is, I no longer care what people think about me.'

'What I'm saying, Gill, is I can't afford to be that cavalier. Frankly, I'm reluctant to associate the museum's reputation with one of your projects until I know exactly what you're working on.'

'I'm afraid I can't divulge that at the moment.'

'Why? Because you're saving the big reveal for your magazine?'

Gill shook his head. 'For this stone to be what I think it is, another stone has to be a fake. At the moment, my publisher has me sworn to secrecy.'

'Okay', said Adina, gathering herself to leave. 'If you want my closer cooperation, I'll wait to hear if you change your mind.'

'Sorry, I hope I haven't offended you. Thank you for coming over. And for your thoughts on the stone.'

Adina got to the door where she turned and shook the rather flimsy handle. 'Get a better lock, Gill. Just in case you're guarding something precious.'

Cassy, Mhairi and Gill watched nervously as Tony paced around the conference room in continuous circles. Gill had never seen him so agitated.

'Let me check I've got this right', he said, the finger of his right hand splayed by his side. 'We have a sandstone slab from Airth, with the same microfossil fingerprint as the *Stone of Destiny*. And you're certain this slab is genuine?'

'Yes', said Gill.

'And that slab led you, somewhat tenuously, to find a wreck off the Isle of May. On that wreck, you find a long, slim basalt stone, originating from the Jordan Valley, in the same general area as the mythical *Jacob's Pillow*?'

'Aye.'

'And now you want to float the idea the *Stone of Destiny*, newly enthroned in its shiny-new Perth Museum, is a fake and we've got the real one, tucked in a university storeroom?'

'That the existing stone in Perth is a substitute for whatever the Scots brought with them on their sojourn is almost beyond doubt', said Gill.

'Though a big question mark hangs over its link to the *Jacob's Pillow* myth', stated Tony. 'Meanwhile, the *Stone of Destiny* has been revered these last seven hundred years and was the stone acquired by Edward the First, yes?'

'That is true', said Mhairi.

Tony leaned forward. 'I can't see how we can proceed with this story without ridiculing the *Declaration of Arbroath*, or the *Stone of Destiny*, or both.'

'The *Declaration* doesn't mention the *Stone of Destiny*', countered Gill.

'No, but it claims a Middle Eastern origin for the Scottish people. The implication is that we gathered the *Stone* during our sacred journey', said Tony.

Gill nodded. 'Which is why most serious scholars see the *Declaration* as propaganda by the Scottish nobility.'

'Great!' said Tony, throwing his hands out wide. 'We'll be debunking the *Stone of Destiny* and the *Declaration* in the same issue of the magazine. Just before a mob armed with pitchforks attack us in the street!'

'Thing is Tony, that's what the facts on the ground are saying.'

'Facts? Are we one hundred per cent certain?'

Gill thought for a moment. 'Nine-nine point nine.'

Tony leapt towards Gill and held two fingers in front of him, squeezing them together like he was about to pick a fleck off Gill's shirt. 'And with that tiny amount of uncertainty, they will crucify us.'

'Who's they, Tony?'

'The nationalist government in Holyrood. The British government in Westminster. Basically, anybody that loses face if we debunk the *Stone of Destiny*.'

Gill looked at Cassy and Mhairi in turn. 'What would you have us do, Tony?'

'For once, I'm praying you've got it wrong. Look, I'm going to have to think about this. Please, on the pain of dismissal from *Mys.Scot*, don't do anything with this until I've figured out the implications.'

With a final gasp of exasperation, Tony left the room.

'I thought we did good work', said Cassy. 'Personally, I love it when Gill plants metaphorical bombs under tracks of beloved Scottish mythology.'

'What ARE we going to do?' Mhairi demanded. 'We can't just sit on a wonderful story because it's commercially expedient.'

Gill sighed. 'Ultimately, we might need to go back to Adina Mofaz. She said yesterday she might be able to offer us more insights if she took the stone to her lab.'

Cassy screwed up her nose. 'I thought you wanted to keep this a secret?'

'I think she's already suspicious. Not necessarily that we have *Jacob's Pillow*, per se, but that we have our hands on something special.'

'I've not had contact with anyone else even approaching her level of expertise', said Mhairi.

Gill nodded. 'Tony needs us to be absolutely certain about this. If he demands more evidence that we have the *Fated Stone*, then I think Adina will be the person to help us.'

'What are you going to do?' asked Cassy.

'I'll message Adina, thanking her for her time today and asking her what further tests she'd run if we transfer the stone to her lab.'

Chapter 33

Four hours later, Gill was writing an article when Tony came by his desk. 'Gill. Remind me where exactly we're storing this stone of yours?'

'The Hammond Building. At the back of the genetics facility.' Gill looked up. 'Why do you ask?'

The colour drained from Tony's face. 'Why have I just had a call from Roddy Canmore's team demanding we meet him there immediately?'

'How can he know about that location?' Gill rocked back in his chair. 'Hang fire, Tony. We need to think this …' But Tony was already walking away. Gill grabbed his waistcoat and limped in Tony's wake.

Tony ordered a taxi for the short journey to Dundee University. They sat in the back together, Tony texting for the entire journey and Gill trying to make a mental note of the things he still wanted to cover in his article. When they arrived at the facility, they found a large BMW parked in a loading bay. The bonnet and sides of the vehicle were liveried in Scottish Saltire blue and white, with the words, *New Scotland* painted on the sides. Gill studied it while Tony paid for the taxi. 'Please don't tell me we're doing this', he said.

'Doing what?' barked Tony.

'Stepping into the jaws of Scotland's angriest man, without any kind of game plan.'

'We need to sort this, Gill. He obviously knows about the *Fated Stone*. We have to grab the bull by the horns.'

'He really doesn't like me, Tony. If I was to grab this particular bull by the testicles, he couldn't get any angrier than he is now.'

'Regard this as an opportunity. If he's persuaded we've found something valuable, it might open up a debate. We could yet see both stones exhibited in Perth, each with the kudos they deserve.'

Gill moaned loudly. Like a petulant teenager, dragged home and away from his mates, he followed Tony into the building's reception area, ignoring the glowering bulk of Roddy Canmore while he fumbled with the keys.

'What's this all about, Roddy?' asked Tony.

'A wee bird tells me you're about to slur Scotland's *Stone of Destiny*.'

Tony offered Roddy his best team-building smile. 'Archaeology uncovers history. If we get new evidence, our theories need to evolve to fit the facts.'

'I don't see how finding a new stone changes anything', Roddy sneered. 'What is it anyway?'

'I'll let Gill explain the details.'

Gill left the key in the door and buried his hands in his pockets. 'I will. But first I want you to tell me how you knew the stone was here?'

Roddy scratched his head and did a poor job of smothering his irritation. 'I dare say you're good at your job, Mr McArdle. Let's just say I'm good at mine.'

'And what exactly is your job?' asked Gill, pushing into the man's personal space. 'Now you're no longer the Cabinet Secretary for Justice?'

Roddy held his ground. 'Why, I'm the next king of Scotland, you moron.'

'Come on, Gill', said Tony, placing a hand on Gill's chest to block him getting any closer to Roddy.

Once he had Gill contained, Tony switched his attention to Roddy. 'If you won't tell us how you know it's here, can you at least explain why you're so threatened by Gill's discovery?'

'I don't feel threatened. It took us seven centuries to get the stone back from England, I'm just pissed off that he's trying to discredit it.'

'I'm not trying to discredit anything. I'm just helping us recover something precious we lost along the way.'

'How do you even know if you've got anything more than a random rock?' said Roddy. 'We know where the *Stone of Destiny* has been this past seven hundred years. I doubt yours has better credentials.'

Gill's indignation rose again, but Tony grasped his wrist. 'Come on. Let's show him the stone so he can make up his mind.'

'Aye, well', Gill grumbled. 'It's not like it's a secret anymore.'

Tony propelled Gill into the room containing the finds from the shipwreck and gesticulated to Gill to point out the stone. But Roddy caught them both by surprise by striding ahead. He marched over to the rows of ballast laid out on the floor and pointed at the stone labelled MS12.

'This it?'

'Yes', said Gill.

'Tell me about it.'

Drawing a deep breath, Gill decided to go all in. He outlined the discovery of the *Airth Slab*, leading to the Isle of May wreck and the preliminary identification by Billy Whyte. Finally, he explained the credentials of Adina Mofaz and her confidence the stone came from the Jordan Valley.

Roddy held a hand in the air. 'If I cut through the science crap, you're telling me you're almost certain that at some point in history, this lump of rock was considered to be the *Stone of Destiny*. Yes?'

Gill nodded. 'Though it was known as the *Fated Stone* in our early history.'

Roddy sniffed. 'Okay. Help me understand why I should care?'

Gill threw Tony a *told you so* look. 'We know the stone in Perth Museum was quarried within half a mile of the town centre. There's no way that particular stone undertook a long arduous journey from the holy land as implied by the *Declaration of Arbroath*.'

'An interesting puzzle', said Roddy. 'I'm sure your readers will love it. But here's the key question, and I want you to grasp it very clearly. Is the stone in the Perth Museum the same stone seized by the English seven hundred years ago?'

'Yes. Of course.'

'Then that, and that alone, is the *Stone of Destiny*.'

Gill clasped his hands together and worked to keep his professional face. 'Surely the attribute that made that stone special in the first place was the myth around its Middle Eastern provenance. Its link to a Jewish patriarch, and its transportation over fifteen centuries to the land we know as Scotland?'

Roddy laughed heartily. 'That's a load of religious bollocks. What makes the stone special is its captivity by the English and its eventual liberation to become part of the crown jewels of an independent Scotland.'

In disbelief at Roddy's deceitful grasp of history, Gill shook his hands in front of him. 'Even though you acknowledge it's most likely a substitute?'

Roddy walked towards the door. 'Don't ever go into politics, Mr McArdle. You'd be shite at it.' He paused to stand near Tony. 'To answer your original question, Tony. What we're about is this. Scotland just spent £20 million rehousing the *Stone of Destiny*. And to save this country from the people who're trying to tiptoe their way to an independent Scotland, I've launched a new political movement on the back of the goodwill engendered in that proud moment.'

'By "people who tiptoe", do you mean moderate nationalists?' asked Gill.

The sneer was back on Roddy's face. 'You, McArdle. You're a Scot?'

'My mother was from the south of Ireland, but I was born and raised here. This is my home.'

'Ah! You're Irish.'

'I'm not Irish …' began Gill, before Roddy cut across him.

'Why're you set against Scottish independence?'

Gill thought for a moment. 'I'm not. On a certain romantic level, I actually quite like the idea. On a warm Saturday evening after a wedding, with a glass of whisky in my hand and bagpipes playing in the background, it really quite appeals. But soon it's a wet Monday morning again and I remember I haven't yet seen enough evidence we'd prosper as an independent state.'

Roddy drew his hands to his hips. 'You watch me for a couple o' years and I'll give you evidence.'

'But you've split nationalism in half. And your extremism could push people away from the idea of an independent Scotland.'

'Could …', said Tony, not normally lost for words. 'Could we get back to the issue at hand?'

Roddy spun to face him. 'I stand for stability and strength. The stone enthroned in Perth is the one and only *Stone of Destiny*. If either of you tries to discredit it, I'll make your Orkney mess look like nine holes at Camperdown *pitch 'n putt*.'

'Another example of unpopular science', said Gill, defensively.

'There's even a few folk wondering if yon waterhorses weren't faked as well', said Roddy, cracking a sarcastic smile. 'When it comes to faking evidence, I gather you've got form.'

'There's no way …' shot Gill, but Roddy dismissed him.

'Thanks for the wee tour, gents. But I'll have no allegiance to your new stone.'

They followed Roddy outside and watched him climb into his car.

Tony sighed. 'That's one mean son-of-a-bitch.'

'Ah! Finally we agree', Gill snorted.

Tony stood with his hands on his hips as the blue and white car roared away. 'Not sure what we can do, Gill.'

'Roddy Canmore shouldn't get to arbitrate on what is, or is not, a precious national object. Not when politics is his only guide.'

'But if we go against Canmore's judgement, he'll swing the argument away from science and use politics as a big stick to beat our brand.'

Gill nodded furiously, desperate to find another route to harness the court of public opinion. 'Are you still matey with any of the tabloid editors?'

'One of two.' Tony's eyes narrowed. 'Why do you ask?'

'I need to stretch my legs. Think for a bit.' Gill started to walk away. 'Let's get a proper debate started.'

'Hang on, Gill. What are you proposing?'

Gill spun around and swung his arms out wide. 'We need to democratise this decision. Let's swamp Canmore's dissenting voice by throwing this out to the public. Let them judge between a cherished substitute and the real thing.'

Chapter 34

The *Mys.Scot* team gathered in the conference room trying to decide how to respond to Roddy Canmore's dismissal of the stone. For the first time in Gill's experience, tempers in the room were fraying.

'Hey, hey', said Gill, raising his voice. 'Let's not make this personal.'

'This is aboot Scotland, pal', said Larry with an edge to his voice. 'Of course it's personal.'

'This is a minefield, Gill', said Cassy. 'Before we blow ourselves to pieces working on what is essentially a political story, we should all lay our cards on the table.'

'What do you mean?' asked Gill.

'Scottish independence. It's ten years since the last vote. How would we feel if there was another referendum? Everyone in the team should explain where they stand. Get it all out in the open. That way we'll avoid any misunderstandings and we can more forward, treating each other with dignity and respect.'

'That's braw', said Larry, sarcastically. 'Do ye want us tae tak' oor clathes off as weel?'

'Larry!' Mhairi protested.

'I think Cassy's got a good idea', said Gill. 'Next week could be quite tough, so I agree with her. Let's start by clearing the air. Make sure we aren't double guessing each other's motives as the story develops.' Gill glanced around the room. 'Everybody cool with this?'

Silently, everyone nodded.

'I'll go first', said Larry, tapping the table in front of him. 'Scotland shuild be free. Simple as tha'. Noo an forever. Whativer the cost.'

'Tick one for independence', said Gill, diplomatically. 'Who's next?'

Craig shook his shoulders. 'I'm not a flag-waving radical like Larry here. But I was raised on a croft and you cannae tell me life on the Scottish rural margins could be any tougher under an independent government. So yeah, as a matter of principle, I'm with Larry.'

Gill nodded his thanks and glanced at Cassy.

Cassy folded her arms in front of her. 'For me, it's all about Brexit.'

'That waz years ago', muttered Larry. 'Anither Westminster cockup.'

'No', said Cassy. 'My point is this. In my limited experience, our country hasn't got any better by getting smaller and shunning its neighbours. I don't always like it, but I'd stick with the union.'

'Indie-pendance would fix yon Brexit', said Larry.

'Sorry, Larry', said Gill. 'We're not reheating the debate. We're just saying where we stand.'

Larry folded his arms. 'Right, pal.'

Gill flicked his chin at Mhairi. 'What about you?'

Mhairi jiggled her palms in front of her. 'Oh no, I'm English. Keep me out of this.'

'But you live here', said Craig. 'In the eyes of the state, you're a Scot. So bring it on. If there was another referendum, how would you vote?'

'I'd hate to see it become harder for people to travel over the border', said Mhairi. 'People moving for jobs, or trade or whatever. I guess I'd stick with the status quo.'

'Okay', said Craig. 'Boss. That leaves you. What 'ya think?'

'Oh, man', said Gill. 'I'm an on-the-fence kinda guy.'

'Nae surprises there', said Larry quietly.

'Come on, Gill', said Mhairi. 'I had to choose. You need to as well.'

'Heart of hearts', said Gill. 'I'd love to see Scotland, living as a good neighbour to England, but completely running its own affairs.' He stopped and looked at the faces around the room. 'But I'm a data guy. I look for evidence. And I've witnessed a quarter century of devolution and so far, it hasn't come close to convincing me we'd thrive on our own.'

'Aw, man', whispered Larry.

'Don't get me wrong. I think Scotland needs nationalism. We need a little prodding to consider what might be possible. And I'm quite concerned that the current ruptures within nationalism risk pushing us to extremes. It increases the danger that nationalism never earns the trust of a majority of

Scots and the whole idea of independence becomes so tarnished that even devolution comes into question.'

'Enough words, Gill', said Cassy. 'Independence. Yes, or no?'

'Fifty-five to forty-five per cent, I'd keep things as they are. And spend the next few years urging our politicians to do better.'

'Or becoming one yourself', said Mhairi.

Everyone else in the room sniggered.

'See yon', said Larry, pointing at Gill. 'Ma gerbil's got mare chance o' bein' elected than him.'

'Is your gerbil a unionist or an indie?' Cassy shot back.

Larry withdrew his finger and thought. 'The wee bugger can only kip in torn-up strips o' Th' Daily Mail. Dae ye think the Tories might hae brainwashed him?'

'Yep', said Cassy. 'Larry's gerbil is a unionist lackey.'

'Thinking aboot it, when I checked on him the o'r mornin' he'd licked the shape o' the Union Jack in his fud bowl.'

'Thank you, ladies and gentlemen', said Gill, smirking. 'Hands in the middle, please.'

Following his lead, they leant into the middle of the table and formed a five-way handshake.

'Friends regardless?' asked Cassy.

The team affirmed their agreement and hung in a brief moment of unity. Then Larry lit a touchpaper, and the gentle name-calling began again.

The following day, after much debate and finally, with Tony's reluctant permission, the *Mys.Scot* team inserted a new lead article in issue 22 before it went to the printers. Setting out the credentials of the old stone and the new, the frontpage headline simply declared, *Scotland's right to choose*. The article wouldn't be in the shops until Monday by which time Gill planned to have a public debate already underway. On Friday, just in time for the weekend papers, a dossier outlining the facts held by *Mysterious Scotland* concerning the two stones went up on the magazine's website. To fuel the fire, Tony leaked a summary to the Scottish press, tossing a pebble into the calm pool of what was otherwise a quiet day for news. On Saturday, the nationalist broadsheets were quick to rally to the established stone, their writers sensing an English plot to cast doubt on Scotland's grasp of history. The tabloids were more circumspect. Some websites saw the news-worthiness of celebrating the freshly discovered stone, while the biggest printed daily decided to oppose both candidates and reignite a campaign for a massive excavation at Scone where they were confident the true stone would lie. Their reasoning was that the very original and authentic stone was hidden from Edward the First and still lay buried on the grounds.

The story continued to flare across the front pages for two days, but despite the column inches of newsprint and online deliberation, the debate didn't grab the public's imagination. To most folk, a stone was just a stone. On the third day, the story dropped off the front page. On the fourth day, a survey organised by a national polling company produced a thin majority in favour of the old stone, against a backdrop of widespread public indifference.

The following weekend, The Daily Record had the final word in the debate. Asking their readers what should happen to the new stone, 12% of responses wanted it added to the display in Perth, 18% advocated its return to Israel, and 70% thought it should be despatched back to the Forth. In service of this democratic mandate, a Fife trawlerman called "Bobby", was offering to do the job for free.

The impact on *Mys.Scot* was mixed. Sales predictions for issue 22 were sky-high, but the authority of the magazine seemed further diminished.

Gill had backed the wrong horse.

And lost.

Twelve days after Gill and Tony's confrontation with Roddy, they admitted defeat. In the court of public opinion, the basalt slab from Israel would never usurp the sandstone block from Perth. And at the end of the day, Gill could live with that. It's just he had a strange feeling that somehow, Scotland, the land he loved, was missing out.

He was still thinking about this on Monday morning when a text came in. It was from Solomon. Blunt and to the point. '*Jacob's Pillow*. Can I see it?'

Gill grunted to himself. She'd have read about it in the papers rather than hearing it from him. Given his promise to her, he should have mentioned it to her.

'If that's what we've got, you are welcome to see it', he texted back.

'When?'

He glanced at his watch. 'It's almost lunchtime. I can be there in half an hour.'

Solomon responded with a thumbs-up. He sighed. Her brevity probably wasn't a good sign.

'We don't know for sure', said Gill, back at the Hammond Building, as they stood side by side looking down at the basalt rock. 'But the data suggests it's the genuine article and my instinct concurs.'

Solomon sank to her knees and placed her palms on the surface. 'Just imagine for a moment it's real, Gill. That Jacob, one of the most famous names in *The Book*, had laid his head on this rock to sleep, and in doing so, had an encounter with God that changed his life. Then, recognizing its importance, the Jews hauled it around for hundreds of years. And if the old stories are correct, then the Scots carried it for thousands more. Perhaps the only important Biblical artefact still in existence; I wonder what it could tell us, Gill. If it could speak?'

'It's just a rock', said Gill. 'I don't think we should idolize it.'

'You're right. And I'm not. But I am slightly in awe.' Solomon flexed her fingers on the surface of the smooth black rock as if she were trying to grip it with her fingertips. 'You can't underestimate the potential importance of this object. I do hope you're protecting it.'

'You saw how we got on last week', said Gill. 'The Scots don't want it. No one else has shown much interest.'

'From what I read in the press you've proven beyond reasonable doubt this was *Jacob's Pillow*. I'm certain there'll be people out there who'd love to get their hands on it.'

'Like who?'

'I don't know. Collectors? Religious groups? Cults?'

He raised an eyebrow. 'Is that divine inspiration?'

'No, Gill. It's plain common sense.'

'Maybe they should have it then.'

'And then what?' she growled. 'It disappears again for another thousand years? If there's even the possibility this thing is real, you need to safeguard it. Guide it into the hands of people who will study and protect it.'

He looked her in the eye and saw how serious she was. Solomon was making a good point. At the same time, he caught himself listening out for the rumble of a faraway heavy motorcycle. But the noise didn't come. Instead, his internal alert had started to pulse red, and somehow, he knew he needed to act.

Chapter 35

Adina is working late. Partly because she's busy. Partly because the atmosphere at home is frosty. She still hasn't told Douglas what's going on, and as things stand, she never will. And he doesn't know this version of Adina. This rendering of herself has been stored away and hidden since before she and Douglas became a couple. This person with clipped military precision. A zealot, willing perhaps, to sacrifice her family for her cause. She shakes her head. Even now, sitting alone in her office well into the evening, she can't just be Adina Mofaz; head of 'International Culture'. Reflected on her computer screen, she sees her mask slip and an altogether different person blinks back at her.

Alongside the work she's doing for the museum, a timer idles over the icon for a program, sitting minimized on her desktop. Using her skills and dark web resources, she's hacked the CCTV at Dundee University, and now a motion sensor scans the footage, activating whenever someone enters or leaves Gill McArdle's storage room. There have been comings and goings, but so far, the exercise has been mundane.

So far, she has hidden her failure from Commander Yuri. That the stone lay virtually undefended for four days and she didn't exploit this vulnerability seems in retrospect to have been a tactical blunder. But she'd had an email from McArdle the day after she'd viewed the stone, hinting that he might simply give it to her for analysis. She'd had a foretaste of triumph; anticipating the moment she'd hand over the stone to Yuri in the safety of the museum laboratory. And even now she smiles at the irony - she could have had a substitute manufactured and flown in from Israel in a matter of days. McArdle would never have known!

Instead she paused, waiting for McArdle's decision. Rather than hand the stone to her, he exploded a media bomb around the so called *Fated Stone*. And it has been in the news ever since. She was appalled at first. At her own mistake, but also the elevated risk that the artefact might be transferred to a more secure location. And while it remains in the public eye, she can't attempt to secure it. That would risk rewarding it with an air of mystery that even McArdle hasn't quite achieved. Instead, she keeps tabs on where it is stored. When the fuss dies down, she'll alert Yuri. With the stone's location in his grasp, their mission could be over in a matter of hours. Then she'll be free of him.

In the meantime, she has the stress and tedium of monitoring the CCTV feeds. And nothing interesting has happened for a week. She hadn't been around to watch the incident live but has reviewed one interesting piece of footage during a moment of privacy. Gill McArdle, and his boss, Tony Farquharson, plus another man; a face she vaguely recognized. The facial recognition software had him soon enough. Roderick Canmore. An MSP and until very recently a member of the Scottish cabinet. Her heart had leapt with alarm. If McArdle was showing Canmore the stone, they might be preparing an announcement. And if the stone should be embraced by the Scottish authorities, the personal cost of acquiring it would destroy her.

And so, she watches the footage several times. The recording has no sound, but as she studies their gestures, she detects hostility between the men. Disagreement! That's good. It seems the stone isn't going anywhere for a while and that suits her fine.

That had been a week ago and, in the meantime, the Scottish press has poured scorn on the new stone's credentials. Its theft now will mean nothing more than an amusing footnote to the story. And so, she's informed Yuri of the stone's whereabouts. Tonight, his team will go in around 2 am when the city and university are at their quietest. It will be a swift, bloodless task and a plane, scheduled under dubious diplomatic papers, is ready to go. If all goes well, by breakfast time tomorrow, this Sword of Damocles over her life will be gone.

Musing on this happy thought, she sees the app's icon start flashing on her screen. Double-checking that no one is around, she maximises the image and watches. Two men, hidden under dirty black baseball caps present security passes to the door mechanism of the Hammond Building and walk inside. A few minutes pass before they return to fetch a large rectangular box from their van and place it on a trolley. Then they go back inside. With rising alarm, she realises what is happening. By the time the two men emerge again, they are struggling with the weight of the box. In desperation, she considers calling Yuri. But he's no fool, and he'll not be laying clues by hanging around nearby. Instead, he'll be hiding in the countryside, well away from cameras and chance encounters with the law. And she's sitting in Edinburgh. Even if she leaves right now and dashes to Dundee, the men will be long gone.

Reviewing her options, she realises she can't hack all the systems necessary to follow the van around the city. She needs to find a different way of tracking them. Digging into her training, she accesses the mobile phone network and tabs to the cell tower nearest to the university. She pulls up the list of mobile numbers currently linked to that cell and dumps it into a spreadsheet. Her fingers flashing over the keys she uses a lookup table to identify any contact details already in her mission file. She expects to see Gill McArdle's mobile, but instead, the table returns a different number. And this one belongs to Billy Whyte.

Adina stops and thinks. Is this an error? If it's right, the geologist must be in the area. She notices the van doors are closing and is about to move away. Deftly, she hunts online for an image of this man whom she's never met. Success only takes her a few seconds, and she uses this image to retarget the facial recognition software, tasking it to the half dozen university cameras she has under her control.

The van pulls away.

Thirty seconds later, the software has a hit. Zooming in, she finds Billy in the passenger seat of a red Ford Focus. She copies his number and the car registration across onto her tracking system and releases a ragged breath. It looks like Billy is also watching the *Fated Stone*. To what end, she has no idea. But now, while she has his mobile phone signal, Adina is following Billy.

Again, she considers contacting Yuri. But the man's ruthless streak makes him a threat to her if suddenly the artefact is on the move. During her training, she and two others were summoned to a rendezvous in central London. They were each given ten thousand dollars in cash and told to achieve a circuit of the globe within seven days. They were to achieve this goal independently and undetected, because, in that training mission, Yuri would be tracking them. And he duly found them all, chasing Adina down at a regional airport in Nebraska, and her colleague at a street food venue in Seoul. The fate of the third candidate was a mystery. He didn't return to London and was never heard from again. So, while Adina respects Yuri's skills, she doesn't need his show of force. And if she's honest with herself, she doubts her long-term value to him once the stone is secure. The more she chews on the problem, the more she realises that intercepting the stone herself might be the best bargaining chip she can muster. Then tonight, when Yuri breaks into the university and discovers the stone is gone, she'll have leverage again. Better to keep him in the dark for now. That way, she can keep control and negotiate an exit. But first, she needs to secure the stone. Grabbing her laptop and her bag, she heads for the lifts.

She is crossing the floor of the Grand Gallery when she feels it again; the ominous presence of the waterhorses. A grown woman, Adina should be able to shrug and walk on past. But she feels compelled to stop. Taking a breath, she appraises the risks ahead of her. Turning slowly through 360 degrees, she takes in the sights and smells of this place she loves. Tonight, instead of being a professional curator; of going home to be a wife and a mother, she will walk the short distance to Waverley Station to collect a gun. Then she's going into battle for the sake of an oath she'd sworn when little more than a child. And, honestly. She doesn't know if she's coming home.

'Hey, boys', she whispers to the skeletons. 'It's all been so much fun. Look after it for me.'

Chapter 36

Six hours after he met with Solomon, Gill sat in the sunroom of his father's house in Stonehaven. The dusk had fallen, and the room was cold through lack of use. In places, he thought he could detect a little dampness in the walls. He'd switched the heating on, but it would be several hours before the old house warmed up. He gathered a blanket off the back of a chair and tugged it around his shoulders and waited.

In the days since Roddy had confronted him at the Hammond Building, Gill still hadn't figured out how the man had known about the new stone and its location. Sitting on his own for the first time in days, he had a sudden thought. Googling Billy Whyte, he tabbed to the man's company web page. Reading his client references, it seemed Billy was legitimate, and held in high regard by his lengthy customer list. Returning to the search engine, he looked for other references. The research didn't take long.

'Damnit', muttered Gill to himself. 'I'm a mug.'

He drafted a quick email to Cassy and the team, alerting them to Billy's credentials. Cassy would be cross; she hated this kind of sloppiness. And it was all down to Gill. Billy, it transpired had been a county councillor in Aberdeen until a finance scandal had cut short his career. He'd been prosecuted, though the charge had been defeated with a verdict of 'Not Proven', a judgement unique to Scottish courts that essentially declared, while you weren't found guilty, you'd not been found innocent either. The ex-councillor remained defiant and had announced he would be running again at the next election, switching teams to run for Roddy Canmore's *New Scotland* party. It wasn't exactly a smoking gun, but when you added this coincidence to Gill's chance meeting with Billy in the Fisherman's Tavern, it looked like a reasonable conclusion.

Twenty minutes later, the sound of a delivery van reversing along the harbourfront distracted him. Gill pulled back a curtain and watched. After a few clumsy attempts to get into the narrow side street, the vehicle came to a stop outside Gordon's front door. There was a muttering of voices, then one of the van doors slammed and a figure approached the house, silhouetted against the street lighting around the harbour. A man in white overalls came to the door, his uniform carrying the same high street logo as the livery on the side of the van.

'Got a delivery for ye, pal', said the man, waving a clipboard at Gill. 'Says here it's a fridge freezer.'

'Thanks', said Gill. 'I'm expecting it.'

The man jerked a thumb at the van where his colleague was already lowering a robust cardboard box on a hydraulic ramp. 'It's awfie heavy. Ye wouldnae be able to gie us a hand?'

Gill blinked twice, then pointed at his crutches leaning in a corner. 'Sorry. I've hurt my legs.'

'Nae bother, pal. Me and Johnny will hae it sorted in just a jiffy.'

Gill watched as the two men huffed and puffed the box onto a trolley and dragged it down the close. 'Where'd ye like it', said the first man, struggling to catch his breath.

'The loft', said Gill with a straight face.

The second, taller man uttered a quiet expletive.

'The kitchen, sir?' said the first man. 'Right ye are then.'

Gill stood aside as the two men grunted and swore their way into the house. Closing the front door, then the porch door behind them, he followed them into the kitchen. 'Next Christmas, you two should consider doing panto', he said.

'Aye, panto my arse', said Larry, dropping his disguise.

'That thing weighs a bloody tonne', said Craig. 'If I've put my back out tonight, I promise, I'm gonna be on sick leave for a month.'

'One hundred and twenty-five kilos', said Gill. 'Not quite a tonne.'

'Any chance of a cup of tea?'

'Don't you have more deliveries to make?' said Gill.

Larry and Craig looked at each other. 'You know we don't.'

'But, if you're to stay in character, you'll have been seen delivering this box and then dashing off to your next appointment.'

'Seriously?' moaned Larry.

'Meanwhile, the back door of your van is lying wide open to anyone who passes by. Where'd you get it anyway?'

'My uncle runs a breakers yard', said Craig. 'We're lucky it still works.'

'And the uniforms?'

Larry looked away. 'Ask me nae questions an' ah'll tell ye nae lies.'

Gill tried to camouflage a smile. 'Thank you, guys. Seriously. And safe home.'

He opened the doors for them and watched their languid steps, back to the van. 'Fancy going tae a trucker's café?' he heard Larry say. 'Coz a've niver been a trucker afore.'

Gill shook his head and went back inside. He didn't need to, but he wanted to check the contents of the box. It did indeed contain an upright freezer (second hand), and inside, wrapped in a blanket was a long, black stone.

The following morning, Gill was the last to arrive in the office. Pleased with his night's work, he gave Larry a tight-lipped nod as he walked in.

'You're looking chipper, boss', said Craig.

'Legs are feeling better. Hopefully, I'll be able to start running again soon.'

'Dinnae rush it', muttered Larry, rubbing the base of his back. 'Might wanna try weight lifting for a while.'

Gill smiled and laid his laptop bag on his desk. Cassy was on her way back from the coffee machine when she saw Gill and the others. Her eyes darted from one to another as her female intuition kicked in. 'What's going on?'

'Operation *Ice Tray* was a complete success', said Craig.

'Where did you take it?' asked Mhairi.

Craig winked at Larry. 'We could tell you the town, but when you think about it, the clue's in the name.'

Mhairi pulled a puzzled face then, after a few moments, she giggled. 'Actually, that's quite funny.'

Cassy sniffed and sat down at her screen. 'Honestly! You boys …' She stopped and thought for a second. 'After all this effort, have you munchkins left the stone unprotected in a deserted house?'

Gill shook his head. 'Salina came up first thing and I'll be back up there before dark.'

Cassy blinked three times. 'You have the love of your life home-sitting a rock? That woman will do anything for you. Marry her, quick, before she comes to her senses.'

'Will do', said Gill. 'As soon as I find a half-decent ceilidh band to lead the dancing.'

Cassy reacted to this gentle provocation with her trademark snort of indignation. She ignored the back-and-forth banter behind her and sat staring at her emails for several long seconds. 'No, sodding, way', she said quietly.

'What's up?'

'Could I have a word, Gill? Privately if possible.'

'Aye, don't mind us', said Larry.

'We're just the hired help', muttered Craig.

'Just a pair o' ol' truckers', added Larry, laughing at his own joke.

Gill hadn't got as far as sitting down, and the conference room was already occupied, so he followed Cassy out to the stairwell, with its glass walls overlooking the street.

'How did you know?' she said.

'Know what?'

'We just had an email from the university. They're reporting a break-in at the Hammond Building.'

'Oh, dear. Anything stolen?'

'They didn't say. They need us to go down and take a look. But when we go down there, we both know the only thing missing was the subject of operation *Ice Tray*.' She stopped and jabbed him in his chest. 'My point is you knew.'

Gill flinched. 'I suspected.'

'How?'

He glanced down into the street. 'I had some intelligence.'

'Who warned you? Salina? Billy? That museum woman?'

Gill let out a long slow breath. 'You wouldn't believe me if I told you.'

'Try me.'

'It's not a short story. And we've both got work to do.'

'So, I'll pull a late shift. Gill. The break-in. How. Did. You. Know?'

'Grab your coat', he said. 'Let's get across to the university and check if anything's amiss. Then I'll buy you a coffee and tell you the craziest story you've ever heard.'

Gill sat opposite Cassy with her coffee cooling in front of her. She'd only spoken in grunts and murmurs for the last several minutes and Gill was starting to feel nervous.

'Aren't you going to say something?' he asked.

She half shook her head and looked away from him. 'You're telling me you're guided by a higher power?'

'Not all the time. Just when … when I need an intervention to keep me on track.'

'You think you're Jesus or something?'

'What? No. Far from it.' He fought for the right words. 'I've come to believe there's order in the created universe and that I'm finding my place within it.'

'A created universe? God made the world in seven days, and all that?'

'Created, yes. I think if you look at what *The Book* actually says, the quoted seven days is a gross simplification. It reduced an impossibly complex topic to something humanity's earliest thinkers could grasp.'

'And the fact you and Salina chose to dive the May Isle, based on what, weird lightning? You took that as a sign from God?'

Gill thought for a second. 'Yes.'

She crouched over the table towards him. 'Do you have any idea how bonkers that sounds?'

He laughed unintentionally. 'You should have seen how we found the waterhorse bones. That was a whole separate level of crazy.'

'What do you mean?'

Gill waved a hand in front of his face. 'Never mind. Long conversation for another day. The point is, we dived where the lightning fell, and we found the wreck. Cass, the lightning led us to the *Fated Stone*.'

Cassy was shaking her head now and seemed to be fighting back tears. 'But you usually seem so logical. Utterly scientific. And now this! What's next, Gill? Will you be reading tea leaves?'

He shrugged and battled to find simpler words to explain how he felt. 'Sometimes I know God is speaking to me, Cass. And he's probably speaking to you too if you'd stop and listen.'

'No, no!' said Cassy, her anger rising. 'Don't try that with me. I don't want to be your wee evangelism project, so you can earn brownie points or whatever. Or drag me along to some cult.'

'There's no cult, Cassy. And there are no brownie points', Gill sighed. 'You're my friend. I've stumbled across something important. The time has come to tell you about it, that's all. Didn't mean to offend you.'

'And if God wanted to talk to me, he coulda done it a long time ago when I needed him', Cassy continued, colour rising in her face.

He peered at her. 'You've been down this road before, haven't you?'

'Ach', she snarled. 'I was just a kid. It's all garbage anyway.'

Gill sat back while Cassy fumed in front of him. 'Okay, I'm sorry that ... whatever it was, didn't work out for you. And it's not like believing in God is a ticket to a trouble-free life. I can tell you that for nothing.'

Cassy's long dark hair had fallen forward off her shoulders, and she now sat back and flicked it out of her face. 'What's the point then?'

Gill thought for a few seconds. 'Having a sense of your own destiny. Getting a little help along the way. I dunno. I'm quite new to this.'

Cassy looked at the coffee shop door and Gill could see she was still blinking away a tear.

'Cass, if there's anything I can help with?'

'Maybe. A long time ago, Gill', she said, slapping the table so hard, other customers turned and stared. 'Nothing to be done about it now.' She pushed away her coffee. 'I'm going back to the office. Lot's to do.'

'Sure', he said, letting his shoulders slump as she walked away. 'Me too.'

Chapter 37

Roddy Canmore speared half a sausage and thrust it into his mouth. At mid-morning, this would be his second breakfast, but he had a busy day ahead of him and needed fuel for the fire. The café was his regular haunt when he wanted to avoid the Holyrood crowd. Situated deep down an alley off Cockburn Street, it was only yards from Edinburgh's Royal Mile and yet, priced like a Glasgow greasy spoon. He looked up at his security guy, blocking the entrance to stop any wasters from getting in. It meant lost business for the café, but Roddy would leave a tip.

He let his phone ring three times so he could at least partially chew the sausage. Glancing at the number he could see from the last four digits that it was one of the burner phones Stevie had procured for off-book comms. He tapped his phone and picked up the call. 'Yeah?'

'Boss. It's Billy.'

'Awright, pal. What's happening?'

'Last night, some guys came for that item we discussed. Used a team to take it north.'

'North, where?'

'Stonehaven. A wee place by the harbour. I'll send you the address.'

'You're sure they didn't see you?'

'Stevie drove. They didn't even know we were following. That guy's a pro.'

'You still there?'

'Aye. But we're knackered. Can somebody relieve us?'

Roddy thought for a moment. He wanted the fewest people in the know about this. 'You kip in the car for a few hours. After that, you get the night shift. Stevie can find a B&B or something.'

'Boss, we don't have spare clothes or anything with us.'

'They have shops in Stonehaven, don't they?' Roddy barked.

'I guess.'

'Right. The pair of you get organised. I'll have a think about what to do.'

Roddy hung up before Billy could protest and continued chewing his sausage. McArdle's stone was discredited. The man himself had been difficult to take off the board, but here was a chance to take the stone out of play altogether. He speared a whole fried egg and pushed it in on top of the remaining sausage. Taking the *Fated Stone* would be low risk, but by stealing it, would he hand McArdle a gift by renewing public interest? Possibly. But it was too good an opportunity to miss. He scooped at the remaining food and arrived at a decision. He'd order his guys to go in tonight and take the stone. Under the cover of darkness, they'd shift it down to

Pittenweem and onto a trawler. Then this imposter *Fated Stone* would end up back in the Forth, as mandated by the people of Scotland. He smirked. Or at least, the portion of Scots that read the Daily Record. And McArdle? Roddy would have to deal with that nuisance another time.

With these decisions made, he used a piece of bread to wipe up the remains of his breakfast. After rubbing his hands on the seats, he dragged himself out from the fixed gap between the table and chairs, tossed a twenty-pound note on the table and left without a word.

Gill spent the rest of the morning working on issue 23, aware that Cassy was studiously avoiding him. As it wore around to the end of the day, he realised he'd have to clear the air.

'Are we okay, Cass?' he said, stopping by her desk.

Cassy looked up and gave him a sad smile. 'We're okay, Gill.' Her eyes darted left, then right. 'I mean, I think you're mad. But actually, in a way, I'm pleased for you.'

'Tell me why?' he said gently, leaning his weight against her desk.

She paused, and this time there were real tears, falling silently down her cheeks. Cassy shielded herself, using the cover of the adjacent partition, plus Gill's body and her own hands. 'It's very sweet that you ask, Gill, but I'm absolutely, definitely not going to talk about it.'

'Okay', he said, inching closer to give her more protection. 'I won't pry.'

Cassy was recovering quickly, wiping away the wetness, even as her expression hardened. 'There was a time in my life when I tried talking to God', she whispered. 'Got on my knees and begged for help. If I coulda got what I wanted, I woulda signed my soul away right there and then to the highest bidder. But I got nothing. For me, God is dead. Or maybe he thinks I'm dead, which in truth, I pretty much am. But I gave him his moment and he didn't come through for me, so yeah, I've no truck with that stuff, even though I'm glad it works for you.'

Gill released a deep, sad sigh. If they'd been on their own, or in a coffee shop, he would have hugged her. He'd had a sense of Cassy's pain before but never known for sure. It lurked under the surface of her emotions like an iceberg. She offered her left hand up to him and he gripped it gently in his. Without any further words to say, he leaned over and planted a single kiss on her knuckles, nodded once, then got up and hobbled back to his desk.

Adina sits in a restaurant overlooking Stonehaven Harbour as she stretches out a small meal. The light finally faded an hour ago and she's almost ready to make her move. She's smartly dressed, but all in black, with her hair pulled into a ponytail so no surprises will throw it in her eyes.

She has been in Stonehaven all day. Her reconnaissance of the target house revealing a pretty Asian woman of about her own age, frequently visible at the windows, but always moving. Not that Adina could enter the house during daylight. Although it sits back from the harbourfront, the tumbled-together layout of the houses means she can't affect an entry without being observed. And of course, there's the problem of the geologist, Billy Whyte. Working with another man, they've come and gone all day. Their body language displaying boredom combined with agitation. They're tense and Adina suspects that like her, they're making ready to move on the stone.

She's distracted from her thoughts by a conversation at the door. The manager is talking to a new arrival, laughing with the man and pointing to his table. Adina steadies herself and prepares for what is coming.

'Commander', she breathes. 'So nice of you to join me.'

Yuri slides into a chair. 'I hope you're not offended. Myself, I'm feeling a little slighted you didn't see fit to invite me.'

'I have the situation under control', she says, calmly looking out the window.

'I'm so glad.' Yuri smiles, then adds. 'And the men watching the house? More uninvited guests. Do you have plans for them?'

'I do.' Adina turns and meets his gaze. 'Though I suspect you'd have me kill them.'

Yuri laughs gently. 'You're a clever and beautiful woman. I'm sure you'll be more resourceful than that.'

'How did you know I was here?' she asks bluntly.

Yuri offers her a shallow shrug. 'Trade secret.'

Refusing to be fobbed off she shakes her head. 'My phone is off', she says quietly. 'I've screened myself for bugs.' And then she realises. 'The Glock.'

He picks up a menu and begins to read. 'If you ever get into a firefight, perhaps the twenty-second bullet might not work as per manufacturer specifications.'

'A tracker! In a bullet?'

He points at the menu. 'I'm told the scallops are wonderful tonight.'

'If you're tinkering with my firearm, then I'm glad my life won't depend on it.'

He dips his head left and right. It doesn't seem he agrees with her.

'Shit', she murmurs, looking out the window. 'McArdle just arrived.'

'The numbers are still in our favour', says Yuri, raising a hand to attract a waiter.

'You're going to eat?'

'Why not? It's going to be a long night.'

After Gill had kissed Salina, he held her tight for several long minutes.

'Loving this', she whispered in his ear. 'But I'm starving.'

He pushed back from her. 'What do you fancy?'

'Something spicy', she said. 'Is there anywhere decent?'

Gill nodded. 'On the high street. I'll go in a second.'

'Are you kidding? No offence but I've been cooped up looking after your rock all day long. I could so with some fresh air.'

'If you're sure? I could catch up on some emails. Maybe get the wood burner going?'

'Now you're talking', she said. 'I'll order the food then go for a walk till it's ready. What do you fancy?'

'You choose. Get a few things we can share.'

He kissed her again and held the door for her as she walked towards the harbour and disappeared from sight.

'Right', said Billy, watching a tall, dark-skinned woman leaving the house. 'Let's get this done.'

'It's too early', said Stevie. 'Best to wait until folk are properly asleep. At least midnight.'

'Sod that. I want to be in my own bed by then. Besides, right now, it's just McArdle.'

'Aye, and the guvnor said not to attract attention.'

'You could take him, yeah?'

'If we catch him by surprise. That's not likely at nine in the evening.'

Billy swore under his breath. 'You're the boss.'

'Aye', spat Stevie. 'In this particular situation, I am. Crawl into the back and sleep if you want. I'll tell you when we're ready.'

When Salina had been gone an hour, Gill started to worry. He reminded himself that she loved Stonehaven and appreciated a little exercise in the evenings. Having walked the length of the esplanade and back once, she'd probably decided to do it again. He shrugged off the worry and battled to write some philosophical words about what the *Fated Stone* should mean to Scotland.

By 10.30 pm, he was genuinely concerned. He called the curry house and asked if they'd seen Salina. Confirming that they had, they grumbled that she'd never returned to collect their order. Gill gave them his credit card number and asked them to ring him if she came back. Then he stepped out of the house and walked the few steps to the harbour so he could look around. It was late now and unsurprisingly given the cool, damp evening, there wasn't a soul around.

Spotting a parked car with two men in it, he glanced back over his shoulder at his father's house and then slowly approached the car. He waved to the occupants, but besides turning to look at each other, they didn't respond. Suspicious, Gill tapped the window on the driver's door. The man moved his face to the window but did not open it and did not speak. Perplexed, Gill looked into the man's face. It was only then he saw the man's mouth had a wrap-around of transparent tape. Glancing down, Gill saw his hands were also taped, most likely strapped to his own thighs. Instead of being angry or concerned, the man's eyes were wide with fear. Gill took a step back. He didn't stop to examine the passenger, but by his posture, he looked to be similarly restrained. Only as he walked away did Gill realise the man bore a strong resemblance to his 'pal' and erstwhile geologist, Billy Whyte.

Back in the kitchen, Gill fought his rising anxiety. Salina's safety was his sole concern. Sod the stone with all its mystery. All he wanted was Salina, safe beside him. Distracted by a sound in the house he froze. Gripping the back of a kitchen chair he remained absolutely still for almost a minute. He half expected to hear the throaty sound of a motorbike, and honestly, he felt let down when it didn't come. Instead, he heard the smooth click of a bullet being pulled into a firing chamber and felt the presence of another human being in the room beside him.

Chapter 38

Gill turned slowly to face the direction of the sound and stared into the shadowed face of his assailant. He had to swallow twice before he was able to speak.

'What are you doing here, Adina?'

Adina sighed. 'Bottom line, I'm taking the stone.'

She stepped silently across the room with the gun gripped in both hands, her arms fully extended. Moving closer to him, she slid sideways to use the stone as a shield. If he was to lunge at her, he wouldn't stand a chance.

'As my brother used to say, you and who's army?' he whispered with more bravery than he felt.

'Trust me, Gill. You don't want to go there.'

'All I want is Salina. You can have the damn stone.'

'And when I'm clear, you can have her.'

'Where is she?'

'Nearby.'

'Not good enough, Adina. Before we go any further, where is Salina?'

'There's a bridge in town. You know it?'

Gill nodded. The local council had recently spent several years rebuilding it.

'My associates are guarding her there. She's not in the water, but no one can see her.'

Gill clenched his fists. 'You're willing to put all our lives at risk. Over a rock?'

'It's more than just a rock. We both know that.'

'And I worked hard to recover it. Salina worked even harder.'

'And now, after all your dedication, Scotland doesn't want it. What are you planning to do, Gill? Put it in your garden?'

Gill shifted his weight from his good leg to his bad and back again. 'When we think a little on the facts, Scotland might yet change its mind.'

'They've already said no, Gill. No one wants it.' Her gun barrel had drifted down, but she steadied it again. 'Get used to it.'

Gill's hands dropped wearily to his hips as he tried to conjure up words to justify Scotland's remaining claim on the stone. After twenty seconds of silence, Adina spoke again, more gently this time.

'Maybe we're not so different, you and me? I know my people are capable of rejecting an idea that has overwhelming proof. And that's why I need the stone.'

'And you'd be prepared to kill me to take it for yourself?'

'Not myself. For a generation who might yet believe.'

'Believe in what?'

'Think about it. Apart from the *Ark of the Covenant*, Jewish sacred writing references no object more sacred than *Jacob's Pillow*. If my organisation recovers the stone, we demonstrate to our people the story is true. The Old Testament becomes more believable. The patriarchs, the kings and the prophets. The road to the messiah.' She dipped her head in an almost sympathetic gesture. 'Gill, most people don't believe. That's why I need the stone.'

'A way-marker for a messiah yet to come?'

Adina's eyes flashed. 'Or a testimony to a messiah who's already here.'

Gill raised his eyebrows. 'And how will it accomplish that?'

'It's a signpost. A physical reminder of the earliest seeds of our faith.'

'You're talking about Jacob and his dreams?'

'As a "modern" Scot, I don't expect you to believe. And what's easier to accept? That a weary and guilt-ridden Jacob, fleeing the brother he'd wronged, spent a troubled night in a wilderness, bothered by bad dreams? Or that he has his eyes opened and saw angels coming and going from their missions to earth?'

'Actually, I've no trouble with that last part at all.'

She snorted. 'You believe in angels?'

'I didn't get a choice. And I didn't believe in God either, but it now seems logical to believe in him as well. Now I'm living every spare moment reading *The Book* the angel showed me.'

Her eyes narrowed. 'I doubt that. In my experience, most academics are MUCH too clever to be deceived by holy books.'

'Granted. But now I've encountered God, I can't un-meet him. *The Book* is my only way to make sense of what I know in my heart to be true.'

'Well then, that's nice. Maybe we're standing on common ground after all.' She studied him for a few moments, before adding. 'Listen, I'm loving the empathy here, but I'm still going to take the stone.'

'We think we know what it is, but we can't be sure. You're taking a hell of a risk with no guarantees.'

'I know exactly what it is', said Adina.

'How?' Gill spluttered. 'We know its approximate source and I can thread together a plausible-sounding story that implies it might be the *Fated Stone*. But really, Adina? How can either of us be totally sure?'

The shake of her head was just a shiver. 'If I explain, will you let me take the stone?'

Gill didn't reply. Instead, he kept all emotion from his face.

'Jewish tradition holds that *Jacob's Pillow* was incorporated into Solomon's temple in Jerusalem. It became the plinth in the holy of holies that the *Ark of the Covenant* rested upon for hundreds of years.'

'Another myth we cannot prove', said Gill.

Adina's eyes narrowed. 'Actually, we can.'

'How?'

'This next bit is a secret', said Adina. 'If you ever repeat it, I'll deny all knowledge.'

Gill grunted his ascent.

'In the earliest days of the modern Jewish state, archaeologists discovered a cache of scrolls. They weren't originals, just copies of copies, but like the scriptures, faithful to the primary texts. And one of those scrolls, painfully reconstructed from flakes no bigger than your fingernail had a plan for Solomon's temple.'

'A plan?'

'Measurements, Gill. Of all the primary indoor spaces. Including the holy of holies. And the plinth for the *Ark of the Covenant*. The most intimate space of the holiest building ever constructed by human hands.'

'You have the dimensions of *Jacob's Pillow*?' spluttered Gill.

Adina met his gaze and let her left hand drift down to the surface of the stone. 'To the millimetre.' She used the barrel of her gun to point at the stone. 'I've measured it, remember? It's real, Gill.'

Gill stepped towards her slowly, and she stepped back as he laid his palms on the black surface of the stone with newly felt reverence. He stood like this for a full minute, basking in the knowledge he'd been instrumental in recovering one of humanity's most precious objects. He wasn't sure whether to laugh or cry – to walk away and leave it to Adina, or call Roddy Canmore right away and beg another audience.

'Do remember', whispered Adina. 'At the end of the day, it's just a stone.'

Gill turned his face sideways to look at her. The builders of the so-called *New Scotland* had rejected the basalt pillow and now he needed to move on. Peering at Adina, an idea occurred to him. But first, he had to decide if he could trust her.

'Maybe there's a compromise here', he said at last.

She took a step backwards and straightened her arms again to be sure of her aim. 'What are you proposing?'

'You don't get to just walk out of here with the stone. I need something in return.'

'I'll give you Salina.'

'For now I'm taking you at your word you haven't hurt her. But she recovered the *Fated Stone* in thirty metres of water. There's no way she'd want me to squander all her hard work.'

'I could just shoot you.'

'Well, maybe you will. But I've come too far to simply let this go. And I'm willing to risk my life on the hope you'd rather strike a deal.'

Adina glanced at the kitchen door and back again. 'What kind of deal?'

Gill shrugged. 'Some good has got to come of this situation. For a fee, *Mys.Scot* could endorse the transfer of the stone to a worthy organisation. I can think of at least one prominent politician who'd be glad to see the back of it. And what's the alternative? That the mysterious death of a local journalist is immortalised in the name of the magazine he used to lead? And a prominent museum curator exits Scotland suddenly, hopefully with her family, though you never can be sure, leaving a wonderful career behind her.'

She considered this for a moment then sniffed. 'You're proposing to sell it to me?'

'It's not my first choice, but yes, reluctantly I would. If we can agree on terms.'

For the first time since the start of their encounter, some warmth crept into her dark brown eyes. 'We're negotiating now, are we?' She lowered the muzzle of the gun down parallel to her right hip. 'What are you proposing?'

Chapter 39

After they shook hands in a taut gesture, laden with risk, Gill looked down at the stone. 'It's brutally heavy. How are you going to shift it?'

Adina's gun was still drawn, but remained pressed against her thigh. 'I've got help on the way. In the meantime, I'd like to stay here, if that's okay?'

He stared down at the stone, brushing his hand against it one last time. 'I hope it speaks to your people more than it spoke to mine.'

'That's my next battle', she said. 'To ensure it goes on display and isn't locked away in some vault.'

'Allow people to see it and make up their own minds?'

'Yes.'

He nodded. 'Just pull the door behind you.'

'You're not staying?'

'Your people have Salina, incarcerated under a bridge. Of course, I'm not staying.'

'You could collect her and bring her back.'

Gill imagined Salina, cold and frightened, then released from whatever restraints they had conjured for her. She'd turn into a fireball if she knew the perpetrators were close by. He considered saying all that then decided to use more tact.

'To see the *Fated Stone* slip off into the night? No, thank you.'

Adina finally holstered her gun and opened the door for him. 'Stay well, Gill McArdle. Please give Salina my personal apologies.'

Gill stepped out into the dark with a heavy heart. The stone was precious. But, being realistic, if it was politically inconvenient for the artefact to reside in Scotland, then Adina's people should have it, whoever they were. That was the pragmatic choice. And somehow his finder's fee had a certain justice to it as well. The hairs on the back of his neck tingled with the thought of what he would do with the kind of money they'd agreed.

And still, with mixed feelings, he shoved his hands in his pockets and started to walk briskly into town, and towards Salina. He wondered how her experience this evening would affect her warmth towards Stonehaven. Maybe, after this experience, she'd be happy to see Gordon's house sold after all.

He turned left towards the harbour and immediately found his way blocked by three men. The two younger ones stood like gunslingers, their hands ready to dive into action, their faces shadowed by hoodies. But it was the older man who spoke. His neatly cropped hair and acne-scarred face just visible in the streetlight.

'Mr McArdle. How good to finally meet you.'

Gill glanced at them in turn. 'I take it you guys are Adina's muscle?'

The older man gave a sloppy shrug. 'Crudely put, but yes. If the shoe fits …'

Gill jerked a thumb over his left shoulder. 'She's inside. We've done a deal.'

'Have you?' said the man, flatly. 'That's excellent.'

Gill nodded once and moved to step around them, but a young hoodie immediately blocked his way.

'There might be a problem with Adina's little deal', said the man slowly.

'What's that', said Gill, impatient to reach Salina.

'I feel it leaves too many loose ends'.

'I'm telling you. We've got it figured out.'

'Yes, yes. And the moment you're out of danger, this deal you've agreed blows away like a fart in the wind, and you expose Adina in your magazine.' He thrust out his hands. 'Please forgive her. She's inexperienced. Naive.'

'Listen. I gave her my word.'

'Words, words, words. I expect you've produced a lot of them in your time.' He nodded to the hoodie on his left and the two younger men started to advance on Gill.

Gill felt anger rise within him. But not an anger he'd ever felt before. It was a bellow that rose from deep inside, refusing to witness evil win the day. Refusing to let Salina become the innocent victim in a war she didn't start. He felt his left shoulder sag under the weight of the crystalizing object.

'Listen, guys', he said, trying to keep anger out of his voice. 'It's already been a hell of an evening. And I've had my fill of being pushed around. If you think I'm going down without a fight, let me disabuse you of that miscalculation.'

The two younger men glanced at each other and smiled. His words had done nothing to slow their advance.

'Last warning!' cried Gill, his fingernails digging into his palms as his body titled back into fight or flight.

They were almost upon him when they simultaneously drew knives from their belts.

Gill unsheathed his sword without having to think about its position, swinging it in front of him, the sword guiding his hand as it expertly lunged at his attackers. In two swift slashes, the young men fell left and right, their arms gashed to the bone and their free hands diving to stem the rush of blood. One instant later and the blade tip rose up to stroke the older man's throat. He froze, his hands arrested somewhere between attack and surrender.

'In the last few weeks', Gill whispered through gritted teeth. 'I've had masonry thrown at me and been hounded off a cliff. And tonight, I'm having a *really* tough evening. So maybe you didn't hear me the first time. I said, I. Gave. Adina. My. Word.'

'Those attacks had nothing to do with me', the man hissed.

'And yet, here we are', said Gill.

The man's right hand flew down to his belt, but before he could deploy his weapon, the sword leapt forward a fraction. The man yelped in pain as it opened up a shallow wound along his jawline and his blade clattered to the ground.

'Adina seems honest. Principled. And I've promised I won't give her up to the authorities', whispered Gill. 'But I didn't make her any assurances about you. If you want to live, go now. If you want to have your freedom by this time tomorrow, go further.'

The man retreated now, blood streaming down his neck. Slowly. Wary of provoking Gill. He gathered his wounded comrades by their good arms and steered them, staggering, out of the street.

Breathing deeply, Gill sheathed his sword. The weight of it bore down on his left shoulder and was a comfort to him. And still, in the heat of battle, he sensed Adina running up behind him.

'Those guys with you?' he demanded.

'Yes and no', she stuttered. 'They're freelancers. What did you just do?'

'Defended myself', said Gill, spinning around to take a defensive posture. 'Do you have a problem with that?'

'No. I ...' She pointed at the sword. 'What is that?'

Gill held his hands loosely in front of him, ready for anything. 'You can see it?'

'Yes.' She staggered backwards a few steps. 'Where did it come from?'

'That's too a long conversation to have when my fiancé is trapped under a bridge.' He thumbed over his shoulder. 'Was that your transportation crew?'

Adina nodded.

'Well, they're gone now.'

'Are you still going to give me the stone?'

'Well, now. That depends.' He restrained his anger and studied her dark eyes, brimming with urgency and alarm. 'I'm no zealot, Adina. And I'm sure as hell no imperialist. What I need to know from you is this. If I give you the stone, will I be stoking violence?'

Timidly, Adina shook her head.

'To convince me, you need to tell me who you're working for.'

'Who do you think?' whispered Adina.

'You don't keep good company and that's becoming a problem for me. I suspect you're with some militant offshoot of British Zionism. You want the stone so you can prove the British are descended from the Jews. That somehow, we are God's chosen people.'

'You're close, and yet, you're so far away.' Adina said, looking at her feet. 'I'm with a department of the Israeli Security Services.'

Gill felt his jaw drop. 'You're working for Mossad?'

She glanced away. 'I can't say.'

'What does Israel want with the *Fated Stone*?'

She edged towards him. 'You forget, Gill. Before it was Scotland's stone, it was Jacob's. It's a vital part of our history.'

On a cultural level, she was right. He gritted his teeth and pondered what to do.

She shivered. 'We can't stay here all night. What's it to be, Gill. Deal or no deal?'

'You still threatening to shoot me?'

Adina looked down at her holstered weapon. 'I was never going to shoot you.'

'Okay then', he said at last. 'Then the deal's still on.'

Adina swallowed. 'I can't move it on my own.'

'I can organise some help', said Gill. 'As long as Salina's okay. If she's not, the deal's off and you're in a world of trouble.'

'I understand.'

He took a few steps backwards in the direction of the town while pulling out his phone. 'Quickly! Tell me where you need me to take the stone and when. Then I'm off to find Salina. And I strongly suggest you're not here when we get back.'

'When I said you could flog it on eBay, ye ken I was joking?' said Corrie as he and Gill watched a van backing up to the front door of Gordon's old house. It was early morning and Gill's plan had been to keep a low profile. But this was Stonehaven. A fishing harbour. Always at the mercy of the changing tide, it never really slept.

'This way the *Fated Stone* stays safe. Ultimately, if it's the real thing, it belongs to Israel. At some point, we would probably have ended up giving it back.'

'Fair enough', said Corrie. 'But it was braw, gettin' to lay my hands on it. All yon history gave me a bit of a tingle.'

Gill nodded. He knew exactly what Corrie meant.

'How's your girl?'

Gill nodded over his right shoulder. 'Inside getting warm.'

'She okay?'

'She is', said Gill, before adding. 'Why are you helping me?'

'Helping?'

'Come on, Corrie. Money. Logistics.'

'Just movin' an old fridge, ken', shouted Corrie over the sound of the reversing van.

'You know what I mean.'

Corrie banged the rear doors a couple of times and the vehicle halted. 'You remember a band called *Dark Reaper?*'

'No.'

'US outfit. Big in the eighties. An early version of *Black Scabbard* supported their European tour in '88.'

'Okay.'

'Their manager. Big butch fella, but fine; very professional. He said the tour would have been a disaster without us.' Corrie nodded at something in the far distance. 'Last words he ever said to me. "Corrie, you make a great wingman".'

Gill threw Corrie a puzzled look.

'You know, as in fighter pilots.' Corrie made wings with his arms and waited for Gill to signal understanding before he continued. 'Anyway, a very good pal of mine repeated yon phrase to me, just a few days ago. "Corrie", he said. "You make a great wingman." And right away I knew I needed tae help you.'

'This friend ...' Gill began.

But Corrie was already holding up his hands. 'I think what my friend ... our friend, was tryin' to say, was, let's get this job done.'

Gill nodded, then faced up to a question that had been bothering him. 'Would this be a bad time to ask who the anonymous donor was?'

'You talkin' about the guy puttin' up the last share of the money to recover the *Fated Stone*?'

'Yes.'

Corrie twisted his mouth to suppress a smile. 'That was me.'

'It was a huge lump of cash. Why was it so important to you?'

'Wingman, Gill. Orders were orders.'

'And was that the whole deal?'

Corrie stopped to pull on a pair of sturdy gloves. 'Roddy Canmore made a song and dance, ken. I wanted him to know, beyond any shadow of a doubt he was buildin' his whole story on a poor imitation.'

'You used the *Fated Stone* to get back at him?'

Corrie flicked his chin. 'I tol' you I'm on my way to becoming a good person. Didnae say I was there yet.'

Gill didn't respond.

'Problem with that?'

Gill permitted himself a thin smile. 'None at all.'

'Okay then.'

Gill stepped back to give Corrie space to yank open the van's rear doors. Then he whistled at two aged roadies to come and help him shift an unremarkable, but brutally heavy fridge freezer.

Chapter 40

In the rising sun of the new day, Gill stood with Salina at the perimeter of Aberdeen airport where a small private jet had just taken off. He had no idea how Adina had managed the paperwork, export licenses, or even if she'd travelled with the artefact. That was her business and his role in the matter was over.

'How are you?' he asked Salina.

'My face hurts and my feet think they'll never be warm again.'

'I'm so sorry about what happened to you.'

Salina sniffed. 'I fly DSVs into the jaws of ocean-floor volcanos for a living. So really, tonight was a breeze.'

Gill laughed.

'But ...' Salina continued, if I ever meet your museum friend again, I'm going to be restraining a very unchristian desire to do her harm. Understand?'

He pulled her towards him and pressed his forehead against hers, raising his hands against her palms so their fingers interlocked. 'This extended engagement thing we're doing', he said. 'How's that working for you?'

She didn't reply, but pushed back from him a little, then pulled forward again so she could bite lightly on his right ear.

'You need a shower', she mumbled against his face.

'No offence, but you too.'

'We should probably check on your dad's place', she breathed. 'Make sure it's okay.'

'We could freshen up.'

Her words were just a whisper. 'That would be so good.'

He swung an arm around her and together they watched until the jet completely disappeared, and then turned for his car. Glancing, habitually, at his phone he realised the noise of the jet had masked three missed calls. Looking at the number, he saw they were from his father's care home.

Suppressing a moan of exhaustion, he tossed his mobile onto the dashboard. The airport was well north of Aberdeen. Even using the bypass, it would take an hour to get to Montrose.

'I'm really sorry', he said, starting the engine. 'But I need to make a house call.'

'Gill?' said Gordon. The old man's demeanour had changed. Where he'd been distant before, his watery blue eyes now looked right into Gill. And where his body had been calm, almost serenely vacant, it now shook with effort.

'I'm here, Dad.'

'I've been thinking. Where's Davey?'

Gill took a deep breath. Cassy had warned him these moments would come.

'Davey's not here, Dad. He died. A few years back.'

'Yes, yes.' Gordon's face was suddenly full of the irritation Gill had known while growing up. 'But *where* is he?'

Gill leaned in closer. 'They didn't find his body, Dad. Don't you remember?'

Gordon flapped his right hand as if dismissing a child. 'I know where your mother is.' He looked up and brightened. 'She's safe. But Davey…'

Gill studied the old man's face and suddenly caught the sense of what Gordon was grasping for. His mother had been a woman of faith. Nominal, in Gill's humble opinion; taking comfort from the annual rhythms of the church. Perhaps receiving the promises it had on offer and in return, meeting a saviour in the private margins of her life. But Davey? He'd been a rig worker. An oil man since leaving school at seventeen. Over-weight on company food and burdened with the chauvinistic carapace demanded by his peers, he didn't strike Gill as a man who'd ever had a brush with belief. Gill grasped Gordon's question and answered as honestly as he could.

'Dad, I just don't know.'

'I want us all to be together.' His gaze drifted for a moment. 'Someday.'

Gill picked up his father's hand from where it rested on the bed. 'I do too, Dad. I do too.'

He felt Gordon grip his hand for a few minutes, and then his father yawned, and without another word, drifted back to sleep.

Gill held on long after Gordon's grip slackened. The old man's choice of words had been revealing. If he perceived Gill's mother as "safe", then, by that logic, he understood her to be somewhere else. Gill leaned over and held Gordon's floppy hand against his own forehead. Wherever he thought his wife had gone, one thing seemed certain – Gordon believed he was going there too.

Mid-morning on the following day, Gill gazed up at the Kelpies; twin horse heads thirty metres high and manufactured from brushed steel. Placed along the M9 motorway, the horses were the most dramatic sculptures in Scotland. Following the waterhorse discoveries in the early 2020s, some folk suggested their appearance be updated. The original architects had reacted with alarm, realising the structures couldn't carry extra weight. And then the authorities reminded everyone the horse heads celebrated the contribution of working horses to historical Scottish industries. Especially in the canal system where the sculptures had been located. For his money, Gill thought they were perfect just the way they were.

The park was also a convenient halfway point between Dundee and the town of Bathgate. And an opportunity for Gill to meet an acquaintance on neutral ground.

'Thought you'd like the irony', said Wiley as he strolled up, pulling on a cigarette. 'Mind you, doesn't look like they've done it right. No tusks.'

'I'll be sure to contact the Scottish government and tell them', said Gill.

Wiley stopped and looked at the sculptures. 'Nah. I wouldn't bother. If they didn't buy your tale about the *Fated Stone*, the powers that be won't take kindly if you start slagging off our newest monument.'

'It wasn't a tale', said Gill firmly. 'I researched the facts and presented them as clearly as I could.'

'Folk didn't buy it, though. Looks like your stock is in freefall, McArdle.'

Gill sighed. The last few days had certainly held disappointments. To deflect Wiley he asked, 'How's the new job, Inspector?'

'Bathgate nick is a dump. Full of small-town coppers allergic to hard work. But personally, I've got a better package and my own team. Talk about a promotion too.' Wiley took a last drag on his fag end and discarded it. 'Our trajectories are quite different, you and I.'

'Well, I hope you continue to dazzle us with your detective skills.' He turned away from the Kelpies and looked at Wiley. 'Which reminds me. My little incident on the Isle of May …'

'You want an update?'

'That's the reason I'm here.'

'Our enquiries aren't finished yet, so technically, I'm not obliged to tell you anything.'

Gill gave him an exaggerated, pained stare.

'I could offer you a favour', said Wiley, sounding like he was still making up his mind. 'But then you'd owe me.'

Gill turned to fully face the short, bald man. 'Stick it on my tab.'

Wiley pulled out his phone and scrolled to an image. 'Are these the guys?'

Gill studied the photo for several long seconds. It wasn't very clear, but the resemblance of the two men to Mick and Monty was undeniable. 'Almost certainly.'

'Almost?'

'It's not a clear photo. Who are they?'

Wiley glanced around and kept his voice low. 'The Galloway brothers. They're a Drumchapel outfit.'

'They're already known to you?'

'On the face of it, they run a small haulage firm. Despite the meagre profits the business reports, the Galloway brothers enjoy a very affluent lifestyle.'

'Are you going to arrest them?' asked Gill.

'For what? I might get them a rap on the knuckles for tax avoidance or VAT fraud. Nothing more.'

'What about trying to throw me off an island?'

'My initial discussions with the Procurator Fiscal haven't been promising. We'd be unlikely to secure a conviction based on existing evidence.'

'But they tried to kill me!'

'Maybe. But from the Fiscal's perspective, no one died, and at the end of the day, you weren't pushed off the island – you jumped. Basically, it's your word against theirs.'

'What about impersonating the warden? And removing our phones?'

'A decent lawyer would make mincemeat of that lot. Better we leave them in play and wait for them to properly trip up.'

'Meaning someone else has to die before you do anything?'

'Not necessarily. We know who they are, and we have them on a watch list.'

Gill drew his hands to his hips and sucked in a deep breath. 'I just don't like the thought of those brutes being free to walk around.'

Wiley shrugged. 'I'd say the most pertinent fact from your perspective is finding out who this crew were working for. In your shoes, I'd want the client behind bars, not the hired gun.' He must have seen something flicker across Gill's face. 'Unless you already know who it was?'

Gill looked away. 'Suspicions. No evidence. Maybe they'll leave me alone now.'

'Anything you'd like to share? Anything at all?'

Gill shook his head. 'Not at this time, no.'

'Okay. But just so you're aware, the night you were attacked in Airth, the Galloway brothers were somewhere else. Which means there are two separate crews trying to kill you.'

Gill slid his fingers over his temples and into his hair, interlocking behind his head, trying not to dwell on the implications of this information. 'Looks like it', was all he could say.

'You don't sound surprised.'

'Did you track down the bird watchers I mentioned?' said Gill.

Wiley nodded once. 'I had them brought into Bathgate on Tuesday. They almost crapped themselves. But it turns out we have them recorded on Ed Johnson's CCTV. None of them ventured into the church that night so those boys are clean.'

'I see.'

'That means we've zero leads for that incident.' He pulled out a cigarette packet and lit up again. 'Have you remembered any details?'

'Just what I've told you already', said Gill. 'My attacker looked well over six feet tall. Exceptionally lean. Scarred face, maybe some kind of mask. And weirdly long fingers, with fingernails running to dagger points.'

'Give me strength', said Wiley half turning away. 'What else? Red eyes? Long pointy tail?'

Gill smiled weakly, suddenly struck by a terrible idea.

Wiley started walking away. 'That's all I've got. But I'll be in touch if there are any developments', he called over his shoulder.

As Gill watched him go he bit back frustration that Mick and Monty still walked free. Over the past days, he'd wondered if they'd had a role in his attack at Airth, but Wiley had confirmed their alibi. And the attack happened before Adina's crew had been in play, so it meant they couldn't be responsible. As Gill thought back to what he saw that night, and the darkness he'd sensed, he suddenly grasped the identity of his assailant at Airth.

Chapter 41

At the end of his working day, Gill found Solomon, waiting as usual under the cover of the V&A museum. As he'd expected, she wanted to talk about the stone. For his part, Gill wasn't keen to disclose all the details of what happened in Stonehaven.

'I saw the news', were Solomon's opening words. 'You let it go.'

'Scotland didn't want it', he replied. 'Israel did.'

'I hope they asked nicely?'

Gill's shrug was non-committal. 'What were we going to do with it? Leave it lying in a storeroom? Besides it's more about their story than ours. Let them study it. Revere it.'

'You seemed to give it up so easily. Did you decide it wasn't relevant to modern-day Scotland?'

'I thought it was *very* relevant. And it could have been the starting point for a very interesting discussion. Who we are? Where have we come from? Where are we going? Unfortunately, Scotland didn't agree.'

'You must be disappointed?'

Gill had been thinking about this. 'I am, but I realise I'm not destined to win every battle.'

She nodded but said nothing as they started walking along the river away from the city.

'In related news, I've come into a sum of money', said Gill, changing the conversation.

'I'm glad for you. I'm sure you're ready for a holiday.'

'A large sum of money', said Gill.

'Did you win the lottery?'

Gill remembered Cassy's five-pound note still tucked in a waistcoat pocket. 'Yes, in a manner of speaking. And I've decided to start a charity.'

Her eyes flickered. 'To do what?'

'I'm not sure about the details; just the calling. I want to help our colleges teach struggling young people how to read.'

'That is very admirable.'

'And as you were a teacher, I'd like you to help me.' He stopped and looked squarely at her. 'If you're willing.'

Solomon took a few steps beyond him before speaking. 'Big task, Gill. How much money are we talking about?'

He took a breath. 'Two and a half million pounds.'

She stopped abruptly and turned. 'Are you serious?'

He nodded. 'A proper charity, with experts, and a bevvy of volunteers. And a board of local high school and college teachers who understand the problems. That's where you come in.'

A smile twisted the corners of her mouth, and they started walking again. 'I'll certainly consider it. I do see merit in us spending more time together.'

'Thank you', said Gill, grateful for the connection they were making.

Her eyes flashed to his unbandaged hand. 'You look better.'

'Yeah. Healed up within a couple of days of our last chat.'

'What a coincidence', said Solomon flatly.

Gill looked down at his hand and realised what she'd implied. His skin didn't even carry a scar.

'Are you ready to talk to me about that night? The night you *cut* yourself?' she said with emphasis.

Gill considered his words carefully. 'I was attacked that night.'

'And who attacked you?'

'A tall man. Disfigured and incredibly tall. He appeared human, but looking back, I don't think he was.'

'Interesting. What makes you say that?'

'He was like Raphael. I mean, he just suddenly appeared, and he didn't seem to be in any doubt who I was.'

'Really? Like Raphael?'

'A malevolent version. Where Raphael only ever comes to my rescue, this creature wanted to destroy me.'

'And yet he didn't. Please, Gill. Tell me what actually happened?'

Gill stopped while he remembered. 'I was poking around somewhere I shouldn't have been; an archaeological site. And a creature attacked me, driving me to the ground. The creature had a weapon and as he swung it against my body, Raphael's sword manifested in my hands. It blocked the blow but drove the sword blade into my palm.'

'Very good.'

'You think that's good?' Gill's exasperation escaped before he could check it.

'That you were protected. That the sword appeared. I'm sorry you were cut, but *The Book* often does that. It can seem unpleasant, even when something good is happening.' Solomon peered out over the water, then closed her eyes, seeming to enjoy the reflected sunlight dazzling on her face. The sun was making her eyes stream and when she opened them again, her face was wet. 'You carry something special, Gill. You and Charlie, and probably others we haven't yet met.'

'Yes', said Gill. 'I believe we do.'

For the first time, in a vulnerable gesture, she reached out and touched his arm. 'I hope it all becomes clear to you both, in due course.'

There was sadness in her tone, and he realised her face was streaked with tears. 'You'll see it too, Solomon.'

'Will I? I've not met Raphael. I've certainly not been presented with any magical gift. I'm realising my role in this may simply be to connect you and Charlie together.'

Gill frowned and stepped over to the railing, grasping it in both hands. 'I can't see what Charlie and I would achieve without you. I only know enough to realise I know almost nothing. I need a mentor, Solomon, and I'd like that person to be you.'

'I see', said Solomon, wiping her face. 'In that case, let's go back to Airth church and your assailant. Do you realise what he was?'

Thrown back into his moment of terror in the ruined church, Gill's mind struggled to articulate the words that needed said. 'The creature brought darkness with it. I had a sudden sense of horrible foreboding. To be honest, that's how I knew it was there.'

'It was evil?'

Gill nodded. 'The very antithesis of Raphael.'

'So, it was like your angel friend, but the opposite. Which makes it what?'

Gill was back in the classroom, and he wasn't enjoying this afternoon's lesson. 'I believe the creature I encountered that night was a demon.'

Satisfied, Solomon nodded. 'Angels and demons, Gill. You really are off the deep end.'

Gill pushed off the railing and growled with frustration. 'I didn't ask to be in this battle. Didn't want to be in a position where I'd have to defend myself. I just wanted to get on with my life.'

As he twisted back to face the river, he felt the weight of the sword as it expressed itself physically in a scabbard on his back. He heard a little gasp from Solomon, and he peered over his shoulder and found her staring at him. 'You haven't seen this before?'

'No', she said quietly.

'It's happening more and more often.' He wanted to flash a smile but couldn't. 'I'm beginning to feel like an extra in a Marvel movie.'

'Looks good on you.' She thought for a second. 'Do you realise what it's costing you?'

'Costing me?'

'Every special power carries a cost. What price do you pay to exercise yours?'

'Raphael carries his sword with huge dignity. I'm a little embarrassed by mine.'

'That will pass, Gill. And I don't think that's your problem. Again, what is it costing you?'

He muttered to himself. The cost had weighed on his conscience since that night in Stonehaven. 'I imagined the sword would be for ceremonial purposes. I never thought I'd ever have to use it. Physically. To the point of drawing blood.' Angrily, Gill shook the railing. 'Defending myself against a demon seems fair. But to use it against another human being? I'm really not sure.'

'I see.'

'I mean, what happened to turning the other cheek?'

'But you did. You gave up the *Fated Stone* when in fact you could have used it to embarrass our political leaders. The fact you had to defend yourself against demonic and human attackers, Gill. I believe that's allowed.'

'And where do you draw the line? When does defence become offence? At what point does standing up for your faith mutate into an armed crusade?'

'That's a nuance you're going to have to consider for yourself.'

'Will you help me, Solomon?'

Solomon peered at him. For a moment he imagined she was going to embrace him, but suddenly she paused, caught with a faraway look as some other thought came crashing into her senses. 'Gill. Something's happening.'

'Yep', he replied. 'I've got a magical sword on my back, and I'm being hunted by a demon. My life's a laugh a minute.'

'No. Something else.'

He quit joking and stared at her, waiting for her to grip whatever was going off in her brain. 'In town', she said. 'You need to go.'

'When?'

'Right now.'

'Where?'

'I'm still trying to get clarity. Head into town. I'll let you know exactly where.'

He pushed off the railing. 'Okay.'

'Quickly, Gill. And I'll text Charlie.'

Seeing the urgency in her eyes, Gill shook some energy into his part-mended legs and started to trot towards the city.

Five minutes later, the ache in his right leg had slowed him to a fast walk. As he passed the railway station his phone pinged. 'DD 6 pm', he read. It was from Solomon's number. He glanced at his watch. The appointment was four minutes away. He checked his weapon and with new purpose, strode towards the centre of town and the *Desperate Dan* statue where he and Charlie had first met. He ignored the startled looks of the very few people who saw what he carried. Maybe he figured, it wasn't a big deal to openly carry a translucent crystal sword through the streets of Dundee on a weekday. Probably wouldn't be noticed at all during weekends. As he stepped onto Whitehall Crescent, Charlie emerged from a lane and fell into step beside him. Strapped to Charlie's left arm was a deep rectangular shield of the same material as Gill's sword.

'Nice kit', said Gill by way of greeting.

'Ye kin see it noo?'

'I can.'

'Somebody's git tae keep us safe. Ah ken that's mah job.'

They walked on a few steps, knowing the statue was less than two minutes away.

'Guid tae see ye brought yer blade.'

'Not sure what I'm going to do with it. Do you know who we're meeting?'

Charlie shook his head. 'Ah just ken th' Big Man's awa tae gies one mair.'

'One more what?'

'Piece o' th' armour 'n' someone fit tae carry it.'

'But who, Charlie? How will we know who we're meeting?'

Charlie gently shunted Gill with his free hand. 'Ah think we'll ken them whin we see them.'

Gill's mind churned as they walked. Who had he met recently that might fit the bill? There was Wiley's new man, Lillico. But he was Mister Average; in height, build, and temperament. Nothing about him struck Gill as someone called to carry the sword or the shield. There was Solomon herself; that felt closer to the mark. Her passion for this journey they were all on already made her a mentor to him. And then there was Corrie. Old and scarred, but with a lifetime's rich seasoning of experience to draw on. A man no longer defined by his mistakes. A man who could silence a room just by walking in.

'Aye', said Gill after a moment. 'I think we might.'

'Just hae yer wits aboot ye.'

Gill and Charlie emerged into the busy high street and watched a tide of people flowing around the bronze statue of the comic book character.

'The Big Man', said Gill, glancing at the statue. 'You've got to admire His sense of humour.'

'Keep ye humble ye big dafty.' Charlie nodded at the figure, sitting cross-legged on the ground, at the foot of the statue, their head hung low. 'Is that somebody ye ken?'

Gill was standing open-mouthed. Only after another jolt from Charlie did he gather his faculties and nod.

'Git oan wi' it then.'

Sighing, Gill drew his weapon and carefully approached the sitting figure, their arms gathered around something resting in their lap. As Gill approached, he could see a crystalline object. Getting closer he identified a battlefield helmet, with heavy sides and a single eye slit cut in the shape of a flat V. He gently tapped the ground with his sword tip and the figure's face flashed up to meet his gaze.

Adina's eyes were red and her face wet from crying. Her shoulders were shaking, and she looked so vulnerable – a shadow of the deadly agent who had confronted him in Stonehaven two days before. Gill immediately wanted to crouch beside her. Instead, he signalled Charlie, who moved in and placed his shield between them and passing crowds.

Gill studied her for a few moments, seeing utter confusion on her face but at the same time, sensing that she'd arrived at a terrible, dreadful conclusion she could not deny. He knew what it was like to be sitting where she was sitting, and he felt nothing but compassion for her.

'You have the helmet', he said at last.

Through her tears, it had taken her a few seconds to register who he was. Without hesitating she thrust a palm out in front of her. 'There was this guy. Big guy on a motorbike', she shouted, spittle flying from her mouth. 'I've just been trying to do the right thing. By everybody. But now I'm here and I don't know what to do.'

'And yet you accepted the helmet?'

'Gill. The things I've seen these last few days; if I told you, you wouldn't believe me.'

Gill swung up his sword and sheathed it. 'You know, I just might.' He nodded at Charlie, guarding the edge of their space, his eyes alert for trouble. 'And he might too.'

'I wouldn't have killed you, Gill. You do know that?'

'I believe you.'

'But I don't understand what's happening!'

'Then come with us and we'll tell you what we know.'

'Where are you taking me?'

'Just down here. Charlie knows a place.'

Chapter 42

__Editor's comment, Mysterious Scotland, Issue 23.__

Like me, do you ever find your life can turn on a pinhead? If tomorrow, you turn left out of your front door, you'll face one set of hazards and opportunities. Turn right, and maybe you'll encounter something completely different. No matter how much we plot and plan, our day-to-day choices affect our ultimate destiny. Multiply this effect across families and towns. Multiply it over the generations and factor in the decisions of other people in other lands. This great tower of human endeavour implies so many separate decision points. Physical and practical. Social and moral. Most of our decisions are mundane, while others impact the very fabric of our society.

Recently, I had the opportunity to offer one such choice, to the folk you might call the high-heidyins of Scotland. I'll not go into detail because, if you're interested, you'll have already read about it in the papers. And the choice on offer was simply this: To reconsider the authenticity of Scotland's 'Stone of Destiny'. The existing sandstone block, which unquestionably has held the title for 740 years, is a revered historical object and justifiably sits in the new Perth Museum. Just an old rock, but a national treasure nevertheless. And then to muddy the waters, we discovered a new pretender - a slab of black basalt, plucked from the bottom of the Firth of Forth by a Mys.Scot team investigating a wreck.

And here's the problem. We know the incumbent was quarried from a pit near Scone, whereas the new discovery can be traced to a river bed in Northern Israel, making it a much closer fit to the 'Jacob's Pillow' myth attached to the 'Stone of Destiny'. This issue of our magazine sets out the scientific and archaeological facts as we know them. We'll also scrutinise the almost implausible possibility, first popularised by the Declaration of Arbroath in the year 1320, alluding to a Scottish destiny story originating in the Middle East. Consider this carefully, because, this puzzle is about far more than a stone. Did our Celtic roots simply emerge out of Ireland, or are we convinced the Scots, already identifiable as a tribe, left the holy land before the time of Christ? Left turn, right turn – what decisions did we make along this jagged way to become a settled people, here in the northern half of these British Isles? It's a fascinating question. Chew on the pages that follow – I promise you a hearty meal.

Unless you've been hiding on a mountain, you'll know of course that Scotland is sticking with the old stone. And I'm fine with that – it's an item with an impressive and undeniable history. Our analysis showed the basalt stone originated in Israel, so that is where it has been returned. With the permission of our co-sponsors, it's been sent to a university team in Tel Aviv who will examine its possible connection to the Biblical story. I wish them well.

In another sharp and unexpected right turn, the city of Dundee is to be the home of a new national charity. I mention this because an anonymous donor has provided an immediate multi-million-pound grant, with the stated aim of boosting literacy levels amongst our young adults. This gift came with the explicit condition that I become the patron of the charity being established to fulfil this worthy cause. And here's the thing - if we apply that money to boost the chances of the most disadvantaged in our society, that's a right turn that could boost our city's destiny. Goodness! This could help all of Scotland, because I'm continually amazed by how many folk suffer the indignity of undeveloped reading, undermining their continued learning and diminishing their opportunities. So, join me in thanking this donor. Join me in choosing a better future for our precious youth. Because at the end of the day, a stone is just a stone. And this is, Mysterious Scotland, where our stones are like our histories – we've plenty of them around.

The End

Author's Note

There's a loose end in this tale and it concerns old Conall Canmore, last seen falling to his death from Stirling Castle. Did he die, taking his dreams of a different Scotland with him, or did a whole new adventure present itself? Tuck that thought away as we might be hearing from him again.

Meanwhile, if you have enjoyed 'This Jagged Way', I would be so grateful if you could leave a review on the site where you bought this book. And please stay in touch. This story is just getting going.

Tormod Cockburn

The next adventure is …

The Ice Covenant

In the moment where the darkness of a Scottish winter meets the saddest moment for a human soul, promises have been made.

DI George Wiley is calling in a favour. As head of a new unit tackling cold and unusual cases, he presents Gill McArdle with a bag of human teeth. His evaluation – a serial killer has been operating undetected in Scotland for decades. With no leads in the case, Wiley wants Gill to leverage his contacts. But Gill McArdle feels under no obligation as he has a puzzle of his own to solve. Roadworks in the Scottish Highlands have uncovered an old battlefield site and now the race is on to complete an archaeological dig before the site is buried under tarmac. Making steady progress under challenging conditions, Gill and the team are suddenly wrong-footed by a disturbing discovery. Face to face with a powerful new enemy, Gill walks into the darkest moments of his life.

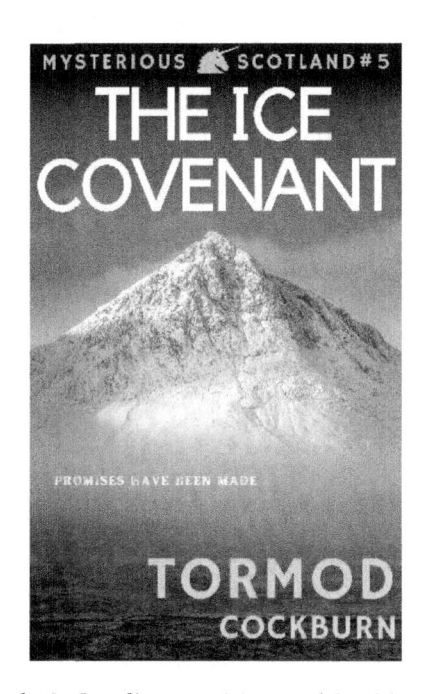

Join the Reader's Syndicate at TormodCockburn.com

Or click on the thumbnail

Mysterious Scotland Reader's Syndicate

Join our Readers Syndicate at TormodCockburn.com for new publication alerts and for free material. We'll shortly be adding more free material, exclusively available to members of the Syndicate.

Mys.Scot

Acknowledgements

I'm fortunate to live on a beautiful part of Scotland's coastline. While Corrie McCann is the work of my imagination, I want to thank and acknowledge all the individuals and organisations that work so hard to keep our shores free of litter. Especially, Fife Coast & Countryside Trust, who do the heavy lifting.

The *Stone of Destiny* has a complex history of fact and myth. I am indebted to Mark Naples and David Bews for their detailed book on the subject. And for their delicate handling of the politics that have surrounded the stone for seven centuries. If I've managed to replicate even a fraction of their tact, I'll be well pleased.

And a big thank you to Hannah for her detailed tour of the beautiful May Isle and all the wildlife we find there. If I've made any errors while applying that information, they're all my own.

My thanks to fellow indie author, Jack Murray who's taken me under his wing of late. Twenty years ago, Jack and I used to work in London together. We'd slip away for tea and bikkie breaks where we'd tell each other jokes and dream about what we'd do when we grew up. He now writes the successful Kit Aston series.

A big, big shout out to my beta-readers, Audrey, James and Julia. Your sharp red pens made this a far better book.

And finally, as the Firth of Forth is my home port, I have to acknowledge the anecdotes and rumours I've gleaned in many conversations, during long days at sea, or in our various local bars. Oh, my goodness, but this old land is bursting with stories …

Printed in Great Britain
by Amazon